WHY, MR. FERGUSSON, ARE YOU FLIRTING WITH ME?

Good heavens, he had been, hadn't he? Was she remembering that ill-fated kiss in the tavern? How humiliating. "Mrs. Mendoza," he said with feeling, "I assure you we Scots never engage in anything so undignified as flirting."

"Yet . . . " Her bottom lip disappeared between her teeth for an instant. "I believe you were."

He started to deny it again, more firmly this time. But the torchlight turned her eyes to pure gold and revealed a wistful longing trying so very hard not to be obvious.

"Would it be an unwelcome thing if I were flirting?" His hand rose to her hair, his fingertips making the merest contact with those loose wisps framing her face. "Would you despise me for it?"

"No, Mr. Fergusson," she whispered. Her eyes, those great gold sovereigns, shimmered in the wavering light. "You can't know how long it's been since . . . "

"Since a man made an ass of himself over you?"

Her nose wrinkled when she laughed. He loved that.

BOOK YOUR PLACE ON OUR WEBSITE AND MAKE THE READING CONNECTION!

We've created a customized website just for our very special readers, where you can get the inside scoop on everything that's going on with Zebra, Pinnacle and Kensington books.

When you come online, you'll have the exciting opportunity to:

- View covers of upcoming books

- Read sample chapters

- Learn about our future publishing schedule (listed by publication month *and author*)

- Find out when your favorite authors will be visiting a city near you

- Search for and order backlist books from our online catalog

- Check out author bios and background information

- Send e-mail to your favorite authors

- Meet the Kensington staff online

- Join us in weekly chats with authors, readers and other guests

- Get writing guidelines

- AND MUCH MORE!

**Visit our website at
http://www.kensingtonbooks.com**

MOSTLY A LADY

LISA MANUEL

ZEBRA BOOKS
Kensington Publishing Corp.
www.kensingtonbooks.com

ZEBRA BOOKS are published by

Kensington Publishing Corp.
850 Third Avenue
New York, NY 10022

All Kensington titles, imprints, and distributed lines are available at special quantity discounts for bulk purchases for sales
promotion, premiums, fund-raising, educational, or institu-
tional use.

Special book excerpts or customized printings can also be created to fit specific needs. For details, write or phone the office
of the Kensington Special Sales Manager: Attn. Special Sales
Department. Kensington Publishing Corp., 850 Third Avenue,
New York, NY 10022. Phone: 1-800-221-2647.

Zebra and the Z logo Reg. U.S. Pat. & TM Off.

First Printing: May 2005
10 9 8 7 6 5 4 3 2 1

Printed in the United States of America

To Mom and Dad,
For setting me on the right road,
To Paul,
For being there for me at every turn,
And to our daughters,
Just for being who they are.

And to my editor,
Kate Duffy,
Who made this possible.

CHAPTER 1

Dylan Fergusson lay back against the pillows feeling sated, contented and deliriously in love with the curvaceous and quite naked woman sleeping beside him. Or, he might amend, thoroughly in lust, but couldn't the one usually be counted upon to spring readily and happily from the other? He was thinking he'd rather like to put that theory to the test when he opened his eyes and made a startling discovery.

He was seconds away from having his brains scattered across the pillows.

A seething arsenal of hulking shoulders, jutting jaw and scorching gaze loomed over him, the barrel of a pistol trained on the portion of skull that lay directly between his eyes.

Dylan thrust backward until his spine thwacked the headboard. His first thought was to toss the intruder his purse, but a quick assessment of his adversary revealed expert tailoring, valet grooming and a manicured trigger finger.

Not a thief.

A cold gaze raked over him with the calculation of a hawk on the hunt. "Prepare to meet your maker, gutter scum." The pistol lurched closer.

Dylan's gut hit his throat as that trigger finger flexed. Instinct sent his hands out while his knees shot up, tenting the coverlets in an ineffectual barricade between him and impending death.

Beside him, Isabel stirred with a sleepy sigh. The intruder's gaze shifted toward her and visible hesitancy settled over his features. "Isabel, wake up."

He *knew* her? Was he her father?

Keeping one eye on the threatening barrel and the other on the ominous scowl behind it, Dylan nudged Isabel's exposed shoulder, the one he'd likened to alabaster only yesterday.

"It's too early, darling. Go back to sleep."

This time it was his turn to urge her from slumber. *"Isabel."*

"Oh, good heavens." One lovely violet eye opened as she rolled to face him. "What time is it? We can't have slept more than an hour or two." The other eye opened. A smile dawned. "You're quite relentless, darling, aren't you?"

"Isabel." He gestured with a flick of his gaze. Her own followed.

"Oh." Her mouth widened on a yawn. "Reginald."

Reginald? Her utter lack of surprise struck Dylan a blow and assured him of two things. His would-be assassin was not her father, but she knew him. Knew him well.

Her golden and meticulously shaped eyebrows surged. "Good morning, darling. I didn't expect you. Did you just get in?"

"Move away from him, Isabel. Now."

She smirked. "Really, Reginald, don't be ridiculous." Sitting up and shaking a shower of golden curls from her face, Isabel gathered the coverlets to her breasts in a show of modesty contrary to everything Dylan knew about her. "Why on earth would you risk the gallows over a triviality?"

"Triviality? The cur has violated you and insulted me beyond endurance. Move out of the way."

Insulted him? Then wouldn't that mean . . .

"*Now*, Isabel."

"Wait." Dylan held up the flat of his hand. "I'm sorry, I don't know who you are, but—"

"I am her husband, you revolting sliver of offal."

"Husband?"

The single word sucked the oxygen from his lungs. If the

sun and moon switched places Dylan would not have noticed. He'd met Isabel several weeks ago at the Covent Garden Theater, where they'd both gone, singly, to view one of the Season's final performances.

During the intermission she'd tripped over a rumpled corner of carpet and spilled her wine on his sleeve. When he'd expected cold indifference and a halfhearted apology, he'd instead been treated to genuine concern, then laughter and charming conversation. Following the performance they shared a light supper. Dawn saw them in each other's arms, as had the next and the next and all the dawns thereafter.

But never—not bloody damn once—had Isabel bothered mentioning the existence of anyone remotely resembling old Reginald here.

"Darling," she said now, and Dylan wondered which one of them the wanton addressed. Extending one of those graceful, slender arms he'd kissed up and down countless times these past weeks, she casually wrapped her fingers around the pistol barrel and redirected its aim to the mattress. "Perhaps you should get dressed while I have a word with Reginald."

"Why the devil did you not tell me you were married?" His Scottish brogue, so carefully smoothed during his weeks in London, now broke through with the rugged insistence of his seacoast home.

She had the audacity to shrug. "I assumed you knew."

"How could I know?" He glared from her to her fuming if slightly subdued husband and back, challenging either or both to supply a rational answer. Good Lord, her features captivated him even now, despite this sudden glimpse of a less-than-desirable underbelly. God save him, she was beautiful, clever, funny, passionate and quite possibly the most devious individual he'd ever met. He shook his head sadly. "Isabel, I'd begun to believe you and I had . . ."

"Something special?" She tilted her pert little chin. "Darling, we did. But now my husband's home and it's time for you to go."

The words sliced at both his pride and the part of him that truly had *stupidly* believed he'd found something extraordinary. Something that had promised, perhaps, to lessen the envy festering in his heart each time he looked upon his sister's growing family. His chest tightened around a withering, relentless sort of pain as a piece of that dream flitted away with a coquettish wink.

"He's not going anywhere." Seeming to have recovered his ferocity, Reginald swung the pistol back to its former menacing position. Dylan went rigid.

Isabel laughed, a haughty, disdainful sound. "Reginald, I swear to you this boy means nothing to me, absolutely nothing. You've been away nearly two months, for heaven sake. And don't try telling me your bed went unwarmed in all that time."

By St. George's ear, had the woman no mercy, no discretion and utterly no shame?

Reginald stood immobile, his features as implacable as stone. "What if the whoreson has got you with child?"

"Then our acquaintances shall all congratulate you on having finally sired an heir."

No, by God, not an ounce of shame. Nor honor, nor conscience nor . . .

"Ah, Isabel, how could you?" The mattress sagged beneath Reginald's weight as he sank to its edge and let his head droop between his shoulders. The gun dangled dangerously from his forefinger, but with relief Dylan noted that, should it discharge, the only casualty would be the man's own foot.

Isabel stole that moment to shove Dylan to the opposite side of the bed and hiss in his ear, "Grab your clothes and go." Then her arms went around her husband from behind as she pressed her unabashedly naked length to his back. "There, there, Reginald, darling, it's quite all right. He's just an amusing boy who happened along at a lonely moment. Let's not have a row over it, for that would utterly ruin your homecoming."

Dylan made for the door with the briskness of an ocean gust, gathering up his shoes and scattered clothing as he went, leaving behind nonessentials such as collar and cravat. He wouldn't need them, by God, not where he was going. He'd had enough of London and English society to last a lifetime. This hadn't been the first insult; ah, no, there'd been plenty of others though none so cruelly humiliating as this.

Isabel's slamming boudoir door shut out the placating murmurs within. On the landing he stepped into his trousers and yanked them to his waist, jammed his bare feet into his shoes and started down the stairs. Never again would he endure another condescending smile or quip designed to make him appear as most Englishmen saw him: an ignorant, provincial Scottish farmer. Though Scottish he was and just as certainly a farmer, despite his university education and the fact that he was the brother-in-law of the very English Duke of Wakefield.

Shoving his arms into his shirt, he couldn't help but admit that this attempt to experience something more of life had failed—miserably. To Scotland he'd return, then, and do what he did best among people who appreciated him for the man he was.

The only problem was, that no longer existed for him either. Not really.

Bugger it. Bugger all of it.

Rain trickled into Eliza Kent's collar, soaked through her plaid woolen coat, many sizes too big, and inundated her skirts, stockings and worn leather boots. Her toes squished in the water pooling between them. One would have thought a woman of Eliza's wit, spirit and resources would know enough to go in out of the rain. But her wits were dulled with cold, her spirit doused with rain and she'd long ago run out of resources.

With nowhere to go and no one to help her, she lay cheek-down on the heath and allowed her few remaining tears to mingle with the downpour. Eliza Kent had climbed to the crest of this sweeping rise in the Yorkshire moors with a single intent in mind: to die.

But even in that, luck refused to turn in her favor. Nathan's musket—the only means of self-annihilation at her disposal—made the task nigh impossible. It was too long, too unwieldy. She couldn't quite aim it at her head and pull the trigger, never mind that she tried doing so with her toe. Besides, the thing was ancient, with a rusty priming pan for the powder—which was wet—and a ball for a bullet that kept rolling down and out the barrel whenever the weapon's weight proved too much for her arms. She couldn't manage it, leaving her no choice but to live, shivering, here on a moor in the rain all alone.

Nathan—gone from the world these six months, and nothing to show he'd ever existed but his unworkable rifle, a threadbare coat and a widow with a stomach so empty it echoed.

She'd lost the farm but three months after losing him; lost the babe inside her the following week. Her first and only glimmer of hope came when an old acquaintance secured her a position in a fine house in Dewsbury. She'd emptied chamber pots and scrubbed bed linens till her arms ached and her hands bled but what matter? She'd eaten daily, slept in a dry bed nightly.

Ah, yes, nights. That was when the trouble came. Trouble in the form of a master with too little to occupy his hands and too many notions occupying his head. One of those notions involved Eliza and brought him skulking below stairs when most of the other servants had gone to bed. She didn't like him talking to her, liked it less when he reached out to smooth her hair. He crossed the line when he yanked her skirts; she crossed another when she smacked him away, one that forever barred her from working in that house or any other.

Dismissed without a reference. Cast out, to starve or whore. Her choice. Odd how easy that choice had seemed before the hunger pangs threatened to wrench her stomach inside out. Ah, not so easy then, not nearly so.

She'd wandered after that until two nights ago, when she'd stumbled into the tiny hamlet of Heverton Gorse. With Nathan's musket tucked at her side beneath his ragged coat, she'd stood against a tree outside the Raven's Perch Tavern contemplating the men striding in and stumbling out. Hidden in the shadows of low hanging branches, she'd pondered with whom to cast her lot, one sober enough to disdain her or one too drunk to care.

In the end she'd made no choice, for as the butt of Nathan's rifle jabbed beneath her arm, the one remaining memento of her marriage acquired a whole new meaning. That was what had led her here, to the blackening heath of the Yorkshire countryside, with no one but the crows and hawks to witness her wretched, God-forsaken luck.

Bugger everyone and everything.

Thunder rolled across the weeping sky and set the tips of the dying heath trembling beneath her ear. Eliza prayed for lightning, just one well-aimed strike. None came while the thunder growled on and on, building to an urgent rumble that shook the hillside.

Sitting up and shoving sodden shanks of hair from her eyes, she searched the heaving vista that scraped the horizon. She'd chosen this spot, some five miles outside of Heverton Gorse, for its visibility. Although remote, the post-chaise would pass through at least once a fortnight. She'd hoped someone might spot the moldering heap of plaid and come to investigate, perhaps provide her a decent burial.

It was no post-chaise or plodding public stagecoach that topped a rise and came into view, but a gleaming black barouche that mirrored the pewter clouds and flashed their bleakness back at the sky. Her first thought was, *thank you for coming, but you're much too early, for I won't likely starve to death till next Tuesday.* But the morbid reflections scattered as she comprehended the source of her would-be thunder.

Coming from the north, the coach barreled along at breath-stealing speed, the four horses pounding the fury of their chase deep into the earth. Behind the matched bay pairs, the cab jostled and jounced over the road while the driver dug his heels into the iron footboard and pressed backward, hauling on the reins with all his strength.

"Slow down . . . Oh, slow down." Eliza pushed the words through teeth that clamped her bottom lip. The carriage raced toward a narrow bend that rounded an incline strewn with boulders and scattered with rowan. Her hands fisted in the heath, ripping it from the ground as though it too were reins and she might, by sheer force of will, halt the horses' frenzied pace.

But neither the driver's frantic efforts nor her own proved enough. Had this been the city and the road smoothed and leveled, they might have made it with nothing worse than bruised bottoms. But this was lonely Yorkshire moorland, the road as pocked and pitted as an old drunkard's nose, slick with mud and rain besides.

The horses cleared what the vehicle could not—a gouge wrought by countless icy winters. The carriage wheels struck it and plunged, caught for an instant, then skipped and bounced, sending the barouche high into the air to reunite with the ground with a teeth-shattering crunch.

Eliza was on her feet but too bewildered to move, held immobile by the sickening prospect unfolding before her eyes. A dreadful clank rang through the air as the linchpin broke free. The whiffletree splintered and snapped. The horses lurched away from the cab, connected to one another now only by their harnesses and traces.

The force of their flight yanked the driver off his seat, headlong, limbs flailing. The reins were ripped from his hands midair. As if tossed—as Eliza had once tossed her rag doll in fits of childish temper—he flopped hard against the low rock wall bordering the road. He balanced there a moment, face up, before his torso slid off the opposite side, so that all Eliza could see of him were the soles of his boots. The horses ploughed blindly on, splashing away down the road to a destination of their choosing while . . .

Amid plumes of spray, the coach veered wildly and struck the wall, the momentum hurling it up and over and down the incline amid a torrent of trunks and parcels. Jagged boulders upended the vehicle, sending it rolling with a deafening clamor as its sides bashed the rocks. Somehow it righted, but struck the trunk of a rowan with a violent shudder that spilled showers of rain from the leaves and sent crows fleeing like black sparks in the sky. The coach's front corner crumpled like a bit of tin.

A horrible silence fell, broken only by the drizzle and the wind and Eliza's panting breaths that couldn't quite decide to become screams or not. Then her legs were moving, hurtling her down the hillside.

Her pace slowed as she crossed the road and approached the driver, or rather his boots, perched almost comically atop the wall as if he'd decided to break from his daily toils, prop up his feet and gaze at the sky. But when Eliza peered over that low stone barrier between her and calamity, she knew the man would never toil again. Knew it even before the blood already congealing in the corners of his mouth, in his nose and beneath his head registered as the inevitable sign it was.

Even so . . . Even so, she gathered her wet, weighty skirts and clambered over the wall. She crouched beside the poor fellow and placed two fingers where the pulse in his throat should be.

Yes, she had known. She pushed to her feet.

A path of brightly colored debris led the way to the carriage. Silks, muslins, snowy linen underthings, shoes, hats, gloves and more lay scattered amongst the rocks and trees and heath. A wooden box lay in splinters mixed with bits of glass, the ground around it gleaming with ink and littered with quills as if some great bird had died there. Open books fluttered halfheartedly, their pages already becoming weighted with raindrops.

The barouche, though upright, stood tipped on the uneven ground, so that one back wheel turned with the push of the wind. Nearly half its roof, Eliza saw, had been ripped off. One door, hanging awry from a single hinge, swung lazily back and forth as if working off a last scrap of energy.

Such complete destruction. What hope then, for the passengers?

A sound, little more than a gasp of the wind except that it ended with a queer bubbling, sent Eliza rushing to the wreckage as fast as the rugged terrain and devastated possessions would allow. Through the door that hung limp she spied a gloved hand, palm up against the floor. Slight, slender fingers gently curled. Eliza reached in.

Those fingers closed around hers with startling strength. Eliza flinched and started to pull away when the grip just as suddenly released. She realized the act had been involuntary, as involuntary as the twitching of the arms and legs swathed in luxurious folds of midnight velvet.

Wiping the rain from her eyes, Eliza squinted to see into the murky interior, to detect any spreading stains on all that rich velvet. She saw none, only the petite figure of a gentlewoman prone on her side across the floor, her jet hair streaming in all directions like more spilled ink. Eliza lifted a handful and swept its heavy length from the woman's face.

"It's all right, miss. Don't worry. I'm here to help you." Yet even as the whispered promise hovered in the air, Eliza couldn't deny the irony of her helping anyone—her, brought to this desolate place by a death wish.

The woman's eyes opened—deep, sapphire blue eyes—and her lips worked weakly. Eliza heard a feeble murmur and felt relief. But that relief lasted all of an instant as she discovered a stream of bloody saliva flowing from the woman's mouth to puddle beneath her cheek.

Those gemlike eyes found Eliza and adhered. A fine-boned,

patrician face tilted ever so slightly up at her, the features contracting with the pain the movement cost her. "Don't . . . Don't let them . . . have it."

The words trembled and slurred. A gurgling in the woman's throat sent more pink-tinged saliva spilling from her mouth.

"Don't talk. Don't try to move. It'll be all right." Oh, such a lie, but what else could Eliza say?

Just as she had known immediately about the driver, she foresaw this lovely woman's fate. She'd witnessed death too many times not to recognize its warnings. Even in the wan light emitted through the clouds, she saw that the woman's lips were nearly white, her breathing shallow and labored, her limbs gone weak and still but for the spasms. And the shivering, the pitiable shivering that proclaimed the slowing of the blood through a body shutting down.

As carefully as if she were placing eggs in a basket, Eliza laid a hand on the woman's shoulder for no other reason than to impart the warmth of another human being who cared. "I'm going to find something to cover you with. I promise I shall be right back. It's going to be all right, miss."

She hadn't far to go, for mere paces behind the coach she came upon a sturdy woolen carriage blanket that must have slid out when the coach rolled. She shook it out, sending pellets of mud and leaves flitting away on the rain. On her way back she detoured to yank an ivory satin petticoat from a twist of bramble.

"Here I am, miss, never fear." She balled the petticoat and, gently lifting the woman's head, slipped it beneath for a pillow. Then she climbed inside the coach and spread the blanket from the woman's chin to her patent-leather-clad feet. "There now, it's mostly dry. That's better, then, isn't it?"

No answer came, not that Eliza expected one. No, she merely meant to fill the silence, to reassure by sound as well as touch.

Too well did she remember the last hour or so of Nathan's life. Up until then, he'd fought to keep talking, using up precious energy as the life flowed slowly out of him. But he'd had so much to tell Eliza, about the farm, about what he wanted for her in life, about how much he'd loved her though he'd never said it before.

How she wished he had uttered those words sooner. Perhaps then she might have made time in her busy life to love him back as he deserved. They'd made a good partnership, worked a successful farm together. They'd been the best of friends, surely. But love. . . ?

In the final hour when he could no longer summon the breath or the strength to speak, Eliza had done the talking for him, assuring, reassuring, promising she'd be all right.

Bugger life.

She reached for the woman's hand. "Well, now, miss, I suppose we'll just hunker here together until another coach passes by. They'll be sure to see us. They couldn't *not* see us if they tried." She forced a soft laugh. "I'm afraid all your lovely things are *everywhere,* miss. Ah, but no matter, they'll wash, won't they? Meantime, we'll get you to a physician, just as soon as that coach comes by."

But Eliza knew the prospect of anyone happening by in time was as likely as the summer sun returning to the September landscape.

The woman's hand convulsed in hers and Eliza tightened her grip, only to notice the braided cords wrapped around a slender wrist. They were attached to a reticule cut from the same fine velvet as the gown and trimmed in dark amber satin. Gold thread curled and swooped to form initials: EM de L. It was as pretty a thing as Eliza had ever seen. She reached for it.

"I hope you don't mind my prying, miss, but perhaps I might learn who you are."

The gentlewoman seemed to have lapsed into a fitful doze punctuated by those rasping, bubbling breaths. Beneath her cheek a new stain crept across the petticoat, deepening steadily from pink to scarlet. A chill swept Eliza's back. She worked the purse free from that delicate wrist, tugged it open and turned it upside down.

Keys clattered, a handkerchief fluttered, a large locket encrusted with marcasite and tiny pearls flashed as it thudded to Eliza's lap. A smaller drawstring purse tumbled after, the telltale jingle hinting at the assets inside. She shook the larger velvet bag, and a letter slipped out.

She squinted to make out the direction. Mr. Raphael Mendoza de Leone, Six Harrowby Street, Marylebone, London.

"Forgive me, miss. But if I don't, who will ever know your fate?"

She broke the wax seal with fingers trembling from the knowledge that rummaging through a gentlewoman's possessions could land her in stocks. She held the letter close to her face to read in the dim light.

The words, *Dear Raphael,* had been scratched over and replaced beneath with *Dearest Brother,*

If you are reading this, then I am dead and the woman standing before you is my wife, Elizabeth. We married a year ago here at Folkstone Manor in York, the sale of which is to take place shortly. I write to you now at her encouragement in hopes that I may achieve in death what I failed to earn in life: your forgiveness.

Though our last words were spoken in anger—(again, here, the last word was scratched out and replaced with "fury")— remember that we are nonetheless brothers who shared many dreams, many secrets and as many sins. Lay the past to rest with me, and believe that what I have done came not out of malice but from a sincere yearning to right the grievous wrong we committed years ago, which led to the sundering of our brotherhood.

Elizabeth knows nothing of these matters. You shall jointly inherit the profits from the sale of my home, and I leave it to you to manage her finances. It is my hope, my dying wish, that you will welcome Elizabeth into the family and watch over her, for she is alone now in this world.

    Ever your brother,

    Anselmo

So full of mystery, not the least of which was why this woman had been traveling this road, an odd choice for someone intent on reaching family in London. This was not the main route south, but an older byway that meandered from village to tiny village.

Eliza picked up the locket—so large it filled her hand— and flicked it open. A pair of faces gazed up at her, handsome and youthful, with similar features captured in meticulous brush strokes. The brothers? They were both dark-eyed, sable-haired, olive-skinned, as no Englishman tended to be. In the European style they wore matching blue coats with scarlet sashes, and looked as noble as their name implied.

Eliza gazed down at the purse in her lap. Her finger traced the elegant gold initials: EM de L.

"Elizabeth Mendoza de Leone." She drew a breath. "It's like music. Just as your entire life must have been a song." She grimaced. "What am I thinking? You're a widow like me." Her gaze shifted back and forth from Elizabeth's velvet-clad form to her own ragged calico trailing from under Nathan's old coat. "Perhaps not quite like me either, but certainly too young to be left alone in the world. Too young to die."

Eliza's throat pinched and burned while ebony hair and blacker velvet blurred before her eyes. Tossing the letter and the reticule aside, she scooped Elizabeth's limp hand into her own and leaned close to the ashen face. "Don't die, ma'am, please don't. Oh, you have so much yet to live for. You're young and beautiful and you've a family waiting for you in London."

She paused, trying to swallow the unbearable urge to weep, unable to quell the sob that burst forth to be borne away by a rainy gust. "I'm the one who should have died today. Eliza, not Elizabeth. Bugger fate—got it all wrong again." She brought a fist down against her thigh. "Oh, ma'am, please, please live."

A tremor ran the width of the woman's shoulders, and her eyes flew open.

CHAPTER 2

"Give me one good reason, Dylan Fergusson, why you insist on running off so soon."

He regarded his sister Charity's snapping green eyes and knew he'd better give a quick excuse and go or he'd never make it off her husband's estate intact. Across the circular sweep of Longfield Park's front drive, a groom stood holding his horse and pretending to be too fascinated in the workings of the fountain to notice the argument taking place at the foot of the steps.

"I need to get back to the farms," Dylan said. "I've been away far too long."

She gave him a look—the *look*—that demanded to know who he thought he was fooling. When she'd married Luke Holbrook seven years ago, they'd spent the better portion of their time in Scotland, raising sheep and some of the finest wool to be found in Great Britain. Dylan, too, had never imagined any other sort of life. Hadn't wanted more.

But the world was a fast-changing place, and he'd soon learned a man who refused to swim with the tide was destined to drown. These days, the St. Abbs farms constituted little more than a pastime, for him and the Holbrooks both.

Charity and Luke split their time between England and Scotland almost evenly now, and he could foresee the day St. Abbs would become merely a place to visit on holidays. But changes set in motion long ago by America's independence, the wars on the Continent and Britain's own shifting economy had touched Dylan's life profoundly too. Nowadays he spent the lion's share of his time overseeing the family investments that ranged from American cotton to West Indies sugar to textile manufacture in Scotland's cities. In his heart, he'd remained and would always be a farmer. But in his purse, Dylan Fergusson had undeniably joined the new bourgeoisie.

It was something he didn't always like about himself. It was something many of his old neighbors didn't like about him either, nor the women he'd once courted. Odd, but he'd never stopped to consider that his growing wealth might prove a deterrent to marriage.

Sure but you've grown too grand for the likes of me, Dylan Fergusson. Perhaps it's a duchess or a countess or the queen of England herself you should be setting your cap for.

He sighed. Right now, with Isabel's duplicity still stinging, all he wanted was to remember the youth he'd been, happy in a life as natural and simple as breathing.

"You need to get back to the farms?" Charity's hands snapped to her hips as she shook curling copper tendrils from her face. "Rubbish. You're no more needed on the farms just now than we are. The flocks are still roaming and will be for several weeks. Were it time for the autumn breeding, do you think Luke and I would be lingering here in England?"

He might have pointed out that they'd left St. Abbs before the spring shearing had ended. But he only shrugged, knowing a peevish reply would earn him a cuff on the shoulder from his older and far-too-bossy sister. It didn't help matters when Luke stepped out the front door and sauntered down the steps, the slant of his eyebrows mirroring his wife's admonishments.

"Charity's right," he said. "You've only just arrived. Stay a few more days at least. Especially since Helena and Wesley should be here in a day or two."

"I saw them a few weeks ago in London."

"Think of your nieces and nephews, then."

"Nephews, eh?" Dylan raised an eyebrow. "One isn't even

born yet and how do you know I won't have another niece? Or two, like the last pair."

"Bite your tongue." Charity wagged a finger and exchanged a pointed glance with Luke. The birth of their twin daughters nearly three years ago had been an exhilarating but exhausting experience for them. "Born or not, this child can hear you, Dylan, and I daresay he or she disapproves of your hasty departure. Isn't that true, my darling?"

"Indeed it is." Luke slipped his arms around Charity's waist from behind, pulling her to his chest. "Besides, William will be inconsolable if you don't tell him another swashbuckling bedtime story tonight."

"I beg your pardon but it's the other way around. William tells *me* the stories." Dylan stole a quick glance up at the nursery window to see if the young man in question was listening and planning to charge down to champion his parents' cause.

"You know you're all he talks about lately," Charity reminded him, succeeding—the sneak—in tugging one of his most vulnerable heartstrings. "Ever since he learned the story of Rob Roy he's been insisting you're him in disguise."

"Rob Roy was a Highlander."

"Nonetheless." Charity stepped out of her husband's arms and placed a hand on Dylan's shoulder. The bossiness gone, she appealed with a sister's affectionate smile, one that reflected all their years of confidences, quarrels and capers. "I'm sorry you found London not to your liking—"

Luke moved forward. "What happened in London?"

"Nothing."

"That's not how you told it to me." How like his sister to press the matter.

"Is it something I can take care of for you?"

"No, Luke, it isn't." Dylan pushed out a frustrated breath. "I don't need my brother-in-law the duke to intervene every time things don't go my way. I'm neither a child nor a hapless country bumpkin."

Luke and Charity traded looks that made the hair on Dylan's neck bristle. They saw him as stubborn and unreasonable, of course, but how could either of them understand his burning need to be gone from England? By some astonishing miracle, Luke and Charity managed to establish lives in both worlds, as Scottish farmers *and* English aristocrats. Of course, they had each other, and a love that transcended every social barrier yet invented.

He would never find that kind of harmony leading two lives. He'd tried for nearly two months, hadn't he? In that time, all he established with any certainty was that he didn't belong in this country and that he understood the English about as well as he understood the will and whim of the Yorkshire weather. And that he liked them about as much.

"No one is suggesting you're anything of the sort." Luke's wounded expression made Dylan regret having spoken harshly. It surely wasn't his brother-in-law's fault, nor Charity's, that Isabel had played him for a fool, or that at least a dozen other Englishmen had found sport in subtly ridiculing him as if he were too brutish to comprehend.

"I'm sorry," he said, meaning it. "I appreciate your concern and your offer to stay. But I simply need . . . " He trailed off, wondering how best to stem the tide of their persuasion. Then he hit upon it. "I'd just be *happier* at home in Scotland."

Charity let loose a sigh. "Oh . . . We do want you to be happy."

Yes, he knew they would. Happiness was one commodity in which Luke and Charity invested heavily. It was what had given a duke and a farmer's daughter the courage to announce their secret marriage to the world.

How he envied them. How he wished . . .

He gestured for the groom to bring his horse. "You'll forgive me then."

"Of course." Luke extended a hand; Dylan pumped it with enthusiasm until Luke reached round and slapped his back so hard he coughed. "We'll have your things sent with the next post-chaise. Stay out of trouble."

"And take care of yourself on the road." Charity put her arms around him. "We'll see you in a few weeks' time."

When she released him he gave her slightly protruding belly a pat. "Take care of my new niece or nephew."

Then he swung up onto his horse and started on his way.

She was dead.

Gazing down into those wide, sightless, sapphire eyes, Eliza felt despair gather into an icy ball inside her. A roar of anguish—and anger—began deep in her belly and pushed its way up, up past her lungs and heart and into her throat and mouth. It filled the battered coach and spilled out, ripping through the rowans and grinding over the boulders to echo on the barren moor.

Eliza pounded her fists on the carriage seat, wanting to pound fate itself. It didn't matter that she hadn't actually known Elizabeth Mendoza de Leone or that, in life, Eliza could never have been more to such a woman than her maid. She, Eliza, was supposed to have died today, not this young gentlewoman with the musical name, who for all appearances had everything in the world to live for.

She lowered a hand to those radiant eyes, closing them for the last time. Oh, she wanted to lift her face to the sky and demand, through the rain and wind and clouds, why the buggery blazes this had happened. Why someone who walked in the full light of fortune's grace should be so violently cut down while she, Eliza, who had nothing, was nothing, must live on in a world she despised.

A breeze rolled through the coach, lifting the letter from where she had dropped it and depositing it at her fingertips. She grasped it, crumpling the page in her fist. An impulse nearly sent the missive sailing out into the rain and mud. Then Eliza's fingers opened.

For long moments she stared down at those words, fashioned in so elegant a hand. The signature was markedly different, shaky and faltering. With illness? *If you are reading
this then I am dead.* Like Nathan, this husband, Anselmo, had
glimpsed his end and dictated this letter, probably to his wife.
Eliza searched for the date. The twentieth of August, nearly a
month ago.

As she reread the letter, a notion stirred.

*. . . I am dead and the woman standing before you is my
wife, Elizabeth.* These brothers had been estranged for years;
for at least the year of Anselmo and Elizabeth's marriage.

*It is my hope, my dying wish, that you will welcome her
into the family. . . .* A family. The very thought ran through
Eliza like warm milk and honey on a winter's night. She
tipped her head back, savoring the sensation. This Raphael
would have a wife and a house full of children, all as beautiful and elegant as their Aunt Elizabeth.

Elizabeth, who should have lived.

How many times in these past weeks had Eliza asked God
for a sign, some small assurance that her fortune might turn,
that there were, in fact, reasons to keep living?

Eliza and Elizabeth. As different as two women could be
and yet, not entirely dissimilar either. In age, proportion and
wretched, rotten luck, they were of a measure. Even their
names were nearly the same. With the mere smoothing of a
vowel and a gentle syllable riding the end, the coarse and
common Eliza became the refined and feminine Elizabeth.

Their paths should never have crossed, and yet they had.

Signs?

She climbed out of the carriage, sending streams of cold
mud squelching into the holes in her boots. She blinked rain
droplets from her lashes and surveyed the wreckage—the
gaping trunks, the spilled possessions—strewn at her feet.

A notion broadened to a plan.

* * *

"Help! Please stop. Oh, please. I need help."

But the wind battered the moors at a roar today, and her pleas were as quickly whipped away as uttered. Eliza scrambled up the incline, her damp, muddied skirts doing their utmost to haul her back down.

Two endless, sodden, shivery days she'd spent here. Two pitch-black nights as well, huddled on the carriage seat beneath a pile of Elizabeth's clothing. She'd found food among the scattered luggage—a loaf of bread, some cheese, a meat pasty. There were a few apples as well. But Eliza had eaten sparingly, rationing like a miser in the event no one came for days and days. Even so, it was more than she'd eaten at any one time for weeks previously. She was still weak, too thin, but no longer plagued by the dizzying, heightened sensations of the starving.

As she struggled to reach the road before the rider passed out of view, she couldn't help but wonder. Had she made a rational decision the day Elizabeth died, or had her choices been shaped by a hollow stomach?

Even before she topped the rise, the rider halted his horse and dismounted. Holding the reins in one hand, he stepped toward the incline, going quite still as he surveyed the wreckage. Eliza could make out little of him, half-hidden as he was beneath a woolen greatcoat that swirled with the wind. But even through the hair blowing across her face, she saw the cloak's three-tied collar, its braided trim, its velvet lining. And his boots, buffed and only slightly soiled from his travels, were so well fitted as to form a second skin over the muscular swell of his calves.

A gentleman. Grabbing hold of a sapling and dragging herself, sodden hems and all, to the wall, she steeled herself to play the role of a lifetime—one that would save her life.

She all but collapsed against the low barrier, catching her balance with the flats of her hands against the stones. It was then he saw her.

"By God." He dropped the reins and ran toward her, cloak

billowing behind and all around him like lapping black flames. When he reached her she was still hunched and panting for breath, her bedraggled hair in her face despite an earlier attempt to secure it. From across the wall he reached for her. His hands, gloved and large, closed around her shoulders—around the shoulders of Elizabeth Mendoza's flowered muslin gown. Ever so gently, he raised her up.

"Madam, are you hurt?" A gaze the color of the Yorkshire hills at dawn, not green nor gray but a shade in-between, darted toward the carriage's awkward stance against the rowan. "By St. George, what happened here?"

"The horses . . . They were going too fast, and the rain and the road, all muddy and pitted, and then the bend and the driver fell and . . . " She stopped, her head drooping and her teeth clamping her lip. She was babbling, yes, but more. She blinked and tried to stop the tears, quell the rising grief and guilt. And the numbing fear that she'd never manage this plan of hers, that she'd been addled even to have thought of it.

As if she, and not Elizabeth, had survived the crash but only just, she began shaking so violently the man's hands and arms shook too, until his grip on her shoulders tightened and he straddled the wall to stand before her.

"It'll be all right now, madam. My name is Dylan Fergusson. I will bring you to safety. You'll soon be warm and dry and taken care of." His voice, husky, nearly a baritone, penetrated the wind and rolled over her like soft, sturdy flannel, making her believe, for a precious instant, that everything could and would be all right.

As if the gift of that voice weren't enough, he enfolded her to his chest, wrapping his cloak tightly around her, securing her in the shelter of his arms.

The tears became a torrent. Gentleman that he was, he went on holding her, patting her back and putting his solid presence at her disposal. Which of course only made the tears flow more furiously. It was the first time since Nathan died that anyone had shown her any kindness at all.

"Forgive me," she mumbled after some minutes into the second tier of his cloak's collar. He wore an open suit coat but no waistcoat beneath, only a fine linen shirt that smelled of an autumn meadow.

She was loathe to pull her face away, to relinquish her first haven since she'd lost the farm. Somehow she found the strength to lift her chin, straighten her shoulders, step back. "Forgive me," she repeated louder, more firmly this time.

"Not at all." He spoke with a soft brogue, a lovely lilt that softened a voice otherwise gruff and gravelly. His face, too, possessed an almost blunt, rugged quality smoothed by the fine arch of his eyebrows beneath fire-shot brown hair that wanted trimming. "You've been through a terrible ordeal," he said. "How long have you been stranded?"

"Two days."

"By God, and in the rain."

"Most of the time, yes. I stayed inside the coach, except when I tried to salvage the luggage."

He glanced over her head, not hard to do for one so tall. "Where is your driver? Your horses?"

"The linchpin and whiffletree broke, and the horses galloped away. We were headed south. They're probably halfway to London by now." She ducked her head, not wishing to answer his first question, hoping he'd let it pass.

He did not. Removing a glove, he placed his hand beneath her chin and raised it, and all Eliza could think of as she met his concerned gaze was that there was a callous on the tip of his thumb, and how rough and reassuring it felt against her skin. How masculine in an honest, unpretentious sort of way.

"What happened to your driver?" he asked, his voice as gentle as a misty rain.

She shivered and turned her face to where the incline leveled and the rocks were not as dense. She'd rolled first the driver and then Elizabeth onto the blanket that first day and dragged them both there. Side by side she'd laid them, covered them with the only cloak she'd found and Nathan's old coat, and weighted it all down with stones. Thus she had kept the buzzards away.

Mr. Fergusson followed the direction of her gaze, then looked back at her, one eyebrow upraised in a question that didn't need asking. She nodded. His gaze returned to the makeshift mound.

"Are there two deceased?"

Again she nodded. "The other was . . . my paid companion." She'd planned this story the first night but stumbled over the voicing of it nonetheless. Lies had never come easy to her. This one sat like a stone inside her chest.

"How on earth did you survive unscathed?"

She felt a lick of panic. How to explain her utter lack of injury? She opened her mouth hoping something believable would come out, but he spoke again first.

"That you're standing here now is nothing short of a miracle, sure enough." His thick brows drew low. "Do you know of their families?"

The question startled her. Of course she didn't know a thing about the driver's background, and precious little about Elizabeth's. Mr. Fergusson eyed her, waiting and expectant.

"An aunt." She paused and thought back to the scant clues in Anselmo Mendoza's letter. "In York. They'd been recently hired, you see, and . . . " She cut short the fabrication, not at all feigning the sudden dizziness that made her teeter in the unfamiliar high-heeled boots she wore.

"Easy, lass." Mr. Fergusson's arm went round her waist and she once more found herself pressed to his warm, solid length. "I fear you may have been injured more than you realize. I won't rest easy till we get you to a physician."

For a wondrous moment she let him hold her steady. He didn't feel as she'd thought a gentleman would, not soft and purposeless but powerful, substantial, resolute. She felt a world of determination in the crook of his arm, tempting her nearly beyond endurance to remain against him forever, protected, cared for, no longer alone.

She eased away. "I haven't eaten much these last two days. I didn't know how long I'd be here and thought I'd best conserve."

"Pardon me for saying so, lass," he said with the beginnings of a smile that caused an odd flipping sensation in her stomach, "but I'd say you don't eat much most of the time. You're a mere slip of a thing."

Indeed. The corset she'd somehow wrangled her way into had delivered the same taunting message. She'd had to tighten and retighten the laces, yet even so whenever she moved the wretched thing twisted and gaped and poked where it shouldn't while her breasts kept disappearing inside. Where Elizabeth had been slender and graceful, Eliza was unfashionably gaunt.

Still, it took her aback that he'd mentioned it. And when, exactly, had he proceeded from madam to lass? Had he sensed something amiss, some slovenly bent in her posture or tone of voice that proclaimed her less than a lady? Would a lady have leaned so readily against a complete stranger? Flames rose in her cheeks.

"That was rude of me," he said, lowering his chin to search her face. Her first instinct was to turn away, hide her face in her hands. But the contrition in his misty hazel eyes held her trapped. His lips curved ruefully. "I'm very sorry."

In the next instant he shrugged out of his cloak, tossed it around her shoulders and tucked it tight beneath her chin. She all but disappeared inside its abundant folds while the hem thudded to the soggy ground with fabric to spare. It felt, oh, like heaven, the velvet lining impossibly soft, incomparably warm with the lingering heat of his body.

She slipped her arms free. "No, Mr. Fergusson, it's quite chilly and your suit coat will never suffice. You'll catch your death and I . . . I have a shawl in the coach."

He was already shaking his head. "You keep it, lass. This isn't considered at all cold where I come from. But you, now, you're as shaky as a newborn lamb."

He stepped closer, again tucking his chin low as he regarded her in that familiar, intimate way of his. Eliza thought a lady might find his manner intrusive; might step away while issuing a firm warning to mind his distance. She didn't.

"Have you nothing warmer than this summer frock?"

She shook her head, basking in his concern. There might have been warmer dresses in the piles she'd gathered, but she had never dressed the part of a lady before. The corset had been difficult enough. This dress had few buttons and no lacings, a welcome respite for her cold and aching fingers.

She had, of course, searched for a black gown, for Elizabeth should appear in mourning. She'd found none among the scattered luggage. At first this puzzled her, until she determined it to be another clue to Elizabeth's immediate past. Her husband must have passed away so recently she'd only had time to have one mourning dress made—the one she wore.

"There's a village a few miles back." The young man's bare hand closed around her shoulder through the bulk of his cloak. "We'll stop there and hire someone who looks trustworthy to come and collect your luggage. Is there anything of value you wish to take now?"

"Only my purse and—" She'd started to add Nathan's rifle, but how could she possibly explain her attachment to the filthy, rusted old weapon? She shook her head, shivering again. "Just my purse. It's in the coach."

He nodded. Surely he recognized her awkward hesitations and sudden flushes for the signs of a liar. Or was he too much of a gentleman to read them accurately?

"Let's get it and be off. We'll need to search out the nearest undertaker as well. Your servants need a proper burial. What did you say their names were?"

She hadn't said. She'd thought up identities that first night, too, but when she opened her mouth now something entirely different, unexpected, appalling, came rushing out. "Nathan and Eliza Kent."

She very nearly clapped her hands over her mouth. And yet

those names made perfect sense. In order for Elizabeth to live, Eliza of course must die. And as for Nathan . . . She might as well have followed him into the grave six months ago.

"A married couple?"

"Yes," she said, nodding and looking away. "Recently."

"Poor souls." They started down the incline toward the coach, his hand firm at the small of her back in steady counterbalance to the uneven ground. "I'll see to it suitable markers are made for their graves."

She came to a sudden halt and nearly sent them both tripping over his trailing cloak hem. "You'd do that, sir? You didn't even know them."

"I may not have, but I daresay Nathan and Eliza Kent deserve as good as anyone else. And I see no reason to burden their aunt with the cost of it. When you write to her, assure her that her relations were well tended."

"Thank you, Mr. Fergusson," she whispered.

He didn't reply; he merely took her hand to help her across the rocks.

Ah, his kindness made her throat throb with the desire to tell him the truth, made her wretched and ashamed. But then again, his generosity was offered because he believed her to be a gentlewoman. Had he known her for a common farmwife turned laundry maid turned almost-whore, he'd surely exact a lewd price for conveying her to the nearest village. Then he would go on his gentleman's way while she returned to the Raven's Perch to decide whether to whore or starve.

At the coach she wrapped the cords of Elizabeth's reticule— the velvet one that matched the lovely carriage dress—around her wrist. She'd fretted over that frock, wondering what to do. What would people say about a paid companion wearing such expensive clothes?

She'd considered exchanging the gown for something less sumptuous, more appropriate for a genteel servant. But strip-

ping those beautiful velvets from Elizabeth's cold body
seemed an insufferable insult, an indignity the gentlewoman
would never have forgiven.

Eliza so hoped she might have Elizabeth's forgiveness, not
only for what she'd done thus far, but for . . . everything.

Mr. Fergusson found a small satchel among the baggage
and handed it to her. "You might wish to fill this with neces-
sities. I believe my horse can manage that much."

She packed a change of underthings, stockings, an extra
pair of gloves. She reached for a silver and gilt hairbrush,
then quickly shoved it inside when she realized the hair
caught in its bristles didn't match her own sandy brown in the
least. She stole a peek over her shoulder. Again, Mr. Fergusson made no acknowledgment of her odd behavior.

She selected a final item: a tortoiseshell trinket box that
had been locked until she had tried one of the keys in Elizabeth's reticule. Inside she'd discovered money, a great deal, so
much she hadn't bothered to count. Perhaps more importantly
she'd found further clues into Elizabeth Mendoza's life: a
copy of the bill of sale for Folkstone Manor and records of
annuity and stock accounts that Eliza despaired of decipher-
ing. It didn't matter; she'd let Raphael Mendoza de Leone
handle such financial matters.

She slipped the cache inside the portmanteau. After taking
a moment to twist her hair and pin it up, she secured a satin-
lined bonnet on her head. Then together she and Mr. Fergusson made their way back up to the road. He secured the bag
and swung up into the saddle. Leaning low, he extended his
forearm. Eliza took hold of his triceps with both hands, astonished all over again at how muscular he was, how thoroughly solid. With as much ease as if she were a child, he
swung her up behind him.

He twisted around to face her. "Perhaps it's time you told
me your name. You do have one, don't you?"

In spite of everything her life had been up until that moment, she found a smile for this man. "I do. It's Elizabeth

Mendoza de Leone." And then her smile shriveled, consumed
by her lying tongue.

   This, too, went unnoticed. He grinned. "That's like music."

   As he clucked his horse to motion, Eliza pressed her cheek
to his back and squeezed one last tear into his woolen coat.

CHAPTER 3

Dylan hadn't planned to enjoy the feel of this woman, this Elizabeth Mendoza-whatever-the-rest, against him for the next several miles. When he set out from Wakefield, he'd chosen this road for its isolation, for the opportunity to be entirely alone after the conniving crowds of London. Much good it had done him. He could not have got any closer to an Englishman—or woman—than he was at this moment.

His resolve to sit stiff and uninviting in the saddle in front of her lasted exactly as long as it took those slim arms to encircle his waist. Not that he believed she meant to cuddle. No, she was exhausted and bedraggled, done in by two days of withstanding the elements and worrying if rescue would ever come. She clung so tight she constricted his ability to draw a decent breath, and his determination to withstand the allure of another English lass melted away into the heat of her body.

Not that there was much of it. Heat, that was. Or body, for that matter. She wasn't at all like other women he knew, not strong and sturdy like the farm girls at home in St. Abbs, and not soft, plump and buxom like the women he'd met in London.

Then again, he'd discovered that oftentimes endowment was merely a trick of clever corsetry. Even Isabel, now that he thought of her with a clear head, had proved somewhat less spectacular once her clothing hit the floor.

But as he'd boorishly pointed out minutes ago, this woman was scrawny, to put it bluntly. Thin and rather flat-chested. Of course, he should never have implied as much. The moment the observation escaped his mouth he'd wanted to kick himself.

By St. George, he *was* provincial.

If not bodily curves, then, what drew him to her? Perhaps it was that lost look in those great golden eyes of hers, as if she couldn't quite grasp what had happened to her, to her servants.

"Are you warm enough, Miss Mendoza . . . er . . . Forgive me, I've forgotten the rest."

She lifted her face from between his shoulder blades, taking the warmth of her cheek with her. It made him sorry he'd spoken and roused her. "Mendoza de Leone," she said, "though Mendoza will do. And it's missus, not miss."

"Ah. Where then, may I ask, is your—"

"I am a widow."

"I see. I'm very sorry."

"Thank you, Mr. Fergusson." Her voice turned soft, breathy. A shiver ran through her arms to vibrate against his torso.

"Don't be afraid to hold tight and lean against me, Mrs. Mendoza. You'll stay warmer and I daresay under the circumstances no one would think to raise an eyebrow."

Her grip immediately released and her arms slid away. Damn, he hadn't meant to insult her. Just as he despaired of ever saying the right thing to any Englishwoman, she encircled him again, this time dragging the edges of his cloak around his shoulders so that it covered them both.

"Now we'll both stay warm, Mr. Fergusson." Like a kitten basking on a sun-warmed pillow, she pressed her length to his back, tightened her hold and returned her cheek to his spine.

Either the woman was the most brazen flirt he'd ever encountered, or the most guileless, ingenuous soul this side of the Cheviot Hills. He felt inclined to believe the latter. There'd been nothing coquettish in her voice, no seduction in the pull of her arms. Everything about her seemed genuine, unaffected, unspoiled.

Even her readiness to swing up behind his saddle spoke of an obliging nature. He'd taken his foot out of the stirrup so she might use it for leverage, but she'd neither noticed nor needed such assistance. Once up, she'd settled astride without a hint of complaint for all she must be unused to the position. Even the most accomplished horsewoman sat sidesaddle. This could not have been comfortable, yet she bore the inconvenience, not to mention the indignity, bravely, with a practical concern, even, for his welfare.

Yes, he was warm. Toasty. For a cold, damp Yorkshire day, he was about as comfortable as a fellow could be. And he liked it, liked it rather much.

He just didn't want to.

"I don't know this area, Mr. Fergusson." Her chin, round and soft, prodded his back as she spoke. "Where exactly are we going?"

"South to Wakefield, to my sister's home. They've a good physician in town. But I passed a small village a few miles from here. We'll stop there first to make arrangements for the burials and to have your luggage collected."

"A village? Do you mean . . . Heverton Gorse?"

"Aye, I believe that was the name. How did you know?"

"I . . . remember my driver mentioning it. But must we stop there? Couldn't we go on to Wakefield?"

"Surely you wish to tend to your servants as soon as possible."

"Yes. Yes, of course."

Reluctance. He heard it in her voice, felt it in the tension in her arms. He wondered why but knew he had no right to question her; no business indulging his curiosity about the woman. Once they reached Wakefield he'd see to her welfare as any concerned stranger would—not that there'd be much for him to do once his sister and her mother-in-law learned someone needed feeding and fussing over.

He, meanwhile, would be free to hire her a new coach and inquire around if her horses had been found. After that he'd send her on her way with a fond and final farewell.

They reached Heverton Gorse by midafternoon. It wasn't much of a village even by lonely Yorkshire standards. In fact it made his seaside home of St. Abbs seem cosmopolitan in comparison.

Not far from the fork where the old and new London roads converged, a third lane branched, rutted and muddy, spanning the hamlet from start to finish. A sprinkling of establishments hunkered against the moorland winds: a blacksmith's shop, an apothecary, a barber shop, a butcher and a tavern, all laid out beneath the supervisory eye of a stone church and its gaunt yard of headstones.

Beyond the town a few homes straggled, small, thatched-roof dwellings where stubby chimneys belched soot into the cloudy afternoon sky. Wire-fenced kitchen gardens promised little more to be had from the autumn soil, while sheep-dotted pastureland rolled away to meet the moors.

There were a few people about tending livestock, hauling firewood, setting off a clamor of pings from the smithy. Their drab forms blended with the grays and browns of the village. They paid Dylan and his charge scant attention.

He saw no sign of anything resembling a coaching inn, just the tavern. Like its neighboring structures, the building was of gray stone, weathered timber, and stucco that had centuries ago ceased to be white. The sign above the door, creaking in time to the wind, displayed a stout black bird posing proudly on a branch; below it, black letters proclaimed the Raven's Perch Inn.

Yes, the place looked about as foreboding as those scavengers of death. But it boasted a stable at the rear, so it would do.

"Here we are, madam." He twisted in the saddle to regard her. "You can take your rest while I make inquiries."

He discovered her staring at an aspen tree opposite the tavern, studying it with a puzzling intensity. Then she shut her eyes and drew a breath, turned, and took in the Raven's Perch with a weary sigh.

"Must we linger here, Mr. Fergusson?"

"There's nowhere else."

"Surely you won't leave me alone inside?" She shivered in a gust of wind, raising a hand to pluck strands of hair from her eyes. "It's so very . . . grim."

Obviously the place didn't meet with her approval. Perhaps he'd misjudged her; perhaps now that she no longer feared succumbing to the elements on a deserted moor, a spoiled English aristocrat had emerged.

"I don't see that we have any other choice, Mrs. Mendoza." He guided his horse into the stable yard. "I'll try to secure you a private room, if they have such a thing, where you won't be disturbed."

She slipped her arms from around his middle. "So be it, then."

Tucking her chin and nearly her entire face into his cloak, she clung to his arm as he brought her inside. Well, he supposed this common public house offended her lady's sensibilities. Did she not realize her great good fortune in simply being able to walk into such an establishment, unlike her driver and companion who'd never walk anywhere again?

Yet even he had to admit that if given a choice he'd gladly have ridden on to Wakefield. The interior of the Raven's Perch proved everything its cheerless exterior promised. Dim and musty, with the sour odors of last night's ale tumbling with today's pungent cooking aromas.

The place was empty but for a man working in the far shadows near the hearth, his back bent over the task of wiping down the pine tabletops. He saw them and straightened, dangling a rag as damp and gray as the rest of the place from his less-than-clean hands. "We've mutton and cabbage stew today. Will you be wanting any?"

"We would, thank you," Dylan said. The menu had needed no announcement. By the smell of the place, he guessed they served mutton and cabbage most days. "We need lodgings for the night," he added. "Two rooms."

"Those we have. Nothing fancy and none too large, but the missus keeps 'em clean." The proprietor's lips pulled in something approaching a smile, revealing one missing front tooth and another that protruded at an awkward angle from his gums.

Dylan glanced away. "We'll take them."

"For the night?" Mrs. Mendoza's face inched out from its woolen shelter.

"It's already growing late," he told her, "and we have arrangements to make before continuing on."

"Yes . . . All right." And with that she all but disappeared back inside his cloak.

And perhaps she had good reason. As the tavern keeper moved closer, his bloodshot gaze wandered her length before settling on the small portion of her face visible above the cloak's collar. Dylan felt a surge of protectiveness. He didn't normally give a fig about class or its privileges but surely the man had no business ogling a lady of Mrs. Mendoza's station. Common courtesy dictated that much.

"Have you somewhere private where we might warm ourselves and have a meal?" he asked the man, as much to distract his attention as to obtain the desired accommodations.

"Aye." Scratching several days' growth of beard with the back of his hand, he inclined his head toward a doorway. "Through here."

He led them through the kitchen, where a woman chopped vegetables at a counter while another stirred the contents of a kettle hanging over the hearth. Mother and daughter, Dylan guessed, judging by the difference in age and similarity in features. The older of the two acknowledged the intrusion with the lift of an eyebrow and the chop of a turnip.

They filed through another doorway into a bare little room

as grim as the main one. Not a single rug brought any sense of comfort to rough-hewn floorboards, nor was there a cushion to be found on the four spindly Windsor chairs that surrounded a pine table. Still, despite the lack of luxury the room was thankfully private or would be once they closed the door behind them.

"Will this do, milord?"

A note of sarcasm in the last word raised Dylan's hackles. "I am Mr. Fergusson merely and yes, it will do if we may have a fire."

"Surely." The innkeeper sauntered out.

Mrs. Mendoza sank into a chair and finally let his cloak fall away from her face. A long sigh escaped her lips.

Dylan chose the chair directly opposite. He leaned a little forward as an impulse prompted him to ask, "Do you know that man?"

Eliza flinched, then tried to cover it with a cough. Yes, she knew that man. Merely four nights ago she had wandered into this very same tavern, only to be ordered out with a stern warning to ply her trade elsewhere.

Not that she believed for a minute the owner balked at allowing bawdy women to frequent his saloon, for a practiced courtesan would be a boon to his business. But a lank-haired scarecrow of a strumpet in a man's plaid coat? *Out,* he'd bellowed, and so she'd skulked away to cower beneath the tree across the road.

Did he recognize her now? Perhaps he found her familiar, yet couldn't quite place her dressed as she was. Her change in appearance and circumstance might confuse him, but she must be careful all the same.

"Indeed not, sir," she said in reply to Mr. Fergusson's question. "Why on earth would you ask such a thing?"

"Forgive me." He looked toward the door, shaking his

head. "It was just the way he looked at you, and how you hid your face within my cloak. I thought perhaps . . . "

"If I hid my face, sir, it was to—"

"Spare yourself his rude gawking. Of course. When he returns, I'll see to it he gets on with his business and leaves us in peace."

What *had* she been thinking, snapping at him that way? Already he'd done more for her than anyone since Nathan died. Surely he deserved her forbearance for what was, after all, merely a question. She wondered, is this how all gentlemen behaved toward the ladies of their rank—solicitous, gallant, tolerant? Or was this something particular to this man, this Dylan Fergusson?

"Thank you, sir, and do forgive my rudeness." She untied her bonnet and set it on the table. "I promise I'll be far more cordial company after a warm meal, even if it is mere mutton and cabbage."

Did that sound convincing? The thought of the coming repast made her stomach growl, but she supposed a lady would show disdain of such simple fare.

He tilted his head at her, a smile curling his lips. "Nothing wrong with a heaping plate of mutton, now is there? Perhaps we might impose upon our friend to part with a bottle of wine, if such a thing exists in this village."

"Ale will do if it must, Mr. Fergusson."

He approved with a chuckle. At least it sounded approving. Would a lady ever drink ale, even if left with no other choice? Eliza hadn't the faintest notion what ladies drank.

When the innkeeper returned to light the hearth fire and set wooden trenchers of food on the table, Eliza shrank back into Mr. Fergusson's cloak. Perhaps she needn't have bothered. Mr. Fergusson not only encouraged the man to make haste in that civilized, gentlemanly way of his, but managed always to position himself between Eliza and the other man's curious eyes.

He saw to it she had enough of everything, including the

wine he'd suggested, mulled to a sweet warmth over the hearth fire. Gradually Eliza relaxed, delving into her meal with a good deal of concealed enthusiasm, forcing herself to eat slowly but privately savoring every bite. Between the fare, the fire and Mr. Fergusson's amiable regard, she soon felt warm enough—and brave enough—to shed his cloak, albeit she draped it conveniently over the chair behind her where it could be quickly retrieved if necessary.

"Where do you hail from, Mrs. Mendoza?" he asked as he rose to poke the fire.

"York," she replied, and prayed he'd never been there, that he wouldn't wish to discuss particulars she knew nothing about.

"I suppose you've spent many a Season in London. I've just come from there myself."

"No, Mr. Fergusson, I've never been to London."

He took his seat and reached for his wine. "That surprises me."

"Does it?"

"It's my experience that most well-to-do families scramble to quit their country homes each spring and converge on the city."

How could she be so careless to have forgotten? She'd never fool anyone if she blundered on the simplest details.

"Don't worry," he said with a dismissive shrug, "you haven't missed much, in my opinion."

"Perhaps you might tell me all about it. It's where we were headed when . . . " She trailed off, looking down at her plate.

His hand inched across the small table until it reached hers, enveloping it in his sure, steady warmth. "I'm sorry, lass, to have brought it up."

There was that word again: lass. Despite a niggling conviction that it conveyed a familiarity a lady would never have brooked, Eliza liked it—the sound of it, the gentleness of his soft brogue when he pronounced it, and yes, the intimacy it invoked.

His fingers curled around hers. She thought he'd give a sympathetic squeeze and release her, but he just held on and on, looking contrite.

She met his misty dawn gaze and offered a smile that was purely hers, Eliza's. "Mr. Fergusson, have you noticed the frequency with which we apologize to one another?"

"You're right, lass. I'm—"

"No, no." She held up her free hand. "You mustn't say it. You saved my life, more than you know. You've nothing to be sorry for."

He shrugged and took his hand away, then cleared his throat and looked as Eliza had never seen a gentleman look—embarrassed and disconcerted and pleased all at once. She felt a little stab of . . .

Oh, she didn't know what. Gratitude? More than that, so much more. Affection. Yes. Unabashed, unfettered affection toward this gentle, generous, aristocratic stranger. Yet she must not show it, must not jump up and reach her arms around his neck as she felt wont to do, for a lady would never indulge in such an undignified display.

Of course, a lady could never comprehend a fraction of the relief, the enormous sense of solace, that Eliza gleaned merely from the sound of kind words, the heat of a fire, the fullness now suffusing her stomach.

And so she must suffer the loss of his wondrous hand with a tolerant smile, must offer prim thanks that reflected but a shadow of what glowed inside her.

He slid his napkin from his lap and laid it on the table, drawing Eliza's gaze back to his hand. Here again he surprised her, for his hands were not white and smooth as one might expect, but broad, muscled and callused. He'd been in the military, perhaps. He also rode horseback when most other men of his class would have hired a coach. Yes, that would explain his sturdy strength, the power that might have frightened a lady but reassured Eliza.

"If you have all you need," he said, "I'll leave you for a time and make arrangements for your luggage and . . . "

"And my servants. It's all right, Mr. Fergusson, I won't fall apart at mere mention of them. I'm very grateful for your generous offer to—"

This time *his* palm went up, his dark brows gathering in mock severity. "If there are to be no apologies between us, neither shall there be talk of gratitude. I'll return as soon as I might, and I'll leave word you're not to be disturbed under any circumstances."

With that he left her, securing the door behind him with a soft but resolute thud.

The room felt cavernous without him, cold and echoey. She drew his cloak around her shoulders, holding a corner of its velvet lining against her cheek. It was childish, an indulgence the Eliza of old would never have countenanced. As Nathan's wife she'd been sensible, decisive, robust and perhaps a tad more independent than her husband had wished.

When had she changed, become fragile and needy? The evening Nathan died? The day she lost the farm? Or perhaps that awful night she'd been turned out of her employer's house in disgrace. Or . . . Had assuming a lady's identity somehow robbed her of herself, like trading one's soul for the devil's favor, so that with each passing day she'd be less and less Eliza, until that woman no longer existed?

She pulled the cloak more tightly around her and sunk deeper into its masculine embrace. It was like having a man's arms around her. The fire sparked and crackled, sending a piney smell into the room. Eliza slid lower still, propped her feet on the seat beside her and tipped her head against her chair. Elizabeth's corset poked like a nudge to her conscience. She shifted, wriggled, relieved the pressure.

Her eyelids drooped but she forced them open. Sounds from the kitchen reminded her she was not safe, far from it. She sat up straighter. The innkeeper might return at any moment. Might remember her. Might bring this last chance for survival to ruin.

Yet more than that, a different sort of desperation kept Eliza awake, a burning need to savor what she hadn't known for so very long . . . Warmth, a full stomach and Dylan Fergusson's lingering scent inside his cloak.

Ah, she was wicked to enjoy it.

CHAPTER 4

An hour later, Dylan returned to the tavern to discover Mrs. Mendoza curled in her chair, wrapped in his cloak and fast asleep. Her lips were parted, slack and plumped as a child's, and the angle of her chin against his cloak collar deepened a dimple he'd so like to explore with the tip of his finger.

As he watched, her lips moved, forming silent words. What? Had he seen correctly? Was it a trick of the firelight or had she just mouthed the words, *bugger it?*

Surely not. Not a lady of Mrs. Mendoza's quality. Still . . . He mouthed the words himself. Bugger it. Then grinned. It had certainly looked to be what she said. Perhaps there was a side to Elizabeth Mendoza concealed by day, only to be unleashed under cover of night. Or perhaps Dylan Fergusson was a damned fool who saw in a pretty woman only the things he wished to see.

He knew he should wake her. Not with a nudge or anything so familiar and cloddish, but with a footstep, a cough, something to let them both pretend he hadn't noticed her slumber. Isabel had somehow always managed to fall asleep after him, waken before him, so that he never witnessed her at her most vulnerable. Except for that last time, when a jab from a pistol had cut his dreams short.

Now, standing over this woman, he wanted only to lift her from the chair, fill his arms with her, carry her upstairs and tuck her beneath the softest coverlet available.

And would his instinct to take care of her prevent him crawling in beside her?

Hardly.

Dylan Fergusson, you're incorrigible. Aye, he could all but hear his sister's chiding. And incorrigible he was, though not in the usual way, not like a rogue looking to take advantage of a young widow dependent on his help, but a bloody dreamer. One night with the lovely Elizabeth Mendoza and he'd be fantasizing about children again, about a life like the one shared by Charity and Luke.

Again he wondered what attracted him to her. She was pretty, true, but not fashionably. Her hair didn't curl and her eyes weren't blue. Her nose didn't taper to an aristocratic point nor were her eyebrows plucked and shaped to delicate arches. No, her features were soft and rounded, her cheeks broad, her lips full, her nose the slightest bit too wide.

Wide enough to accommodate a man's playful kiss. Only the thought of her reaction prevented him. A scream, a slap, perhaps a kick to the shin? Especially if she learned who he was. What he was. So much less than her equal.

Thus far she seemed to believe he was a Scottish gentleman, perhaps even an aristocrat. Not that he'd set out to fool her. It had simply become his habit that while in England he did as the English, or nearly so. He'd learned success alone held little weight among these people; in the end a man's worth nearly always came down to the circumstances of his birth.

But perhaps this woman, who uttered such delightful phrases as *bugger it* in her sleep, would break tradition and judge by altogether different standards.

The notion brought him to his senses and reminded him not to make a fool of himself a second time. He'd been beguiled by Isabel, too, with her wide-eyed admiration and her ingenuous praises. Ingenuous? Ha. Those stunning violet eyes had held cunning designs from the first. He understood now. She'd ventured to the theater the night they met with a goal in mind. He had been her holiday from a dull, loveless marriage.

Taking no pains to subdue his boots' report against the floorboards, he strode to Mrs. Mendoza and laid his hand on her shoulder.

"Madam, wake up."

She flinched and shot upright, feet kicking over the chair they'd been propped on, sending it crashing. As Dylan lurched sideways, her cry echoed against the opposite wall. Her knuckles whitened around the arms of the chair and in her great golden eyes a fierce, defensive fear churned. Panting, she drew back as if trapped in a corner.

"It's only me." Dylan crouched beside her. He reached for her hand, then thought better of it; it would only embarrass her further. "Calm yourself. You must have been dreaming."

"I . . . yes . . . dreaming." Her fingers strained around the Windsor chair's curved arms. Her eyes darted here, there, then lighted on his face. "I didn't mean to sleep. How long . . . ?"

"I've been gone about an hour. I've arranged for your things to be collected in the morning and brought to Wakefield."

She nodded slightly but seemed hardly to hear him. He rose and moved away, stooping to right the fallen chair but also to give her a private moment to gather her composure. When he faced her again, however, the wariness still peered from her eyes.

"It's no wonder you dozed off, after all you've been through." He set the chair closer to the table and settled into it. "I daresay the sleep did you good."

"I suppose." She relaxed her grip finger by finger as if releasing her fears one by one. As she brushed strands of hair from her eyes, Dylan wondered what could have so frightened her. A dream? One that made her say *bugger it?*

Only once before had he seen anyone so disoriented, so perplexed. His brother-in-law. How well he remembered the morning Luke awakened insisting he was an English duke and remembering nothing of his yearlong marriage to Charity. Luke had been angry, frightened and quite desperate to understand how he'd come to be in a Scottish farmhouse among strangers. His memories of his Scottish life had been dashed the night before during a fight, scattered by a blow to the head with a bottle. Only weeks later did they discover that it had been an earlier attempt on his life that erased his English memories and sent him to Scotland in the first place.

Mrs. Mendoza seemed clear enough on who she was, but what did *he* know with any certainty about her?

Enough to know she was none of his business.

Chin tucked inside his cloak, she leaned a little forward, staring past him into the flames lapping in the hearth. Her eyes darkened as her pupils dilated. He cleared his throat.

"I've arranged for the burials. A simple graveside funeral, for I thought you might rather wish to arrange a memorial in York, or simply send a stipend to that aunt of theirs or to their home parish."

That set off a puzzling spark of alarm in her eyes, but so fleeting he might have imagined it. "How considerate of you to have thought of that, Mr. Fergusson." She raised her face and met his gaze. "Thank you."

"You're welcome. If you give me the proper direction, I'll see it's done the moment we reach Wakefield. There's a bank there that can handle the transfer of funds."

She blinked. Her teeth nipped at her bottom lip. "No, you've done so much. I'll do it, if you'll be good enough show me where the bank is."

Her gaze again drifted to the fire. Her response troubled him. He knew it shouldn't, for it hadn't been unreasonable by any means. She may already feel more indebted to him than she cared to be. She might not want him involved in her financial affairs. Still, he experienced a vague but stubborn uneasiness, and a growing curiosity.

"Come, our rooms are ready." He stood and gestured to the

door. "It's growing dark. We might as well retire for the evening and start out early in the morning."

She wobbled getting out of the chair. He caught her elbow, holding her steady until she gained her balance. How insubstantial she was—made more of light and air than flesh and blood—far too thin for a grown woman. Her grief in losing her husband, perhaps, had taken its toll. He glanced at the wooden trenchers on the table. Hers sat empty, so clean it almost might have been washed. At least she was eating.

Their rooms adjoined, it being necessary to walk through the first to reach the second. He gave her the further one to ensure her privacy and—yes, he had to admit—to put himself between her and anything that might disturb her in the night. Before he extinguished the lamp he tapped at her door.

"Have you all you need? I'm afraid these barren little rooms fall far short of what you're accustomed to."

He had expected to speak to her through the door. She startled him by opening it, surprised him further still by appearing wrapped in his cloak, her bare toes sticking out from under its hem, her hair spilling down her back.

"The room is splendid, Mr. Fergusson. Thank you."

"I, er, wondered if you needed more blankets. Another pillow perhaps?"

"I want for nothing, sir, I assure you." She pulled his cloak tighter around her as she regarded him expectantly. He guessed she wore little beneath, for the garment hugged her hips more snugly than it had previously over skirts and petticoats.

He released a breath. "If you're certain, then."

"Are you forgetting I spent two nights in a battered coach?" Her lips curled in a soft smile. "Compared to that, Mr. Fergusson, this is heaven."

She ended with a shake of her head that sent her hair swaying around her shoulders. Loosened from its pins, it plunged as straight as it had when rain-soaked, but what it lacked in curl it surely made up for in gleam and gloss, like polished sandalwood. He imagined such hair would glide through a man's hands like pure satin, cool and slippery across his skin.

He might not have made his colossal error had she not laid her hand on his arm just then and stepped closer to whisper, "Thank you so much, Mr. Fergusson, for all your kindness. You cannot know what it means to me."

"Good night, then, lass," he said. Then, taking momentary but complete leave of his senses, he leaned and brushed a kiss across her lips.

For one thunderous instant she didn't move a muscle, other than her eyes which widened like two gold sovereigns. Dylan, too, went utterly still, horrified and wishing he could undo the deed, disappear and die. Then Mrs. Mendoza whirled, her hair whipping his chest. The door shut in his face.

His forehead fell against it with a thud. "I'm sorry," he murmured to chipped, worn paint. He pushed away and groaned.

The funeral, sad little affair that it was, occurred early the next morning. Mr. Fergusson arranged and even insisted on paying for everything, from the transporting of the bodies at first light to the little graveside service performed by a village elder, since the church boasted no permanent rector. When Eliza promised to repay Mr. Fergusson for his generosity, he had refused with a shake of his head and firm *no*.

The sun made a feeble appearance through a gauzy haze that threatened to thicken and send rain across the moors. Eliza could scarcely bare to watch as the flimsy coffins, hastily assembled by the local carpenter, were lowered into graves that would remain unadorned until markers could be fashioned. The churchyard of Heverton Gorse offered a bleak resting place at best, a barren slab of ground beside the cheerless stone church.

A chill wind slapped her cheeks. Elizabeth Mendoza de Leone deserved far better. She deserved flowers, music, a gleaming black casket lined in satin. She deserved friends and mourners. She deserved to be remembered in as elegant a manner as that in which she had lived.

As the obliging villager, a Mr. Todd, intoned an appropriate if uninspired bible verse, Eliza offered a silent prayer of her own. In it she acknowledged her crime—the stealing of Elizabeth Mendoza's identity, future and, yes, even her death. In exchange Eliza pledged a solemn and binding oath. The rest of her days would be spent honoring Elizabeth and the life she might have had, spending every ounce of energy she possessed in good works and dedicating those works to her deceased patroness.

When she arrived at the home of Raphael Mendoza in London, Eliza would place herself utterly at the family's disposal. She'd become a devoted aunt to the children, friend and confidante to the wife and conciliator to the husband, doing her utmost to ease the rift that had separated the Mendoza brothers.

A twinge of fear rippled through her confidence. If someone there recognized her for an imposter . . . but no. Anselmo's letter assured her that his family in London had never met Elizabeth, that she was alone in the world. Like Eliza herself.

A hand closed on her shoulder, yanking her from her London daydreams back to the dreary Yorkshire village.

"It's over. Let's get you indoors." Mr. Fergusson stared at a point somewhere above her head. He'd avoided eye contact all morning and spoken precious little besides. The funeral cast a solemn pall over the morning, true, but the familiarity that had so perplexed her yesterday had vanished in a single moment—when he'd leaned in and kissed her the night before.

Still, his gentleman's honor had not abated. In silence he escorted her into the tavern, staying close, a constant presence between her and the proprietor's continued stares.

At the threshold of her room he tipped a polite, very correct bow. "The cart with your luggage has already set out, but I've been unable to find any sort of coach for you. This village has precious little to offer. I could, if you wish, return to Wakefield alone and send a carriage back for you."

A practical plan, true, but one that would leave her here alone with a tavernkeep who might at any moment remember when he'd seen her last. "If there's any way at all, Mr. Fergusson, I'd much prefer to leave today."

He nodded. "I understand. I'll ask around some more. In the meantime, I'll order a meal for you in the private room below."

Before she could reply, he turned and left her. Left her with a briar stuck in her conscience. How he must long to quit his responsibility of her, yet how readily he gave of himself, with nary a blink nor hint of complaint. She could not help but marvel what a rare sort of man this Dylan Fergusson was, and she could not help but wish he'd treat her in similar kind even if he knew who and what she truly was.

Her fingertips pressed her lips. Mr. Fergusson surely didn't seem the kind who dallied with women for sport. Were customs so different in Scotland? Or was this something she didn't know about aristocrats? Perhaps they kissed all the time to convey friendship, gratitude, concern, good wishes.

She doubted it. As she packed her few things into the satchel, she thought back on the conversation immediately before their lips met. He'd inquired about her comfort. She'd thanked him. Perfectly civilized. Oh, but then she'd touched him. Placed her hand on his arm and leaned close to murmur her thanks for his kindness. Perhaps she'd stepped closer than a lady should. The rules between noble men and women were subtle, an intricate mystery. How many had she broken, and how far had she declined in Mr. Fergusson's estimate?

His kiss had startled her, bewildered her. It also sent fingers of warmth and well-being throughout her body, her soul. Like hot food in her empty belly, compassion in her harsh world, hope in her barren heart, his kiss had filled her with sudden joy, but only for the briefest of instants. Then all the reasons why it should not have happened trampled the pleasure and left her confused, mortified and, yes, frightened of being turned away yet again.

At a clatter outside her window, she glanced up to see a raven perched on the sill, in perfect keeping with the name of the inn. It shook its wings and glared fiercely at her through the glass before soaring away into the pewter sky.

Eliza shivered. Mr. Fergusson's great coat lay draped over the foot of the bed. She hadn't worn it to the burial. She would not wear it again. Like his kiss, it brought too great a sense of intimacy, a warm temptation that must be resisted. Instead, after fastening her overnight bag she tossed her shawl—Elizabeth's fine, lamb's wool shawl—over her shoulders.

Downstairs, she discovered a generous meal but no Mr. Fergusson, just as she had predicted. Just as well, for what would they talk about with the awkward memory of their kiss dangling between them? Relief vied with disappointment, but her growling stomach ruled the day. Wisps of steam escaped makeshift linen covers, filling the air with the aromas of fresh bread, porridge and a Yorkshire pie filled with, of course, mutton.

Eliza indulged in far more than she might have dared in Mr. Fergusson's company. In short, she ate as no lady would. But when she finally touched her napkin to her lips and leaned back in physical, if not emotional, contentment, the gentleman still had not appeared.

The opening of the door startled her, but it was the tavern-keep and not Mr. Fergusson who poked his head into the room. "The gentleman asked that milady meet him outside in the coach yard. If your bags be packed, I'll bring 'em on down."

"Mr. Fergusson found a coach, then?"

He shrugged. His squinting eyes held her in blatant curiosity, and she wished she hadn't twisted her hair into a tidy knot at her nape but had left loose tendrils behind which to hide. Realizing that any show of evasiveness would only heighten his suspicions and perhaps confirm his nagging memories of her, she met his gaze full on.

"My bag is right here, thank you."

"Carried it yourself, did you?"

Another mistake. She'd have to remember such particulars from now on. Getting to her feet, she slipped the cords of the beautiful velvet reticule onto her wrist and gathered Mr. Fergusson's cloak over her arm.

She tugged the door wider and swept out past the nosy innkeeper with her own nose thrust to an indifferent angle. From the main room, his wife's voice stopped her cold.

"We do have a lady staying here, yes," she heard the woman say to someone out of view in the pub. Eliza's heart began to pound beneath the restricting corset. "But not of that description, not exactly," the woman added.

"Is her name Mendoza?" a man's voice inquired. "Elizabeth Mendoza de Leone?"

"Don't know, sir. You can ask her yourself. She's through there. In the kitchen and to the left."

Heart clogging her throat, Eliza turned and sprinted, nearly slamming into the innkeeper as he exited the parlor with her satchel.

"Forget something?"

"I did," she rasped and shut the door behind her. Looking down, she met with defeat. No key in the lock. What to do? Where to hide? There was nowhere. Not a cupboard, not even a tablecloth to crawl beneath. She ran to the window, flipped the latch and pushed. It didn't budge, not even when she pounded the frame with the heels of her hands.

Bugger it. Oh, *bugger* it.

Footsteps reverberated across the kitchen. Eliza backed into a corner. This was it. Her charade was over. Her chance at life gone.

A knock came at the door. Perhaps if she said nothing he'd

go away. Another knock, louder, insistent. Eliza barely heard it over her thrashing heart. She felt dizzy, sickened, crushed.

The door swung open. A man, gray-haired, a little stoop-shouldered, stepped into the room. His clothing hung limp on his figure, but the black serge declared him, if not quite a gentleman, more than a tradesman. His glance swung first to the table and chairs, then landed on Eliza cowering in her corner. She wanted to curl up into a ball as his gaze searched her, intense and piercing. She raised Mr. Fergusson's cloak in front of her like a shield.

"You . . . you are not . . . " As the breath froze in her lungs, the man's lined features relaxed. "Pardon me, madam." He inclined his head in a gesture of apology. "Forgive me for barging in. I was . . . " He sighed, the gesture accentuating deep shadows beneath his eyes. His fingers quivered where they clutched the doorknob. "You are not the person I'm seeking."

But who was *he?* Not a family member, surely, for Anselmo's letter claimed Elizabeth was alone in the world. The brother-in-law from London?

The thought brought fresh panic. But Eliza detected no trace of the dusky Spaniard in this Englishman's pale countenance. Besides, Anselmo Mendoza's letter indicated his brother, Raphael, had never met Elizabeth, while this man had known on first sight that Eliza was not she.

She stepped away from the wall. "It's perfectly all right, sir. No harm done."

He nodded, started to back out of the room, then hesitated. "May I be so presumptuous as to ask a question?"

"By all means."

"Have you by chance seen a young woman hereabouts, an extraordinarily beautiful young woman with hair as dark as midnight and eyes as bright as the morning sky?"

Oh, yes. Good heavens, yes. Her bravado flitted away. Everything that was honest and good in Eliza goaded her to speak of the horrendous accident that stole that gracious lady's life. She trembled with the urge to do the right and decent thing, to properly lay Elizabeth Mendoza's soul to rest.

But the frightened part of her, the part that remembered every wrenching hunger pang, every cruel injustice and cold, unsheltered night, stilled the truth, at least until Eliza discovered what he wanted.

She moved several steps toward him. "You seem distressed. May I ask why you seek this woman? Is there some emergency?"

Her studied Eliza, drew a breath and seemed to reach a decision. "Emergency? No. The emergency is over. All that remain are questions, ones only she can answer."

Eliza shook her head at his mysterious reply.

He smiled apologetically. "I am her husband's physician. *Was* his physician. I was also his friend, and I wish to find his wife and bring her home where she belongs."

Good heavens, then he might very well continue his search all the way to London, might even show up on Raphael Mendoza's doorstep to destroy Eliza's only chance at a future.

Don't let them have it. All but forgotten, the only words Elizabeth ever spoke in her hearing came rushing back. Don't let who have what? Was someone after Elizabeth Mendoza? Is that why her coach sped so recklessly down that slick and muddy road as though its horses were possessed?

Is that why this physician sought her? To protect her or . . . did *he* pose the danger?

Indeed he did—to Eliza. And she must put an end to his quest here and now, before he spoke to Mr. Fergusson.

"Sorry to have disturbed you, madam." He was backing out of the doorway, about to close the door behind him.

"Sir, do wait one moment," Eliza called. He regarded her curiously. "I . . . might have information for you."

"Do you remember having seen her?"

"No. But . . . " Eliza paused to steel herself for what she was about to do, something she hoped would end this man's search and lay Elizabeth's memory to rest, at least among those who had known her in York. "There's been talk of a coaching accident that occurred several days ago, out on the old Yorkshire Road."

"The old road?" His brows rose in surprise, then lowered. "Yes . . . she might have taken the old road. I hadn't thought of it, assumed she'd take the swiftest route." He questioned her with a look.

"The news was not good, I'm afraid. Not at all good."

"Do you mean . . . "

"Yes. I'm terribly sorry. No one survived." She went so far— oh, she'd land in hell surely—as to lay her hand on the doctor's forearm. "I do hope the lady you seek was not involved."

"Good heavens." His hand rose to grip the lapel of his coat, fist pressing his chest. "Elizabeth . . . "

"I understand there was a funeral this morning. Perhaps one of the village folk might be able to identify the victims." Oh, how easily these lies dripped from her tongue.

"Thank you, madam. You have been a great help."

"Sir, may I ask . . . " She sucked in a breath, steadying her nerves while he waited her for to continue. "May I ask how long it has been since her husband passed away?"

Puzzlement flickered in his eyes. "A week."

She bit back a gasp. So short a time. "How very tragic. I heard you speak the woman's name to the innkeeper's wife. Very beautiful it is, sir. But may I ask you one more thing?"

"Yes?"

"Her coachman's name."

His brows drew together slowly, thoughtfully. "Why do you wish to know?"

She'd made him suspicious, even if he couldn't quite decide why. "I should like to pray that no harm has come to them, or if it has, that their souls may be at peace."

That smoothed his doubts and raised a hint of a smile. "I've known him since he was a boy. Howitt. John Howitt."

Then he turned away and closed the door. Eliza pressed her ear to the scarred oak, listening as his footsteps receded through the kitchen and into the pub. Then she swung the door wide and sped in the opposite direction he had gone, charging out the kitchen door and into the stable yard.

"Easy, there, lass." Tall and solid, Mr. Fergusson caught her when she would have tripped over a loose stone on the path. It seemed he was forever catching her in those sturdy arms of his. "You've got the devil nipping at your heels, to be sure."

Devil? Yes. She'd burn someday. But despite his easy words, Mr. Fergusson's gaze was guarded. Once more, the memory of last night's awkwardness prodded, sending a wash of heat to her face.

She stepped away from him, out of his arms. "Are we ready to leave?"

"Would you please put this back on?" He took his cloak from her and draped it around her shoulders, over her shawl. "And no, we're not quite ready to go yet."

"Whatever can you mean? The innkeeper brought my bag out. He said—"

"I thought I'd finally found the use of a second horse." He gave a shrug. "Now it seems we can't have it until tomorrow. We'll have to stay another day."

"No, Mr. Fergusson, that won't do."

"But—"

"I insist we leave immediately. This very instant."

CHAPTER 5

Ah. Dylan found it astounding what a bit of braised mutton and one night's sleep on a lumpy mattress could achieve in a person. In but twenty-four hours Elizabeth Mendoza had transformed from fragile, grateful damsel to sizzling firebrand spitting orders like sparks.

That won't do, Mr. Fergusson. I insist we leave this instant, Mr. Fergusson . . .

And as quick as that they were back on his horse traveling to Wakefield, she astride behind him and he trying to forget, or at least not dwell, on his deplorable lack of control last night. As his beleaguered horse plodded south—for he dared not hurry the creature while it bore a double burden—he realized he should have seen the transformation coming. It nearly always did with Englishwomen.

Of course, he counted at least one blessing in this debacle. With the woman riding at his back, he couldn't easily twist around and kiss her again.

She still felt so damnably good against him, all but wrapped around him as she was. With relief, then, he watched the rooftops of Longfield Park, his brother-in-law's family seat, poke into view in the distance.

"We're very near Wakefield now," he said over his shoulder. "It won't be much longer."

She gave a start and pulled up straighter, and he realized they hadn't shared so much as a word in more than an hour. She must have been dozing, which would explain that little bounce of her cheek against his shoulder blade each time his horse's gait wavered over a bump in the road.

"Is that it there?" Her voice came as a breath against his ear, sending a pleasant shiver along his nape. Her arm came away from his middle, rising in the air to point.

They'd just rounded a bend that brought the valley into view, a wide vista of peaks and turrets and snug thatched roofs. Barely grazed by the first autumn colors, the farms and pastureland seemed far greener than the surrounding Yorkshire countryside.

"I'd thought it merely a village," she said. "It's practically a city."

"Hardly, though Wakefield is growing and prospering by the day. What was once mere sheep country is fast becoming England's center of textile manufacturing. Still, after York I should think you'd find it rather limited."

"Oh, I . . . well, yes, I suppose I will." Her arm returned to his waist, one hand clutching the other. She leaned to perch her chin on his shoulder. "It does looks to be such a lovely town though."

Her voice was airy, dreamy. His cloak had fallen open around her and her breasts were warm and soft at his back. He wondered, had Wakefield's apparent wealth led her to make assumptions about his family, or about him? Was she calculating his worth and finding him a tad more intriguing than she'd previously thought?

He hadn't explained his connection to Wakefield except to say his sister's family lived there. As much as Longfield Park had become a second home to him, he loathed revealing his circumstances to new acquaintances, writhed inside each time polite interest burgeoned to simpering opportunism. Then he was Dylan Fergusson no longer but the relation of a duke, valued not for the man he was but for what favors he might bestow.

A quiet voice of reason reminded him Elizabeth's opinion

of him didn't matter a whit. They'd part soon enough, and she might take along any impressions she wished.

Elizabeth. Exactly when had he started thinking of her by her given name? Ah, yes, about the time he kissed her last night. Christ.

He skirted the town, taking the New High Road that bridged the Calder River. Longfield Park lay just to the east, beyond its own small village and a patchwork of tenant farms whose pastures billowed like heaving seas flecked with wandering sheep. Here his sister's home sunk out of view again, only to reappear as they approached the estate's textile mill.

Elizabeth's chin pressed his shoulder. "What is that place, the large one with the spires?"

Ah, now it would come—the cooing admiration, the cloying flattery. He released a breath and braced for it. "That's Longfield Park. It's where we're going."

"I've heard the name before."

"I don't doubt it."

"So your relations are tenants on the estate?"

Not a ridiculous assumption. Many tenants did become wealthy in their own right. Ah, but never so wealthy as this. Dylan had never encountered such opulence before his first visit here; he'd been rendered speechless for nearly an entire day.

"Not tenants," he told her. "They own Longfield Park."

Her surprise came as a hot burst of breath against his neck. Then she went rigid as a house beam, depriving his back of her pliant heat.

"Just who are your relatives, Mr. Fergusson?"

"The Duke and Duchess of Wakefield."

"Stop the horse. Please, Mr. Fergusson. Stop right here."

She threw her leg over the horse's rump and slid to the ground before Dylan had the chance to assist her. He dismounted to find her apple-cheeked and moon-eyed. Her hand shot out, forefinger jabbing the distance.

"I can't go there. A duke and duchess? Are you mad?"

Are you? he wanted to counter, unable to fathom what had prompted such a panic. For panicked she was, from her flaming features to her shaking knees, visibly trembling beneath her skirts.

"Noble they might be, lass, but they're still my sister and brother-in-law. You certainly won't come to any harm at Longfield Park."

"You don't understand." She tossed her hands up, let them drop and swung away. "Oh, Mr. Fergusson, I'm not who you think I am. Not at all."

Had he been any other man, his bafflement would have grown at that statement. But her dejected tone and her conquered look sparked an all-too-vivid memory.

His sister had once appealed to him in just such a way. When Luke had awakened that morning in Scotland with his English memories intact and his Scottish ones gone, Charity had agonized over what she could possibly offer him in return for his wealth, connections and duchy. Dylan had insisted her love was enough and in the end that proved true. But in the early days of her marriage Charity's doubts persisted, for she feared she could never be a grand enough lady to exist in Luke's aristocratic world.

She'd been wrong, of course. Entirely wrong. Luke's family adored her while even the staunchest society snobs found themselves drawn to her. In short, Charity had made a smashing success of her life as a duchess.

"Lass." He closed his hands over her shoulders gently and turned her to face him. "I believe I know exactly what's going on here. You needn't pretend anymore, not with me."

A little moan slipped from between her lips. Her eyes shimmered like golden moons on a crisp autumn night. "Forgive me, Mr. Fergusson."

"For what?" He chuckled. "I assure you, Mrs. Mendoza, you are not the first woman to rise above her station through marriage. My own sister, for example, and her mother-in-law, too. Neither were . . . titled ladies until they married."

He left off, aware he'd tempered the truth with a gross understatement, at least in Charity's case. But reassuring Elizabeth Mendoza was one thing. Divulging his sister's private affairs was quite another.

The very real threat of tears prompted Dylan to do the one thing he knew he shouldn't. Promised himself he wouldn't. He put his arms around her, and like a child she let him, leaning into him and pressing her cheek to his shoulder. In an instant her trembling ceased and she simply felt good against him.

His head went down, lips seeking her hair, burrowing in the silky strands that came awry. The pleasure of it, of holding this woman wrapped in his cloak, coiled through him. Desire rumbled like a crouching, waiting beast.

She suffered his intolerable urges for mere seconds before emitting a cough. The sound, a call for discretion, of course, did much to rouse his senses if nothing at all to lessen the pulsing in his breeches. As he eased backward she didn't whirl away, however, but raised her face, her lips almost brushing his. He looked down into her eyes, feeling the heat of her mouth and breath against his skin. He felt kissed without having made contact. He felt . . . like pressing for more.

The wind sent a sharp gust knifing down the road. It sliced between them, stinging his eyes with bits of dust off the moors. Blinking, Dylan stepped away from her and racked his brain to discover how a too-thin, too-English gentlewoman had such power to entrance him.

Ah, but then it really had very little to do with his brain, didn't it?

The horse had wandered to graze at the side of the road. Dylan strode to it and gathered the reins. "Shall we continue on our way?"

She gazed at him, at the horse, at Longfield's rooftops beckoning in the distance.

"Don't worry, lass, you'll hardly have to say three words to them once they hear what you've been through." He placed his foot in the stirrup and climbed into the saddle. "I daresay they'll be too busy plying you with tea and cakes and tucking you into bed to bother prying into your background."

As each time before, she grasped his arm with both hands and swung up behind him, ignoring the fact that he had removed his foot from the stirrup for her. Her nimbleness raised a smile as he again wondered where she'd learned to do that.

"I'm not usually like this, Mr. Fergusson," she said as she settled behind him.

"Like what?"

"You needn't be polite. We both understand what I mean. Weepy and timid. I despise such weakness in myself and I apologize to you for it."

"Ah, but that's against the rules. We struck a bargain that there'd be no more apologies between us." He patted her hands, grasped at his waist. "And anyway, lass, you've every right in the world to be a little less than strong, to let someone else shore you up, for a time at least."

And indeed, perhaps that was the answer he sought, the reason for his inappropriate and inexplicable attraction to her. She needed help and he . . . well, it was one of his weaknesses. He liked to be needed.

They rode in silence as Longfield Park thrust higher above the trees, becoming larger, more distinct, until the rambling house and its sweeping grounds dominated the horizon.

"Aren't we stopping in town first, Mr. Fergusson?"

She spoke as they rounded a bend, as a coach and four came into view at the side of the road. A man in a charcoal suit stood beside one of its open doors. A liveried driver bent to examine one of the horse's hooves. The dark-suited man turned at their approach, surveyed them with an offhand curiosity and nodded a greeting.

Dylan tipped his head in return, then said over his shoulder to Elizabeth, "It is already late in the day. The bank will be closed and will not reopen until Monday." The breeze kicked up and he raised his voice to continue, "I realize that will delay your trip to London, but it will also afford you some much-needed rest. I suggest you take advantage of the opportunity, Mrs. Mendoza."

She made some reply he didn't hear. The man at the coach suddenly swung full around to face them, staring daggers at Dylan. Dark eyes bored into him with an intensity that took him aback. If he hadn't known better, if this man—stout, dusky in complexion, some thirty-odd years in age—hadn't been a complete stranger to him, he'd have believed there to be a matter of contention between them.

Or . . . *was* this impudent baggage staring at him? That hostile gaze shifted to a point just beyond Dylan's shoulder, and he felt a protective and indignant ire rise up at the notion that yet another stranger dared gawk at Elizabeth.

He brought the horse to a stop.

"What is it?" Elizabeth asked, but he hushed her.

"Are you in need of assistance?" he called across the road, injecting a slight note of challenge into the otherwise courteous words.

The liveried servant pushed to his feet. "Threw a shoe, but she'll make it into town."

Dylan gazed from one man to the other, still mystified by an apparent hostility that made no sense. "You'll find a smithy on Old Church Lane. Just south of the cathedral."

The driver touched a finger to his hat. "Much obliged."

His boorish passenger continued glaring, seeming frozen in an antagonism only he understood. Foreign words rode the breeze as someone—a woman—spoke to him from inside the coach. Dylan could make out folds of dove gray trimmed in black lace, a matching bonnet. Nothing more.

He clucked his horse into motion.

"Oddest thing," he commented once they passed beyond hearing.

"How so, Mr. Fergusson?"

"Did you see how that man stared?"

"Did he? I can't imagine why he would."

He cast a quick glance over his shoulder. "To be frank, he

seemed to be staring at you. And could that have been Spanish they were speaking?"

"How in the world would I know that?"

"Mendoza *is* a Spanish name, is it not?"

After the slightest hesitation, she said, "True enough, but I'm as English as can be, sir."

"Still, you must admit it's an unlikely coincidence. In London one wouldn't think twice about it, with people from all over the world spilling from the ships. But here in Wakefield, three people of the same nationality must surely be related." He adjusted the reins as the horse started down an incline.

Her warm weight pulled away from his spine. "Related? That's absurd. Why would you even say such a thing?"

"The way he stared . . . are you certain you know nothing of those people?"

"I assure you I do not. In fact, I've never met a Spaniard. Other than my husband, of course. And I'd thank you to stop insinuating otherwise. If the man chose to stare, perhaps he was simply being rude."

Dylan released a breath. "I've no doubt you're right, lass. I suppose if it weren't for our bargain, I'd have to apologize again, wouldn't I?"

She relaxed back against him with a rueful chuckle. "I suppose you would at that, Mr. Fergusson."

Eliza's eyes grew wider and wider in the effort to take in all of Longfield Park. There was so very much of it, all but blotting out her lingering qualms about that Spanish couple on the road. Could they somehow be connected to Elizabeth Mendoza?

Oh, but surely not. Despite Mr. Fergusson's claim to the contrary, England was a modern country in a world where people traveled, and Wakefield lay between London and any number of bustling cities: Liverpool, York, Carlisle . . .

No, Longfield Park became her immediate concern. It

seemed to go on and on, both the house with its confusing jumble of towers, turrets and terraces, and the park with its lawns and gardens and artfully placed woodlands.

The closer they got, the more the enormous prospect filled her view and unsettled her nerves, or what were left of them. The Duke and Duchess of Wakefield. The very notion twisted her stomach in a dozen different directions. Thoughts of how she'd surely do and say all the wrong things made her queasy. Fooling a Spaniard who hadn't seen his brother in years nor ever met his wife was one thing. But this . . .

Oh, she'd got herself into more than she could handle—far, far more. But the simple act of regretting her mad decision wouldn't save her now. No, to escape she'd first have to confess to Mr. Fergusson, as she almost had when he revealed his sister's identity. But then what? Go . . . where? The nearest tavern? And do . . . what? The very thing she'd rather die than do.

The memory of the night she'd stood outside the Raven's Perch sealed her lips now. And so did her stomach, full for the first time in many weeks. She could only hope Mr. Fergusson spoke true when he said she'd barely have to talk to his relatives, that they'd feed and pamper her and tuck her into bed. And soon after, they'd set her on her way to London, where she need never fear blundering in front of them again.

Yes, please let it happen that way.

Winding beneath canopies of oak and birch and pine, the drive stretched on longer than any private drive she'd ever seen. And then it ended all too suddenly in a circle that rounded a fountain fashioned with two large, graceful fish that looked to be leaping from the bubbling basin.

That was merely the first and smallest indication of how distantly above her these people were.

From behind the shelter of Mr. Fergusson's formidable shoulder, she peeked with a sinking feeling at the front of the house, at elaborate brickwork laid in a diamond pattern that matched the many—good Lord, *so* many—mullioned windows. From the ground floor she counted four stories below the roof. At least a dozen steps led up to the front door. Soon she must climb them, but what on earth would she do once she reached the top?

Mr. Fergusson turned in the saddle before she had a chance to smooth away her dismay. "Chin up. You'll be astonished at how ordinary they all are."

Ordinary? Out of the question. Not while living in a palace like this.

At the same time she marveled that Mr. Fergusson could so accurately read her thoughts, could understand her so thoroughly without actually understanding a thing about her. Despite her ridiculous outburst on the road, he still believed her gentle born or nearly so. And he didn't seem at all fazed by her reluctance to enter a duke's home. Perhaps everyone, even the gentry, battled bouts of nerves when faced with meeting a peer.

She summoned a brave smile only to feel it dissolve as the front door burst open. Chaos spilled through and down the steps, a noisy gaggle of people talking, shouting and laughing to the accompaniment of a pair of barking dogs.

Mr. Fergusson helped her down as the crowd closed around them. The dogs, little more than snowy fluffs tipped with black button noses, scurried in circles and darted at their heels, little mouths trumpeting a welcome that far exceeded their size. Vibrant hues, pastels and somber blacks filled Eliza's vision. She glimpsed flashes of red hair, blond, brown, peppered gray; heard tones of voice ranging from delighted squeals to rumbling baritones, all competing to be heard above the barking. Eliza wanted to press her hands to her ears.

"Uncle Dylan!" A boy no more than waist-high literally jumped into Mr. Fergusson's arms. "I knew you'd come back!"

"Did you now, lad?"

The child's vigorous nod sent hair very like Mr. Fergusson's—dark auburn streaked with flame—for a tumble over his freckled brow. "Did you find Bonnie Prince Charlie and restore him to the Scottish throne?"

"You've got to leave off about that, William, or you'll get your papa tossed out of Parliament."

"They can't toss him out, it's his birthright. Mine, too, someday."

Mr. Fergusson tousled the child's rich, reddish hair before extending the same hand to greet the adults. From within the confusion of handshakes and hugs, a pair of slender, freckled arms, bare from the elbows down, found their way around his neck and squeezed. "Ah, Dylan. We're thrilled you've come back but tell us, what on earth's happened?"

The woman spoke with the same light, lovely brogue as Mr. Fergusson. For an instant, a riot of golden red curls blocked him from Eliza's view, making her feel quite alone in this bevy of strangers. Then the woman turned to regard her.

"Tell us who you've brought," she said. "A cart filled with belongings arrived earlier but your note gave us precious few clues."

In that brief moment Eliza realized several things at once about this woman. First, her complexion and coloring declared her the little boy's mother beyond doubt. Secondly, the loose style of her muslin frock announced the impending birth of yet another child. Eliza experienced a quiet but nonetheless painful tug, deep, deep inside, but as she had learned to do these past months, she shoved the sensation aside and acknowledged the third and perhaps most important detail about the woman before her.

She was Mr. Fergusson's sister. The duchess. Eliza guessed it without anyone telling her, for the woman's features were the very likeness of his, subtly realigned to present a pert, pleasing femininity.

Those sun-dappled arms now closed around Eliza with such tenderness tears gathered in her eyes. "Welcome to Longfield," the woman said warmly in her musical English.

Eliza blinked and said nothing. The embrace—so familiar,

so filled with compassion despite coming from a complete stranger—stunned her and wiped her mind clear of every proper greeting she'd silently rehearsed on the journey.

Without releasing her hold on Eliza's shoulders, the duchess stepped back to study her from arm's length. "My brother's note said he discovered you on the road, that there'd been a accident. Were you injured? Shall we send for our physician?"

"Of course we must send for Dr. Farlow."

"I'll have Mortimer see to it at once."

"Let's get the poor dear inside."

"Yes, before she catches a chill."

"Skiff, Schooner, down lads. Stop pestering our guest."

The voices swarmed Eliza's ears as she found herself conveyed across the drive, up the steps and through the front door in the midst of all those people. There were seven adults in all, she now counted, four women including the duchess, and three men besides Mr. Fergusson.

That gentleman moved to her side as they stepped into a hall whose sheer enormity made Eliza dizzy. Under the cover of footsteps pattering on the marble flooring, he whispered, "You see? Ordinary, just as I told you."

"She's quite pretty, Uncle Dylan." From his perch in his uncle's arms, the boy craned his neck to take unabashed assessment of Eliza. She ventured a smile and he grinned back, revealing several missing front teeth. "I like her nose. Have you kissed her? Are you in love with her?"

"Shouldn't you be in the nursery with your sisters?"

"They're napping and so are my cousins." His thumb tapped his chest. "I outgrew naps a year ago. I'd only keep them all awake and make Nurse cross."

"Aye, you would at that."

A man at Mr. Fergusson's other side chuckled. He was the eldest of the group, a balding, rotund gentleman tottering with the aid of a cane. Beside and a little behind him, a tall and willowy blonde kept careful hold of his shoulder, though he seemed not to notice.

"And to think, my boy, we almost missed you by a day." The old gentleman's voice rose in merriment, echoing into the vastness of the hall. "What splendid luck, eh?"

"Aye, Sir Joshua. It's good to see you again. How is your newest grandson?"

"Delightful." An expansive grin brought a flush to the man's face. "But you'll see him for yourself later. He's one of those napping children up in the nursery."

"Yes, Father, and no waking them this time," said the blonde over his shoulder.

Eliza was feeling overwhelmed, a little faint. In fact, she found herself longing for Mr. Fergusson's capable arms to support her through this latest ordeal.

For an ordeal it was. Which of the three men was the duke, she wondered. Surely not the elderly man, with his overgrown mustache and ivory-handled cane. She could not for the world imagine the youthful duchess married to such a one despite his twinkling eyes and ready smile.

The other two men were young, though not quite as young as Mr. Fergusson. They were dark-haired, tall, and walked with the self-assurance of those accustomed to the deference of others. They were also handsome in strikingly similar ways. Brothers, she decided. But again, which was the duke?

So far she hadn't bobbed a single curtsey. For the first time in her life it hadn't seemed at all necessary or expected or even desired, not with the way the duchess embraced her as though she were a long-lost cousin.

They brought her into another huge room, so big the entire farmhouse she'd shared with Nathan and even some of its barnyard would have fit inside. A barrage of paintings, carvings, brocades and gilding crowded her senses but it was the utter quiet of so many footsteps that astounded her most. She'd never trod on anything finer than a braided mat before.

Not even when she worked as a maid, because she hadn't been permitted anywhere near the family's private rooms.

Now her feet positively sank into the deep pile of colorfully woven wool, so soft and thick she might have curled up in the middle of the floor and slept.

Oh, but not so.

"Put her in the wing chair, it's our most comfortable."

"No, let her stretch out on the settee, with her feet up."

"Here, put this pillow behind her back."

"Schooner, down this instant. Skiff, do stop poking your nose in our guest's hand."

"Has anyone rung for tea?"

"Never fear, I shall do it."

It wasn't until the refreshments had been brought in—by an entire company of servants—that the adults began to settle down and the tide of their concern was stemmed, or at least calmed to a level that didn't make Eliza's mind reel.

As though forming an audience they dragged chairs from various corners and ranged them around Eliza's settee, a striped affair of some elegant fabric they insisted, against her protests, that she place her feet upon. As their gazes settled on her, she nearly felt obliged to perform in some manner, to break into song or delight them with an adventure story. Then, thankfully, the duchess distracted their attention by pouring tea and passing round cups and saucers.

A plate was thrust—however gently—into her lap. At first she thought it contained some kind of cake, so creamy white and smooth did it appear. On further inspection, however, she discovered carefully sliced bread of a texture finer than she'd believed possible, embracing juicy slivers of chicken, or perhaps pheasant. Her stomach growled in approval.

One of the women rose to assist the duchess. She was petite and round, not quite elderly but past her prime. Her eyes were dark, like those of the two brothers, leading Eliza to surmise she might be their mother and the dowager duchess. With cup and saucer in hand she crossed to Eliza and carefully handed them to her. "If you want for anything, my dear, anything at all, you must not hesitate for one instant in asking."

"Thank you. All of you." These were the first words she'd spoken; these people hadn't given her a chance previously. "You're much too kind."

A mistake, for the comment released a flurry of denials.

"Not at all."

"You mustn't think of it."

"We're only doing what decent folk should."

It was then she noticed Mr. Fergusson's nephew grinning at her from behind the settee. "I'm an earl. The Earl of Lynhurst."

"Oh . . . that sounds very important."

The boy nodded, then rolled his eyes. "Only Mama and Papa won't let me use my title until I'm older."

"I'm sure that's very wise of them."

He hooked his two small hands over the sofa frame and pressed his face closer. "Are you Scottish?"

She blinked in surprise. "Why no, dear. Why do you ask?"

"You sound a little bit Scottish. Like Uncle Dylan when he tries to pretend he's English. Doesn't she sound like that, Uncle Dylan?"

The elderly man let go a chuckle.

"I hadn't particularly noticed." Dylan leaned to place his teacup on the sofa table.

"Mama can do it, too," the boy went on, blithely unaware of the disapproval simmering from beneath the duchess's reddish gold eyebrows. "She's much better at it."

The turn in the conversation whipped Eliza's misgivings to a froth. If the child had noticed the Yorkshire rhythms in her speaking, were the adults already thinking she sounded more like one of their servants than a member of their class?

"But she only ever does it in London." William rested his chin on the back of the settee. "It's to fool the . . . the . . . who is it to fool, Mama?"

"Why don't you let our guest drink her tea, now, William."

"Now I remember. It's to fool the bluebloods."

"William, darling." His mother's brogue darted crisply across the space between them. "Time to go upstairs."

"Oh, but I don't want—"

"William." The single-worded warning—deep, stern, indisputable—came from one of the dark-haired gentlemen, the slightly taller of the two. Given how quickly that word silenced the boy, Eliza knew this man must be his father—the duke.

The warning made her scalp prickle and sent an irrational fear pressing down on her shoulders. But perhaps not so irrational, for it had been in just such a tone that her former employer had sent her away without a reference. Here, again, was a man of authority and power over others.

Eliza would do best to avoid him if she could.

Without another word but with much heaving of breath and arm swinging William pushed away from the settee. A parting grin in her direction before he trotted away assured her she hadn't seen the last of him.

The duchess offered an apologetic smile. "I dread to think you might judge us based on my son's manners, madam, but I suppose we can hardly boast any better." She raised an eyebrow at Mr. Fergusson.

For an instant he looked blankly back. "Ah. Introductions. Of course. I've all the manners of a barbarian, haven't I?" The resulting titters led Eliza to suspect a private joke apparent to everyone but her. "This is Mrs. Mendoza, Mrs. Elizabeth Mendoza de Leone. Of York."

He cleared his throat, then continued more quietly, "There was a horrific accident on the old Yorkshire road, the one that winds to the northwest before twisting back toward York. Mrs. Mendoza's coach went off the road and down an incline. I'm very sorry to report that her driver and companion did not survive."

All at once they jumped up from their seats or leaned far forward to express their dismay, sympathy, condolences and relief that she, at least, had escaped unscathed.

"Thankfully," Mr. Fergusson continued as the family again fell quiet, "when I last left Longfield Park, my broodings sent me in that lonely direction, or Mrs. Mendoza might have waited much longer than two days for rescue."

"Two days? You poor creature."

"My word. How *did* you survive?"

"It must have been terrifying."

"I'd have expired of sheer fright."

"Settle down, gooses."

This last drew Eliza's attention to the blonde she'd noticed earlier, young, slender and quite possibly the most beautiful individual she'd ever laid eyes upon. Where the duchess was of a slim but sturdy frame and pretty in a lively if not quite fashionable way, this woman was sleek, elegant and impeccably groomed.

The lady leaned across the space to extend a hand—one that had never seen a laundry tub—to Eliza. "I am Helena Holbrook, and I am very pleased to make your acquaintance. The dashing gentleman beside me is my husband, Lord Wesley Holbrook. He represents the district in the House of Commons."

"Darling, must you always brag?"

"Always, my love."

A duke, a duchess *and* an MP? What next? The king? Eliza's teacup rattled in its saucer. While the others pretended not to notice, Mr. Fergusson reached over and took the delicate and obviously costly porcelain from her hands, placing it beside his own on the sofa table.

"There now," he said, "you may eat your sandwich."

She returned his comprehending look with one of gratitude. How swiftly and tactfully he'd rescued her from embarrassment. With equal ease, he continued the introductions. "This is Dahlia Holbrook, the dowager Duchess of Wakefield."

Ah, Eliza had guessed correctly. The woman with the dark eyes smiled. "Welcome to Longfield, Mrs. Mendoza."

"And this is her mother, Lady Mary Fairgate."

"How do you do, my dear?" The older woman, ensconced in black from her lace cap to her buffed high-heeled boots, raised a silver-handled quizzing glass and studied Eliza. "Welcome to Longfield Park. We're very happy to have you."

At that moment one of the dogs stood with his front paws propped on the settee at Eliza's elbow. His button nose worked eagerly.

"Skiff or Schooner or whichever little devil you are," Lady Mary said, "leave off begging food from Mrs. Mendoza's plate."

"I'm pleased to meet you, and very relieved to be here," Eliza managed, all too tempted to offer the little dog a treat but not about to cross that dignified woman's edict.

"And this is my father, Sir Joshua Livingston," Mrs. Holbrook said, or did one call her Lady Holbrook or perhaps Lady Wesley? Eliza's head began to ache.

"Delighted, my dear." The portly man used his cane for leverage as he leaned forward to shake her hand. "Tell us, was it brigands that caused your coach to veer off the road? If so, never fear, the boys and I shall ride out to apprehend them."

"Oh no, sir, nothing like that." With the ghastly images replaying in her mind, Eliza drew a shaky breath. "It was rainy. The road was wet and slippery and . . . my driver simply went too fast."

"Mrs. Mendoza, did not my brother-in-law say you are from York?" William's father, the duke, balanced his cup and saucer on his knee and focused his attention on Eliza until she wanted to sink into the striped cushion beside her. "May I ask why you were traveling the old road? Especially in such weather."

"This is my husband," the duchess put in before Eliza could think of a reply. "Luke Holbrook."

Eliza's brows gathered. Luke? Why hadn't the duchess introduced him by his title? Shouldn't she have said *my husband, his grace the Duke of Wakefield?* Why, after but a few moments' acquaintance with these people, she was practically on a first-name basis with them. How utterly mystifying.

And how to answer the duke's question? She'd no idea why Elizabeth had traveled the old road rather than the swifter, safer route; could not fathom a reason anyone bound for London would choose such a roundabout way.

Perhaps a truthful response would best serve under the circumstances. "I cannot tell you why my driver chose that road. Perhaps he had business of his own along the way. I am unfamiliar with the roads beyond York, and knew only that we were headed south and would eventually reach London."

Her conscience prickled. Had she laid unfair blame on poor John Howitt, a man unable to speak in his own defense?

"Where in York are you from, might I ask?" The dowager duchess's eyes brightened with interest.

"Folkstone Manor, ma'am."

"Do tell! Why, I know of it."

CHAPTER 6

If Dahlia Holbrook's announcement came as a surprise to Dylan, he realized that was nothing compared to the reaction it produced in Elizabeth. A jolt of astonishment nearly sent her sandwich tumbling from her lap. Her mouth gaped. A little stutter came out and nothing more.

"I remember it well." Dahlia warmed to the topic. "Mama, you remember my old friend, Miss Jane Thomason, do you not?"

"A frivolous child, if I recall."

"Nonsense. She was among the sweetest creatures ever born. At any rate, her home, Willow Hall, was about a half-hour's ride from Folkstone, and whenever I visited Jane, our afternoon carriage rides took us right by Folkstone." She turned back to Elizabeth. "Are you acquainted with the Thomasons, my dear? Jane moved away after she married, of course, but I'm quite certain the rest of the family still summers at Willow.

"I . . . No, I'm afraid I don't know them."

"No? How very odd. But then I suppose the area's not as intimate as it was twenty years ago. In those days Folkstone was owned by the Carlton family, but I learned from Jane that when the old gentleman died the family decided to sell out. Their interests lay primarily in the south, and keeping up the old place proved more of an expense than they deemed prudent. But tell me, were the renovations ever completed?"

"The renovations?"

"My goodness, yes. You know the place is positively ancient, predating this house by a good century or two. It had a reputation for being rather dismal and cold, I'm afraid. According to Jane, old Mr. Carlton had boasted of adding an entirely new wing that would quite bring the house into the nineteenth century, but then she and I lost touch and I don't know if his plans ever came to fruition."

Elizabeth's apparent consternation turned to out-and-out dismay when Dahlia Holbrook sat back in anticipation of some comment that would satisfy her curiosity. Plainly, Elizabeth did not wish to discuss the matter of whether her home had been improved or not, a sentiment made quite clear by her heightened color, pinched lips and her refusal to meet anyone's gaze.

Dylan believed he understood and felt a moment's mortification for her distress. "Dolly," he said gently, "Mrs. Mendoza has also recently suffered the loss of her husband. She may not wish to discuss the home they shared."

Dahlia's hands flew to her heart. "My dear child, do forgive me. Oh, I would not distress you for all the world, and after all you've been through. Had I only known—"

"Please don't fret, ma'am. You could not have known and so have done no wrong." Elizabeth's gaze darted from face to face. A little smile wavered on her lips, like a chick wanting to fly but unsure of its wings. "How can we speak of forgiveness when you've already shown me such generosity in the short time I've been here. Me, a perfect stranger to you."

Contradictions flew at her, beginning with Sir Joshua's declaration of her being a stranger no longer and ending with Dolly's promise never to pry again. It was then, however, that Dylan noticed the one quiet member of their group. His sister's lashes rose and fell repeatedly as she silently perused Elizabeth from head to toe and back, and Dylan knew by the perplexed ridge above her nose that something puzzled her.

He glanced back at the lady and realized that he, too, had been nagged by some contrary sensation since meeting her.

True, her ordeal had left her out of sorts and her moods wobbled from moment to moment, but those things were understandable under the circumstances. She might not, perhaps, be quite the aristocrat he'd initially thought, but that certainly didn't lower her in his estimate. No, there was something else . . . .

As he mused, Charity's head gave a discreet turn toward Lady Mary, held that position a moment, then centered again on Elizabeth. And then it struck him.

Flowers. She'd been wearing a floral print dress when he found her. Once her luggage had been retrieved she'd exchanged that frock for this one—a darker striped pattern of violet and gray but still not black. Not widow's weeds, to be sure. For her to be out of mourning, her husband had to have been gone a year at the very least, though ofttimes more.

He'd been so certain her loss had been recent. Her skittishness, her thinness, and that lost look that so often shadowed the gold of her eyes . . . .

He nipped his musings short. This was far more curiosity than he need indulge. The woman's affairs were her own and if he were smart he would let them remain so. He'd already become more involved than he cared to be, though he supposed he couldn't very well have walked away and left her shivering on the moors.

Now, however, he could relinquish his responsibility to the others. They'd be only too delighted to oblige, as they lived to cosset and fuss. When Charity had first described her new in-laws to him, he'd accused her of exaggerating. His first meeting with them had proved every claim true.

Aye, so why not leave Elizabeth Mendoza in their capable hands, mount his horse tomorrow and continue the journey he'd been so bent upon only a day ago?

Well and good, then, he'd be off tomorrow. Or perhaps the day after. Better to allow his horse a day of rest.

* * *

Eliza watched the door of her bedroom close with a soft thud behind the duchess and her beautiful sister-in-law. Fatigue seeped through her, bone crushing and spirit dousing. Yet, at the sound of their retreating tread along the corridor, she threw back the eiderdown coverlets of the vast canopied bed.

Elizabeth Mendoza's trunks sat against the wall beside an elegant marble-topped dressing table, and this was her first chance to continue examining the contents since Mr. Fergusson rescued her. She had already gone through most of the clothing back on the moors when she'd gathered them from the ground. Now she wished to search through the smaller items in hopes of finding further clues to Elizabeth's life. At least then she might no longer feel as if she were treading so blindly into the unknown.

Tiptoeing across the room, she pressed her ear to the door and turned the key in the lock. Then she opened the closest trunk, lifting the lid with the utmost care to prevent its creaking as it was wont to do. Not that anyone would hear through the manor's thick walls, but Eliza couldn't dismiss the sensation of sneaking where she didn't belong, of dipping her hands into forbidden riches.

Nonetheless, she pored through the contents of small cases and bags, most of which held toiletries, accessories and jewelry. Among the last were many lovely necklaces, brooches and earbobs, but nothing, Eliza surmised by close inspection, of great value.

It must have been nearly an hour later that she sat back on her heels, gazing down in puzzlement at an object that had just tumbled out of a satin evening glove and into her night rail.

Rising and moving closer to the lamp on the dressing table, she examined the oddly shaped ornament that more than filled her palm. Forged from black metal that gleamed like polished iron, the piece seemed incomplete, half of a shield.

Part of a crest, perhaps. Within intricate etchings and

scrollwork, stones of russet and blue and icy white twinkled. Her pulse thumped, then calmed. Surely the stones were mere glass, for who would set precious gems in a base metal?

At what appeared to be the broken edge she discerned the smooth tracing of a letter, or half a letter. An M for Mendoza? Beneath it lay an empty half circle rimmed with prongs as if in want of a stone more than an inch across.

A sense of having seen this shape before sent her to the bedside table. Delving into its single drawer, she retrieved Elizabeth's reticule. She fished through it until she found what she sought, and then returned to the light.

Eliza experienced the chill of discovery upon opening Elizabeth's locket and gazing down at the two miniature portraits inside. Each young man wore, pinned to the sash crossing his blue coat, what looked to be a smaller but quite whole version of the very ornament in her other hand.

There was one marked difference. According to the artist's renderings, their crests were fashioned in gold rather than the somber iron of the one Eliza held. Tiny dabs of paint depicted what must have been rubies, sapphires and diamonds.

This larger piece, then, must have served as a model for the jeweler. She wondered briefly how it had come to be broken and then decided it didn't matter. It was no doubt worthless.

"There's something about her . . ."

Seated at her dressing table, Charity leaned her head back to allow her maid, Esther, to remove the pins from her hair. But it was to Luke's reflection in the mirror that she spoke. "I can't quite put my finger on it . . . ."

"She's like a wounded bird," he replied from the easy chair beside the hearth. He lowered the account ledger he'd been studying to his lap. "So fragile it makes one afraid to touch her for fear she'll break."

"Yes, but that much is understandable considering her recent circumstances." Charity picked up a silver-handled brush from its tray and handed it to Esther. "I'm rather ashamed to admit this, but she gives me an uneasy sensation. Am I simply imagining things?"

"Perhaps, my darling, your misgivings are due to the way your brother looks at her."

She sighed. "I'd noticed that too. Not that it's any business of mine who my brother looks at. Not at his age, at any rate. But I do wish he'd be . . . careful."

Luke met her gaze in the mirror. "Do you disbelieve her story?"

"Not entirely." She frowned, trying to make sense of the conflicting emotions that had sprung up soon after Elizabeth Mendoza's arrival. "I suppose there are quite logical explanations why a widow might travel in a striped gown."

"She hasn't had time to see her modiste?"

Charity ignored the comment. "Dr. Farlow couldn't find a thing wrong with her."

"For that we should be grateful."

"But isn't it odd after such a violent carriage accident?" Charity winced when Esther ran the brush through a snarl.

"Sorry, ma'am."

She smiled up at the girl, then considered. "And another thing. As our astute son tactlessly pointed out, Mrs. Mendoza doesn't quite speak the king's English, does she?"

Luke laid the ledger on the brandy table beside him. "No, and while many a country-bred gentlewoman speaks in the local dialect of her home, I believe I can tell you this much. Mrs. Mendoza is not as gentle born as she'd have us believe."

"How do you know?"

He inclined his head. "It is an area in which I do have some experience, my love."

They exchanged furtive smiles in the mirror, reflecting shared memories of Charity's very first visit to Longfield Park six years ago.

"Do you think the others realize?" she asked.

"I've little doubt they have their suspicions, but I daresay no one will breathe a word of it. If Mrs. Mendoza married above her station, who are the Holbrooks to judge?"

"You're absolutely right, darling. Still . . . " She contemplated the reflection of her own freckled cheeks and for an instant regretted spending so much time outside without her bonnet this past summer. "She is rather jumpier than someone who merely married above her station."

"Perhaps we make her nervous. Or . . . " He shrugged. "There may be matters she doesn't wish to concern us with."

"Or simply doesn't wish us to know."

"What are you proposing we do?"

"Do? Nothing." She absently twisted the sapphire ring on her left fourth finger. "It's not as if she's making demands or planning to stay for a prolonged length of time. She told me she wishes to continue on to London as soon as possible."

"Well, then, no harm in extending her a few days' courtesy and seeing her safely on her way."

"Quite so . . . ." But those little tugs at her better sense didn't cease; quite the contrary. She of all people knew the signs of a woman with something to hide.

"My darling, if it will help smooth that ridge above your nose," Luke said, "I'll make some inquiries and see if any of our acquaintances in Leeds has heard of the Mendoza family."

Her gaze snapped to his. "Would it be terribly unbecoming of us to do so?"

"Not where your peace of mind is concerned, my love."

The next morning dawned crisp and bright, a perfect autumn day and a welcome relief after the chilly, rainy moors. Dylan hadn't seen Elizabeth since the ladies spirited her away to a guestroom last evening. They'd insisted she be served supper in the privacy of her room, where she had also been seen by Dr. Farlow, who pronounced her shaken but in sound health.

Dylan, meanwhile, had spent the evening hours entertaining and being equally entertained by his nephew William, along with Wesley and Helena's older son, David, amid a foray of lead soldiers and their wooden horses.

Now, entering the fragrant recesses of Dolly Holbrook's rose garden, he followed the voices—Dolly's, Helena's, his sister's—until he found them seated on iron benches made more hospitable by bright cushions. Just as yesterday in the drawing room, Elizabeth's feet were elevated and extra pillows plunked behind her back. A blanket swathed her from shoulders to toes.

Again he detected no trace of black on her person, the small part of her visible above the blanket revealing soft russet wool. On the somber side, perhaps, though no more so than his sister's autumn wardrobe.

"*Never* been to London, my dear?" Dolly was exclaiming as he came around the marble fountain. "*Never?*"

"Well, Dolly, after all," Charity said, "I'd never been to London before I married Luke."

"Oh, but you were from another country entirely."

"And I rarely traveled to London before my marriage," Helena put in, "though I can with all honesty admit I never much missed it. If not for my cousin, Tess, and of course Wesley's obligations in the House, I'd be perfectly delighted to remain here year-round."

She and Charity traded nods of agreement and even Dolly concurred with a *hm.*

"It's simply unusual," the elder woman concluded.

As so often since her arrival here, Elizabeth sat chewing her lip, eyes darting from face to face as if to glean as much wisdom as possible from her companions before offering an opinion. Her expression brightened considerably upon spotting him, an occurrence he could not deny put a slight swagger in his step.

"Good morning, ladies. I trust you all slept well? Mrs.

Mendoza, how are you faring today under the watchful eyes of the Holbrook lionesses?"

Elizabeth gave a little laugh at the word, but the others only smiled wisely.

"We Holbrook women are most fierce when it comes to safeguarding anyone or anything we care about," Helena explained.

Elizabeth's smile turned wistful, a little sad. "You're all exceedingly lucky to have each other. I've always wished to be part of a large, rambling family. Loud and boisterous, the kind that drives one another and the servants to distraction during the holidays." She pulled the blanket nearly to her chin. "The kind that draws complaints from nearby neighbors."

"I daresay we're a bit too far from our nearest neighbors to set them complaining," said Dolly with a chuckle, "but as for driving each other to distraction . . . yes, I believe that's been done a time or two." She aimed a sly look at Charity. "Wouldn't you agree, dearest?"

His sister had the good grace to blush as she nodded her assent. Her very first visit to Longfield Park, six years ago, had been shrouded in deceit. Under an assumed name, she'd followed her English duke all the way from Scotland to steal back his heart despite his previous engagement to Helena. Her furtive plan had ended in chaos, danger and startling revelations but, in the end, forgiveness all around.

"Mrs. Mendoza plans to journey on to London as early as Monday," Charity announced. Dylan would bet the farm she did so to steer the subject back to more agreeable and less controversial matters.

"Then I'll make arrangements today to hire her a coach. I am also considering starting out for home on the morrow, seeing as how Mrs. Mendoza will be quite well looked after by the lot of you." Unbuttoning his suit coat, he flicked it back and took a seat beside his sister.

"Hire a coach?" Charity swatted his wrist. "Mrs. Mendoza is perfectly welcome to use one of ours."

"Oh, thank you, ma'am, but I couldn't . . . "

"Of course you could. We've more than enough coaches in our shed. For the time it takes to reach London and back, it shan't be missed."

"Yes, but at any rate, I hope you'll agree to stay on a few more days at least, Mrs. Mendoza."

As Helena looked for concurrence among the others, Dylan discovered a surprising particle of the same sentiment where he'd least expect—beneath his own breastbone. He could not but admit, at least privately, that he didn't want Elizabeth rushing off to London any more than the ladies did. For once she went on her way and he on his, he'd likely never see her again.

Whereas if she remained at Longfield, he'd know where to find her, should he wish to.

Would he? Find her again, that is?

He opened his mouth to tell her London would be a jostling, jarring place for anyone so recently recovering from a great shock, but Helena spoke first. "Surely your brother-in-law can spare you a few more days."

Brother-in-law? This was the first he'd heard of that. He'd come to think of her as not only widowed but orphaned at well. A lone, fragile flower in a world of thorns and only he there to—ah, the notion made him groan—protect her, romantic idiot that he was.

"You can write to him and explain the situation." Dolly tightened her shawl against the breeze that kicked up. "The poor man can have no idea what horrors you've endured."

"That won't be necessary." Elizabeth shifted, drawing her knees up beneath the blanket and wrapping her arms around them. "You see, he doesn't know I'm coming. Doesn't even know I exist."

As the ladies exclaimed their surprise over that, a voice hailed from the direction of the house. Luke came into view between the rose bushes. He looked perplexed, out of sorts.

"We have two immediate dilemmas that need feminine

attention as quickly as possible," he said when he reached them. Then he paused and tipped Elizabeth a bow. "Mrs. Mendoza, good morning."

"Good morning, your grace." She fidgeted beneath the blanket, drawing her knees up tighter.

Charity smoothed her skirts and stood, kissing Luke squarely on the mouth and eliciting tolerant grins from Helena and Dolly. "What disaster has befallen us now, darling?"

He blew out an audible breath. "The three little ones woke early from their naps in the fieriest of tempers. William and our nephew David are causing a ruckus and making matters worse. The nurses are practically in tears. That's the first." He looked beyond his wife to his mother. "The second involves a delivery from your dressmaker which your maid insists is all wrong and must be sent back at once."

"How tedious. I suppose I'd better intervene." Dolly eased to her feet, pausing to give her son's hand a squeeze as she passed him on the garden path.

"Can't you and Wesley handle the babies?" From her seat beside Elizabeth, Helena wrinkled her nose at Luke. "It isn't as though they each have one parent only, is it?"

"Yes, but you see Stephen caught Lena's finger in his mouth and wouldn't let go. Not that he hurt her much without any teeth, mind you, but the insult started her wailing. Lara attempted to restore order by using her new doll as a gavel and I needn't tell you the face is cracked beyond repair. Now all three are shrieking at the tops of their lungs. William and David meanwhile have taken advantage of the commotion to have a pillow fight. There are feathers everywhere. To top it all off, the dogs are running wild and barking at everyone."

"That doesn't answer my question," Helena replied in a patient tone. "Why are the children yours and Wesley's when they're laughing, and Charity's and mine when they're cross, naughty or need changing?"

"Changing. The babies all seem to need that, and with poor Miss Jenkins crying and all . . . "

"The cloths are in the linen room, in the lower right-hand cupboard," Charity told him with a sweet smile.

He peered down at her, brows knotting, lips pressing tightly together. His head sagged until his forehead touched hers. "Please."

"Oh, for heaven's sake." She grasped his shoulders and gave him a shake, then another kiss. "Let's go restore peace to the kingdom."

"I'd better come as well. You can't be expected to enter the fray without reserve troops." Gaining her feet, Helena smiled down at Elizabeth and held out her hand. "Mrs. Mendoza, would you care to come meet our adorable but apparently barbarous brood?"

"Oh, why, I'd love to—"

"Do you think that's a good idea?" Dylan stood, lodging himself in Elizabeth's way and preventing her standing. "They're quite a handful, and after all Mrs. Mendoza's been through, now might not be the best time."

"What was I thinking? You're quite right."

"Yes and in the meantime, I'll keep our guest company." He sat back down. "She won't be lonely, I promise."

Helena patted his shoulder, then swept away to join Luke and Charity on the stroll back to the house.

He suppressed a sigh of relief but only just. Love them though he did, he couldn't deny a certain exasperation with the Holbrook ladies—all of them. For one, they made it a near-impossible task for him to insert three complete words into a conversation. And when he did, they were usually three entirely wrong words.

Ah, but he was used to that. Charity, Helena and their mother-in-law were all of a mind, able to read each other's thoughts and moods as gypsies read the stars. And those who lagged in such skills often bore the insult of being tsked at, however cordially.

Usually he laughed it off, but this morning he'd found himself wishing them and their good intentions away. Since yesterday they'd effectively rendered him unnecessary in Elizabeth's life, just as the blanket covering her now rendered his cloak unnecessary.

Even as the resentful thought reached its conclusion, Elizabeth sat up and set her feet on the ground. The blanket drooped from her shoulders. A little sigh escaped her lips.

He caught her eye and the two of them shared a smile he felt fairly certain arose from a similar thought. "They mean well," he said, "but they can be a bit relentless, can't they?"

"Mr. Fergusson, you have a wonderful family." Her chin jutted, and for an instant he thought she'd misunderstood his meaning. Then she shook her head. "But yes, they do bewilder me at times."

"I can assure you that while their concern for you is completely genuine, their bid to persuade you to stay is spurred by somewhat more selfish motives."

"Selfish? I can hardly believe so, Mr. Fergusson."

"Oh, aye, they've laid claim to you, Mrs. Mendoza, and they aim to keep you. I've seen it before. In fact, I myself have been the victim of several kidnapping plots."

"Kidnapping!" She laughed, a light, airy sound that made his heart stop and listen. "Goodness, am I to understand I'm in danger, then?"

"Danger of being smothered with kindness."

"I can think of no more pleasant way to meet my demise than among these people." One velvet-slippered toe nudged the gravel on the walk. Lifting her face to the breeze, she inhaled audibly and gazed out beyond the garden to the lawns that rolled away to the forest. "How beautiful it is here. I've never seen the like."

"Care to explore more of it?"

"I surely would, Mr. Fergusson."

"Are you up to walking?"

The look she slanted him both disdained and teased. "Despite the ladies' ardent beliefs to the contrary, Dr. Farlow was quite correct in his conclusion. I'm healthy as a horse."

"Good." He stood and offered his arm, delighting in the eager way she sprang to her feet. She paused just long enough to carefully fold the blanket before sliding her hand into the crook of his elbow as if it were the most natural thing in the world.

He liked that she hadn't demurred as most Englishwomen would have, debating the possible injuries to their reputations. Perhaps her being a widow rather than a debutante on the marriage mart accounted for it, but it seemed his blunder of two nights ago, that ill-timed, ill-fated kiss, had been forgiven.

But forgotten? Nay, not by him.

He took her first across the lawns to the pond, and there he resisted the temptation to kiss her beneath the concealing sweep of a willow. It was no easy task, especially when her lips parted in wonder at the sight of the folly on the far bank. A Greek temple in miniature, the gleaming marble structure presided over both the pond and the brook that fed it, with a man-made channel directing the flow down a bubbling cascade and into a stone pool filled with lily pads.

"It's merely for show?" She shook her head, clearly as taken aback at the notion as he'd once been. "It serves no function at all?"

"It brought a smile to your face didn't it?"

Afterward, when they climbed the broad steps of the tiered gardens, temptation again prodded as the breeze tugged her shawl from her arms and nearly sent it flying. He caught it quick in one fist, then shook it out and wrapped it around her shoulders, thinking how fortunate its fringed edges were and wouldn't his arms like to be in their place?

On their way back to the house they stopped to play a quick game of bowls on the green. That left her a little breathless, disheveled, a lock of hair drifting across her cheek to the corner of her mouth like an arrow mocking his restraint.

As the sun angled above the highest level of Longfield's

rooftops, they doubled around to the colonnaded walkway and up onto the terrace outside the drawing room.

She'd taken it all in like a child, with wide eyes and gaping lips, the occasional *ooh* and *my goodness* slipping through. Aye, Longfield Park was impressive, but his enjoyment came most from the dawning realization that her home, Folkstone Manor, must be a good deal more modest and perhaps not as far removed from his own home as he'd first believed. It made him feel rather more her equal.

"Thank you, Mr. Fergusson," she said as they strolled across the terrace. Her smile, wide and genuine and as pretty as a Scottish summer day, did much to banish his earlier disappointment at feeling so damned unneeded. "I enjoyed that immensely."

"There's much more. I could show you round the tenant farms on the morrow."

A shadow obscured her smile but before he could wonder why, she brightened again. "I thought you were leaving tomorrow. Have you changed your mind?"

Had he? There *was* his horse to think about. What kind of master would he be to run the beast lame?

"My staying on another day or two would make my sister very happy."

At that moment both drawing room doors swung wide and Charity came striding out. "Dylan Fergusson!"

She didn't sound the least bit pleased.

"What are you thinking? I went out to the garden to collect Mrs. Mendoza over an hour ago to find nothing but a folded blanket on an empty bench."

"Your grace, I'm so sorry, I—"

As a startled Elizabeth stuttered apologies, Charity's blazing green eyes cooled to a gentle glow. "Oh, no, dearest, I'm not angry with you in the least, though I will entreat you to be more heedful of your health in future." The fierceness returned just as quickly in the sizzling glare she turned on Dylan. "How could you drag our guest the length and breadth of this estate when you know good and well she should be resting?"

"She said she's feeling—"

"Of course she did, polite darling that she is. You, however, should have known better."

"Please don't blame your brother, your grace." Elizabeth moved forward, a brave gesture on her part and one Dylan didn't care to emulate until his sister's temper eased considerably. "Longfield Park is ever so lovely, ma'am. I enjoyed our walk very much. And perhaps you'll be pleased to know your brother has agreed to stay on another few days rather than rush off tomorrow."

Charity's chin tilted. "Has he now?"

"He has." Dylan avoided those searching green eyes, shrewd and pitchfork sharp. Did she fathom the reason for his sudden change of heart—a reason that stood but an arm's reach away? If she hadn't yet, she would. She always did. "If you'll still have me that is."

Her lips curved slowly in a rueful smile, one that pretended disinclination while assuring him of the opposite.

"Charity, Dylan," came a call from inside the house. Luke stepped out onto the terrace looking flushed and winded. "I've just come from town." He paused, bending to catch his breath. His gaze found Elizabeth's and locked. "Mrs. Mendoza, your horses have been found. And from the looks of things, I fear the accident may have been the result of foul play."

CHAPTER 7

"What?" Eliza's hand flew to her throat. The duke must be mistaken. She'd witnessed the entire accident. There'd been no one else involved, only the deplorable weather and the wretched state of the road.

The blood drained from her face, leaving her dizzy, wobbly. Mr. Fergusson's arm went around her, supporting her about the waist.

"Easy, lass." His breath was warm against her ear, the words a deep and soothing reassurance. "Let's all go inside and sit down."

He didn't release her until she was safely delivered to the settee. But it was the duchess who slid in beside her, who scooped up her hand and held it firmly in her lap. Oddly, this calmed Eliza more than she would have expected. Surely people who were willing to offer such kindness to a stranger would be equally willing to listen to her and not jump to conclusions.

As she must remember not to do. "Please, your grace, explain what you mean by foul play."

The duke leaned forward in his chair, clasped hands dangling between his knees, expression deadly serious. "Your team was found by a farmer a few miles to the north. They stumbled onto his land exhausted, still connected by their traces. Two of them are lame, and all four of them suffer from hunger and thirst. That is to be expected, of course." He paused and drew a breath. "Mrs. Mendoza, do you know of any reason why anyone would wish to do you harm?"

"Harm me? Good heavens, no." Elizabeth Mendoza's words coursed through her mind, louder and stronger than ever. *Don't let them have it.* Eliza wanted to grab the duke by his coat, shake him and demand that he stop toying with her and give her some clue as to what she suddenly faced.

"What else did this farmer discover?" Mr. Fergusson's Scottish lilt restored a measure of her composure. She released the breath she'd sucked deep into her lungs and pondered how he always managed to step between her and adversity as if he comprehended her need to be shielded. Indeed, she wondered if her self-appointed guardian angel could read her mind.

"There was a good portion of the whiffletree dragging at the ends of the traces," the duke said, "with part of the shaft and roller bolt still attached. I'm told with the way it all broke up, it appears as if the carriage had either been tampered with, the bolts and linchpin loosened, or hastily and incompetently hitched in the first place."

"Incompetently hitched," Eliza repeated. Again the blame would fall on the driver. On poor John Howitt who may or may not be responsible for the accident but who nonetheless could not speak in his own defense.

"Yes." The duke's dark eyes searched hers. "You'd mentioned your driver may have had business on the old Yorkshire road. Could that have been the cause of his haste?"

"I couldn't say for sure." She swallowed a sodden lump as Mr. Fergusson—*dear* Mr. Fergusson—sent her a message of sympathy from beneath his heavy brows, a look that said he would spare her all of this if he could.

"I don't mean to upset you, Mrs. Mendoza." As his grace spoke, his wife's hand tightened around Eliza's. "It may well be that your driver caused his own death and that of your companion, who was, I believe, his wife?"

Eliza nodded, staring down at the linked hands, hers and

the duchess's, willing her fingers not to clench and convulse as they felt wont to do.

"Had he lived, the man might well be facing criminal charges," the duke went on, each word a thorn in Eliza's conscience. "But since we cannot prove his guilt we must allow for the possibility that he was as much a victim as you. If you could supply me with the names of the villages you stopped in along the way, I will raise an inquest into the matter."

She yanked her hand from the duchess's grip. "Please don't!"

Astonishment shivered in the air between Eliza and her three saucer-eyed companions. In that instant she glimpsed her downfall, saw her utter disgrace and her lonely walk back to the moors, with the image of Mr. Fergusson's horrified disappointment burned forever into her mind's eye.

"I'm sorry . . . I . . . " But there was nothing, no explanation for her outburst. No excuse for the things she'd done.

The duchess slipped an arm around her shoulders. "I understand exactly what you mean, dear. You needn't say another word." She raised her chin to address her husband. "What are you thinking, Luke Holbrook, to speak of inquests at a time like this. The poor thing has been through the worst of nightmares. Sweet mercy, people in her employ have died. Can you imagine if we lost Mrs. Hale or our dear Esther? Why, it would be akin to losing members of the family."

"I realize that, my darling, but—"

"But nothing. I'll not have you driving this poor woman to distraction when what she wants is rest and time to grieve."

Eliza's growing dismay stemmed from her need to quell the duke's suspicions, true, but also from a desire to diffuse the argument now brewing between him and his wife.

"Please, your grace," she implored, "there isn't any need for an investigation because . . . I fear it may have been my fault we hurried so." She'd grabbed fistfuls of skirt, twisting the fabric as if wringing it out. "You see, the house had been sold and I'd nowhere to go. I simply wanted to leave York and reach London. Perhaps my driver used undue haste to please me and . . . "

"There, there now." The duchess patted Eliza's cheek. "You mustn't blame yourself. Of course you wanted to be gone from York and be with family. Anyone would." Her gaze darted to her husband. "It was simply an accident and we shall speak no more of the matter, shall we?"

That evening as Eliza prepared for supper, the duke's discovery replayed in her mind. As she brushed out her hair and attempted to braid and twist it into something resembling a stylish coiffeur, she wondered if she'd done the right thing in convincing the duke not to conduct an investigation. Safer, surely, for her but . . .

Don't let them have it. Had Elizabeth's mad flight down the old Yorkshire road been an attempt to outrun an assailant? There had been that doctor in Heverton Gorse, and then the Spaniard on the Wakefield Road, the one who stared. What if . . .

She set the hairbrush down on the dressing table and frowned at the anxious face staring back from the mirror. A Spaniard who stared. No crime in that. And the doctor had only wanted to bring Elizabeth home. He had denied any emergency, alluding merely to questions Elizabeth could answer. Again, nothing sinister about that. If anything, the man had been acting as Elizabeth's benefactor.

And Elizabeth's last words? Why, in her delirium she might have been thinking about her home, Folkstone Manor. Perhaps she had regretted selling it, and loathed having turned the place over to the new owners.

That left the broken linchpin and whiffletree, but coaches plunged off country roads all the time and no one cried foul.

She pushed off the cushioned bench and turned to face the room, her gaze skimming the elegant bed hangings, the pillows, the daintily painted furnishings, and all the lovely details that made this room fit for a queen. She'd spoken one truth in the duke and duchess's presence. She had nowhere else to go. No other options. The duke's allegations simply must be wrong because Eliza could not turn back, not now, not ever. Not to the life she'd left behind.

No, her immediate concern was not how a linchpin had broken. If there were mysteries to be solved about Elizabeth Mendoza's life, she'd solve them eventually and move on. More pressing at this very moment was how to fake her way through her first-ever supper in a nobleman's dining room.

Last night she'd eaten in the privacy of her room. The meals earlier today had been informal, either in the morning room or in a room the Holbrooks called the conservatory, which didn't seem a room at all to Eliza but a glassed, tiled garden abloom with all manner of peculiar plants.

Her first quandary now lay in what to wear. She knew that nobles wore particular fashions depending on the time of day and the room in which they planned to gather. A muslin gown with short sleeves might be acceptable for luncheon in the family parlor, but never for evenings in the drawing room. A lady might wear bright floral patterns to receive guests at home but never for walking or visiting abroad. A silk, shoulder-baring bodice was expected at balls but would scandalize at an afternoon tea. There were morning dresses and afternoon dresses, at-home dresses and carriage dresses. Evening gowns, ball gowns, reception gowns and even boudoir gowns, as if ladies of quality were expected to entertain in their dressing rooms.

When her friend, Nancy Miller, explained all these details, Eliza had wrinkled her nose and laughed at the absurdity. At the time, her wardrobe had boasted five everyday frocks, two Sunday to-church dresses and a gown for village assemblies. She'd considered herself luckier than most to own those.

Alone now in her room, she struggled to remember all Nan had told her. The largest trunk lay open like a jewel box, spilling amethysts, garnets and sapphires . . . silks that gleamed, moirés that shimmered, muslins that absorbed the warm glow of the candlelight.

Supper would be served at eight. Evening, so not the flowered muslin. There would not be dancing, therefore not a ball, so she decided the less bosom exposed the better. There were no other guests arriving, so she needn't wear the finest of the lot.

But not a one of them suited her, not really, for all they dazzled her eyes and delighted her fingertips—or because of that, really. Such finery had been fashioned for the exquisite Elizabeth and not for the likes of Eliza—plain, ordinary, inconsequential. When she held any of those dresses before her in front of the tall swivel mirror, she uttered a grim laugh at the audacity of a farmwife turned laundress turned almost-whore thinking she might wear anything so grand.

In the end, common sense suggested a deep, inky crimson silk for its elegance. The sumptuous fabric would suit the grandeur of the dining hall while the somber tone remained appropriate, for, like her, Elizabeth had been a widow. And perhaps this was the one color that suited her perfectly. Red—blood red—for Nathan and their baby and Eliza's broken heart. Blood red for poor Elizabeth and unlucky John Howitt.

With the decision made she pulled the bell tassel. She did so reluctantly. She'd much prefer to slip into her pilfered clothes in private, but the duchess had expressly forbidden her the exertion of dressing herself. As if tossing a gown over one's head could be considered toilsome. The duchess could have no idea what true exertion entailed—would recoil at Eliza's memories of back-breaking labor as both a farmwife and a laundry maid.

She heard a soft knock at her door.

"I'm Esther, ma'am," said a plump young redhead when Eliza opened the door. "Her grace says I'm to help ready you for supper, if you please, ma'am."

The young woman, about Eliza's own age, smiled, bobbed a curtsey and stepped into the room. Her easy manner reminded

Eliza of the above stairs maids at Quibley Manor in Dewsbury, and brought back how much she had envied their starched white aprons, their tidy hair, their comfortable tasks that raised nary a blister nor callus. While Eliza had hauled and scrubbed and rinsed and ironed, the abigails had lovingly tended their mistress's needs while snubbing their fortunate noses at the scullery maids and washerwomen.

She was tempted now to make the maid's task difficult. But then Esther faced her sporting a genuine smile, her freckled face filled with a patient and honest desire to please. Eliza could not but acknowledge that this woman had never done her a bit of harm.

As the silence stretched, Esther turned toward the bed and touched a fingertip to the garnet gown. "Is this what you're wearing tonight, ma'am?"

Had there been approval in her tone? Criticism? Neither exactly, Eliza decided, but perhaps the girl would prove useful in more ways than one. "Will it suit, do you think?" She gave what she hoped was a careless laugh. "I must confess I've never dined with a duke and duchess before."

"Oh, you could come in sackcloth and the Holbrooks wouldn't mind, ma'am."

What an odd thing to say, and how impertinent of this servant to voice it aloud. Eliza didn't know quite how to react, so instead she joined Esther by the side of the bed.

"Shall we tighten your corset first, ma'am?" Esther sounded as if the act would bring her as much enjoyment as opening a birthday present.

Eliza obliged by slipping out of her dressing gown and, standing in chemise and stockings, turning her back to the girl. Esther wrapped the corset round her waist and began the task of pulling and adjusting.

"Pardon me, ma'am," the young woman said with a tug, "but this doesn't fit exactly, does it? A size too large, I'd say."

"I've . . . lost weight recently. Do what you can with it."

Esther gave another firm yank; Eliza winced as the stays

pinched her side as if a stone were lodged between her ribs. A wiggle or two helped set it to rights.

"You might consider ordering a new one, ma'am, if you don't mind my saying so. There's a shop in town that services all the ladies in the house."

"Is there now?"

"Oh, indeed, ma'am. A fine shop it is."

She chatted on merrily about the shop, the village of Longfield, the larger town of Wakefield, paying no heed whatsoever to Eliza's silences and fleeting replies. Such banter would have earned her a reprimand at Quibley Manor, and it led Eliza to believe the Holbrooks were indulgent masters indeed. Perhaps too much so, for when Esther had finished with the corset and prompted Eliza to step into a petticoat, she exclaimed, "Lord save me, ma'am, you *are* slight as a reed!"

But it wasn't until she'd gathered up the folds of that radiant silk gown and draped them over Eliza's too-thin figure that Esther's smiles gave way to frowns. She smoothed and plucked, fluffed and tucked, all the while with a worried pout.

Hot needles prickled Eliza's cheeks. Thus far she'd managed to fool Mr. Fergusson and his family, but a lady's maid? Who better understood the very essence of what made a woman a lady than the servant who bathed her, dressed her, listened to her secrets and dreams? Perhaps it wasn't anyone so lofty as a duke who might prove her ruination, but a mere servant who knew more about the nobility than they knew themselves.

And so Eliza waited for Esther to suddenly snatch her hands away as if they'd encountered something soiled and repulsive. She braced for her to back away with glaring eyes and an accusing finger. *Fraud,* she'd charge . . . .

"If you can spare me a moment, ma'am, I'll be back in a trice."

Esther didn't wait for a reply but scampered from the room, leaving Eliza to contemplate herself in the mirror. As predicted, she looked like a common wench who'd stolen a gown. Or worse. She'd once heard of bawdy women who rented gowns from their fancy men in order to attract a higher sort of clientele as they plied their nighttime trade.

Esther didn't leave her brooding over her disappointment for long, but returned minutes later with a small gingham-lined basket—a sewing basket as Eliza discovered. "There now, ma'am, let's see what we might accomplish with this. We'll do a quick job of it tonight, but tomorrow I'll make the alterations permanent. Mind you I'm no seamstress, but I am known for a smart trick or two with the needle."

The little gilt clock on the escritoire ticked away as Esther worked and Eliza, her gaze fixed on the mirror, watched the curve of her breasts appear from out of nowhere. Soon a tight waistline took shape, smoothing to hips that, if not entirely filling the skirt, at least fit more snugly within.

After some twenty minutes the maid stood back with a proud grin. Eliza's breath caught at the sight of her own reflection. The gown almost, but for that half-inch of hem dragging the floor, might have been made for her.

Esther's grin faded as Eliza began shaking her head.

"Does it not please, ma'am?"

"Oh, Esther . . . it's perfect. Why, it's—"

"Perfectly beautiful on you, ma'am." She shook out one side of the skirt, an unnecessary but lovingly bestowed adjustment. "Shall I dress your hair, now?"

Eliza's hand went to the braided twist she'd fashioned earlier, but she only just stopped herself from mentioning her efforts to Esther. "Yes, if you wouldn't mind."

"It's my job, ma'am, and a bonnie job it is when the hair's as lovely as yours."

She recognized that for the swinging great lie it was, but she couldn't begrudge the false flattery, not after the magic Esther had worked on the gown. Her nimble fingers set to work on Eliza's lifeless hair, pulling, lifting, twisting, hurting a little but Eliza held her tongue. Finally the clock rang out its single half-hour chime: seven-thirty.

Moments later there came a soft tapping at her door.

"Wait," she whispered to Esther. She swept closer to the mirror, entranced—stunned, really—by the fashionable, sophisticated, almost shapely stranger staring back. Using pins set with tiny jewels, Esther had swept her hair high on her head in a loose tumble that elongated her neck with a graceful curve. She'd left a few strands floating about her face, lending shape and shadow to her cheeks and making them appear so much less round.

As that charming, confident woman stared back at her, Eliza felt the farmwife turned laundry maid turned almostwhore begin to fade from existence, until all that remained was a gentlewoman's tragic memory of the companion and driver that died in a coaching accident.

Days ago she'd feared that very occurrence, feared losing herself within her own deception. But she didn't feel lost or forsaken at all. She felt . . . filled with hope for the future. And for Eliza, that was extraordinary indeed.

Another knock came and this time she signaled to Esther with a decisive nod.

"Yes sir, Mrs. Mendoza's ready," the maid said at the partially open door. "And just wait till you lay eyes on her." With that she swung the door wide.

Eliza and Mr. Fergusson gasped simultaneously. He, too, was resplendent in a coat of deep wine, a crisp white shirt and tapering charcoal trousers that revealed the muscular legs of a true horseman. She realized how closely his colors complemented hers, and once again his uncanny ability to know her mind left her flabbergasted.

"Mrs. Mendoza . . . " His gaze was pinned on her, drinking in every detail. He took several strides into the room, his elegant, masculine presence seeming to fill even that large space, so much so Eliza, finding difficulty in drawing breath, drew a step back. He came to an abrupt halt as if only just remembering he'd entered a lady's bedchamber. "You're positively . . . "

She heaved a breath and raised her eyebrows. "Transformed?"

"Not the word I was groping for." Not for the first time, his smile sent her stomach for an odd but not unpleasant flip. "Nor were any of the others that sprang to mind adequate by any means."

His praise brought on a conflicting wash of warmth—of delight and the desire to believe him, of a lingering inability to do so. "We have Esther's talents to thank for it," she said with a shrug.

"No." Without taking his eyes off her, he inclined his head in the maid's direction. "With all due respect to Esther, you have yourself to thank for it."

Just as young William had done upon her arrival here, Mr. Fergusson took open, unabashed appraisal of her, all of her, making her keenly aware—physically, thrillingly aware—of a bosom that had never dared reveal its shape so thoroughly before. Though the garnet dress covered all it should, she felt nonetheless bared beneath the heat of his regard, for that regard was a fiery thing, so intensely did it burn where it roamed.

He made her feel . . . like the most beautiful and most important woman on earth, one who bore no relation at all to the slattern who once stood alone outside the Raven's Perch Tavern.

He offered the crook of his arm. "Are you ready?"

At that moment she'd have grasped that arm and gone anywhere with him. Anywhere at all.

"Oh, not just yet." Esther trotted to the dressing table, returning with a length of black ribbon. "I found this in your jewelry case and thought with that dress and your coloring, ma'am, it would be just the thing." She moved behind Eliza and draped the ribbon around her neck. A cameo set in gold and bordered with seed pearls came to rest just below her collarbones. "Now Mrs. Mendoza is ready for supper."

"Aye, lass," Mr. Fergusson murmured, "Mrs. Mendoza is ready to awe them all."

His claim sent her hurtling from the clouds back to earth, for while her transformation was indeed an awesome feat for the likes of she, surely the others would find her merely acceptable, nothing extraordinary. Yet at her entrance into the drawing room, all heads turned in her direction. The air shivered with an astonished hush, broken finally when Sir Joshua Livingston wobbled to his feet with the help of both his cane and his daughter's arm.

He made his way to Eliza and raised her hand to his lips. "This is quite what we've been after, my dear. To see you with a glow in your cheeks and a gleam in your eye."

They all rather enveloped her after that, inquiring after her health, asking if she'd like to sit closer to the fire, would she like a shawl, a pillow, etc. Someone pressed a glass of something that looked like flaming molasses into her hand. Discovering the taste to be not far off, she dared only the tiniest of sips.

Previously she had been the quiet, overwhelmed recipient of their collective goodwill. Tonight, perhaps as a result of their open admiration, or perhaps due to the spirits, she smiled and laughed and talked as though she had every right to do so.

These were good people. Kind, compassionate and generous, and she liked them very much. Never mind that their largess would not have been extended quite so readily had they known her true identity. Then again, she doubted any of them would have left her to starve on the side of the road either. No, the Holbrook clan had proved themselves better than that, better than the aristocrats she had once despised.

This family was genuine, even if she was not. But those occasional twinges of guilt she shoved away. She hadn't caused Elizabeth Mendoza's death, but she refused to allow that death to be meaningless. What use would two dead women serve, for Eliza surely would have followed in Elizabeth's fate had she not seized the opportunity thrust so unmistakably into her lap.

And it wasn't as if she hadn't suffered, hadn't paid dearly for that opportunity. No, guilt had no place in her life, at least not in the life she was determined to lead.

CHAPTER 8

Some thirty minutes after supper ended, Dylan rose from the dining table barely able to suppress the annoyance that had been building inside him since the ladies vacated the room. At the time, he would have liked nothing better than to follow them out, but courtesy and, damn it all, a thousand years of tradition had dictated that he remain behind with the men to indulge in port and cigars.

He detested cigars and esteemed port only slightly more. But those weren't the only distasteful habits the Holbrook men indulged in. It seemed they never tired of nudging Dylan toward a future they envisioned for him, a course that would take him further and further from the life he loved until he no longer remembered the way home. Of course, they used subtle tactics, speaking in general terms, asking his opinion of that new bill set before Parliament, his thoughts on the newest import tax, his intentions concerning the latest trends in capital investment.

It was with vast relief that he strolled to the drawing room, anticipating his next sight of Elizabeth, hoping he might draw her to the settee near the fire or perhaps take a stroll across the terrace.

He discovered her at the card table, however, surrounded by the Holbrook ladies. She was shaking her head and looking decidedly perplexed.

"I'm afraid I don't know many card games."

"Surely you know whist." Helena stepped gingerly around

one of Charity's West Highland terriers as she brought a deck
of cards from the corner cabinet.

"No."

"Bridge?"

Elizabeth shook her head

"Hearts then," Charity suggested.

"I've never played."

"We'll teach you."

"Yes, it's easy."

From across the room she caught Dylan's eye for an instant, then released a breath. "I'll try."

It was more than apparent that she needed rescuing.
He started toward the table but a hand came down on his
shoulder.

"And just where do you think you're going?"

Dylan met his brother-in-law's gaze and tried to look innocent. "Thought I'd play a hand or two with the ladies."

"You loathe card games."

No more than he loathed port, cigars and hints concerning his future, yet he'd endured those.

"Come, Dylan, sit with Wes and Joshua and me."

Before he could demur they conveyed him almost physically to the chairs near the open terrace doors. Night noises
drifted in on a breeze tinged with the faintest hint of rain.
Dylan hoped the weather wouldn't keep them trapped indoors
on the morrow. He'd enjoyed his walk with Elizabeth today,
looked forward to showing her more of the estate. And to
being alone with her . . . .

"Now then," Luke said, breaking into what might have
proved rather pleasant musings, "I wasn't going to bring it up,
but have you given any further thought to my suggestion?"

"Which suggestion would that be?" Dylan raised his eyebrows. "You make so many."

"You know which. You're fast becoming a man of influence
in Scotland. Isn't it time you assumed the responsibility that
goes along with that?" Luke sipped his brandy, eyeing him

from over the rim. "Edinburgh needs a voice, a strong one. It's time you thought about entering the political arena."

Dylan stole glances at Wesley and Sir Joshua. "Are you all in this together? Why didn't you simply ask me over port and cigars, rather than talking in circles around the matter?"

"Because we know what a stubborn goat you are." Luke's brother shrugged a shoulder, his grin mocking but not entirely lacking a certain warmth. "We've discussed the issue at length. We all agree—"

"Upon the direction of my future? Don't you think I should have been included in that conversation?"

"We're including you now so don't be hostile." Luke leaned over and clapped his shoulder. "It's time, Dylan. You can't bury yourself in St. Abbs forever. At least you shouldn't," he added when Dylan opened his mouth to protest the claim.

Sir Joshua contributed his opinion with a sage nod. They wanted Dylan to enter politics, to eventually represent Lothian—which encompassed not only farming villages like St. Abbs but Edinburgh as well—in the Commons. Luke had first broached the subject earlier that spring. Dylan hadn't appreciated the notion then and he liked it little better now. "I'm no politician," he said. "I'm certainly no aristocrat."

"Lothian doesn't need or want an aristocrat," Wesley said. "It wants fairness and someone who understands the region. You studied both law and economics at the University of Edinburgh. Is all that education to be wasted?"

"No, I use it everyday in managing my family's holdings."

"What better way to secure your family's interests," Sir Joshua put in, "than influencing the laws that govern them."

"A compelling argument." That much Dylan couldn't deny. It wasn't so much what they were suggesting that needled him, but that they suggested it at all, as if he needed fixing. "Despite your praises, however, I'm merely someone with a knack for wise investments and a few good strokes of luck. That does not a politician make."

"Dylan, with Wes and me behind you—"

He held up a hand. "Stop right there."

The brothers exchanged a look. Sir Joshua raised his brows.

"I don't deny we Fergussons have benefited through our relation to the Holbrooks. And I am grateful for it. But we're a family that has always taken pride in working for our own successes and taking responsibility for our failures."

Luke looked dumbfounded. "Good God, do you think I can be married to your sister and not know that?"

Dylan glanced across the room at the ladies, at Elizabeth fanning a batch of cards in her hands and shaking her head with a bewildered air. He wondered, would she encourage him to take Luke's suggestion seriously? Would she support this bid to make him a better and more important man?

By St. George's ear, he hoped not.

He turned back to the Holbrook brothers, those men of great consequence who would never fully comprehend him. "You can't always arrange things for me, Luke. I wish you'd stop trying."

"That's not at all what I meant."

"Rather unfair of you, Fergusson, old boy," Wesley murmured in support of his brother. Sir Joshua turned down the corners of his mouth and angled his gaze at the floor.

"You're right." Dylan stood up and smoothed his coat front. "And I'm sorry. On both counts. I know you mean well, but simply put, I'm not your man."

Luke tipped his head back to regard him. "I still believe you are. You simply don't realize it yet. One of these days we'll knock sense into that thick Scottish skull of yours."

"You might try hitting me with a bottle." Dylan flashed a genuine grin, the kind he saved for his regular bloke of a brother-in-law who farmed sheep in Scotland. "It did wonders for you six years ago, didn't it?"

Luke's expression turned serious. "It made me remember who I am, Dylan. It returned me to my proper place in the world."

"I already know my place." He tipped a bow. "If you gentlemen will excuse me, I believe I detect a slight overflowing of goodwill at the other end of the room."

He approached the card table just as Dolly suggested a game of cribbage.

"Cribbage?" Lady Mary pursed her lips. "If Mrs. Mendoza doesn't know hearts she's certainly not likely to know cribbage."

As Skiff and Schooner clambered around his feet with eager snorts, Dylan placed a hand on the back of Elizabeth's chair. "How is the game proceeding, ladies?" he asked, seeing quite plainly the game wasn't proceeding at all.

"Not very well, I'm afraid, and it's all because of me." Elizabeth tipped her face to peer up at him, looking as eager to be gone from the card table as he was to take her from it. "We never played cards at home while I was growing up. I'm hopelessly ignorant."

"Never mind, then, let's just chat." Dolly absently leaned to stroke the head of a passing Westie. "I've been wondering, where in Spain are the Mendozas from?"

"Wouldn't Leone be the obvious answer?" Lady Mary said in a mild but pointed tone.

Dolly looked fascinated. "Is there such a place?"

"Of course there must be," Charity patiently explained, "or they would not be the Mendozas of Leone."

"Oh, quite so."

Dylan stole an opportunity granted by a lull in the conversation. "I wonder, Mrs. Mendoza, if you've had an opportunity to view the rose garden by moonlight?"

"Why no, Mr. Fergusson, that's a privilege I've not yet enjoyed."

"It's grown rather cold," Dolly observed with a look of concern.

116   *Lisa Manuel*

"Nonsense," Dylan replied, "in Scotland this is considered midsummer weather. Would you care to go, Mrs. Mendoza?"

"Indeed I would." She cast a glance at the others. "It must be breathtaking."

"Oh, it is. Why don't we all—"

Lady Mary silenced Helena's impending proposal with a shake of her head. "We've seen the rose garden by moonlight more times than we can count."

Thank you, Mary. But Dylan wondered, had that shrewd woman guessed at his desire to have Elizabeth all to himself, or perceived Elizabeth's need to simply escape for a few moments?

"Mind you don't stay out too long and catch a chill," Charity cautioned as they left the table.

A cool breeze rippled Elizabeth's skirts around her legs as they stepped out to the terrace together. Despite the hovering scent of rain in the air, a bright, waxing moon illuminated the sky.

"Thank you, Mr. Fergusson."

"For what?"

"For . . . Oh, please don't misunderstand. I adore your sister and her family. But . . . "

"I understand completely. I love them all, yet there are times I feel the need to steal away, too."

She nodded. "I suppose I shall have to learn some skill at cards or I'll be a tiresome addition to my brother-in-law's home."

The mere mention of her intended destination had the odd effect of setting him on the defensive. "I for one am grateful you have no such skills."

"What an odd thing to say."

"Not at all, for had you skill at cards, Mrs. Mendoza, I would not now have the pleasure of your company."

They reached the terrace wall and here she stopped abruptly, turning to face him. A smile played about her lips. "Why, Mr. Fergusson, are you flirting with me?"

Good heavens, he had been, hadn't he? Was she remembering that ill-fated kiss in the tavern? How humiliating. "Mrs. Mendoza," he said with feeling, "I assure you we Scots never engage in anything so undignified as flirting."

"Yet . . . " Her bottom lip disappeared between her teeth for an instant. "I believe you were."

He started to deny it again, more firmly this time. But the torchlight turned her eyes to pure gold and revealed a wistful longing trying so very hard not to be obvious.

"Would it be an unwelcome thing if I were flirting?" His hand rose to her hair, his fingertips making the merest contact with those loose wisps framing her face. "Would you despise me for it?"

"No, Mr. Fergusson," she whispered. Her eyes, those great gold sovereigns, shimmered in the wavering light. "You can't know how long it's been since . . . "

"Since a man made an ass of himself over you?"

Her nose wrinkled when she laughed. He loved that, wanted nothing better than to press his lips to that too-wide-to-be-fashionable nose. William had been right. A man could fall in love with a woman based on a single endearing feature.

But they were standing on the terrace before a pair of double doors open to the inside, where far too many members of his family sat watching. "Shall we continue down to the garden?"

"Yes, but . . . I do hope we haven't offended the others with our flimsy excuse for running off."

"Flimsy?"

"Viewing the rose garden at night? As if there will be anything to see in the dark."

"Ah. There you are wrong." He took her hand in his. "Come with me, madam."

She clearly wasn't believing a word of his claim, not until they descended the wide granite steps and crunched a few

strides along the walkway. Then she halted with a breathy
ooh.

"The blossoms are all aglow. Oh, how lovely."

"A trick of the moonlight and the fact that the flowers are
watered every evening at dusk. Come." He led her further in,
tugging her hand ever so slightly because she'd become like
a bewildered child, dragging her feet, reaching out to touch
and staring over her shoulder to admire the plants they
passed. As they approached the fountain she tugged free and
trotted the last few steps until she stood breathless before
the gushing water.

"It's like tiny diamonds flying through the air." She stuck a
finger into one of the streams, arresting its flow before
snatching her hand away.

"Don't worry, lass, you can't break it."

She spun full circle, then back toward him. "Did the dowager duchess really do all this herself?"

"With plenty of help, of course. But yes, she designed this
garden and tends it every day during the growing season."

She looked around again, her face filled with wonder.

"There's a better way to experience it. Close your eyes."
Her sudden frown made him smile. "On my honor no harm
shall come to you. Trust me."

"Well . . . " She did as he asked, her wary frown persisting.

"Now breathe. Deeply."

Her nostrils flared as she inhaled a long breath. Her brow
smoothed and her lips parted.

Dylan engaged every ounce of willpower, not to mention
that honor he'd just claimed to possess, to stay where he was
and not grab her in his arms. Instead he indulged his gaze on
the honey-haired, unfashionable beauty whose tiny figure became somehow profoundly arousing in a gown that hugged
to perfection.

"Now listen," he said. "To the water, to the crickets and the
night noises. Listen to the swish of the blossoms. And
breathe."

Breathe she did, full, heaving breaths that swelled her bosom, lifting it to the silver moonlight. Her lips fell open on a smile, wide and childlike. A bubble of laughter tumbled out.

He need only lean, and he did—leaned and bowed his face to her upraised one, brushing his lips ever so lightly across hers. Her laughter became a gasp. Her eyes flew open, bright golden surprise meeting his own sensation of shock.

Oh, God, he'd done it again.

Stupid. So *stupid*. Hadn't he already made this very mistake?

But this time Elizabeth didn't whirl and run away. She stood still, utterly so, her gaze that of a startled deer . . . at first. Soon the astonishment faded and something quite different emerged, something knowing and wanting and not childlike in the least, prompting him to wrap his hand into her hair and without ceremony pull her face to his.

His lips came down on the bridge of her nose, suckling for an instant before sliding to the tip. He nipped it softly— couldn't resist doing that—before plunging lower, bringing his mouth firmly against hers. How eagerly her mouth opened for him, without his having to coax in the least.

His tongue sampled the taste of her lower lip, explored the line of her teeth. She made hungry little noises that passed into him, tickling the insides of his mouth and throat. Finally their tongues met, a sweeping greeting that acquainted them fully and left few secrets between them.

There it should have ended, been over and done. But he felt her wobble and stumble against him, that soft, sweet weight seeking the support of his chest. He gave it gladly, gratefully, lustfully as her arms closed around his neck. And he knew then this was far from over.

Her calf rose along his, sending a fire coursing through his trousers. As he continued exploring every warm, wet inch of Elizabeth's mouth, she murmured wordless permission and tipped her head higher, exposing a lovely white neck he would not have ignored for all the world. He slid his lips to the soft underside of her chin, and suddenly they were both stumbling and sinking to the ground.

CHAPTER 9

Oh, it was wrong, entirely wrong and Eliza didn't care. If ladylike warnings blared in her mind, what of it? She wasn't a lady, not really, and so she made one conscious decision to stop thinking and simply held onto Mr. Fergusson, onto the exhilarating sensations as the two of them sank to their knees on the biting gravel of the path.

She ignored the pain as easily as her qualms, until both faded into the acute pleasure of masculine hands touching her, roaming her as his gaze had earlier. But this, ah, this was infinitely more intimate, so much more stirring. A thousand nerve endings sprang to life inside her, feelings she had believed long dead . . . feelings she never knew existed.

He eased her onto the grassy bank bordering a flowerbed. His breath came hot and moist against her cheek, her ear. "Elizabeth," he murmured into her hair, but she seized his face and pulled his mouth back to hers, bruising him for all she knew but determined to silence him.

She didn't want talking, did not want to be asked permission for this shocking thing they were doing, all but lying on the garden floor in the home of these gentlefolk who'd been so kind. No, if she thought about it at all, if he spoke so much as a word, this pleasure would come to a crashing halt and no, Eliza could not have born it.

She found his hand, smoothed the fingers open and, gaze locked with his, brought them to her breast. His eyes flickered in surprise, then eager pleasure as his hand molded to the shape

of her, kneading, fondling in a dizzying rhythm that spawned
an entirely unique thought. She, Eliza, was desirable—this man
desired her.

"You're so beautiful," he murmured as if to prove her correct and this, as much as his touch, spread a sensual, consuming ache all through her.

Eliza felt tipsy with roses and moonlight and Mr. Fergusson's magic. She filled her lungs with fragrant air and shut
her eyes to the glorious friction of his hands on her bodice.
These were no dandy's hands, soft and smooth, but a man's.
They captured her throat, tenderly circled her neck, capered
at the buttons down her back. Then they slid back around and
plunged beneath her neckline, down inside the dratted corset
and beneath her shift.

"Oh." Her nipples beaded against his broad palms, and
passion streaked beneath her skin like fine-veined lightning
fanning the sky.

But Eliza wanted more. She wanted to feel him and know
him beneath his coat and waistcoat and shirt. Her fingers
fumbled at buttons and laces. She yanked them loose but the
shirt wouldn't open nearly wide enough. With a feverish need
she tugged his hems free and thrust her hands beneath, flat-
tening her palms against his chest, learning the lay of his
muscles, fingertips exploring his taut stomach to the border
of his waistband, then dipping lower. Oh, he was . . .

All a man should be. Rock solid and sprinkled with coarse
hair in all the right places. And warm . . . so warm. So in-
trigued was she that for a moment she didn't realize where his
hands had strayed, but now she felt them beneath her hems,
raising her skirts, gliding along her legs, higher, ever nearer
the place that yearned now for his touch, burned for it.

Wrong, Eliza thought, so wrong. And yet so very inevitable. He was her champion, her knight, who somehow understood her better than anyone else ever had. As his fingers
reached the apex of her thighs, he stroked and delved and
opened her with such tender coaxing, such perfect awareness

of how to woo her, her surrender to pleasure was so complete
she could not for all the world have stopped him.

No, he and his capable hands took her away from the
world, away from deception, guilt and fear. She went willingly, eagerly. Eliza and Elizabeth ceased to be. There was
only the rapture wrought by Mr. Fergusson's hands, by his
fingers that slipped in and out of her with an intimacy both
glorious and devastating, that revealed her wholly, that made
her twist and writhe until her insides pulsed and squeezed and
died and were reborn.

Shameful . . . and marvelous.

And then somehow she was sitting in his lap, shivering in
his arms, weeping against his shoulder. Not from remorse or
shame but from the sheer joy of this thing that had happened
to her, this sweet secret taught her by her wonderful Mr. Fergusson. She'd always suspected there must be more to cou-
pling than chafed thighs and a vague sense of satisfaction.
But oh, Mr. Fergusson had sent her soaring, spinning through
the heavens, then caught her fast in his arms.

His face, pillowed between her breasts, swung upward.
"Lass, are you crying? Dear God, forgive me . . . ."

"I'm not crying, Mr. Fergusson, and no fair asking forgiveness. Do you not remember it's against the rules? And
anyway, I'm simply . . . I don't know, I . . ." Without taking
her cheek from his shoulder she raised her gaze to the
strength of his profile silhouetted against the night sky.
"What did you . . . how did you . . . do that wonderful thing
to me?"

He ever so gently grasped her shoulders and eased her from
his chest. He peered into her face a long, solemn moment. Then
he smiled, as tender and gentle as the moonlight gilding his
brow. "Lass, don't you think it's time you stopped calling me
Mr. Fergusson? My name is Dylan, as well you know."

"Dylan. Such a lovely name, Mr. Fergusson."

He grinned. Keeping one arm around her he leaned back
on the other, hand propped on the ground. "I shall call you

Elizabeth whether you give me leave or no, for Elizabeth you've been to me since yester morn, and tonight has made you ever more so."

Can a heart leap and break in the same moment? Eliza swore hers did. Mr. Fergusson—Dylan—had just said the most joyous thing to her and yet, if only he had said it truly to her, to Eliza, to the woman she was beneath Elizabeth's exquisite gown. He wasn't *her* Mr. Fergusson at all, but in an eerie sort of way Elizabeth's. It was her ghost he admired, her elegance, for all it was Eliza's soul he'd touched.

Only now, with the newly created gaps between them, did she realize how heavily she'd been perspiring. The breeze stole into her loosened gown and made her shiver in earnest.

"Here, lass." He grabbed up his coat from where it had fallen to a heap on the ground. "Put this round your shoulders."

But her gown was halfway down her arms. She turned to show him her back. "Please," was all she had to say before he went to work. When he'd secured the dress properly, pausing once to redo a button he'd put through the wrong hole, he wrapped his coat around her.

"I should have had all my coats made in pairs," he teased with a chuckle. "One for me and one for you."

A mere jest, but one that stirred a yearning inside her. To be always inside his sleeves . . . his arms . . . so completely safe.

"Oh, but we must set your shirt to rights." She reached for the laces and worked them straight, tying a neat bow. He wrapped his collar about his neck and secured it, then shrugged into his waistcoat. Smiling, she helped him button the front and savored this new familiarity that made the act so natural.

When he ran his hands through his hair, her own hands flew to her ruined coiffure. "All the pins have scattered. I can't return to the house like this."

"We'll find them." He bent over, making sweeps of his

hands across the grass and gravel. Eliza did the same; between them they retrieved nearly a dozen.

"Do you think these are all?"

"If not, the children are sure to find them come morning."

"I'll never be able to fix it as Esther did." She gathered her hair at the top of her head, only to have it slip through her shaky fingers and stream down around her shoulders.

"Let me try." He combed his fingers through it, swept it off her neck and began securing it with pins.

"Ouch."

"Sorry. Hold still. There. That's a fair approximation if I do say so myself."

"Oh, Mr. Fergusson, really?"

"It's *Dylan* and well, sort of. Nearly so." He made a face that did little to bolster her confidence. "If no one examines you too closely."

She inspected his handiwork with her fingertips. "It isn't at all as Esther arranged it. And we've lingered here so long. What will your family think? Mr. Fergusson, however shall I go back inside and face them?"

"How? Why, at my side, Elizabeth." He helped her to her feet and offered the crook of his arm. "And with your head high."

At the foot of the terrace steps he stopped. "Do you ride?"

The question took her aback. She started to affirm that of course she could but what did it matter now? Then she remembered the style of riding he would expect of her and became wary. "I can, though it's not something I've often done."

"Good. Follow my lead when we get inside."

Still baffled, she let him convey her by one hand while her other continued worrying over her revamped hair.

He impelled her up the steps and across the terrace at a run, and now in addition to her disheveled state she panted for breath. Why had he made their appearance so much more disordered; why deny her even the smallest amount of dignity before his family?

"By St. George's ear, it's blustery outside," he announced to the occupants of the drawing room as they stepped inside. He deftly transferred Eliza's hand to the crook of his elbow. "We ran all the way down to the stables and back. Elizabeth greatly admired your White Andalusian, Luke." He turned a broad grin on her. "He's quite a prize, isn't he?"

"He's magnificent," she agreed quickly, taken aback at the lie, yes, but more so that he'd made good on his intention of calling her by her "given" name in front of the others. She darted a look around the room, searching for censure, speculation.

Did this new informality hint at what really happened outside? Could they detect how Eliza's legs and insides quivered still from those extraordinary moments in Mr. Fergusson's arms?

"Elizabeth has expressed an interest in seeing more of the estate." He started toward the settee and, her arm still linked through his, she followed as naturally as any young lady who'd enjoyed an innocent evening stroll with a gentleman. "If the weather permits," he went on, "we shall saddle up after breakfast. Anyone care to join us?"

This sparked a lively discussion of the merits of such an outing, and Eliza knew her secret was safe. She hid a smile, a wicked one, yes, but one filled with sweet delight all the same.

She allowed herself to relax, enjoying both the warmth of Mr. Fergusson's coat around her shoulders and the relief of his having deflected attention away from the sorry state of her appearance.

How cleverly he'd explained her ruined hair, her shortness of breath. A windy night, an impulsive race across the lawns. *Thank you, Mr. Fergusson, for rescuing me yet again.*

Then she became aware of the one voice that had remained silent as the others proceeded to debate a possible turn in the weather by morning. At the card table in the far end of the room, the duchess slowly came to her feet.

"A ride, Dylan?" A little ridge defined itself above her nose as she approached them. "I hardly think it a good idea after all Mrs. Mendoza has suffered these past days."

Indeed. Eliza had been so grateful for Mr. Fergusson's clever ruse, she hadn't stopped to consider how a desire to ride would be seen by the others. Would they think it the height of callousness that she wished to partake of any sort of enjoyment when her employees lay barely two days in their graves?

"I believe it the best of suggestions," he countered. His fingers closed around Eliza's. "The physician has declared Elizabeth in good health. Why then must she sit about the house with little else to do but dwell on the tragedy that took the lives of her employees . . . and perhaps fall to fretting if she might in some way have prevented it."

"Oh, dear . . . " A surge of her eyebrows transformed the duchess's disapproval to regret. "I hadn't thought of it that way. You are quite right, Dylan. My dear Mrs. Mendoza, do forgive me for being insensitive. I assure you we've no desire to make this time any more difficult for you than it must be."

"Oh, no, ma'am, you haven't—"

The duchess would have none of Eliza's protest. Sitting at her other side, she placed a hand on Eliza's cheek. "I sometimes forget what a wise young man my brother can be." She smiled gently, startling Eliza at how much she resembled her brother. "Our instinct has been to pet and cosset you, but Dylan has reminded me that ofttimes activity is the far better remedy. Each of us must grieve in our own unique way. Longfield Park is at your disposal, dearest, in any way it might be of comfort, whether you prefer to sit snug in the garden or gallop across the countryside. It is for you to decide."

"Your grace's kindness is the best remedy of all," Eliza said around the dumpling-sized lump in her throat, made all more unmanageable when Mr. Fergusson's thumb traced the underside of her wrist.

The duchess made a rueful face. "It seems my brother has already breached formality with his use of your first name, though I suppose his having rescued you does give him leave to do so."

"And I am a barbarian, after all," the gentleman interrupted, eliciting a titter of laughter around the room. It wasn't the first time Eliza had heard this joking reference to Mr. Fergusson's character, and she wondered . . .

"Yes, quite right," the duchess agreed. "But since Dylan has taken that first step, do you think, Mrs. Mendoza, that we all might dispense with formalities and titles?" She leaned in closer and whispered, though loud enough for all to hear, "I must admit I've never grown entirely comfortable with mine. Would you be terribly affronted?"

Affronted, no. Mortified, yes. As Eliza tried to forbid her mouth from gaping, she doubted her ability to ever address a peer or his wife by their given names. She might not know much about the world, but one thing she understood with certainty. Someone of her station never, ever placed herself on equal footing with her betters. It wasn't prudent, wasn't safe, for such an insult would rob her of any compassion they might otherwise feel toward someone as inferior as she.

And yet, the expectation on the duchess's face assured her that any disinclination on her part would be met with great disappointment.

"I told you they were ordinary," Mr. Fergusson murmured in her ear. "And now they've claimed you for their own."

"Yes," Helena Holbrook called from the card table. She rose and started across the room. "And we do intend to devise some way to keep you, Elizabeth. So you might as well grow accustomed to the idea."

One by one they vacated their seats and, in a way that touched Eliza to her very core, reintroduced themselves. Sir Joshua even raised her hand to his lips as though meeting her for the very first time. Of course, this new development would make her days here much more difficult, for now "your grace", "my lady" and "sir" would no longer do; now she must remember each individual name.

But oh, her qualms aside, how lovely—and how seductive— to be welcomed into this family. True, a sense of sinfulness tinged her pleasure, as did all good fortune when granted by the devil. Someday, she knew, there would be a reckoning. But like the fool who has bargained his soul, Eliza would bask in this inconceivable gift and shut her eyes to the inevitable consequences. For now. For tonight and tomorrow, and however long she dared linger at Longfield Park.

Oh, but tomorrow. Good gracious. She'd nearly forgotten. Her reckoning might come sooner than expected. Mr. Fergusson's quick thinking had preserved her respectability in the eyes of the others, but dear heaven, tomorrow she would be required to ride and make a decent show of it. Not that she couldn't jump fences, span streams, take an open field at a gallop—so long as she rode astride. That was the only way she knew, but it would never do in front of these genteel people. Oh, no, she must ride as a lady, with her legs tucked to one side and Elizabeth's velvet riding habit flowing out behind her.

Eliza had never ridden sidesaddle before in her life. How would Mr. Fergusson rescue her from that predicament?

Acting on a hunch the next morning, Dylan went down to the stables early to make arrangements with the groom. On his way back to the house across the dew-kissed lawns, he decided his plan had sprouted less from a hunch than an educated guess. He'd noticed—and pondered—Elizabeth's ability to swing up onto a horse with little assistance. It had both puzzled and amused him and aroused a sneaking suspicion. Now he'd put his theory to the test.

He hoped they might steal off alone today. Helena had expressed an interest in the outing, had poked her husband in the biceps when he'd failed to match her enthusiasm for

it. Ah, but Dylan saw through that gracious lady's smiles
sure enough. He would lay a hefty wager her wish to join
them had little to do with exercise and everything to do
with observing propriety and providing proper chaperones.

Ah, if they only knew. He believed his little ruse last night
had forestalled any budding suspicions concerning his and
Elizabeth's lengthy absence from the house. Sir Joshua had
been quick to note the heightened color in Elizabeth's cheeks,
but with his usual good cheer he had declared a good scam-
per just the thing for young people from time to time.

Dylan knew good and well what raised that color, what made
her eyes gleam so in the lamplight. He had done it to her, and
he regretted it not in the least. Did she? The notion robbed his
step of some of its bounce as he crossed the gardens.

Had she spent a sleepless night repenting their colossal
breach in decorum? He hoped she didn't see it that way.
Not for the world would he cause her the smallest scrap of
embarrassment or distress, but neither would he undo a
moment of their encounter in the rose garden. Even now,
images of her sweet face gone taut with ecstasy sent his
pulse for a wild dash.

Her response to his touch had left him fairly certain, not to
mention elated, that he'd introduced her to something new
and heretofore undreamed of. At the risk of disrespecting the
dead, her departed husband must have been a dithering old
fool to have never taken the time to love Elizabeth as she deserved. Mr. Mendoza had cheated himself, too, of the joy of
her soft cries, the melting heat of her trusting body.

Despite having sworn off English gentlewoman, taking
her in his arms last night had been like plunging headlong
down a winding, wooded path. He hadn't the foggiest notion where it might lead but, ah, getting there would be
such an adventure. He needn't foresee the ending, not just
yet, and this morning all he burned to know was when and
where he'd hold her again, and how he'd manage it with so
many well-meaning people underfoot.

He let himself in through the drawing room, hoping the others hadn't yet left their rooms; hoping, too, that he'd find Elizabeth ready to leave. His search sent him into the Grand Hall, where, by good fortune, he caught sight of her swathed in the deep blue folds of a riding habit. Good. She was ready to be whisked out of the house and away from well-intentioned interference.

He almost called out to her, then closed his mouth and leaned against the doorjamb, watching. With the train of her habit looped over one arm, she stood on the threshold of the dining room, her hand on the knob and neck craned as she peered inside.

After a moment she shook her head and closed the door. Like an apparition in the morning shadows she moved on to the next door. Dylan knew this to be Luke's study. He waited, head tilted, as she opened that door, peeked in, shook her head again and heaved a sigh.

Ah. He'd once spent the better part of a week losing his way around this house. "Good morning, Elizabeth," he called. "May I help you find something?"

She screeched, drowning out his echoing question. As she spun about in search of his voice, her train slid from her arm and hit the floor with a swoosh and a thud. Her startled look vanished as she spotted him across the hall.

"Oh, it's you, Mr. Fergusson." Her hand went to her heart. "You mustn't sneak up on people like that."

So it was still Mr. Fergusson, was it? He'd wanted her to call him Dylan, but perhaps she found the notion too presumptive, too familiar. Or perhaps he *had* crossed a line last night, and she wished to make it clear she had no intention of furthering their . . . acquaintance.

But no, her *Mr. Fergusson* of today plainly differed from her *Mr. Fergussons* of old—bouncier, crisper, no longer stiff with the respect afforded a stranger but . . . challenging, bantering in a frolicsome sort of way.

In a way he liked. Very much.

He tsked. "Perhaps you shouldn't go sneaking about the house."

"I was doing no such thing." Her adorable nose hefted for all of an instant before she released another sigh. "The truth is, Mr. Fergusson, I'm hopelessly lost. Esther told me I'd find breakfast waiting in the morning room, and I hadn't the courage to tell her I couldn't remember the way. I know it's through a door and down a hallway. Am I at least on the right floor?"

"Right floor, wrong wing. But don't take it to heart, lass. Longfield baffles many a first-time visitor." He pushed away from the jamb and started toward her. She moved to meet him part way.

A misstep sent her stumbling over her hems. He hurried forward with little hope of catching her in time, but she prevented a fall with an awkward little dance across the marble floor. She was still teetering when his arms closed around her.

"Easy, lass. A little early to be tipsy, wouldn't you say?"

Grinning, she struck him a blow to the shoulder. Then her gaze darted to the staircase. "Do let me go, Mr. Fergusson. Someone else may happen down at any moment."

That did little to persuade him. He held her tighter still and coaxed her face upward with a nip at her lips. "Is that the only reason I should release you? For fear of what the family would think?"

"For fear of . . . what has already occurred between us," she said in a voice gone quietly somber.

"Do you regret it?" His hands slid to her shoulders. He raised her to her toes, face to face with him. "I do not. Not a blessed minute of it."

"It's different for you, Mr. Fergusson. A man may indulge in such dalliances without fear of ruination."

"Dalliances?" His grip tightened. "Do you think so little of men?"

"It doesn't matter what I think. It is the way of the world."

"Not my world. If you believe last night meant little to me, then by God, lass . . . " He could think of no claim strong enough to dissuade her of her illusions, so he kissed her, hard and deep, and pressed his tongue into her mouth on the odd chance she possessed any lingering doubts. "There. Does that speak to you of regret or indifference?"

Blinking, pressing her fingertips to her lips, she shook her head no.

"And you? Do you regret our acquaintance? Do you believe it any less than Providence that of all the men traveling the roads of this country, I am the one who found you?"

She tucked her chin and contemplated her feet, and he instantly regretted having demanded she acknowledge feelings she might not, in fact, share. But then her lips twitched, and with a surge of overwhelming relief he realized she was fighting a smile.

He grasped her chin. "You *are* glad it was me. You can't deny it, can you?"

The tiniest nod was her only concession.

He bowed his head to study her face. "Then you don't regret last night?"

Though she compressed her lips tightly, they persisted in a grin that would not be conquered, that utterly conquered him. But she said sternly, "Last night was an indiscretion that must not happen again, Mr. Fergusson."

"Nor will it."

"Won't it?"

"Do I detect a note of disappointment?"

"Not in the least." She stooped to gather her train in her arms as if it were a bundle of hay. "Would you be good enough to point me in the direction of the morning room?"

"I'll do better than that, for I am headed that way myself." He extended the crook of his elbow.

She narrowed her eyes and gave a little snort. "The last time I took your arm, Mr. Fergusson, the devil came of it." That nose lofted in the air once more as she pivoted and started off—in the wrong direction. And no sooner had she

taken a handful of steps than she stumbled again over her too-
long skirts. Somewhere in York, he decided, there presided a
modiste unworthy of the thread she plied.

The morning room was empty when they reached it but
the main sideboard held an assortment of dishes. A maid,
who must have been listening at the servant's entrance for
footsteps, scurried in to pour their coffee. Elizabeth thanked
her before crossing to the sideboard and ladling porridge
into a bowl.

The morning room windows were tall and broad and faced
south, and now that Dylan saw her bathed in sunshine he decided she was nothing short of stunning in all that deep blue
velvet, however ill it fit her petite figure. The color was so
richly dark her hair shined nearly blond while her eyes turned
a more lavish shade of gold.

"Allow me." He took the bowl from her hands before all
that heavy velvet sent both her and it facedown onto the rug.

"I'm perfectly capable." She tugged her train higher over
her arm.

"Capable of what?" Charity came into the room, followed
by Wesley and Helena. To Dylan's disappointment, the latter
two were dressed for riding—and chaperoning.

"Good morning." Elizabeth strode to the table where she
and Charity exchanged an embrace. "Your brother witnessed
one tiny misstep and now judges me the clumsiest creature
ever born."

He stifled a chortle.

"He *is* impertinent," his sister agreed.

"A barbarian." Helena smiled fondly at him.

"Quite impossible to train, really."

He aimed a glare at Wesley. "True, but I daresay, Wes, I
haven't the benefit of a military background to set me jumping through hoops."

Charity's lips contracted into a tight little circle as her eyebrows shot up. Helena winced and bit her bottom lip. Elizabeth

went still, a worried frown working above a gaze that darted from person to person.

"Ah, a verbal backhander. Touché, my boy." A corner of Wesley's mouth pulled. "You'll learn to spar with the best of them yet."

"You mean the nastiest of them." Dylan continued to hold the other man's gaze. "And no, I will not."

"Stubborn." Shaking his head, Wesley strolled to the sideboard and lifted a plate. "You'll never live up to your potential that way."

"Well, then," Helena said in a singsong voice clearly designed to change the subject, "what are our plans for today?"

As the others discussed the day's intended ride, Dylan helped himself to poached eggs and a slice of glazed pork. When he settled at the table Elizabeth slid into the seat beside him. "Are you and Lord Wesley angry with each other?"

"Not in the least. Why would you think so?"

Looking puzzled, she rose and returned to the sideboard. From behind his back, Dylan heard her exchange a word and a quiet chuckle with Wesley. Luke entered the room, kissed his wife, bid everyone good morning and crossed to the buffet.

Dylan didn't see what occurred after that; he only heard a thud, a soft cry and a stumbling step. Twisting around, he saw Elizabeth's hand grope for the back of her chair. The plate she held in her other hand skidded onto the table. A scone went flying, spewing crumbs as it bounced and rolled.

Dylan pushed to his feet, but by the time he turned with outstretched arms, Elizabeth had hit the floor, knees first, her skirts heaped around her.

Everyone moved at once. Charity and Helena flanked Elizabeth on either side while Luke and Wesley hovered above, the former looking mortified.

"I'm so sorry, I didn't see you turn . . . ."

"Have you twisted an ankle?"

"Can you move?"

"Can you wiggle your toes, dearest?"

"Did she hit her head?"

Despite the attempts to coax her from the huddle she'd become, Elizabeth would not be budged. Her face lay all but hidden in her hands, the small portion that was visible turning an alarming shade of crimson. Dylan pushed her chair out of the way and crouched in front of her. As gently as his too-large, barbarian's hands would allow, he grasped her wrists. "Lass . . . ?"

She shook her head. Her shoulders trembled.

"My dear Elizabeth, are you terribly hurt?" From behind her, Luke bent lower, his face gone pale with remorse. "It was entirely my fault, wasn't watching, didn't see you step away . . . ."

"We must send for Dr. Farlow at once," Charity announced in her most take-charge duchess tone, the one even Luke never dared argue with.

"No, please . . . " Elizabeth shook her head, still firmly cradled in her hands. Dylan heard a sniffle, a sharp breath and knew a moment's true concern. "Don't send . . . for anyone. I'm . . . fine," she said between gasps. "I'm just . . . so . . . very . . . "

"Just so very what, lass?"

"So very embarrassed." Finally she raised her face, revealing, not tears of pain but laughter—bubbling, hiccuping, belly-shaking laughter.

It became infectious, spreading among the others. Dylan grinned, enjoying a good dose of relief that she hadn't injured herself. Lowering himself until he sat on the carpet beside her, he swung an arm about her shoulders. "You gave us a good scare, lass."

She peered over her hands. "Did I break the plate?"

"Bother the plate." Hand pressed to her belly, Charity moved down the table and sank into a chair with a sigh. "We've plates aplenty in this house."

"Ah, but nonetheless, this one's as sound as ever." Helena

lifted the offended porcelain from the table and held it up for all to see. "Can't say as much for your scone, though."

"Good gracious." Elizabeth wiped mirthful tears away on the back of her sleeve. "If this is any indication of how the day will progress, perhaps I daren't climb atop a horse."

"Perhaps you're right." Charity propped her chin on her hand. "Dylan could drive you about in the curricle instead."

"Yes, that would be much safer," Helena agreed. "Or we could all go in one of the carriages, and bring the children as well."

Not if Dylan had anything to say about it. "Surely, Elizabeth, you're not going to let one small mishap frighten you out of our morning's ride."

"Frighten me?" For a moment he'd have sworn a speck of fear flickered in her great, golden eyes. She blinked, and the look was gone, replaced by sheer determination. "Not a chance, Mr. Fergusson."

CHAPTER 10

The horses and mounting block had been brought out to the front drive. There were two chestnuts, a bay and a dappled gray. The horse she and Mr. Fergusson had previously ridden was not among them. Eliza wished it was. These four animals were a mystery. From beneath her brows she watched them swing their heads, swish their tails and paw the gravel as if itching to spark the ground beneath their feet.

Whatever made her think she could do this?

She'd always considered herself a passing good rider. But that had been on broad-backed work horses and stout draft ponies. These were thoroughbreds, tall and sleek and fitted with such narrow saddles she despaired of keeping her seat at any pace swifter than a walk.

Last night she'd practiced sitting sidesaddle on the chaise longue at the foot of her bed. That was safe. Climbing onto one of those slender, impatient giants seemed nothing short of suicide.

"The bay is for Mrs. Mendoza," Mr. Fergusson said to the groom. Wesley had already claimed the taller of the two chestnuts. Helena strolled to the dappled-gray and ran a palm along its sinewy neck.

The groom led the bay to the mounting block. Eliza sucked air through her clamped teeth and decided she could always claim some minor injury from her earlier fall. Yes, that would explain her disinclination to canter. Or trot, an even more precarious gait for all that bouncing.

"Let me help you." Mr. Fergusson took her hand as she placed her foot on the bottom step. Before she reached the platform he stopped her short. "What the devil is this?"

Eliza looked about in confusion. Mr. Fergusson spun on his heel and glared at the groom. "This isn't a side saddle. Didn't I make it clear two of the ladies would be riding today?"

"Did you, sir?" The groom, little more than a youth, scratched his tawny head. "Could have sworn you said Lord and Lady Wesley, yourself and his grace."

At the first sign of Mr. Fergusson's scowl, Eliza leaned from her perch to whisper in his ear, "Don't scold the boy, please. It was an honest mistake. I don't mind."

"His grace?" Mr. Fergusson repeated as if he hadn't heard her. He glowered at the groom. "Tell me, Ben, how does 'Mrs. Mendoza' in any way resemble the sound of 'his grace?'"

The groom shrugged, tugged a lock of hair from his brow and reached for the reins. "I'll bring the mare back round to the stables and switch her out, sir."

Dylan regarded the others. "Sorry for the delay."

"There's no need to delay." Eliza placed both hands on the saddle before Ben could lead the horse away. "I don't wish to trouble you."

"It's his job, Elizabeth."

The groom made a little bow. "No trouble, ma'am."

"Yes, but you see, I've ridden astride before and I'm perfectly comfortable with it." Eliza stole a glance at Helena, another at Wesley. "I know it sounds rather shocking, but I truly don't find it objectionable at all. It the truth be told, it's rather a treat. It's so much more . . . er . . . "

"Natural," Mr. Fergusson suggested.

"Just so. Natural."

Helena studied the saddle on her gray. "I used to ride astride as a child, and I must admit there are times I miss it. Perhaps next time I'll give it a go." She ended with a challenging heft of her chin aimed at her husband, who only smiled and shrugged.

"If you're certain it won't be an inconvenience," Mr. Fergusson said hesitantly.

"None whatsoever," Eliza assured him.

He grinned. "Let's be off then."

With her petticoats tucked beneath her and her riding habit spread out over the horse's hindquarters, Eliza clucked to the animal to follow the others. She needn't have bothered. The moment the lead horse, which happened to be Mr. Fergusson's, set off at a walk, the others obediently followed.

They started off down a forested trail, a dark, damp tunnel of ancient growth that closed out the sky above them. A series of turns, however, soon brought them into open pastureland. Though vast and rolling, this countryside little resembled the moorland Eliza knew so well, a land both wildly beautiful and cruelly dangerous, ruled by forces no man dared scorn.

By comparison, Longfield Park and its outlying regions seemed tamer, kinder, as if reshaped by the careful hands of the lovely Helena riding beside her, by the warmhearted Charity, by the dowager duchess whose own hands had sculpted the wondrous rose garden beside the house.

Mr. Fergusson led them up steeper ground to a ridge that thrust upward like the backbone of a gaunt giant. Two valleys stretched on either side, to the east and to the west, each dotted with roaming sheep, stone farmhouses, and rimmed by craggy hills. In the far distance, sunlight crystallized the snaking line of a river and sparked the topmost spires of a cathedral.

The sights dazzled Eliza's eyes. The freshness of the breeze and the scents of autumn wildflowers filled her lungs and wrapped her in a sensation so alien, so removed from her recent life she could not immediately put a name to it, could only identify it by the qualities it lacked: fear, guilt, remorse, sorrow. Of those she felt nothing at all.

Peace. Yes, it surrounded her, flowed through her. She shut her eyes, tipped her head and filled her mouth with the very taste of it, rolling it about with her tongue to better learn the flavor of this astonishing gift and remember it always. She drew the essence deep, deep inside in the hopes of somehow storing a part of it away for another time, when no other source of comfort came her way.

Upon opening her eyes she gazed from one friendly, smiling face to another. These benefactors of hers, these new friends, would never know the part they played in breathing new life into a dying soul.

Mr. Fergusson reached across the distance between them to grasp her hand. "Glad you came?"

"Oh, yes."

He flung a glance out over the east valley, to the distant peaks and crags. "How about a race?"

"Across the valley?" Her heart scampered at the thought. The breeze nudged at her back, urging her on.

"No, it's too dangerous." Helena swung her gray around. "Dylan, you should know better than to suggest any such thing."

He only pursed his lips in a smile that assured Eliza there would be no danger, that he would not let there be. But Helena's censure remained all too evident in her worried frown, and Eliza felt lost between trusting Mr. Fergusson and being unwilling to cause that dear lady a moment's distress.

An involuntary sigh escaped her. "We shouldn't."

"No." The abrupt and quite adamant protest took her aback, coming as it did from the least unexpected source. Helena brought her horse alongside hers. "No, dearest, you should. I can see how very much you want to. Forgive me. There was a time I'd have spurred my horse at the mere mention of a race. Being a mother has made me cautious and tiresome."

"Then it's settled." Mr. Fergusson slapped his riding crop against his boot. "We'll meet you and Wesley in the village."

Carefully he and Eliza made their way down the ridge. Once on level ground a shout from Mr. Fergusson sped their horses to a canter. A burst of fear whitened her knuckles around the reins, but soon instinct took over and Eliza gripped with her knees and leaned into the pace.

It was soon apparent they weren't racing at all. Mr. Fergusson could have left her far behind from the first had he wished, but instead rode hard at her side, eyes squinting into the wind, his own careful hold on the reins setting a pace they would share the length of the valley.

They came to a brook that meandered through the meadow. He flashed a grin. "Jump it, or dismount and walk across?"

"Jump it!"

The momentum of the hurdle grabbed her hat off her head; held on by the ribbons tied beneath her chin, it bounced against her back when her bay touched down on the far bank. The beat of the hooves and Mr. Fergusson's unbridled laughter filled her ears. Sheer exhilaration replaced her earlier sense of peace. She felt alive, utterly so, as she burst free of the constraints of being Elizabeth, as she experienced a rushing back of the Eliza she once was, that happy, carefree, oblivious girl. . . .

They rounded a farmer's pasture, skirted a mill, sent flocks of sheep scattering in their wake. A stone wall loomed ahead and Mr. Fergusson shouted his query like a blast from the wind.

"Over?"

"Over and beyond!"

"And the next?"

"And the next and the next."

She loosened her reins and tried to pull ahead, urging her horse with cries of laughter. She succeeded in putting several horse lengths between them, only to hear a determined thudding behind her as Mr. Fergusson allowed his mount a burst of speed that brought him solidly beside her.

No, this was not a race. This was a sharing.

Far sooner than she wished, her legs began to tire from clutching so tightly. At the same time, without any discernable signal, she realized Mr. Fergusson had already slowed the pace and was heading them to a tree-shaded slope. The last farmhouse they'd passed lay indistinct in the distance, little more than a gray smudge on the rolling landscape.

Eliza gazed back across the valley to the ridge where they'd begun and couldn't believe how insignificant it appeared, no more than a ripple. She could see no trace of the town beyond the sloping hillsides. They might have been in the very middle of the world, protected on all sides from intrusion.

She ignored the voice inside her that insisted this was the same world that had once cast her out—the same she had almost quitted, gladly, but a handful of days ago.

"You're quite a rider," Mr. Fergusson said as he helped her down from her horse. "It was all I could do to keep up."

She smiled at the lie, at his gallantry. It proved what a gentleman he was, how little he needed to prove his superiority over a woman.

When her feet touched the ground he didn't remove his hands from her waist, but held her fast and close. His head bent over hers, his eyes veiled, misty, heavy-lidded. Something inside her clenched with anticipation. His lips parted with a tender smile that sent her heart for a twist.

"I believe I'm going to have to break my word, lass."

Before she could consider what exactly that meant, his intentions became clear by the slant of his lips across hers. His arms slid around her while the deepening pressure of his kiss forced her head back, her chin up, until she lost all balance. She remained on her feet only because Mr. Fergusson held her there, tightly against him, fusing their bodies from their lips down.

It was a kiss that went on and on while they explored each other's mouths and tongues, while Eliza's limbs turned liquid one moment only to feel his strength surge through them the next. It was a kiss that ended oh-so gradually, with lots of little, lingering kisses, until they simply stood with lips touching, nuzzling, loathe to part.

That relentless voice inside her spoke again, advising her to step away. After all, this man was too good for common Eliza and too honorable for counterfeit Elizabeth. Yet it was a feeble voice at best and easily ignored.

He brushed his nose against hers. "You may smack me now if you wish."

"I should. You lied, Mr. Fergusson, about the possibilities of further indiscretions."

"Sure enough."

"And you contrived to separate us from the Holbrooks, didn't you?"

"Guilty as charged." He nipped her bottom lip, holding it an instant or two between his own. "What shall my sentence be?"

"Hm. Perhaps an afternoon watching all the children while the others and I enjoy an excursion to town."

"Ah, then you maintain your innocence, do you?" He kissed the tip of her nose. "You'd let me shoulder all the blame?"

Their gazes held a long moment. Eliza shook her head. "No, Mr. Fergusson, not all."

He took her hand and with a little tug drew her to the base of a tree, and again, she ignored the whisper of caution from inside. He sat with his back against the trunk and pulled her down, turning her so that her back rested against his chest, her hips cradled between his thighs. His arms went around her, holding snug beneath her breasts.

He rested his chin gently on the top of her head. "Do you realize, lass, that you're now on a first-name basis with a duke, a duchess and a member of Parliament, yet you still insist on addressing me, the man you're forever kissing behind the foliage, with the utmost formality."

"Kissing behind the foliage?" She wiggled to break free of

his hold, an effort that met with no success. She was forced instead to content herself with backward jab of her elbow.

"Oof! Watch it, lass, you'll crack a rib, and then who'll arrange a standard saddle for you and take you racing across valleys?"

"You arranged that saddle?"

"The groom and I made a fairly convincing performance of it, wouldn't you say?"

"But what made you . . . "

"Come now, Elizabeth. You rode hours behind me on our way to Wakefield. Did you think I couldn't sense what kind of rider you were? By St. George, you must have been a little hellion in the saddle as a child. I'll wager your parents turned gray and your servants went lame trying to rein you in."

She couldn't help settling back against him and pondering how he always guessed right about her without knowing the first thing about her. There hadn't been any servants in her childhood home, of course, but she *had* worried her parents with her madcap rides across the farm.

It was magic, she supposed, pure and simple. *He* was magic.

"Won't you call me Dylan?" he whispered in her ear.

She remained silent, wondering, just as he did, what made that simple request so difficult.

"What makes me so special?" he asked after a moment, "It's not as though I'm a duke or duchess or a member of Parliament."

That raised a chuckle, though a brief one as she considered. Then she angled her head against his chest and said to the rugged line of his jaw, "But neither did a duke nor a duchess nor a member of Parliament save me. You did."

His strong hands turned her sideways in his lap until they stared into each other's eyes. He frowned faintly. "I didn't save you, lass. I found you, true enough, but a higher power than I possess saw you through that accident."

"Oh, no, Mr. Fergusson." She placed her hand against his cheek, letting the indescribable dearness of him fill her palm. "It was you who saved me. It was."

His face filled with a boyish astonishment that grasped Eliza's heart and squeezed. But then he was thoroughly a man again, tipping her back in his arms and kissing her deeply and tenderly. Desire roared instantly to life inside her, threatening to take complete possession of her body and her will. And that might very well prompt her to . . . commit further acts of indiscretion right there on the open fields.

He leaned away, grinning. "You owe me then, don't you?"

She eyed him askance. "What knavery is this now?"

"If I indeed saved you, then you owe me, and the price I shall exact is . . . my name. Dylan. Henceforth you must call me Dylan or forfeit. . . ." His eyes went narrow and devilish. "Whatever I wish to have of you."

The words set loose a rush of heat that licked and tugged at Eliza's sensitive places. She tried to look scandalized, furious. She failed miserably, if Mr. Fergusson's satisfied smirk was any indication.

He brought his lips against hers and whispered, "Say it."

When she hesitated the tiniest instant his fingers tug into her sides, reducing her to uncontrollable giggles. "Say it."

"D–Dylan."

"There. Not so hard." His fingertips prodded, more gently now but enough to make her squeal in a decidedly unladylike fashion. "Again."

"Dylan."

"In a sentence."

"Dylan, stop tickling me this instant or you'll pay dearly."

"Aye." The fingertips eased away, replaced by his open hands running up and down her sides. "I've no doubt of that. I look forward to your taking revenge."

"Your sister is right, you really are a barbarian."

His expression sobered. "She *is* right. I am."

She laughed. "Whatever do you mean?"

He glanced up at the branches overhead, then smiled albeit without the mirth of moments ago. "There is something you should know about me, Elizabeth."

She shook her head. "You needn't tell me a thing. I can't imagine there is anything of significance I don't already know about the kind of man you are."

"You may be surprised." His arms tightened for a moment, then relaxed until his hands lay loose against her thighs. "You take me for a gentleman, don't you?"

"Of course. Everything about you convinces me of the fact."

Each somber shake of his head seemed to portend something Eliza suddenly didn't wish to hear. "I'm the brother-in-law of a duke," he said, "but certainly no gentleman. That is neither who I am nor what I wish in life. I am as common as common can be. I was born a Scottish farmer's son, Elizabeth, and although I've been to university and my family has prospered through the years, I am and always will be a farmer at heart."

"A . . . farmer?"

"Aye."

As he spoke of sheep and land and his Scottish home, the words became indistinct and his handsome face blurred. Eliza went utterly still, straining to hear the faintest of sounds that seemed to echo her own faltering heartbeat.

He was a farmer—just a bloody farmer. Not a gentleman, not superior and beyond her reach, but a common nobody like her. He might have been perfect *for* her, if only she'd told the truth.

Dare she now? *I am like you. I am a farmer's daughter, a farmer's widow. I am . . .*

A liar. A cheat. A coward. How could she confess it and watch the regard fade from his eyes? Witness the gathering storm of anger and disappointment that would surely brew once he realized the depth of her deception, and what fools she'd made of him and his family. She'd be cast out again. Alone again.

Oh, what a hideous, ghastly mistake she had made.

But what *was* that awful sound, that nagging discord riding her thoughts, making her ears ring, her head pound? Ah, yes, now she recognized it. Laughter. God's and fate's. They were sharing a good snort over her stupid, wretched foolishness.

Bugger life.

CHAPTER 11

"Uncle Dylan, catch me!"

Dylan barely had time to position himself beneath the rambling yew tree before the impetuous William leaped from the branches. He landed with a thud against Dylan's chest—a thud drowned out by the excited yipping of the matching West Highland whites and Charity's cry of dismay.

"William Holbrook, have you lost your wits?"

"It's all right, Mama, Uncle Dylan wouldn't let me plunge to my death."

"Sweet mercy." Charity released a theatrically shaky breath and turned an exasperated expression on her husband, beside her on their picnic blanket. "Will you please tell that child he'd best not be doing that again if he knows what's good for him?"

"No more diving out of trees, William. That's an order."

"Yes, sir," the boy said with a wink at Dylan.

"That goes for you, too, David." Helena, on another of several blankets spread out across the grass, shifted her infant son, Stephen, to the opposite shoulder. She jabbed a forefinger in the air toward her oldest boy, perched in the same tree not far from the very branch his cousin had just vacated. "I'd like to enjoy one picnic without turned ankles, sprained wrists and bloody lips, thank you."

"Not fair. Uncle Dylan caught Will. Why can't he catch me?"

Dylan set his nephew's feet on the ground, tousled his hair

and peered up at the other boy. "Because Uncle Dylan's arms are tired from playing windmill with Lara and Lena and he might miss you, lad."

The child made noises of disappointment but, as lithe as a cat, made his way down to the lowest branches. Once there he caught his cousin's eye, squinched up his own and pushed off into the air.

Dylan only narrowly caught the imp in his arms. With a wide swing that made David yelp, he tossed him over his shoulder and returned him to his parents. His mother immediately embarked upon a lecture on the necessity of obedience, albeit a hushed one, for the baby had finally drifted off to sleep. Wesley echoed his wife's sentiments, but with an unmistakable note of pride at his son's daredevil courage.

Beyond the yew tree, the four horses he, Elizabeth, Helena and Wesley had ridden there grazed at their pickets. The rest of the family had driven out to meet them in two carriages, now parked a few dozen yards away where the drivers, footmen and Charity's maid were enjoying a picnic of their own.

Sir Joshua leaned on his cane not far from the horses, swinging a net with his free hand in pursuit of the autumn butterflies flitting among the season's last burst of gorse and heather. The dogs, Skiff and Schooner, capered near Sir Joshua's legs, leaping and snapping at those same butterflies. Yet, as if aware of the elderly man's infirmities, the Westies maintained a safe enough distance to avoid upsetting his balance.

On another blanket, Elizabeth sat with Dolly and Lady Mary. Charity's two-year-old daughters, Lena and Lara, sat beside her, busily tracing patterns with their fingertips in the rich blue velvet of her riding habit. He noticed, too, with a twinge of affection, how the elderly and usually stoic Mary studied the progress of the little girls' designs and every so often leaned to add a line of her own.

But mostly he watched Elizabeth amid a jumble of conflicting feelings. He'd certainly guessed correctly about her. The woman rode astride and often, and the fact that she'd been so adamant about not letting the groom change the saddle set him to wondering if she ever rode sidesaddle at all.

A woman unafraid to hug a horse between her knees . . . The notion sparked other ideas that had nothing whatsoever to do with riding, at least not horses.

Aye, he'd guessed right about her and much good it had done him. Everything had changed since their morning excursion. Of the high spirits that had sent them galloping across the valley and into each other's arm, not a hint remained. He hadn't thought his confession would make a difference. Not to her. He had believed her . . . well . . . a cut above the average English gentlewoman. Better, certainly, than a woman like Isabel.

Ironically though, Isabel hadn't raised the slightest objection to his being a farmer. No indeed, his baseness had proved the very thing that attracted her to him, and with no small amount of irritation he acknowledged how thoroughly she'd enjoyed her few weeks' fling with the barbarian Scot.

Not so Elizabeth, apparently. Oh, he tried rationalizing that any number of reasons might have sparked her abrupt change toward him and sent her pushing out of his lap. Her quiet reminder that they had promised to meet the Holbrooks in the village had done little to reassure him. Especially as they'd barely exchanged three words ever since.

No, her sudden reticence could only have arisen from one of two sources. Either his origins flat out appalled her and made her feel the fool—which would set any gentlewoman seething—or he'd simply pushed this young widow too far too soon.

Why had he done so? It had only been a handful of days since they'd met. But theirs hadn't been a casual meeting at some social affair. There'd been no initial flirtation, no gradual but growing acquaintance. On the contrary, they'd been thrust into a kind of intimacy from the first. He'd literally ridden into what surely had been one of the most traumatic moments of her life, stumbled right into her fear and grief and by necessity had taken her into his protection. And into his arms. Small wonder, then, that physical intimacy followed so quickly.

But was it more than that? Not long ago, he'd equated love and lust with all the bombast of a fool who deserved to awaken with a gun to his head. Had he, these past days with Elizabeth, been loading the bullet and priming the pan all over again?

An unsettling sense of having lost something he'd never in fact possessed curled around those thoughts even as Elizabeth curled a lock of Lena's red-gold hair around her finger. She happened to glance up at him then. In the instant their gazes met he thought he saw some his own sentiments reflected back at him. There was certainly a dispirited cast to those lovely gold eyes. Shades of regret, too. Or did he only wish it were so?

Her lashes flitted downward. She reached out to stroke first one little curly-topped head, then the other. She traded smiles and a few quiet words with Dolly and Lady Mary.

He didn't like guessing games. English reticence was not his style, but how to question Elizabeth with so many spectators? He thought he'd go out of his mind with frustration until the lads, God love them, began tossing a ball back and forth and calling for their parents to join them.

Mary summoned her grandson. "Come help me up, William."

She suffered the boy's ungainly tugs on her hands and his animated entreaties of "Come, Grandmama, come on, come on. . . ." as she maneuvered aging limbs on the uneven ground. Then she picked up the ball and underhanded it across the blankets to David.

It was Sir Joshua who next played the unwitting conspirator in providing Dylan a private moment with Elizabeth.

"My word," the gentleman called out with a burst of

enthusiasm. Staring intently into the air, he swung his net in a wide arc, took two short steps with the help of his cane and swung again. "I do believe that is a Duke of Burgundy."

"Oh, are you sure, Josh? How very exciting. You must have him for your collection." Dolly gathered her skirts and struggled to her feet, leaving Elizabeth alone on the blanket with Lena and Lara. Dylan stole his chance before someone else decided to join her or worse, coax her into the game of toss just now beginning.

"I wanted to apologize," he began as he settled beside her, but the haughty look she turned on him stopped him short.

"Foul," she said with a righteous lift of her eyebrows.

He stared back, not at all knowing how to respond.

"Apologies are against the rules, sir."

"Ah. Quite so." Stretching out his legs, he settled back on his elbows. Grown weary of drawing, the twins moved to the edge of the blanket and were now plucking grass and heather by the handful and flinging them at each other. After a moment they cast glances over their shoulders, curious to see if the adults disapproved or thought it the cleverest of sports. Dylan made a face at them. They grinned and returned to their grass war.

"No apologies, then," he said to Elizabeth. "But you've grown quiet these past hours. Are you angry with me?"

"Why would I be?" She avoided his gaze as she spoke and tipped her chin away when he tried to grasp it.

"You're disappointed, then." He tried not to let it hurt. Failing in that, he tried not to let it show. He stared up at the clouds scuttling across an autumn bright sky. "I'm not who you thought I was. I should have told you the truth sooner."

"No, Mr. Fergusson. There was never any reason for you to tell me anything. We are veritable strangers. You owe me no explanations. And I have no right to regard you with anything but gratitude and respect."

"I see." He sat upright and made an effort to relax a jaw gone rigid. "So it's Mr. Fergusson again, is it?"

"That is best."

"Is it? Are you afraid this humble farmer might take you in his arms again?"

That sent flames to her face, and with a perverse satisfaction he watched them leap from her chin to her hairline. At least he still had some effect on her. She hadn't become completely impervious to him in so short a time. He thought again of Isabel, who would never have blushed, who would have launched a disdainful glare the length of her fashionable nose and shrugged her shapely shoulders.

He looked away, ashamed at having compared the two women so unfairly, at having found any pleasure at all in flustering or angering Elizabeth with reminders of their intimacy. He had no wish to embarrass her or make her feel . . . as she'd made him feel. He only wished to summon the familiar smile to her face, the laughter to her lips. He couldn't help it. He simply wanted to kiss her and hold her in his arms again.

She pulled up her knees and hugged them. "Is that what you think?" Her words were clipped with a bitterness that took him aback. "That you've lowered yourself in my estimate for telling me the truth?"

"I only know you've made a great effort to avoid speaking to me ever since."

He flinched at the jerk of her chin, the snapping of her eyes. "Gentleman or farmer—it makes no difference. Not when I shall go south to London and you north to Scotland, and we'll likely never see each other again. Two such people have no business kissing in the foliage as you put it, Mr. Fergusson."

With that she pushed forward onto her knees, leaning to brush grass from Lena's hair, Lara's shoulder. By the tension across her back he thought she was about to gain her feet and stalk off. He placed a hand on her arm to coax her back down beside him, thanking his good fortune when she didn't resist.

"Must it be inevitable that we go our separate ways?"

"Don't do that, Mr. Fergusson." She slid her arm free and he felt his luck draining away. "Don't try to dissuade either one of us of the simple truth. I am bound for London while you . . . " A fine mist brought a sheen to her eyes but she blinked it angrily away. "Any man who calls himself a farmer cannot bear to be parted from his land for long."

"I admit you are right about that. I miss it so much sometimes I ache. But what of you? My sister tells me you've never been to London, that you've never met this family awaiting you there."

"And what does it matter?" Her brow furrowed and he braced for a glare meant to put him in his place.

At that moment, however, Lara scooted along the blanket and eased her way into Elizabeth's lap. Her little fingers opened wide, letting loose a shower of leaves and broken petals onto the blue velvet gown. That brought a smile to Elizabeth's face, though her next words shot out at Dylan with all the challenge of a dueling pistol.

"Those people in London are Mendozas. They will accept me. I shall have a place among them, a place where I belong, where I need not fear . . . "

She trailed off, her startled look hinting that she'd uttered more than she had meant to.

As he pondered this unintentional disclosure, Lara reached up and wrapped one dimpled fist around the ribbon of Elizabeth's plumed velvet cap. Elizabeth let the child tug the bow free. Then she plucked the hat off her own head and set it on Lara's, tilting it this way and that as if she hadn't a care.

"Mine," Lara said, grinning.

"Yes, darling." Elizabeth tied the ribbons in a wide bow beside one round, rosy cheek. Leaning, she kissed the other cheek, tapped a finger to the end of Lara's pert nose and gazed at the child with a wistful, almost pained expression. "It's far prettier on you than me."

Lena glanced over her shoulder. Spying her sister's

newfound prize, she scrambled crab-like across the blanket, rumpling it as she went.

"Something for Lena," she declared upon reaching Elizabeth's knees. She held out her hands and waited for some treasure to be placed in her palms.

Elizabeth gently placed a hand beneath the child's chin and raised it, smiling down into the little face. Then she appealed to Dylan with a perplexed frown.

"If I'd worn a hat I'd give it to her," he said with a shrug.

"I wish I'd worn two. Oh, I know." Quickly she pulled off her beige kid gloves. "There you are, Lena, dearest. A lovely pair of gloves to protect milady's hands."

Settling back on her haunches and looking happily satisfied, the girl shoved her hands into the gloves. Dylan could see by the uneven bulges and sags in the kidskin that the leather maze bewildered those tiny, childish fingers. Lara reached over to help her sister disentangle the mystery. The result was a tug of war with Elizabeth caught in the middle.

"Oh, you two." Her arms encircled both twins, scooping them close. Her eyes fell shut as she inhaled a deep breath, her lips traveling from the top of one head to the other.

Unprepared for the sudden and acute constriction in his chest, Dylan raised a hand to his breastbone and pressed. For an instant that would be forever burned into his memory and his heart, he glimpsed the thing he yearned for most. A family. For the briefest of moments he experienced the pride and contentment of being a husband, a father. Perceived with absolute clarity his place in the world as a man. Understood exactly what his future required of him.

It was an instant of recognition caught in the flash of a pair of impossibly bright little heads—a color that would inevitably darken and fade in the years to come, as did all dreams, all meticulously laid plans.

And then the moment was gone. Impatient to devise some new game with which to amuse themselves, Lena and Lara pushed their way out of Elizabeth's arms.

Lara lost her balance and tumbled face first onto the blanket. Expecting a wailing complaint, Dylan grasped her shoulders and righted her. Instead of tears, however, a squall of laughter pierced the air. It brought the Westies bounding over. With a boisterous invasion of sniffs and licks and mischievous growls they jumped from Elizabeth to the girls to Dylan and back. Soon Helena sauntered over with a smile that revealed her inability to resist the fun despite the infant asleep on her shoulder. Charity followed, and soon after Dolly and Sir Joshua, his net empty at his side. Dylan found himself surrounded by this family he loved, that loved him, but which was not and never could be his own. Not really. Not in the way he so desperately wanted.

Alone in her elegant room the next morning, Eliza opened Elizabeth's tortoiseshell trinket box and extracted a handful of bank notes. The time had come to settle a debt, the first of many, before her life took another irrevocable change.

In the long months since Nathan's death, urgency had been the driving force of her life. Urgency to keep the farm running, pay the rent, stay alive. That same urgency had compelled her, in a moment of despondency, to forsake her very self and transform into the aristocratic Elizabeth Mendoza de Leone.

Then Dylan Fergusson entered her life and the urgency began to wan, first in trickles and then, yesterday in the valley, in a great dizzying flurry. Here among the Holbrooks, Eliza finally, finally began to feel safe and protected, showered by the gifts of hope, time, and future possibilities. She felt able to relax her guard, to trust in people and in fate.

Now that urgency once more rose up to command her life. His guileless confession yesterday had rendered her own deception unbearable. How her lips had burned to speak the truth during the interminable hours of that afternoon and evening.

I am not Elizabeth, I am Eliza. Common Eliza who can be a proper helpmate to a farmer, who can love a farmer if you'll only let me.

Those words had perched on the tip of her tongue longing to leap off during those endless hours. Her courage, meanwhile, had cowered in some corner of her soul, fearing the consequences of that confession.

Dismissed without a reference. Too well did Eliza remember the sudden reversal in her fortune and how it led her, hungry and desolate, nearly to sell her body to drunken strangers. Nearly to end her life. Would she just as quickly be dismissed from Longfield Park? Perhaps find herself locked away in a prison cell, charged with fraud. For why shouldn't the generosity shown her by the Holbrooks transform in an instant to anger and a demand for justice?

Would Dylan understand, or would he back away, his handsome face twisted with horror at what she'd done? She could not but admit the ugliness of that deed, of having taken a dead woman's place. Would he despise her forever?

Dylan. Just as he had declared her Elizabeth that night in the rose garden, her heart had declared him Dylan the moment he made his confession. Dylan the farmer. Her handsome, robust farmer.

They were of a kind, the two of them, and on some level he had known it all along, had recognized her truest self almost from the first. A farmer. That was the source of his magic, his uncanny ability to read her moods and thoughts and needs. Oh, how stupid, *stupid* she'd been to believe Elizabeth's ghost stood between them, that it was somehow Elizabeth he admired and wanted when all along his regard had been for her, Eliza. She'd simply been too daft to see it.

When first she'd struck her devil's bargain she had been thinking only of food and the prospect of a warm, dry haven. She hadn't much considered the rest of her life because life had frightened her so much. Frightened her right out of her very own existence.

Now she wanted that existence back, but the question was how, and when. And knowing what she would do if speaking the truth left her right where she started, with nothing at all.

Today, at least, she would take the first step in righting the wrongs she'd committed in becoming Elizabeth. She would go into Wakefield and arrange to send funds to the family of her driver. She only hoped the money would reach them. Folkstone Manor had been sold, but she knew that ofttimes many of the previous owner's staff remained. She hoped someone among them would be able to locate John Howitt's family, if indeed he had one. If not, she would instruct that the money be donated to the local parish.

Dylan and the duchess awaited her outside on the drive, along with the duchess's maid, Esther, who might have been a Fergusson relation for all her red hair and freckles. Dylan would be taking them in the duke's cabriolet, a sleek, open-air carriage drawn by two horses. It was just the dashing sort of vehicle she would imagine him driving.

When he saw her descending the front steps he gave a curt nod, his gaze barely skimming her before angling away. He didn't understand her change toward him yesterday, thought it had to do with his being less noble than she'd originally thought. Well, yes it did, but not for the reasons he believed. As long as the lies stood between them she had no right accepting his affection or giving hers in return.

Just then little William Holbrook came running from the fountain in the middle of the drive. He saw Eliza and offered a grinning, gap-toothed good morning before clambering up onto the driver's seat.

"Don't touch those reins," his mother warned. She joined Eliza at the bottom of the steps. "I do hope you don't mind my bringing William along. He's been begging for a trip into town."

"Of course not. I'm delighted."

Dylan helped his sister into the gig. Then he offered his broad hand to Eliza. She hesitated, gazing down at that strong farmer's hand marked by calluses and old scars that must date back to his childhood. Ah, those imperfections spoke of perseverance and tenacity, of pride and conviction and self-reliance.

She placed her hand in his, felt his energy and his honor blaze through her and knew a longing so painful it nearly drew tears. Feeling the upward pressure of his grip, she stepped up into the cabriolet, ducking her head until she'd blinked the regrets safely away. In the meantime, William began prattling blithely on as children will, oblivious that anything could possibly be amiss on a day when he was treated to an excursion into town.

As Eliza settled beside the duchess, the boy twisted around to peer at her, resting his chin on the back of his seat. "I've been practicing to sound like a Scot, because I am one, you know. Half, anyway. Would you like to hear?"

Sitting in the rear-facing seat at the back of the gig, Esther tittered. Dylan swung up into the driver's box, giving the boy's head a tousle before clucking the pair of horses into motion.

"I would indeed," Eliza told the boy.

The duchess slipped an arm through hers. "You needn't encourage him."

"I think he's charming," Eliza whispered back as William began some unintelligible discourse that involved a good deal of tongue rolling.

When he finished he flashed an elfin grin. "I still say you must be part Scot because you don't talk like Aunt Helena or Grandmama or Papa. They aren't the slightest bit Scottish, but—"

"William, mind your manners." The duchess leaned forward and caught his chin on the ends of her fingers, turning his face to hers. "Stop badgering Mrs. Mendoza or I promise you, this will be your last visit to town for an exceedingly long time to come."

He mumbled an apology and settled back in his seat.

"Apology accepted, William," Eliza called to him softly. The first time he'd brought up the subject of her accent, she'd fretted about the others becoming suspicious about her origins. That anxiety suddenly rose up again. No matter how kind these people had been, it was far too easy to envision their reaction if they discovered her deceit, to imagine their indignant wrath. And before she might consider the wisdom or lack, words poured from her mouth.

"I am from York, William, as were my parents and my . . . er . . . governess. We're simply none of us London-bred. York is to the north of here. It isn't Scotland, but it is closer to Scotland than Wakefield is. Perhaps that's why I sound just a little bit Scottish to you."

She closed her mouth with a sinking feeling, realizing this new lie plunged her deeper into her deception. But it had risen of its own volition, from the place inside her that could not forget the cold and rain and days without food.

William peeked over his shoulder, searched his mother's face for disapproval and shifted his bright green gaze back to Eliza. "Then you are almost a little bit Scottish."

Eliza nodded and wished she were.

William faced forward again and nudged Dylan's side with his elbow. "I still say you should marry her."

"Hush, William, and I'll let you hold the reins a while."

"It isn't necessary to use currency, madam. Nor is it advisable." The bank clerk plucked his pen from its holder, dipped it in the inkpot and leaned across the counter toward Eliza. "If you simply supply me with the proper account information, I can arrange the transfer of funds for you. That is the safer course."

"Account information," Eliza repeated, trying not to sound utterly mystified. Did John Howitt have an account with the Bank of England? She had no way of knowing. All she had with her were Elizabeth's financial documents. She had hoped not to need them, but this man seemed adamant about not taking her banknotes.

She opened her drawstring purse. "Will any of this help?"

The clerk took the papers from her, smoothed them open and with a tightly knit brow began shuffling through, pausing now and again to squint down at a particular bit of information. Then he slid the pile to Eliza's side of the counter. "The annuities are not yet due to be paid. And you'll need a power of attorney for the stocks."

"A power of attorney?"

"You are, I presume, Elizabeth Mendoza de Leone?"

This is what she'd hoped to avoid. "I am."

His eyebrows converged over his long, thin nose. Did Eliza imagine a sudden air of disapproval, disbelief? Her stomach clenched against a desire to snatch her papers and go.

He cleared his throat. "These documents are in your husband's name. You are, however, indicated as his beneficiary."

"Y-yes . . . he recently passed away."

"I see. However, madam, you are not authorized to access these particular funds without a power of attorney or written permission of the trustee of the estate. One . . . " He squinted again as though reading, but recited from memory, "One Raphael Mendoza de Leone, I believe."

Eliza nodded. "But he isn't here at present. He's in London."

"Perhaps then, madam, you should contact him first."

"But couldn't I simply give you the money I wish to send? It's what I came here intending to do."

The man emitted a long-suffering sigh and reached for a sheet of paper. "The name of the party?"

"John Howitt."

"Does he have an account with this bank?"

"I've no idea. And the money is to go to his family."

"I need a name. His wife? Parents?"

"I'm afraid I don't know."

"Direction?"

"York. Er, Folkstone Manor."

"Can you be more specific? Is there a steward or solicitor who oversees the manor's accounts?"

"I . . . really couldn't say."

Oh, Eliza definitely wanted to be gone from here. The clerk surely thought her daft. What had she been thinking, sauntering into this bank as if she had a right to be here? She'd never entered such an establishment in her life, had no idea how such matters were conducted. Her ignorance could not have been more obvious or more humiliating. Or damning, had Dylan or the duchess accompanied her. Thank goodness she had insisted they take William on a walk through town instead.

"Madam?" The clerk waved his pen to get her attention. "I'm afraid I'll need more information than this. Perhaps you might wish to return another time with the proper documents. Or you might simply seal the money in a small package and send it by post."

"Is that safe?"

"No. There could be thieves along the road." He shrugged. "But I don't see that you have any other choice given the circumstances."

She didn't at all like the way he said that last word, decidedly severe and dripping with mistrust. Eliza gathered up the papers, folded them as best she could with trembling hands and stuffed them into her purse.

"Thank you for your time," she said without meeting his gaze. "Good day, sir."

"Good day, madam."

As she crossed the polished wooden floor, his lingering scrutiny chafed her back and raised the hairs at her nape. The doorman tipped his hat as he let her out to the street, but even that simple gesture seemed to question and mock, as if they all saw through her elegant clothes to the pitiable wench beneath.

The experience left her shaken and wretched, all the more so for having failed poor John Howitt's family. This should have been her first step in redeeming herself. She'd cheated her way into a better life and perhaps cheated the Howitts out of a secure future.

Even if she sent the funds by post, she realized she had no guarantee they'd ever reach their rightful destination. It would be like tossing money blindly into the wind with no idea where it would fall. Meanwhile, a man's family might very well go hungry. Might come to know firsthand the gnawing fear that had hounded Eliza until a mere few days ago.

A passerby bumped her arm. She realized she was standing immobile on the busy street, shuffling through her disordered thoughts as the clerk had shuffled through the Mendozas' account records. She chose a direction at random and began walking, trying to remember where she was supposed to meet Dylan and his sister.

The gilt edging on a sign across the way caught her eye: Harper's Emporium. Was that the place they'd decided upon, or somewhere nearby? The milliner's shop beside it, perhaps? The duchess had mentioned ordering a new hat. Eliza waited until a coach, a cart and several horses passed and then headed in that general direction, lifting her skirts clear of the mud still pooling from the recent rains.

How strange, she thought as she threaded her way in and out of pedestrians and vehicles both, that Elizabeth's husband had arranged his finances so as to prevent his wife all access. Hadn't he trusted her, or was this simply the way of the wealthy? Were the duchess and Helena so cut off?

She and Nathan had never hidden anything from each other, but then, not only had they not had a bank account, they'd never seen an abundance of cash or anything else in their lives. Still, what they did have always seemed more than enough.

Nathan had been adamant about one thing in the hours before he died. He'd wanted Eliza to live out the rest of her life on the farm. His family had enjoyed hereditary tenantship of that land for generations, but of course that hadn't made any difference to the landlord. Not once the rent had become overdue. In a mere three months' time his patience had run out, as had Eliza's chance to prove she could manage the farm on her own and raise the money.

Could Elizabeth have been facing a similar predicament? *Don't let them have it.* Those might have been Eliza's own words the day the magistrate served her notice to vacate the premises. *Don't let him take it, please, not when I've worked so hard. Don't take away my only means of survival. . . .*

"Mrs. Mendoza!"

The sound of William's voice from somewhere down the street snapped her from her reverie. Eliza had come to stand in front of the milliner's wide display window, staring into her own reflection and seeing, not the latest fashions in plumed and beribboned bonnets, but the dark reflections of the past. She shook herself and turned, searching for the boy's face, for those of his mother and uncle on the crowded street.

She caught sight of William pushing toward her at a trot, dragging Dylan by the hand behind him. Of the duchess she saw no sign. William called her name again and waved. Eliza pasted on a smile, waved back and set off to meet them.

She hadn't gone many steps when a hand gripped her forearm. Eliza stopped, startled. Blinking as the clouds unveiled bars of sunlight, she found herself gazing into the vaguely familiar face of a man. He was heavyset, dark in coloring, and neither young nor old, but of an age in-between. Her attention fell to her arm. Why was he clutching her like that?

His lips moved and meaningless words streamed over her in a foreign accent, rapid, slurred, the syllables indistinguishable from one another. She frowned. He leaned in closer and suddenly she remembered. The Spaniard on the Wakefield road.

With a sneer he formed words again, this time slower and with emphasis. "Elizabetta Mendoza de Leone?"

"Y-yes . . . who are you?"

His grip tightened, threatening to leave bruises, and he

began pulling her toward him. Eliza dug in her heels, tugging in the opposite direction, shouting for him to release her at once. Several passersby came to a halt, turning to stare.

A wild possibility gripped her. "Raphael Mendoza?"

"No!" His eyes sparked with instant and unmistakable wrath. "Raphael Mendoza es . . ."

She understood nothing of the rest, but the malice of the words stung nevertheless. Then an arm snaked around her from behind and a baritone thundered into the air, drowning the stranger's unintelligible ranting.

"Let her go, damn you."

CHAPTER 12

When the hand restraining Elizabeth refused to obey, fury pounded inside Dylan's skull. For an instant the person connected to the hand almost didn't matter. Outrage fueled a very real desire to break those fingers open.

But violence proved unnecessary. At Dylan's touch the man's hand sprang open. The sudden release sent Elizabeth stumbling backward, lodging her ever more firmly against Dylan's chest. His arm tightened around her as his gaze narrowed on the brazen offender.

Recognition choked off breath and had him sputtering. The Spaniard whose coach had stopped on the Wakefield road because one of the horses had thrown a shoe. "What in the devil's name do you mean by this!" Dylan demanded, concealing his bafflement beneath surging anger.

The man's mouth opened but just as quickly closed. His features took on the wariness of an animal cornered. He started to back away but Dylan made another grab for his sleeve.

"Now see here." He released Elizabeth and strode forward. The Spaniard continued pulling in the opposite direction until the unintended intervention of a pedestrian sent them both lurching off balance. The Spaniard tugged free. Before Dylan could react, his quarry pivoted and ran, dashing in front of a rumbling stagecoach and narrowly missing being struck.

"Stop!" Dylan shouted after him, fully aware of the futility of doing so. His instinct was to take off after him but

William's voice brought him up sharp. If he ran in pursuit, his nephew might unthinkingly follow. A far too dangerous prospect in this busy part of town.

"Mrs. Mendoza, are you all right?" The boy was tugging her skirt, tipping his head far back to look up at her. His features were pinched, his freckled brow puckered. He reached for her hand and she gave it almost absently, staring off in the direction her assailant had gone.

Struggling to master his spiking temper and charging pulse, Dylan retraced the small distance created by his short-lived chase. "Elizabeth, did he hurt you?"

Although the question brought her gaze focusing on him, she seemed little roused from her bewilderment. As her stunned silence continued, his anger simmered to a low boil to be stirred up another time. In its place rose a vague sense of misgiving along with a powerful desire to protect.

How inconvenient, especially after the way she'd all but shunned him yesterday. *No, Mr. Fergusson . . . we are veritable strangers. You owe me no explanations.* Why should he still care so much, still feel so damnably possessive of her?

That, too, he would ponder later.

"Lass, are you all right?"

"I . . . think so." Her chin trembled. He reached out and cupped it in his palm, suddenly needing to feel something of her against him, to impart something of himself in return.

The door to the hat shop opened upon Charity and her maid. "I thought I heard shouts. Dylan, was that your voice?" She studied the three of them, then turned a worried frown on Elizabeth. "My dear, you look quite shaken. What on earth has happened?"

"There was a man, Mama," William trumpeted, his voice climbing octaves with excitement. "He grabbed Mrs. Mendoza and . . . "

"Grabbed you?" Charity dropped the parcels she was carrying and threw her arms around Elizabeth's shoulders.

"Sweet mercy. Did he harm you? Was he trying to rob you? We must summon the magistrate."

"I don't know what he wanted. . . ." Elizabeth's voice shook; she seemed younger, somehow, little more than a frightened girl.

Dylan's arms suddenly ached with an urge to shelter her, to reassure and console.

"Uncle Dylan saved her, Mama. You should have seen—"

"Hush, William." Charity scrutinized Elizabeth from head to toe. "At least he didn't steal your purse. Come. Let's return to the carriage at once and go home." She slipped her arm determinedly through Elizabeth's. "Luke and Wesley shall see to it the villain doesn't go far."

Dylan was all too happy to escort the women and his nephew to the coach yard and bundle them all safely back into the cabriolet. He was glad, too, to leave curious onlookers behind.

He remembered Elizabeth's curt denial when he suggested she might know the Spaniard the first time they encountered him. She'd been quick to deny it. Too quick, perhaps?

Aye. Undue haste had defined her actions since he'd met her. Her driver's race along the old Yorkshire road, her insistence on a speedy departure from Heverton Gorse. Luke had spoken of the splintered whiffletree, the broken linch pin. Haste and carelessness. And now a Spaniard with some sort of vendetta.

He knew better than to think he'd be able to question Elizabeth once they reached Longfield. Ah, no, first there must be an outpouring of concern and sympathy, comforting and cosseting, tea and cakes. Only when each Holbrook, Sir Joshua *and* the Westies had all had their fill of setting their new friend to rights would he gain any hope of having her to himself.

But have her he would. He'd make sure of it.

* * *

"Who is he?"

The sharp-edged brogue sprang out of the blackness as Eliza stepped into her bedchamber. Before her gasp finished forming, she heard the scrape of metal. A flare burst before her eyes, blinding in the gloom.

A circle of light took shape on the nightstand, its glow giving form to the hulking outlines in the chair beside it. Dylan set the flint and tinder on the tabletop, adjusted the lamp's wink, leaned back and crossed his arms. "Close the door."

Stand or run? Eliza's private debate was a swift one. Stand. He'd only chase her down, and then her interrogation would be a public one.

This came as no surprise. She knew he'd confront her eventually. All evening, his intentions had become increasingly clear with every downward pull of his eyebrows, every comment he didn't make as he silently watched the family fuss over her. He'd been biding his time. And now here he was.

She closed the door without a sound and turned the key. Whatever was about to happen, better it happened without an audience. She walked to the hearth, banked earlier by the maid to a soft red glow. She held out her hands to catch the warmth. Then she turned to face him, her only bulwark of defense the length of the room between them.

He smiled slightly. "Are you quite recovered from today's shock?"

"Quite." A lie, of course. She couldn't be more unsettled, more confused about what to do next. She could no longer fool herself. She couldn't afford to. The man in town today proved beyond a doubt that Elizabeth Mendoza's life involved more than family and estates and pleasant social engagements. Proved a person could be wealthy and beautiful and still face dilemmas and possibly even danger.

Eliza had thought to escape a wretched life. But at what price? Which might be worse, remaining Elizabeth or returning to Eliza? If neither proved possible, where to next?

She folded her hands at her waist, cautioned her pulse to

steady itself and waited for Dylan's next demand. It was not long in coming.

"I asked you the same question several days ago. Please answer me now. Who is that man?"

"I don't know. That is the truth."

"He certainly seems to know you well enough." His arms uncrossed and his hands drifted to grip the arms of the chair, the only visible sign of frustration in his otherwise calm exterior. "I saw what happened. It was William's hail that set the Spaniard on you. He'd just come out of the Emporium when he heard your name called out. It took him only a moment to spot you. And then he moved quickly and grabbed you."

"You needn't recount what happened. I was there."

"Damn it, Elizabeth." He stood up abruptly, his calves sending the chair scuffing backward an inch or two. "He's obviously of Spanish origin, as was your husband. And the sound of *your* name triggered an otherwise unprovoked attack."

He strode closer, considerably shrinking Eliza's safety buffer. She found herself retreating toward the hearth until the heat hit her full on the back. But it wasn't just his proximity that unnerved her, it was that steely look on his face that hinted at— no, laid bare—his determination to achieve answers.

"Then again . . . perhaps it wasn't completely unprovoked." The lamplight behind him cast his features deep into shadow. Eliza could only make out the darkened hollows of displeasure beneath his brows and cheeks. "He wants something from you. Or perhaps he has a *right* to something from you."

For once she wished he'd stop guessing things about her. But at least this time she had truth on her side. "I don't know what that something could be."

Don't let them have it. Is this what Elizabeth had meant? That these Spaniards, the man and the woman traveling with him, intended stealing something from her? But what? She'd been through Elizabeth's belongings and found nothing out of the ordinary. True, her trunks contained a wealth of fine gowns and elegant jewelry, but surely no more so than the trunks of any other gentlewoman.

Even the financial records appeared unquestionable, naming Elizabeth and her brother-in-law as co-heirs and beneficiaries. There was nothing to indicate that someone else had been cheated out of a share of Anselmo Mendoza's estate.

"If you don't believe me, search those trunks against the wall." She raised her chin, at the same time wondering from which part of her imperiled soul the defiance came. "You'll find nothing much of interest."

Dylan shook his head at her. "I'd like to believe you, Elizabeth, if there weren't already a host of doubtful coincidences and evidence to the contrary."

Eliza felt cornered. Not so much by his questions and suspicions as by the awful fear that once he learned the truth there would be no more shows of concern, no more tenderness, no more champion to save her from danger.

Dear God, she wasn't ready to lose him. Not yet. The desperation to keep him in her life, for a little while longer at least, sent a brand new whopper slipping from her lips. "I've done nothing wrong."

"I didn't say you had."

"Didn't you?"

"No, lass." His brogue gentled, settling into the soothing tones she'd grown accustomed to. He reached into the shadowed distance separating them. "Come here. Please. I am not accusing you of wrongdoing."

How tempting that open palm was, how inviting those powerful, wonderfully callused fingers. She wanted to run to him, to her strong, honorable farmer, and let him wrap her in his arms, in his coat, and keep her safe from the dangers that plagued both Elizabeth *and* Eliza.

Ah, but he wore no coat tonight, only a crisp white shirt, its collar abandoned somewhere, its hem tucked into trousers that flaunted nearly every detail of his maleness.

She pulled her gaze away from his tight waist and lean

hips, swallowed and remained fixed where she was. "What is this then, if not an accusation?"

"A desire to understand the truth." He came closer, leaving the severe shadow cast by the lamp. She could see his features more clearly now, saw the sternness melt away into something infinitely more tender, hinting at the boyish nature that every so often emerged from all that masculine vigor. He held up his arms. "How else can I protect you?"

She might have pointed out that it was not his responsibility to protect her. But how *could* she resist him when he said things like that?

She swept toward those inviting arms until they closed around her. The next moments were kisses and whispered apologies and laughter because once again they'd broken the bargain made on that first day together.

"No apologies," she admonished.

"Then perhaps we'd do best not to speak at all." His breath mingled with hers as his hands swept her bodice, spreading fire until she wished nothing more than to succumb to the blaze, to melt away and be reshaped by Dylan Fergusson's magical hands, formed into an entirely new woman with no past, no secrets, no shame.

She dragged her mouth away from his, the cool air plucking at her kiss-bruised lips. "I swear I don't know that man. I truly don't know what he wants. If I did, I'd tell you. . . ."

Careful, Eliza, don't promise more than you have the courage to give.

He grasped her chin and tipped it upward. He stared down into her face, into her eyes. With the imprint of his passion hot on her lips and his gallant spirit warming her soul, if he'd asked for the entire truth just then she'd have told him and been brave enough, perhaps, to face the consequences.

But instead of a bid for truth, he said, "I believe you. But that you and he are somehow connected I am in no doubt. We must discover what that connection is. What can you tell me about your husband's family?"

"There is the brother in London. Raphael is his name. But they've been estranged for years."

"Could this man today be—"

She began shaking her head before he completed the question. "I thought of that, too. But when I spoke the name of Raphael Mendoza aloud, he denied it with such poison in his eyes I believed him."

"I didn't know you'd exchanged words with him."

"You were too busy charging to the rescue to notice."

He kissed the tip of her nose, then sobered. "This rift between the brothers—your husband never explained it?"

"He . . . never wished to speak of it and I . . . didn't think it my place to pry."

"What about your husband's estate? Were there debts?"

Were there? That might explain both the physician's appearance at the tavern in Heverton Gorse and the Spaniard's behavior today.

"If there were I'm not aware of them."

He grasped a lock of her hair that had slipped loose from the rest. Absently he brushed it back and forth across his lips. "Surely you'd have known if your husband owed money. Even if he'd hidden it from you, you'd have made the discovery at the reading of the will."

She turned away, tugging her hair from his fingers. "Must you always be so dogged in your suspicions? Can you not simply . . . believe in me?"

For several moments she suffered the shame of that question in silence. Believe in her? It was a notion deserving of a good snort.

But then his arms encircled her and he turned her to face him. "I believe anything you tell me when you're close like this, when I'm breathing you in and filling my hands with the sweet, soft feel of you."

She smiled in spite of herself. "No trust without seduction, Mr. Fergusson?"

He bent his head for a quick kiss. "Trust and anger make

wary companions. And I'll admit I was angry when you all but told me a farmer wasn't good enough for you."

"I never said that." She balled handfuls of his cotton shirt in her fists, pushing him away then pulling him close. "Never."

"Yet you did set me at a distance."

"Because you and I shall part ways soon. It won't do for us to—"

"Then why are you here?"

"I do believe it was you who came to my room, not the other way around."

"No." His arms tightened, securing her more snugly against him until the throb of his desire penetrated her skirts to beckon at her thigh. "Why are you *here,* lass, right now, in my arms?"

A lady would have pushed him away with a haughty retort. But any wiles Eliza possessed were lost in the undeniable leap of her pulse. As the contents of her heart rushed to reveal itself upon her face, there was nothing she could do to prevent it.

"Dylan." The word emerged as a whisper and she discovered her arms thrust around his neck in kind of fervent, physical prayer that she might never lose him. She pressed her face to his. "Dylan."

"Aye, lass, say my name. Possess it. Hold it close." His lips stirred against hers to form both a promise and a kiss that could not be distinguished one from the other. "It is yours, dear heart. I put it in your keeping."

His tongue prodded her lips and she welcomed it, opening to the moist heat of his mouth. This, at least, she could do without lies, without artifice, purely as Eliza. His farmer's arms—large and solid—hefted her off her feet, and with lips sealed, tongues entwined, bodies crushed, he sat at the edge of the bed with Eliza straddled in his lap.

Her hair came tumbling free—she didn't know how—and tangled around their arms, tying them together. Suddenly the room went spinning and Eliza landed face up on the bed, her legs dangling over the edge between Dylan's. His lips burrowed between her breasts, tongue sweeping the flesh exposed by her gown's neckline.

His hand came down on her thigh, a pressure no less searing for the presence of skirts and petticoats. Slowly his hand rose to her hip, traveled her stomach, swept the fabric of her bodice. As his open palm conformed warmly to the shape of her breast, a vortex began spinning inside her, twisting the many threads that connected her sensitive places into one deliciously, acutely taut skein. Inflamed filaments stretched to breaking. Eliza moaned into Dylan's mouth and arched for more.

When she realized, moments later, that she drew cool air into her lungs, she opened her eyes to find him staring down at her from arm's length. His gaze raked her, intense and probing, making her feel naked despite the layers of clothing. One dark eyebrow quirked before settling to a glowering line that spoke of steely resolve, single-minded desire. Her mind flooded with images of that glorious thing he'd done to her in the rose garden. A fiery chill of expectance swept through her.

"I want you so badly I can scarce breathe, lass."

Her own breath caught. She reached out for him, barely grazing his broad chest with her fingertips. He pulled further back, just beyond her grasp.

"Do you understand, Elizabeth? I want all of you. No more fleeting kisses and interrupted embraces. No more distance between us." His hands seized her cheeks, the calluses rough and remorseless against her skin. From the flare of his nostrils and the glint in his eye, Eliza understood, oh so very clearly, that this would be no repeat of the rose garden.

"Unless you send me away this very moment," he said, "I will have all of you, Elizabeth."

Ah, no, this surrender would be far, far more unconditional, for both of them.

And that terrified her.

She reached two conflicting decisions at once. The first surged from the wild, grappling rhythm of her heart and the impassioned whimper of her innermost places. Yes, she wanted him, more than life, more than any luxury her future as Elizabeth might afford.

But how could she—how dare she—commit the most intimate of acts with so many lies standing between them. How betrayed might Dylan Fergusson feel once he learned, as he surely must, that he made love not to Elizabeth, but to a farmwife turned laundry maid turned almost-whore turned liar?

He spoke of distance. Because of her dishonesty, theirs was a distance that could only be spanned at great risk to both their hearts, to Eliza's future and very life.

"Dylan, wait."

He released her at once, eyes filled with disappointment and . . . yes, pain. As he backed away she quickly sat up, wanting to explain, wanting, finally, to let the truth out. But as she opened her mouth she discovered that wanting and daring were two very different matters. The words curled inside her like old dead leaves.

Dylan backed away from the bed, hands raised in capitulation. Elizabeth might as well have threatened him with a gun. He would not have been more dumbfounded, more crestfallen. He spun away to glare his frustration into the glowing embers in the hearth.

His breath heaved in and out of his lungs. He'd given her the choice, damn it, fair warning as to the consequences of their continuing as they were. But it had been a formality merely. He certainly hadn't expected her to become ice in his hands.

No, because everything about her these past days—every look, every touch, every breath—sang to him of feelings gone deeper than regard or friendship or the regret of someone bent on saying goodbye.

Feelings that ran as deep as his own. He'd given up trying to rationalize what he felt for her. It wasn't protectiveness because he'd found her on the moors. It wasn't compassion because she was alone in the world and seemed so blasted young and vulnerable. And it wasn't sheer lust, either, although for the life of him he could not stop envisioning the unqualified rapture of having her naked in bed beneath him.

It was more than all that. *She* was more. Different . . . in the way he was different. Not quite noble but not common either, belonging neither in one world nor the other. And so she, like him, made her own way, her own rules. Like riding astride. And mouthing *bugger it* in her sleep. And parting with her hat and gloves at a child's whim—she still hadn't got them back from the twins.

Not to mention gazing up at him with passion sizzling in her great golden eyes, but calling him Mr. Fergusson in her prim, respectful way. Dear God, how he liked those things about her.

How he *loved* those things. He wanted to groan. Heaven help him for falling for yet another woman who seemed to have her uses for him but little else.

Thank God he hadn't revealed his heart, at least not entirely.

Behind him came the rustling sounds of Elizabeth sitting up, sliding to the floor, smoothing her skirts. His head went down between his hunched shoulders as he fought to master his emotions and still his rapid pulse.

"I'm sorry," she whispered.

"Don't be. You did nothing wrong." He glared into the dormant fire glow. "It was I—"

"You did nothing wrong either."

He angled a glance over his shoulder. "Didn't I?"

"No. We both . . . " She shrugged. "We both want what we cannot have."

"Can we not?" He faced her full on. "Why do you insist we must part? Where is it written that Dylan Fergusson and Elizabeth Mendoza de Leone must never abide in the same place, except for these few short days here at Longfield Park?"

Her mouth pulled to an ironic slant. "Oh, but it is written. I will show you."

In complete bafflement he watched her stride to one of her trunks and open it. She reached inside and lifted an ornate jewelry cask with bowed panels and gilt carvings. Hurrying back across the room, she set the box on the bed and opened the lid.

"Here it is." She unfolded what looked like a letter, yet didn't hold it out to him. Instead she squinted to make out the writing in the dim light. She tapped her forefinger to the page and began reading, " 'Though our last words were spoken in fury, remember that we are brothers who shared many dreams, many secrets and as many sins.' "

She paused, skimmed the page, and continued, " 'It is my hope, my dying wish, that you will welcome Elizabeth into the family and watch over her, for she is alone in this world now. Ever your brother, Anselmo.' "

After folding the letter and returning it to the casket, she tilted her face expectantly as if he should now understand everything.

He understood nothing.

"Don't you see?" she blurted into the strained silence, "Anselmo and his brother fell out years ago, and it is my task now to heal those wounds. It is the least I can do."

Anselmo. The word sprang so naturally from her lips. It was the first time Dylan heard her speak her deceased husband's name, and it raised his hackles. It shouldn't, he knew. The man was dead, after all. But she'd just rejected his overtures of love—albeit they were cloaked in acts of lust—in favor of carrying out the man's dying wish. Noble of her, true, but he didn't have to like it.

"What will you do in London?" He strolled to a window,

gazing at his own reflection in the blackness and attempting to school the scowl from his features. "Take up residence with a family you've never met, who know nothing about you and never will." He heard the resentment creeping into his voice and felt helpless to prevent it. "If you dwelled with them a hundred years, they'd never come to know you as I have these past days."

"I owe Anselmo that much." Her voice became as forlorn as a Yorkshire gale. "I owe it to . . . "

He dragged a breath through his nose and turned. "So do it and return."

"Here?" A wistful light filled her eyes for an instant. Then she shook her head. "This is not my home."

"Yet it's filled with people who care about you. And I am here. And here I'll wait, if you ask me to."

She turned her face to the floor, retreating behind trailing locks of hair. "I can't do that, for I can make no promises in return."

"Why can't you, Elizabeth?"

"Because . . . " She shook the hair from her eyes and met his gaze. "What if I haven't been honest? What if . . . there are things I've kept from you? Would you forgive me?"

"Lass, how can you even ask that? I kept things from you, and—"

"This is different."

"No, it isn't. Elizabeth, I'm a farmer. I couldn't care less that you're not quite the noblewoman I'd originally thought, or that you married a wealthy man and rose a bit above your station. In fact, I'm glad of it. I'm relieved."

He went to her, taking her face between his hands and kissing first one cheek, then the other. Then he ever so gently placed his lips against hers in a kiss utterly devoid of lust, that sought only to impart his faith in her. "I figured those things for myself because you never tried to hide them. You've simply been you—brave and honest and entirely original." He grinned. "I wouldn't change a blessed thing about you."

"No . . . ?"

"No, not a thing. I want you to be Elizabeth, just Elizabeth. Forget about Mendoza whatever the rest—"

"De Leone," she murmured, looking bewildered.

"It doesn't matter. Just be the woman I know. Stay exactly as you are and never apologize for it."

"But—"

"And another thing." He released her and strolled to the fireplace, seizing the poker and stoking the embers to life. Modest flames rippled through the kindling. "For the time being, you're stuck with me whether you will or no. All the way to London."

"What do you mean?"

"You don't think I'll let you travel alone after what happened today, do you?"

"Oh, but the duke shares your concerns. He intends providing me a driver and an armed footman."

"Good." He replaced the poker in the iron holder and turned. "Then we'll present a formidable front to anyone thinking to molest us along the way."

She looked confused and about to raise a protest. He hefted his chin in his best approximation of Charity's decisive, no-arguments expression. "You won't be rid of me, Elizabeth, until I've seen you safely to London."

He was surprised to see tears fill her eyes. They acted as a magnet drawing him to her. "Why are you crying, lass?" He raised her chin and gazed into twin pools of liquid gold. "Are you so determined to be rid of me?"

"Why are you so determined to stay?" She shook her head at him. "We are strangers. You owe me nothing. Why won't you send me on my way and forget me?"

"Strangers?" His throat tightened and burned. "Nothing could be further from the truth. We are misfits both, and as alike as a wish to a prayer."

As he spoke, his hands slid down her arms. His fingers entwining with hers, he drew her closer to the warmth of the growing fire. The rug beneath their feet absorbed their tread with inviting softness. "You are my wish," he murmured as he coaxed her down beside him with a gentle tug. "And my prayer, Elizabeth."

"If only it could be so . . . " Her next words shattered. Her eyes seemed impossibly large, a gilded reflection of the fire glow . . . and of the emotion and need blazing inside him.

"No, lass, not if only. When we are together, close, like this, we need not make wishes." He reached his arms around her, moving his mouth against her hair. They dipped to smooth a kiss across her lips and tasted the salt of her tears. "Don't you see? The wish is granted, the prayer is answered. And the answer, if you'll only listen . . . is yes."

"Yes." The word came feather soft against his cheek. Was she simply repeating him, or agreeing? He didn't know, didn't wonder for more than an instant before he lowered his shoulder to the cushiony rug and brought her down beside him. His mouth to hers, his hands sought flesh beneath hems, around buttons, through lace and linen.

His trousers came open. Had she unbuttoned them? Had he? Again, the knowledge eluded him, didn't matter. He was consumed by warmth and pliancy and the sweet scent of Elizabeth's hair and skin. He was drunk with it, exhilarated.

When her bodice fell open he pressed his lips to the weight of her breast, suckling the beaded nipple deep into his mouth, adoring it with his tongue. His thigh came up between her legs and she rode him, pressing so tight against him he could feel the wet flame of her lust through his trouser.

Reaching, she captured him in her hands. With a hypnotic rhythm that sent him soaring, tumbling, surging, she brought him to arousal and beyond, to the brink, to wild rutting passion where thought and judgment dissolve into the mindless need to satisfy, to achieve completion.

He shoved her skirts out of the way. "All of you, Elizabeth."

"And all of you." Her thighs opened and embraced him. "My Dylan."

The moment of penetration sent a hammer blow to his chest and a deep, grinding groan from his lips. Elizabeth released a cry and gripped his shirtsleeves, pulling and releasing in counterpoint to each long, slow thrust.

Her soft grunts blended with his own. Their breath raced and heaved and tattered. Their hips rocked to a tempo he knew only they could hear, a song of their making that swept them up and away and sent them crashing like two stars on a collision course, to shatter and die and be reborn more brilliant than ever.

And as Dylan spiraled down from heaven he knew . . . the wish was granted. The prayer had been answered.

He need never be alone again.

CHAPTER 13

Dylan awoke some time later to the distant rumble of thunder and the dismal gray of a rainy dawn. He lay on the floor before a lifeless hearth, covered only with a corner of the coverlet he'd yanked off the bed a hour or so ago. And yet for all that, he felt not the least bit cold, for Elizabeth lay in his arms, her head in the hollow of his shoulder, arms and legs tangled with his.

How like a child she slept, with her lips parted and her cheeks all pink and warm. She didn't so much as stir when he eased out from under her, and let off only the faintest of sighs when he lifted her in his arms and tucked her into the wide, vacant bed. He watched her plump, pretty mouth, hoping she'd say *bugger it.* She didn't, and finally he tiptoed across the room, turning once to blow her a silent kiss before letting himself out the door.

By mid-morning the rain increased, sending unending sheets battering the house and cascading from the rooftops. He supposed the wretched weather would mean a day of card playing, reading aloud, games of charades, an extra-long luncheon. The hearth fires would be lit in the drawing room and the children brought down from the nursery to provide the adults amusing distraction during the otherwise dreary hours.

Aye, it would be a day surrounded by family with little chance of stealing a moment alone with Elizabeth. A day of pretending last night had not changed his life and his very being in ways so profound he had not yet had the opportunity to absorb it all.

He found himself tarrying in his room till after breakfast, knotting his cravat, combing his hair and realizing what a fool he was to be primping in front of a mirror like a damned peacock in full bloom. As if fashion or the lack of it would make a difference to Elizabeth. She knew who and what he was . . . and she'd given him the gift of herself last night all the same.

He couldn't quite take the peacock's swagger out of his step as he descended the stairs and headed toward the voices in the drawing room. If he couldn't be alone with Elizabeth, he'd at least enjoy being near her, sharing perhaps the odd secretive smile, the knowing wink. But he never made it there, for as he reached the bottom of the staircase Luke beckoned from the threshold of his study.

It was the look on his brother-in-law's face that made apprehension gather in Dylan's gut. Approaching the doorway, he saw Charity and Wesley hovering inside, their expressions matching Luke's in seriousness.

"Come in." Luke closed the door behind them. "Have a seat."

It didn't escape Dylan's notice that Luke turned the key in the lock. Amid the familiar onslaught of aged leather, older brandy and Wesley's more recent pipe tobacco, he glanced at each of the room's occupants in turn. "Something is wrong."

When no one made the slightest effort to deny his conclusion, apprehension turned to leaden misgiving.

A sofa spanned the wall beside the door, presided over by a portrait of one of the former Dukes of Wakefield. Luke motioned for Dylan to sit while the others took up grim-faced positions around him. Wesley set an armchair opposite for Charity before settling at the other corner of the sofa. Luke remained standing, ruminating down at his feet.

"Shall one of you clue me in, or is this the first charade of the day?

"No, Dylan, this is no game." Charity looked bleak, as bleak as that morning six years ago when Luke had awakened with no memory of their marriage.

Dylan stole a glance at Wesley, who in turn raised a stern eyebrow at his brother. "There's no proper way to do this, Lucas. Might as well just have out with it."

Luke contemplated the tips of his shoes and cleared his throat. "A messenger made it in this morning before the rain began in earnest. You are aware that I began an investigation into Elizabeth's carriage accident."

Dylan nodded. "Even though she asked you not to."

"Even though." Luke's shoulders bunched. "And in light of what happened yesterday in town, I'm glad I chose not to heed her request. Perhaps it was underhanded of me, but I feared she might be in some sort of danger. The facts of that accident didn't add up. But now . . . "

He and Charity exchanged a decidedly uneasy glance.

Dylan pushed to the sofa's edge. "Have you learned something about the man who accosted her?"

"Not yet, but I'm working on it."

"Then what?"

Charity encouraged her husband with a solemn nod.

"Has Elizabeth explained to you how her husband died?"

Luke's question took him aback. "No. And I haven't asked. I thought if she wished to speak of it she would."

Another round of solemn looks had Dylan's patience unraveling like the edges of a wind-whipped flag. He started to gain his feet, but Luke's hand descended on his shoulder with a weight that could portend nothing good.

"An associate of mine in Leeds has information concerning a rumor out of York, Dylan. There is talk, especially within the servants' networks, that . . . well . . . understand that at this point it *is* just a rumor . . . ."

"Say it, Lucas," Wesley Holbrook urged.

"That Anselmo Mendoza de Leone may have been murdered."

Eliza had awakened alone in her bed that morning, but not lonely. No, Dylan had apparently carried her there sometime earlier and tucked the coverlet snugly around her. She had emerged from a haze of sleep with the scent of him still warm on her skin, sweet on her tongue.

Despite the impossible muddle her life had become, she'd awakened happy and contented and filled with a new sense of who she was. The woman Dylan Fergusson loved. No matter her outward identity, she'd learned in those wondrous hours, even without the words being spoken aloud, that she'd become precious to him. His hands and fingertips and wordless lips had told all.

He hadn't appeared at breakfast, which only worried her the tiniest bit. They'd slept little enough last night, after all. The thought brought a secret smile to her face as she followed the children and the elders into the drawing room. The duchess, her husband and Lord Wesley stole off somewhere else together, perhaps on matters of estate business. Helena had gone up to the nursery to tend her younger child.

Settling now into the settee, Eliza allowed one of the duchess's little white dogs to jump up into her lap. Absently she ran her palm the length of its furry back as her thoughts drifted.

Beyond doubt, her plans to become Elizabeth had run awry nearly from the first. Longfield Park should have been a quick stopover, a chance to rest. But last night changed everything, and nothing could ever be the same because of it. She had given up her identity willingly. She never bargained on losing her heart. And Eliza knew that of all the dangers she faced, that was the gravest.

The Westie's head suddenly popped up from its perch on

her thigh, and her thoughts scattered. His shaggy face swiveled to hers, his dark eyes wet and sad. Eliza realized she had stopped petting him, her hand hovering in midair.

"So sorry, lad. I won't let it happen again."

Helena walked into the room just then with her infant son at her shoulder. "Been trying to get a good burp out of him . . . "

"Have you tried alternating patting with rubbing his back?" Eliza suggested, remembering a neighbor once mentioning the trick. She regarded the baby's sweet face and felt a tug in the deepest corner of her heart. "Round and round in little circles."

"Really?" Helena shifted the boy to her other shoulder and tried Eliza's advice.

"Not too vigorously," Eliza cautioned. "Don't want his breakfast coming back up." She smiled up at the other woman. "I've been wondering, which Westie am I holding?"

"Oh, that's Skiff," Helena replied after a quick glance at the dog. "Schooner is presently helping my father sort through his butterfly collection."

Partway across the room, the other Westie was standing on his hind legs and straining to see over the edge of the writing desk at which Sir Joshua sat. The man, hunched over a large gilt-edged book and using Lady Mary's quizzing glass to study its pages, seemed not to notice the animal's inquisitive snuffling.

At the other end of the room, Dolly and Lady Mary sat at the card table with the twins, Lena and Lara, sorting through old fabric scraps to make clothes for their dolls. William and Helena's older son, David, had dumped a box of lead soldiers and carved wooden horses onto the floor and were busily laying out territory according to the rug's colorful pattern.

Such a contented family scene. If only Eliza could truly be part of it . . . as Dylan Fergusson's wife.

A wish granted, a prayer answered . . . but only, Eliza knew, if she told Dylan the truth. The notion still frightened her. Especially after all he'd said about her being Elizabeth and staying exactly as she was. Those words had dismayed her at first. But after what occurred between them later, she couldn't go on *not* telling him.

The dog in her lap whimpered, prompting her to scratch his neck. "There, there now, Skiff." She glanced again at Helena. "How can you be certain this one is Skiff?"

"The ears." The other woman paused in rubbing little Stephen's back, listened, then patted. "Skiff's are intact, while Schooner lost the tip of his during a dispute."

"A dispute? Over what?"

"Charity said it was with a rat or a weasel or some breed of rodent." She wrinkled her nose, an oddly elegant gesture on her. "From the sound of it, the rodent emerged quite the victor while Schooner learned nothing whatsoever from the encounter." Her gaze drifted to the boys. A frown emerged. "David and William, return that letter opener to the desk this instant. Father, please don't let them take things from the drawers."

She sat beside Eliza and heaved a sigh. "Those two. Can't take one's eyes off them for an instant."

Eliza felt another wistful tightening in her chest. "I think it's truly lovely how involved all of you are in raising your children. I know it isn't always so, that many a family leave the keeping of their young children to nurses and governesses."

"I'll admit our homes shall undoubtedly witness a fair passing of nurses and governesses over the years, but our children shall always have their parents, grandparents, aunts and uncles to contend with. The little devils wear us out and bring us to life all at once."

"Yes. How I wish . . . " No. She mustn't dwell on the child she never had, for it only brought stinging tears and more regrets than she could bear. Helena watched her expectantly. Eliza stroked Skiff's back. "Perhaps someday . . . "

"Of course you will, dearest. You'll find happiness again, you'll see. Would you care to . . . trade for awhile?" Lifting the baby from her shoulder, Helena first untangled a lock of her lovely flaxen hair from his tiny fingers and held him out to Eliza.

"Oh." Her throat closed around anything else she might have said. She'd held babies before, of course, but not since losing her own.

Carefully she gathered the child into her arms, holding him close while Helena lifted the Westie from her lap. She experienced something akin to pain as an unbearably soft cheek pressed into her neck, as impossibly delicate fingers latched onto her lace collar. Eliza lowered her own cheek to the top of Stephen's head and filled her lungs with the warm, precious scent of him.

"Oh, he's beautiful," she whispered when her throat allowed speech. "He's just perfect."

"I think so, but then I'm prejudiced." Helena traced a fingertip down the back of his satin gown. "Dearest, may I ask you . . . how your husband passed away?"

With her nose pressed to the baby's feathery-soft locks, she said, "He was gored by a bull."

Eliza heard those words leave her mouth and flinched in horror. Stephen let out a half-hearted complaint, lifting his head and tugging her collar.

Good God. Why had she said that—why had she told how Nathan died rather than allude to Anselmo's illness?

Because it had become virtually impossible to continue lying to these people. Because last night Dylan had touched the real Eliza and left her exposed and vulnerable.

"Dearest Elizabeth, I am so sorry," Helena whispered after a stone cold pause. Her lovely complexion had drained of color. Her features were frozen in shock. "How horrible, for him and for you. And how despicable of me to have made you speak of it. Do forgive me."

Eliza didn't trust herself to speak, so she clamped

her teeth, closed her eyes and clung to the babe. As rain
lashed the windows, memories of that hideous day flooded
her mind.

The bull had pierced the main artery in Nathan's thigh.
Steady and relentless, the life had drained out of Eliza's husband despite the bandages, the makeshift tourniquet and the
pressure of her own desperate hands as she resorted to wrapping them around the wound. . . .

As gently as she could, she eased little Stephen Holbrook
from her bosom and handed him back to his mother. Then she
smoothed her skirts and stood.

"Will you excuse me? I believe I'll go upstairs and lie
down awhile."

Helena raised a face pinched with remorse. "Of course,
Elizabeth, dear. Would you like anything? Shall I send
up tea?"

"No, thank you." Unable to leave the kindly Helena Holbrook in so obvious a state of distress, Eliza summoned a
smile. "You mustn't think you've upset me. I'm simply tired.
The sound of rain always lulls me to sleep."

The beautiful Helena hardly looked convinced but Eliza
hurried off, fleeing the drawing room at nearly a run. She
intended finding Dylan that very moment, opening her
mouth and trusting that the right words would finally, finally come out. As she reached the staircase, his muffled
voice drew her instead to the closed doors of the duke's private study.

Oh, she should have observed propriety, ignored those
voices and continued on up the stairs to wait for him. If only
Dylan's baritone hadn't rumbled through the doors and spiked
her curiosity.

She thought she heard the duchess's and duke's voices
as well, and by their tones she guessed they were arguing
about something. She stole a quick glance around the hall
in search of household staff. Seeing none, she pressed her
ear to the door.

* * *

"Murdered? By God. How?"

"Are you familiar with arsenic poisoning?"

Dylan stared blankly at his brother-in-law. Of course he wasn't familiar with arsenic or any other kind of poisoning.

"It mimics a slow but wasting illness. Depending on how much is given at a time, death can take days, weeks, even months." Luke worked his fingers into his neck cloth, loosening the knot. "There are rumors that Anselmo's illness looked suspiciously like the work of arsenic."

"That's madness."

"There's more. Apparently he's been dead less than a fortnight."

The revelation jarred through him. "That can't be. Elizabeth and I . . . we . . . " His eyes fell closed but could not blot out visions of his arms around Elizabeth, his lips on Elizabeth. His hands everywhere exploring Elizabeth. Himself inside her, loving her, sharing a passion that could no longer be tamped or put off or denied.

Good God, had it been as mutual as he'd thought? Or had he seduced a grieving woman? Never, never would he have pressed her had he known how recent a bereavement she bore.

And yet, no, he had not been alone in those embraces, those kisses. He'd felt the rising flame of passion on her lips, in her roving fingertips. The very notion of it now soured in his stomach. A widow of less than two weeks . . .

Why would she . . . ? How could she . . . ?

No, he would not judge what he clearly did not understand. Lord knew, she faced a large enough tribunal in these three Holbrooks. He opened his eyes and narrowed them on his brother-in-law. "What are you insinuating?"

"Only that there are facts and particulars we are only beginning to understand. Elizabeth's accident indicated the coach had been traveling at great speeds. Her former servants confirm that she quitted Folkstone Manor in undue haste, though they cannot with any certainty state the reason why."

"It does make one . . . wonder," Wesley added to Luke's summation. "And when the horses were found following the accident, their shoes showed unusual wear, more so than even their frantic flight would occasion." He propped a forearm on his knee as he leaned forward. "As if those horses needed reshodding before the journey, but no one took the time."

The blood pounded at Dylan's temples. "Are you suggesting Elizabeth might have been responsible for . . . " He gained his feet and rounded on his sister. "You've seen her with the children. How sweet she is, how patient. Surely you cannot believe so ill of such a gentle soul."

Charity shook her head. "I can no more see that dear child harming a fly than I could . . . our own Helena." Her expression sharpened. "But I of all people understand what it is to be a woman with something to hide. From the very first I sensed a secretiveness about our guest, an evasiveness. I believe there is more to Elizabeth Mendoza than we currently know."

"Perhaps what we don't know is none of our business."

"Perhaps," Luke agreed. "But she hasn't exactly been forthcoming about her past. And she nearly had an apoplexy when I so much as suggested investigating the accident."

"And that makes her a murderer?"

Wesley leveled him a steady gaze. "It makes her suspicious."

"She's grieving." Dylan shook his head, becoming more disgusted by the moment with his family's meddling. "And she has every right to her privacy."

"If she is innocent." Luke met his gaze head on, unflinching.

"She is."

"How can you be so sure?"

"Because I know her. And because . . . I intend to marry her." The shock registering on the three faces before him paled in comparison to the astonishment he felt as those words left his mouth. But in the next instant he knew only the contentment of a sound decision, the only *right* decision.

"Dylan, you can't mean it." Charity pushed to her feet, her face crumpled with dismay. "You barely know Elizabeth."

"Elizabeth and I know each other far better than any of you can guess. She understands me far better than any of you ever will. And after last night—"

Charity gasped. "Last night?"

"Aye. After last night there could very well be a child on the way. My child."

Wesley pushed a breath between his teeth. Luke grimaced.

Charity's eyes popped wide. "Dylan, how could you?"

"Oh, in the usual way."

Luke stepped between them. "Don't you dare make light of your sister's concerns. She has only your best interests at heart. We all do. Your future is at stake here—"

"Do not make presumptions about my future or what is best for me." Dylan held his ground in the face of Luke's anger. "I've told you before I will not be a creature of your making. I am my own man and I make my own decisions. Whether or not those decisions include Elizabeth is none of your concern and I'd thank you to butt out of my life and stop speaking ill of the woman I love."

"Dylan." Charity stepped around her husband and pressed a hand to Dylan's forearm. "We only wish to learn the truth about Elizabeth, not wrongly accuse her of a crime she did not commit. If someone murdered her husband, she herself might be in danger. If we could only gain some insight into her life before you found her on the moors, it might help us help her. Right now, Helena is attempting to find out from

Elizabeth exactly how her husband died. A lot will depend on her answer, won't it?"

Dylan whisked his arm from her grasp. "Helena is spying for the lot of you? Now you've gone too far."

CHAPTER 14

Eliza strained to make out the words pelting back and forth on the other side of the door, but with little success. If only that door weren't fashioned of such dense oak. Still, she knew by the rise and fall of the voices that they were indeed arguing. She thought she heard her name mentioned several times. Elizabeth's name, that is.

And then she heard something altogether different. A jiggling. The door handle swiveled back and forth.

Bugger it! She dashed for the stairs, praying she made it at least half way up before the study door opened. An angry voice spurred her on—Dylan's brogue, loud and thick with indignation as the door opened.

Dread filled her at the thought of his turning that baritone on her if he discovered her eavesdropping or worse . . . if he'd finally discovered her identity and despised her for the many lies. Daring a glance over her shoulder, she saw him on the threshold facing into the room, hand on the knob.

She made it as far as the half landing before her hems caught beneath her toe and brought her crashing down. Stifling a cry and ignoring the pain radiating from her knee, she gripped the banister and hauled herself to her feet.

A second peek over her shoulder confirmed the worst. Dylan stood below in the hall glaring up at her, a scowl robbing his features of warmth, of the compassion she'd come to depend on so desperately. He just stood there, a silent, brooding pillar of hostility, while Eliza watched her only source of solace in the whole entire world slip away.

Then he was moving, taking the stairs two at a time, charging toward her. She tried to back away but hit the window seat with the backs of her knees. Dylan reached the landing and came to an abrupt, breathless halt.

"I . . . tripped," she stammered.

Beneath his dark brows, his eyes shimmered. His fists were clenched, the knuckles white. "Did you hurt yourself?"

"No. I . . . er . . . "

"You should have your dresses taken up. It isn't safe."

"You are right. I . . . shall."

He took her hand. "Come." But before he could lead her further up the stairs a voice called from below.

"Dylan, please come back."

The duchess. Eliza watched indecision flicker across Dylan's face, followed by firm resolve.

"We've said all that needed saying, Charity. And I believe we've detained Mrs. Mendoza long enough. It's time she set out for London and I with her." Though the words were directed toward his sister, Dylan nonetheless spoke them to Eliza, his gaze locked with hers. Relief coursed through her, making her dizzy. His anger was not directed at her. He hadn't caught her eavesdropping. He hadn't learned the truth about her.

That comfort lasted all of an instant. Not for the world did she wish to see Dylan at odds with his family. She'd rather return to the barren moors than be the cause of a rift between them.

Holding her hand securely in his own, he turned to regard his sister. "May we still use one of your coaches?"

His stiff formality made both Eliza and the duchess wince. "Of course you may," his sister said quietly.

"Thank you. We'll be leaving before luncheon."

"Not in this weather," the duchess protested, but Dylan had

already turned away, had drawn Eliza close to his side and started up the remaining steps.

"How much did you hear?" he asked once they reached the upper gallery.

"Only . . . your voice raised in anger as I left the drawing room," she half-lied. "Nothing more."

"Meddling fools."

"Have you . . . argued with your family?"

"Argued doesn't begin to describe it. I'm furious."

"Oh, I do wish you weren't. And I hope . . . it doesn't have anything to do with me."

That he didn't deny it did little to allay her fears. Had the family become suspicious about her? Perhaps that doctor from York had shown up searching for Elizabeth. Or that man in town. Perhaps the duke had found him and learned something that would destroy her future as Elizabeth *and* Eliza.

Like a life flashing before a dying man's eyes, Eliza's crimes paraded through her mind. Taking Elizabeth's belongings—theft. Claiming to be Elizabeth—fraud. Extracting favors from a duke under false pretenses—the worst sort of skullduggery that would surely lead to her ruination.

They turned into the wing that housed her bedroom. She was shaking and trying to conceal it, trying not to stumble over her hems again.

"How soon can you be ready to leave?"

His curtness unnerved her, so alien did it sound coming from him. And it frightened her, too, that he was defying the family he loved because of her. "Dylan, you shouldn't leave now while you're so angry. Reconcile with your family first."

"They hardly deserve such loyalty from you."

"Then it is about me, isn't it?"

They stopped outside her door. He raised her hand to his chest and bowed his head over it a long moment. Then he turned her hand over and pressed a kiss to her palm. A shiver ran the length of her arm and traveled through her.

"They have fallen into the misfortune of listening to

hearsay," he said. "I am exceedingly disappointed in them. I had believed better of them, you see. So much better."

Every instinct advised letting the matter drop. But if the worst had happened—if the Holbrooks *had* somehow learned her secret—better to have it out now, and confess the whole truth. She took a deep breath. "What hearsay? What do they believe I've done?"

"It doesn't bear discussing. In fact, it's me they wish to censure. I made the mistake of revealing my feelings for you." He kissed her hand again, holding it against his lips before lowering it. "They're simply interfering in my life as usual."

He still believed in her. And that made Eliza ashamed. If only she were worthy of such a champion. If only a wish and a prayer could make her so.

Elizabeth was no murderer. Of that Dylan was certain. And yet . . . miles now down the London Road, he began to wonder. Not about her innocence or the lack, but rather what secret Elizabeth concealed as though her life depended on it.

I know what it is to be a woman with something to hide. His sister's words tugged as memories of the past few days scampered through his mind. Elizabeth's haste in leaving Heverton Gorse . . . her reluctance to visit Longfield Park . . . her denial of knowing the Spaniard, who later accosted her as if with an old and deep-rooted rancor.

Whatever danger she faced, he would face with her. Or *for* her, if he could. She was part of him now. Their lovemaking established that, sealed it, made it forever. But he supposed his first and perhaps most arduous task lay in persuading her there was nothing—not a blessed thing on this earth—she could not share with him.

But like a disease, Luke's parting words ran like ice through his veins. *She lied, Dylan. She told Helena her husband was gored by a bull. Why make such an outlandish claim when her husband's illness is a known fact?*

But then Helena, too, had pulled him aside before he climbed into the coach, insisting she believed Elizabeth's story. *I was there, Dylan, I saw her face. She spoke without forethought or artifice, and was immediately overcome by a grief so raw my heart bled for her.*

Beside him now, Elizabeth sat jostling to the rhythm of the coach, head down, face averted, eyes reddened reflections of the sorrowful farewells at Longfield. Their sudden departure had clearly bewildered the elders, who knew nothing of the recent developments or the suspicions. But they'd embraced her and wished her Godspeed without questions.

To her credit, Charity had seen Elizabeth off with nothing but kind words, though Dylan heard the brittle misgiving that rode them. Luke and Wesley had been polite, thoroughly correct to the point of stiffness. With tearful eyes Helena had pressed a goodbye token into Elizabeth's hand.

William had presented the hardest parting of all, clinging to Elizabeth's skirts and indulging in something entirely out of character, at least since he'd rounded the age of five. He'd cried, prompting Elizabeth to unlock one of her trunks and fish out some damaged trinket from the bottom of an evening glove.

She told the boy it was broken because her heart was broken, and that she wanted him to have it so he would always remember she had left half her heart behind at Longfield Park.

Even Dylan himself had fallen to blinking away a sudden and irksome sting in his eyes.

The strained silence, marked only by the coach's rumblings and the occasional sniffle from Elizabeth, was near to driving him mad. And yet, how to voice the thing hanging between them? *I intend to marry* her. Aye, the intention was still there, as powerful as ever.

A widow of less than a fortnight. It was the one thought he'd tried to shove from his mind, but it kept sneaking back like a foul-tempered mongrel to chomp at his coattails.

"Why do you never wear black?"

She blinked. "I beg your pardon?"

"Why are you not in mourning for your husband?"

Her brows converged. "I mourn my husband more than anyone can guess."

He laced his fingers together in his lap. "How long ago did your husband pass away?"

Even without looking he sensed her utter stillness. "This is hardly a fit time for questions, while you are still so angry."

"What has my anger to do with the answers you might give?"

She hesitated again. Then, "Perhaps it would be best if we parted. If you went back to Longfield Park and settled this dispute with your sister, and I continued on to London alone."

"Mr. Fergusson."

"I'm sorry?"

"I can hear it in your voice. 'Perhaps it would be best if we parted, Mr. Fergusson, and I continued on to London alone.' " His imitation of her carried an edge of resentment. "We are to have distance again, aren't we? And formality. It is how you protect yourself."

"Can you blame me in this instance?" The corners of her mouth pulled downward. "You all but told me I am the cause of this rift with your family. I have no wish to be."

"You are not the cause and I will not leave you to continue alone. I've already told you you're stuck with me till I see you safely to London." He treated her to one of his deepest scowls, the one that made the young hired shepherds at home run for cover. "To London, and beyond."

She eyed him warily. "Beyond . . . what does that mean?"

Did he really have to say it to her? Could she not arrive at the sense of it, the rightness of it, on her own? Was she that thoroughly lost and confused about the ways of the world?

So be it.

"I intend to marry you, lass."

* * *

There it was again, that odd, relentless sound just barely audible above the grinding of the carriage wheels, the wind and rain, and the voice of the man beside her.

Eliza had heard *his* words clear enough. It was that other noise . . . yes, that one. God and fate, sharing yet another chuckle over the morass her life had become.

Her champion, her Mr. Fergusson, had just offered for her. Well, not offered exactly. More like insisted, in that stubborn Scottish way of his.

This morning she'd held a baby in her arms and dared, for the briefest instant, to dream of cradling her own babe to her breast. And now this man, whose very existence was shaped and honed by the strictest principles of honor, wished to take her to wife.

How desperately she longed to grasp Dylan's hands, smile into his eyes and tell him yes, yes, she'd be his wife. She'd love him the rest of her life and take the greatest of pains to make certain he knew it each and every day, and never for an instant give him reason to doubt it.

First there must be truth. But how, *how* could she tell him here in this carriage with his rage simmering and his ties with his family in tatters—because of her.

"Well, Elizabeth? Have you nothing to say?"

Oh, she had many things to say. "Now is not the time. Not here. Not with the way we left things at Longfield Park."

"Forget Longfield."

"I cannot. Your sister's family was so kind to me and now . . . "

"Now there are matters that lie between you and me. No one else."

But there was someone else. There was Eliza Kent, a woman he knew nothing about. A woman he might quickly learn to loathe. "I need time to think. Time to decide what is best to do."

"Lass, have you considered that you made the decision the

moment you allowed my body to enter yours? The rest is merely ceremony." His voice rumbled. His jaw worked. Signs he hadn't yet mastered his ire.

She sought only to lighten his mood and summon the familiar smile as she said, "Yes, well, as I remember it was you who came to my room, who lingered and . . . "

"Seduced you?"

"That isn't at all what I meant," she said and looked away. "You did not seduce me. You took nothing more from me than I wished to give."

He broke into a wide grin—his first all day—and snatched her hand. "Then marry me, lass."

"It is not so simple."

"It will be if we've made a child."

Don't. The word pounded through her as she went stiff against the seat. *Do not toss heavenly notions about so heedlessly, so cruelly.* A child. She carried one once. Inside her. Where it should have been safe. Where it should have grown and thrived until the day it was born. But it left her months before it should have, in violent, bloody heaves that left Eliza half dead herself. And wholly wishing she were.

A child. A wish that would never be, a prayer fallen on deaf ears.

No, not deaf. Indifferent.

"What's wrong, lass?"

She disentangled her fingers from his. "I wish to speak no more of it. Not now."

"As you wish." His gaze held her fast. "But the notion will not go away, and neither will I."

As though with a shove, Eliza tumbled from sleep into cave black nothingness. Yet well enough did she know where she was. A coaching inn just north of Leicester. Dylan would be in the room next door, while their driver and footman occupied a chamber downstairs off the kitchen.

Something had yanked her from a dreamless sleep. A noise.

As if the coverlet could protect her from danger, she dragged the patchwork to her chin and pricked her ears. Nothing, only the wind hitting the eaves, the rustle of leaves skimming the ground, the distant howl of a dog. Instinctively she knew none of those ordinary night noises were what disturbed her slumber. No, it was something closer, more immediate.

Opening her eyes as wide as they would go, she struggled to pierce the darkness. A chill swept her back as an image of the mysterious Spaniard flashed in her mind. Her pulse lashed wildly at the notion he'd followed her here, was right now in her room, a breath away . . . .

Then she knew. There was no one in her room, and the sound that woke her was simply the hammering of her own heart. Her sleep had not been a dreamless one after all, for it suddenly came rushing back. She and Dylan . . . and a baby. Endless wells of love glistened in Dylan's eyes . . . her name rolled softly off his tongue.

Eliza.

Not Elizabeth but Eliza. It was the only wish, the only prayer that mattered.

So very much time had been wasted, squandered in fear and doubt and indecision. No more.

She slid out from between the bedclothes and hurried into the corridor. Within moments she slipped into a second bedroom, shivering in her bare feet and thin cotton night rail.

The sound of Dylan's deep breathing guided her to the bed. She stumbled as her thigh came up against the mattress, and caught her balance by putting her hand down on something rock solid. It heaved beneath her palm, and she found her wrist locked within a biting grip.

"Dylan, it's me."

"Elizabeth? By St. George's hairy toe, woman." He released her, sat up and reached his arms around her. "You shouldn't sneak up on a man like that."

"I need to speak with you."

"Come up here." He half lifted, half hauled her into his lap. His nightshirt lay unbuttoned, and she felt the springy prickle of hairs through her night rail. "Is something amiss?"

All she could see of him were his sturdy outlines and a faint gleam of the coach yard lantern across his forehead.

"No, there's nothing amiss. Oh, everything is amiss. I must . . . " She trailed off. He was stroking the back of her neck, nuzzling his lips in her hair. "Are you listening?"

"I am, lass." His fingers smoothed the length of her braid, then settled warm and steady at her nape.

"Tell me the truth, please. When you said you intended to marry me, was it only because there might be a babe?"

He hesitated only long enough to gather a breath and press a kiss to her brow. "No, Elizabeth. I love you."

Something inside her swelled to bursting. Those words were so simply spoken, so utterly devoid of wiles or seduction, and so brimming with sincerity and promise and hope. She reached her arms around his shoulders and pressed her length to his. His pectoral muscles were hard and solid against her breasts. Love mingled with courage and faith as she pulled back and smiled.

"I love you, too."

She felt the smallest of convulsions deep within his chest. "Then you've come to tell me you'll marry me?"

Joy and dread entwined around her heart. "If you'll have me after you hear what I have to say."

"Wait." His arms fell away as he leaned over the bedside table. He fiddled with flint and tinder, making several scrapes until the spark caught. Then he lit the lamp, adjusted the wick and gathered her once more in his arms. "There, now that I can see you properly, lass, tell me everything that's on your mind and in your heart."

Eliza filled her lungs with the masculine scent of him and dared believe that once, just once in her life, doing the right and honest thing would result in her happiness. "I am not," she said decisively, "Elizabeth Mendoza de Leone."

CHAPTER 15

Dylan was certain he could not have heard her correctly. And yet, what else could she have said?

Anything else. It didn't matter. So long as she wasn't attempting to deny her own identity in an attempt to . . .

His arms released her, fell to his sides.

She lied . . . why would she make such an outlandish claim?

I know what it is to be a woman with something to hide.

As Luke's and Charity's words roared through him, he realized Elizabeth was still talking. Rapidly. But the words made no sense, might as well have been a foreign language. Might have been Spanish for all he knew.

Anselmo Mendoza de Leone may have been murdered . . .

He was moving, dragging his legs out from under her, putting space between them. Cold nausea gripped his stomach.

. . . Arsenic poisoning.

"Dylan, please say something." She looked stricken, sickly pale against the lamp's burnished glow.

But she looked not nearly as ill as he felt. He turned away from her, sliding his legs over the edge of the mattress, falling forward to prop his head in his hands as the reality of his own gullibility wrenched his insides.

Her hand came down on his shoulder, a gentle reminder of all he had thought her to be. The contact roused him from his stupor and sent a fevered fury pounding inside his skull.

He swung round to glare at her. "By God, what do you

wish me to say? That I believe this flight of fancy you've dreamed up to save your neck from the noose?"

She pulled back, eyes and mouth gaping. "Whatever do you mean?"

"No wonder you refused to answer me in the coach. You overheard us talking in Luke's study." He gripped the pillow as if to rent it in two. "I didn't believe a word of it. I defended you. I told them—"

He hurled the pillow across the room, sending his shaving brush and mug crashing from the wash stand. The porcelain cup hit the floor and shattered. "This is what you meant last night, isn't it, when you said you hadn't been honest with me. You asked if I'd forgive you, but how can I, Elizabeth?"

"Dylan, I'm so sorry I lied but . . . noose? Did you say *noose?*"

He braved another glance at her over his shoulder. Oh, she played her part well, even now, with her slim, vulnerable shoulders shaking beneath her delicate night rail, her cheeks drained of all color, her eyes great golden wells of unshed tears.

He came to his feet and faced her, though his gaze focused on her knees drawn up before her rather than on that pinched face with its bewildered expression.

A face that, moments ago, he had held dearer than any other. He had even turned his back on his own sister for her.

He swallowed rising bile and dragged a breath through his nose. "Did you murder your husband?"

She recoiled as if he had struck her, huddling against the headboard. Her head shook back and forth in a denial that did not reach her lips.

"For the love of God, Elizabeth, answer me."

"Murdered . . . "

"By arsenic poisoning."

"That can't be . . . No. I didn't. I couldn't have—I didn't even know him." Her breathing deepened to labored heaves. "You mean to say . . . Elizabeth . . . ?"

"Stop this nonsense this instant." His fingers shook and he clenched them, pressing his fists to his sides. "If you are guilty, admit it and I'll see you are represented by a competent barrister who might salvage something of your life."

"Have you not heard a word I've said?" She crept forward but halted when he pulled back to maintain space between them. "I am not Elizabeth. And I do not believe the real Elizabeth is guilty of any crime save that of preventing someone—the murderer most likely—from stealing something of great value to the Mendozas. She told me as much as she lay dying. *Do not let them have it,* she said. And so I—"

"Enough." He pressed the heels of his hands to his eyes, trying to blot out the nightmare that sprang so cruelly from the one dream he'd almost believed in. But when he opened his eyes again, the beguiling specter of the woman he'd loved remained to taunt him. "What a fool I've been to believe in you."

"Please don't say that. Can't you see that everything you believed in is here, in me. In Eliza, not Elizabeth. It's always been Eliza."

"Eliza?"

"Yes. Haven't you heard me? My name is Eliza Kent."

"You'd use your own dead servant's name in an attempt to deceive me." He shook his head, disgusted to the brink of his endurance. "Have you no shame whatsoever?"

"How certain you are I'm lying. How eager to believe the worst." She was shaking her head again, not in denial this time but indignation. He saw it in the hardened line of her jaw, the swelling of her bosom. Another brazen bit of play-acting. "Why don't you go then, and alert the authorities?"

"Do not tempt me to do the very thing I should."

"What are you waiting for? Go and tell the local magistrate you've captured the bloodthirsty Elizabeth Mendoza de Leone. I'm sure for such a boon he'll take no offense at being awakened at this ungodly hour."

"Then you admit—"

"I'm only repeating what you insist upon hearing."

He'd had more than enough. "Go back to your room and stay there."

She made no move to leave. "What are you going to do?"

What indeed? Logic urged him to do exactly as she'd suggested—alert the local magistrate. Then wash his hands of the entire affair. His only crime lay in his own lamentable naïveté, a provincial ignorance even a university education, wealth and travels could not erase.

Kicking himself didn't help. Neither did brooding over what he should and shouldn't do.

He strode to the window in the effort to look at something other than her. "I'm going to bring you to London as I said I would. And there I shall leave you to whatever fate deals you."

It was a compromise he'd have to live with, but how to live with the bitter dart protruding from the center of his chest?

He heard her slipping down from the bed, heard the swish of her night rail as it slid to cover her legs. "Aren't you afraid I'll murder Anselmo's family?"

"Damn you." The very name of the man who'd possessed her first sent spots of red before his eyes. Had she killed him in passion? For lack of passion? For wealth or freedom or . . . God . . . another man? He spun around. "You wouldn't dare kill again, not if you value whatever chance you may have to go free."

She raised an eyebrow. "Do you think I might get away with it, then?"

"How can you make light?"

"As you said, I am shameless."

"Justice will find you."

"Let it. I've nothing to fear because I've nothing to lose." She walked to the door, then turned, her voice easing to a whispered caress that left him stinging. "After tonight, Dylan, I have less than nothing."

* * *

London teemed beyond the coach window like a living, writhing beast with no restraint, a stinking, soot-breathing dragon with a thousand roaring voices . . . *fish here, get your pies, fresh flowers, live chickens* . . . There were rumbles and blasts and clangs and shouts until Eliza pressed her hands to her ears. She held her breath against the sulfur stench, shut her eyes to the dingy towers blotting out the sun and wished herself anywhere else in the world.

Another whole day it had taken to get here. An entire day of sitting beside a stiff and silent Dylan, wishing, praying he'd relent and see the truth, that he'd look at her just once and see Eliza.

What more could she have offered than the truth? But no, the lie had proved too enduring, too seductive perhaps to be banished by so weak an avowal as that of Eliza Kent. For who was Eliza Kent, after all? Just some common nobody who died many months ago, or should have done, with the world none the worse.

She returned her attention to the sights outside her window. The streets had gradually become quieter, smoother, brighter. In place of grimy tenements, rows of whitewashed town houses lined the way, with tall shiny windows and flowers beside the front doors. Eliza's nerves settled. At least her pulse stopped bucking. She opened Elizabeth's black velvet reticule, stole a glance at Dylan, confirmed that he paid her no mind whatsoever, and dug for the card Helena had pressed into her palm as she'd said goodbye.

She read the name and direction: Mrs. Charles Emerson, Twelve Grafton Street, Mayfair, London.

Should you ever find yourself in need, go to my cousin, Tess, and tell her I sent you, Helena had instructed in an urgent whisper. *She's performed miracles for more young women than I can count, and there's nothing she wouldn't do for a friend of mine.*

Oh, Eliza doubted this Tess would produce any miracles

for the likes of her, but once she paid a visit to Raphael Mendoza, where else did she have to go?

She would tell Raphael of his brother's and Elizabeth's deaths, of Anselmo's dying wish to reconcile, and of Elizabeth's desperate attempt to reach him. She owed Elizabeth, and perhaps Anselmo, that much. Then she would hand over all the financial records in her possession along with Elizabeth's personal effects. They did not belong to her. Nothing of Elizabeth's ever did, ever could.

That the gentlewoman was innocent of her husband's death Eliza felt certain. Not that radiant, graceful lady who traveled with both her husband's and his brother's youthful portraits tucked safe in her purse. Not the sentimental soul who had stuffed a worthless, broken ornament at the bottom of an evening glove rather than toss it away, simply because it evoked memories of the man she'd loved.

After she carried out Anselmo's and Elizabeth's dying wishes, and only after, would she seek out this Tess Emerson and learn if perhaps, by some miracle, there might be a future for Eliza Kent. She doubted it, but what did she have to lose?

The neighborhoods changed several more times along the way, town houses to mansions to sudden slums and then town houses once again, until Eliza could not begin to guess if Raphael Mendoza was wealthy man or no.

An ashen, coal-tinged twilight descended by the time she spied a sign marking Harrowby Street. This would be London's Marylebone neighborhood, and she would meet Raphael Mendoza in a matter of minutes. Her stomach clenched at the thought, and she clutched her hands until the knuckles ached to prevent them from trembling.

The coach pulled up beside a three-story terrace house in a row of identical attached houses. They were none of them grand dwellings, to be sure, but not squalid either. Behind a simple iron gate, two steps led to a paneled front door flanked by walls of yellow brick and stucco only slightly grayed by soot. Some of the other houses boasted window boxes of rather choked looking violets or pansies. The Mendoza house possessed no such embellishment.

The coach listed as the driver and footman descended from the box. Eliza sat frozen where she was.

"Here you are." Dylan's voice was flat, devoid of any emotion save finality. "Henry and Robert will unload your trunks."

"Are you . . . coming in?"

His gaze turned razor sharp. "Here is where we part."

"You have nothing to say to Raphael Mendoza?"

"Nothing. Events shall speak for themselves. I . . . "

The sentence went unfinished. He what? Wished her well? Hoped she'd hang? Surely somewhere in his heart he believed her innocent or he would not now be leaving her a free woman.

"Goodbye, Elizabeth."

"Goodbye . . . Mr. Fergusson."

She almost added that she didn't intend staying here long, that she'd need a ride . . . somewhere . . . after she conducted her business with Raphael Mendoza. But the scalpel coldness in Dylan's eyes forbade it. He had meant to see her safely to London and so he had done. He'd been her savior and her champion ever since he first wrapped her in his cloak back on the Yorkshire moors. How lucky she had been to have such a guardian angel in her life at all.

The driver opened her door, set down the steps, and held out a hand to help her down. A last peek at Dylan revealed a granite-set profile as he stared straight ahead as if fascinated with the opposite seat. And yet . . . the working of a facial muscle suggested this was no easier for him than for her. Her throat closed around all the things she wished him to know. He wouldn't believe her anyway.

"Thank you," she whispered to all that cold indifference

that was, nonetheless, the best and noblest of what life would ever offer her. Then she stepped down from the coach.

From the corner of his eye, Dylan watched her go, careful not to turn his head too much lest she glimpse how damnably much he wished to call out to her. Then her back was to him, and with a thousand regrets reeling through his brain he watched her cross the narrow foot pavement to the stoop of a complete stranger's house.

Those regrets should have been about his having not turned her over to authorities. Or about his having treated his family so unforgivably on her account. He was ashamed to admit his regrets were of a wholly different nature. They were entirely selfish, entirely foolhardy, entirely painful.

The door to the house opened. Dylan clenched his jaw as a man appeared on the threshold, shaggy silver eyebrows raised in query. Raphael Mendoza? No longer caring how it might appear should Elizabeth happen to glance over her shoulder, he turned full on to peer out the coach window. Henry and Robert at that moment hauled a trunk from the carriage roof, drowning out the voices. Then a bit of conversation reached Dylan ears.

"Whom may I say is calling?"

Not Mendoza, then, but a servant.

Elizabeth opened her purse and held out a folded note. The man took it and skimmed the front. With a nod he opened the door wider. It was then Elizabeth cast a backward glance and caught Dylan staring, face all but pressed to the window. He didn't pull back or try to pretend to be signaling Robert. Instead, he allowed himself this one last glimpse of his heart's desire, however much she had been a fabrication of his pitiful longings.

He saw his own sorrow mirrored in her great golden eyes and felt . . . bereft. And seized with an urgency to call her back, believe whatever she wished, love her no matter who she was and what she'd done.

Henry and Robert set the last of the baggage inside the gate. Elizabeth watched the pair return to the carriage. For a moment her head went down and she stood there, looking lost, young, alone. Then she squared her shoulders.

What irony that in his last view of her, she stumbled on her way over the threshold. Those damned hems of hers. It almost brought a reluctant chuckle to his lips, nearly triggered a call of *Lass, find yourself a new modiste before you break your neck.*

Almost, but not quite. Memories burned his throat, singed his eyes. His vision blurred slightly as he watched the steward grasp her elbow and steady her with the quick efficiency of one trained to serve. Then the door closed behind them and she was gone. Out of his life as abruptly as she'd entered. Dylan rapped on the ceiling of the coach and sat back as Robert maneuvered away from the gutter . . . from the life he and Elizabeth might have shared.

And still the thought nagged . . . what if there was a babe?

CHAPTER 16

"Thank you. How clumsy of me. . . ."

And yet how fitting that within moments of Dylan quitting Eliza's life forever, she'd nearly fallen flat on her face.

For a desperate moment she listened for the rumble of coach wheels returning. Then she drew a breath deep into her lungs, swallowed against a rising sob and faced the future.

From beneath a grizzled tangle of eyebrows, the servant ruminated down the length of his nose at her. He made no polite attempt to gainsay her comment about her clumsiness. Instead he sniffed and mumbled, "Wait here, please."

"Oh, but the trunks. Surely we mustn't leave them outside unattended." She blinked in the dusky interior of the foyer—and not because tears had gathered in her eyes. No, the house was simply dark. The walls were covered in what had perhaps once been a deep burgundy damask but was now faded to dull brown, the pattern worn thin along the wall beside the entryway from years of coat sleeves brushing against it.

The man frowned at her with no small amount of censure, though perhaps she couldn't blame him.

"I realize my arrival is unexpected," she added hastily. "It couldn't be helped. But I assure you the contents of those trunks are of the utmost interest to your employer."

"I shall send Peter out directly." His superior tone acknowledged her claim as a dubious one. He started up the staircase, Anselmo Mendoza's letter in hand.

It didn't escape her notice that he'd left her standing in the entry hall rather than escort her to more comfortable quarters. She spied a mahogany settle pushed against the slant of the stairs, an inhospitable looking thing with an ornately carved back and not a cushion to be found on the solid board seat.

While she remained standing, the tense silence was marked by the ticking of a clock in the nearest room off the foyer. After the elegance of Longfield Park, this drab little house felt oppressive, cheerless, devoid of promise or optimism or anything from which to draw courage.

But no, surely it wasn't the house at all. And was she truly so concerned about the baggage left outside? The neighborhood, while modest, seemed safe enough.

It wasn't faded wall coverings or comfortless chairs or abandoned trunks that left her feeling so empty. Something else entirely had been abandoned on the other side of that door—the life Eliza had glimpsed for a scant few days, which would haunt her the rest of her life.

She had only herself to blame. If she'd been honest with Dylan from the first . . . if she'd only . . .

She would *not* cry. *Must* not cry or she'd never stop, never move past the regret.

Footfalls sounded on the upper floor, becoming louder as they negotiated the upper portion of stairs not in her view. She scrubbed a hand across her eyes and straightened her bonnet.

"Dios mio, El—" A man, not the butler this time, came to an abrupt halt on the narrow half landing. A single taper burned in a wall sconce behind him, and she could make out only the dimmest outlines against the damask wall covering. She sensed, rather than saw, a pair of dark, deep-set eyes staring down the length of the staircase. Anselmo's letter fluttered in his hand. "Who are you?"

"Mr. Raphael Mendoza de Leone?"

He descended the remainder of the stairs and stopped just beyond the bottom step. His gaze swept her several times as if he didn't quite trust his senses. He was a tall man, though not as tall as Dylan, and not nearly as young either. Yet the silver threading his chestnut hair and close-cropped beard lent an air of confidence, of conviction; the slight brackets about the mouth and eyes did not detract from handsome, dignified features.

Eliza felt the heat of his scrutiny from the top of Elizabeth's silk bonnet to the tips of her buffed leather traveling boots. He drew a heavy breath.

"I am Doctor Mendoza. And you are?" The long-ago traces of an accent clung to his words.

"I am not, as the letter says, Elizabeth Mendoza de Leone, sir. My name is Eliza Kent. I was a friend of sorts to Mrs. Mendoza, and it would not be entirely false to say she sent me to see you."

" 'Was' a friend?" The man squinted down at the letter, pinching the bridge of his nose with the thumb and forefinger of his free hand. When he looked up, his dark eyes glistened. "I know of my brother's fate. A letter arrived last week from his solicitor. But what of his wife? Has something happened to her?"

Eliza nodded gently. "If I may, sir, there is much I have to tell you."

With a wary gleam he again surveyed her. He seemed on the verge of voicing some private conclusion, but then his expression cleared. "I long to hear everything you have to say, Miss Kent. Please, won't you come up to the drawing room."

On the way up the stairs, carpeted in rose velvet worn to silver in the well-traveled center of each step, Eliza wondered at the utter silence of the house. Why had no feminine voice inquired after their unexpected visitor? Why were there no sounds of children scampering from room to room?

Perhaps his wife and children were out shopping or visiting or any number of things city people do.

At the top of the stairs he led the way into a room that hardly deserved the distinction of "drawing room." The close confines were cluttered with an unmatched assortment of chairs, side tables and a settee whose once rich brocade sagged across the cushions. Eliza stepped onto a carpet that might once have been nearly as grand as the one in the Holbrooks' drawing room, but these twisting vines and flowered medallions had long since lost their bloom.

"Please sit and take your ease." He gestured to the settee, speaking in that gently accented voice pitched pleasantly low, though not quite as deep as Dylan's. She caught herself. What point in comparing the two men? Would she spend the rest of her life comparing every man she met to Dylan Fergusson?

More than likely.

She settled at the edge of the sofa, schooling her features not to react to the sight of the upholstery's frayed edges.

"Please." It was a word he used repeatedly, habitually, as one who had been raised to always observe the rules of polite society. "How do you know my brother and his wife?"

"I did not ever meet your brother, sir." She pulled the ribbons of her bonnet loose, removed it and placed it on the nearly threadbare cushion beside her. "And his wife I knew only briefly . . . at the very end of her life."

"Then she too . . . is dead?"

Eliza nodded. "A carriage accident. Both she and her driver died, he instantly, she some hours later."

"Were you with her in the end?"

"I was." Eliza shut her eyes at the memory of both the accident and her own dishonorable decision that followed. "She died most bravely, sir. Her last words were spoken out of a sense of duty toward her husband. I didn't understand exactly, but I surmised she desperately wished to protect something of great value."

Dr. Mendoza raised his palms. "What could this be?"

"That I don't know, sir. I wish I did. Perhaps it has to do with her husband's property."

"His estate in York?"

"You know of it?"

He nodded solemnly. "Folkstone Manor. My brother's solicitor wrote that the property had been sold."

"I've brought the documents of the sale, along with other financial records."

He glanced down at the letter still in his hand. "If my brother had already sold his property, then whatever his wife meant to protect must be of some other nature. You had her luggage. Did you go through it?"

Was there a note of accusation in that resonate voice of his, or did she only imagine it out of guilt? Either way, hot color flooded her cheeks as she nodded. "I . . . did not discover anything of great value. The lady's jewelry, her personal effects. And the financial records of course."

"I should like the opportunity to look through Mrs. Mendoza's possessions, if I might."

"Whenever you wish, sir. Unless you know of more immediate family members, it is for you to say how her things are to be disposed of."

"You are too kind."

"Hardly, sir." She supposed she should mention that the dress she wore belonged to Elizabeth, and that she had set aside several of the pounds she'd found in Elizabeth's purse for her own use. She intended to pay back every penny, including the price of the dress, as soon as she found the means of doing so.

For now, the money would see her across London to the home of Helena's cousin. And when that endeavor proved less than successful, she'd still have funds to rent a cheap room somewhere while she searched for employment—any employment so long as it was honest; so long as it didn't involve selling her body or her soul.

She averted her gaze, focusing on a stack of books poking out from beneath the settee. A playbill capped the pile: *Doctor Faustus by Christopher Marlow,* the title read in bold black letters. Dozens of texts lay in haphazard stacks all about the room, like those of a scholar too consumed by his studies to bother restoring them to order. Mixed in were more playbills, and Eliza saw that several framed theater bulletins graced the walls as well.

Either he noticed her wandering gaze or read her mind, for he said, "I am a professor of European history at University College."

Eliza smiled politely, realizing that once again she found herself in vastly superior company. A man of education, and of wisdom and honor, too, she didn't doubt. "You enjoy the theater as well, I see."

"Undeniably one of my vices," he conceded with a half nod, as though it were something regrettable. Then he smiled. "I cannot help but feel I owe you a great debt, Miss . . . "

"*Missus* Kent, sir. And you owe me nothing. You see, in a strange sort of way, your sister-in-law changed my life for the better, and I felt I owed it to her to continue the mission she'd set out from York to achieve."

His brow furrowed. "Mission?"

"Yes, sir. To reconcile you with your brother. Or, at least, with his memory."

"She told you this?"

"Well . . . no, sir, not in so many words. But the letter and . . . and this." She tugged open Elizabeth's velvet reticule. Finding the golden locket inside, she held it out to him.

The lines between his eyebrows deepened as he reached for the ornament and flicked it open. He stared down at the images in his palm, then let go a breath laced with weariness. "How long ago this was. Before the war came to Spain. Years before Anselmo and I . . . argued." He flicked a glance at her as his fingers closed around the locket. "May I. . . ?"

"It is yours, sir."

He seemed about to thank her again, then nodded and tucked the locket into his coat pocket. Eliza had the distinct impression the truth had not yet sunk in, that the man had yet to grasp that these family members were truly gone, never to reenter his life again. His lips curved in a thin smile. "May I offer you some refreshment, Mrs. Kent?"

She hadn't eaten since that morning at the inn. Her stomach growled at the notion, but she shook her head. "It is growing late and I should be going."

"Nonsense. It will not take but a moment to have tea brought up." He gained his feet and crossed the room, tugging the bell pull beside the door. When he returned to his chair, he asked, "Where in London do you live?"

"I do not. I am from Yorkshire."

"Ah. Where are you staying, then? With family?" He voiced this guess with the emphasis of a statement, as if there could be no dispute as to where a woman of quality would stay.

"Not exactly." Eliza fidgeted, then admonished her hands to be still. "Perhaps you might direct me to the nearest accommodation. Modestly priced accommodation, that is."

He studied her. "Is your husband not in London with you?"

"Oh, no, sir. I'm a widow."

"Ah. Do forgive me, Mrs. Kent. And yet . . . did you not arrive here in a private coach?"

"That coach will not be returning for me."

"Then you must accept my hospitality for tonight. It is the very least I can do in return for your kindness."

"I couldn't—"

"Of course you can. I will have my housekeeper make up the guestroom. I assure you it is most comfortable."

"It isn't that, sir—"

"And in the morning, perhaps you will help me sort through my sister-in-law's belongings."

"Oh. Yes, I suppose. But what about your wife, sir? She might not—"

"I have no wife, Mrs. Kent."

This struck her something of a blow. "Don't you?"

"No. I have never been married."

Eliza schooled her jaw not to come unhinged. All this time, ever since she first found Elizabeth and read the letter, she'd formed notions about this man, about his family and the kind of life Elizabeth would have led in this very house. Until recently—just last night, in fact—Eliza had indulged in visions of just such a life for herself. So many plans she'd made . . . to be an aunt to Raphael's children, a companion to his wife . . .

She sat back, stunned. How could she, usually so practical, so levelheaded, have let her imagination run so wild? Desperation, piercing hunger and a single thread of hope, she supposed, had colored both her judgment and her common sense.

"If you are concerned about propriety," he said, misinterpreting her silence, "I can assure you the arrangements will be most proper. The guestroom is downstairs, quite close to my housekeeper's. She will be close by should you need anything in the night."

When she opened her mouth to protest again, he held up his hand and treated her to a kindly smile. "And in the morning, Mrs. Kent, perhaps you will be so good as to help me decide if Elizabeth's possessions should be donated directly to the poor, or sold first and the funds donated. I myself will of course choose a token in remembrance of the sister-in-law I never knew, and invite you to do the same."

Eliza could not find it within her heart to deny such a request, however uneasy she felt at the notion of spending the night as this man's guest. And yet, what reason did she have to distrust this scholarly gentleman?

None. It wasn't that, just as it hadn't been the house or the furniture or the unfriendly servant that oppressed her spirits.

Dylan. He would not have approved of her staying here. He would have objected, raised a fuss, insisted she leave with him. She listened in vain for that stubborn Scottish brogue and heard only the silence of Raphael Mendoza awaiting her decision.

The walls seemed to close in around her and Eliza knew she was alone, as alone as she'd been on that barren Yorkshire moor. Only more so, because now she knew the difference.

Knew what it was to have strength and honor and courage beside her, only to lose it through her own wretched failings.

The next morning, Dylan stared out his hotel window into the gray skies hooding the rooftops. For the hundredth time he wondered about that nagging sensation he couldn't shake.

Perhaps it had to do with his lodging here at the Clarendon Hotel. He might have stayed at Luke and Charity's Berkeley Square town house, as he usually did when he came to London. But after their row at Longfield and the way he'd stormed off with Elizabeth, he didn't feel he'd be a welcome guest in their home. No, he didn't feel he *deserved* to be welcome.

Especially when they'd been so right about Elizabeth. A woman with something to hide. Good God, how could he have been so deceived? Ah, but it wasn't the first time, was it?

He swung away from the window and turned into the room, staring into a hearth gone cold because he'd forgotten to stir the coals when he'd awakened. His heart felt the same. Cold and neglected and dry as ash.

Loneliness? Surely. Regret? Aye. Not to mention that twinge of conscience. He'd let Elizabeth enter Raphael Mendoza's house alone. He tried telling himself he worried for Mendoza's sake, but he couldn't quite make himself believe the man would come to any harm at Elizabeth's hands. No, in spite of everything, he feared for her. What if Mendoza turned her away? What if she were lost somewhere in London, right now, wandering the streets. . . .

He drew up straight, squinting into the hearth as if it might produce a sharper memory than the one his troubled mind conjured. Elizabeth at the door to Mendoza's house, speaking with the servant, stepping inside . . .

No, not stepping—*tripping.* She'd stumbled over her hems again. Stumbled because . . .

That was what had been nagging him, tugging at his conscience.

He sprang into motion, rummaging among the bedclothes for his coat, cloak and cravat. He tossed them all over an arm and bolted for the door.

Of course, of *course.* She'd tripped because the dress didn't fit her. None of her dresses fit her. Because they weren't hers. Dear God, she hadn't been lying, not at the end. Not when she'd tried to tell him she wasn't Elizabeth.

She wasn't. She really wasn't.

Eliza arose early the next morning. She'd slept fitfully at best, despite the bed proving comfortable, the room secure and the housekeeper a mere stone's toss away.

She simply longed to quit this house, to put an end to the false life she'd been leading and start anew, no matter what that meant. It wasn't enough to be Eliza Kent again. Being under Raphael Mendoza's roof, maintaining this last tie to Elizabeth, only forestalled the moment she would take her rightful place in the world.

Breakfast was brought to her room, a generous plate of eggs, blood pudding and oatcakes. She ate quickly but consumed every last crumb. Who knew when her next full meal would come? Then she straightened the bedclothes, smoothed her skirts and readied her few remaining things for her departure.

That amounted to precious little, merely the contents of Elizabeth's reticule, her shawl and bonnet. She'd chosen a traveling dress of amber bombazine, for the sturdy fabric would help keep her warm should she find herself without shelter in the coming days.

Eliza turned toward the bedroom door and experienced a moment of panic, of defenseless vulnerability. Elizabeth's luggage had become a kind of arsenal between her and the world. It had given her a sense of identity, property, significance.

When she walked out the front door of this house, she'd have the clothes on her back and nothing more, nothing to distinguish her from London's homeless and hungry. Or London's whores.

No, nothing but her determination never to fall so low again. Never to allow anyone to shove her into the gutter.

For Dylan. Yes, she'd do it for him for she wanted—needed—to make him proud of her, even if she never saw him again. Even if he wouldn't care anyway. He thought her a murderess? She'd show him. From now on her life would be a matter of pride, a lesson in honor, because . . . because . . .

The convictions dissolved into stinging tears. She sank to the edge of the bed, head on her knees, shoulders shaking with the weight of her sobs. For the first time in many days, she thought of Nathan's rusted old rifle. If she had only angled it in such a way and perhaps used a stick to push the trigger . . .

No.

Her head came up. Her shoulders squared. She placed her feet firmly on the floor and stood. All this time she'd thought she heard God laughing at her. Mocking. Well, perhaps He had been. Oh, not because He despised her, but because she'd failed to listen and understand. He'd spared her life on the moors, then given her a new one. Not Elizabeth's, but her own. He'd shown her good, decent people and, however briefly, the love of a man so honorable, so filled with integrity her very soul had stood still in astonishment.

Now, finally, she heard the message. It wasn't laughter. It was God shouting down from heaven. *Stop feeling sorry for yourself, Eliza Kent. Be who you are and live your life.*

All right then. She lifted a corner of the counterpane and wiped her tears away. Raphael Mendoza had requested her help in sorting through Elizabeth's things. And so she would. At the same time, she would tell him about poor John Howitt and suggest attempting to find his family if he had one.

As she turned into the dining room, where Dr. Mendoza's

servants had brought the trunks, Eliza came to an abrupt halt. A hand flew to her lips. Elizabeth's elegant gowns were strewn everywhere, her jewelry scattered across the dining table. Her dainty shoes and boots had been tossed willy-nilly on the floor, caskets were upended, pouches turned inside out, underthings flung over chairs.

And there, just a few feet from the door, Raphael Mendoza knelt before one of the open trunks, his head and shoulders all but out of sight inside. How dare he treat a departed woman's possessions so disrespectfully? The gasp that escaped Eliza's lips held far more outrage than shock.

At the sound of it, the man's head emerged from the trunk. His dark eyes glared at her from above the raised lid. "Where in God's name are they?"

CHAPTER 17

"What?" Eliza backed away, frightened by the venom in Raphael Mendoza's voice, by the rancor in his face. He certainly hadn't looked or sounded so . . . so predatory last night.

"I said where are they." In an instant he was on his feet and advancing toward her. Eliza backed across the foyer until her shoulder blades came up against the stair railing. Raphael bore down on her, one hand outstretched.

His fingers closed around her neck, pinning her to the banister. "What have you done with them?"

"I . . . " She coughed, struggled for breath. His grip eased slightly, enough to allow speech but not escape. "I don't know what you're talking about. I swear. Tell me what you want and maybe I can help."

"Ah, you are going to help, are you?" His olive features showed no trace of the handsome dignity of yesterday, but hovered close to hers with a fierce, florid scowl.

She struggled not to turn away, not to show fear. "I will if you'll explain what you—"

His hand released her neck and flew to her shoulder. He heaved her away from the banister and propelled her back into the dining room. She stumbled through the doorway, came down on one knee, then pushed past the pain to gain her feet.

Turning, she faced him, steeling herself not to cower in the face of a wrath she didn't understand. He strode into the room and slammed the door.

"The crest and the stone. Where are they?"

When she remained mute, a cruel smile curled his lip. "Ah, do not play the ignorant with me. Elizabeth told you, did she not? The thing she wished to protect."

"She never spoke of a crest. She only said—" Eliza's heart slammed beneath her corset stays. Could it be? That broken, worthless-looking trinket she'd given to William?

Given to William. Good heavens.

Raphael wrapped his fingers in her hair and tugged, angling her face beneath his own. "You know where they are. I see the truth in your eyes. Tell me what you have done with them."

He yanked again, bringing tears to her eyes. "I don't have them."

"Liar."

"No. I did have the crest, or at least part of it. I-I didn't know what it was. It was broken and . . . ouch!"

"Not broken, you little idiot. Severed. Intentionally. Now tell me what you did with it."

"I gave it to a little boy."

His free hand once more found purchase around her neck while his other tightened in her hair until her scalp prickled with a thousand pinpoints. His warm breath grazed her cheek as he murmured, "What little boy?"

She almost spoke the Duke of Wakefield's name, but some instinct cautioned against mentioning her connection to the Holbrooks. At least not yet. "The son of a friend. In the town of Wakefield."

"Are you mad?" He thrust her away so abruptly she fell against one of the dining chairs, sending it toppling and her with it. Her shoulder shrieked with pain, her side throbbed ominously. Raphael stood over her. "Loathsome baggage . . . ." His features sharpened. "Did you give this child the stone as well?"

"There were stones in the crest. I assumed they were worthless glass."

"I don't care about those. What of the largest stone? The loose one."

"I don't know what you mean."

"Are we going to begin again?" Reaching down, he caught her wrist and hauled her to her feet, sending blasts of pain to her shoulder and ribs. She no sooner established her balance than he released her and backhanded her across the cheek.

Agony exploded across her face, dizzying and blinding. She reeled backward, but Raphael's hand closed like a vise around her arm, preventing her falling. He dragged her close.

"I shall ask one more time. Where is the stone?"

"I swear I don't know. Perhaps Elizabeth threw it away—"

"Elizabeth would never—"

Raphael fell abruptly silent, and realization thrust Eliza a suffocating blow. "Dear God." Her eyes widened with horror. "You *knew* her."

His scowl blackened like the devil's. "I do not know who you are or what you want. I do not particularly care. I want the crest and the stone. You shall pay dearly unless you find a way to deliver both."

"All right. I can get you the crest, I promise." Eliza forced the next words past a growing lump of dread. "But I never saw any other stone but the ones in the crest. I swear."

"Have you not?" It was not a question that expected an answer. Mendoza's gaze slithered over her bodice, sending a chill across her shoulders. Before she knew what he was about, he gripped the front of her gown. The buttons down the front gave beneath a violent yank, pattering to the floor as the dress ripped free of her shoulders.

The thrust threw Eliza off balance. She wobbled, groped, pitched to her knees. Mendoza followed, relentless in his mad bid to molest her. She tried pushing those violating hands away, but he was too strong, too determined. He slapped her again and then, to her horror, groped inside her corset. He shoved her breasts this way and that, reaching beneath them.

Just as suddenly, he released her with a shove. As she lay,

shaking and dazed and trying to hold together her ruined dress, Mendoza pushed to his feet.

Jaw clamped to control its trembling, she glowered up at him. "I told you I didn't have it."

"A search of the things still in your room shall determine what you do and do not have."

"You won't find anything there either." She sat up and shoved her palms across her cheeks, scrubbing away tears of pain and fear. "I can't give you something I never had."

"Where is she?"

"Who?"

"Elizabeth, you fool. Where is she buried?"

"I told you. In Yorkshire. A village called Heverton Gorse."

"Then to Yorkshire I must go."

She swept a tangle of hair from her face. "Dear Lord, you'd dig her up?"

"If I must."

"What is this stone, that you'd sink so low for it?"

He aimed such seething anger down at her she ducked half under the dining table. "That is not for you to know. But what to do with you while I am away? I can't keep you here. A fellow professor or a student might come calling . . . ."

"Let me go. I know nothing of your wretched stone or your damnable problems."

"Let you go? Oh, no, Mrs. Kent. If I do not find what I am looking for, you shall suffer for my disappointment. Suffer greatly." He strode from the room, locking her inside.

"I need to speak with Mrs. Mendoza."

"There is no one presently at home, sir."

The servant's impassive reply sent a rush of blood pounding at Dylan's temples. "I brought Elizabeth Mendoza here yesterday, damn it, and I demand to see her this instant."

The man sniffed. "That person is no longer here."

"What the devil do you mean, 'that person'?" He resisted

the urge to push past and storm into the house shouting her name. Whatever her name might be. "How dare you—"

"Smitherson, what is all the commotion about?"

The slight but undeniably Spanish tones undercut Dylan's ire as a second man entered the foyer from a room off the hall. The sight of his dark eyes and olive complexion sparked a deduction.

Raphael Mendoza.

"This gentleman wishes to speak with Mrs. Mendoza, sir." The servant took no pains to conceal his disdain. "I told him there is no such person here."

The other man shook his head. "Smitherson, really, what am I to do with you? Invite the gentleman in."

With no subtle show of reluctance, Smitherson opened the door wider. Dylan stepped into a grotto of a foyer, far too small to accommodate three grown men. Smitherson gave a curt bow and retreated down the corridor.

"Won't you come up to the drawing room, Mr. ah . . . "

"Fergusson. Dylan Fergusson."

"Ah, Mr. Fergusson. I am Raphael Mendoza de Leone. You must forgive my man. I told him earlier I did not wish to be disturbed. He can sometimes be . . . overvigilant in his duties."

"Where is—"

"Please, Mr. Fergusson, come upstairs where we might talk privately and more comfortably.

Mendoza led the way to a shambles of a room, a room that could not have seen a maid's services in years.

"Do sit down, Mr. Fergusson. Have you broken your fast this morning? Shall I ring for refreshments?"

"Don't bother." He took a seat on the room's only settee, a threadbare brocade that creaked beneath his weight. "I merely wish to see—"

"Mrs. Mendoza . . . yes." Mendoza settled into an armchair and tented his fingers beneath his chin. "Is that who she told you she was?"

"Yes, at first, at any rate. She might also be using . . . " He trailed off, realizing how it was going to sound. As if he were addled and she a charlatan, a criminal. He didn't know for sure she wasn't. "She might also be using the name Eliza Kent."

Mendoza nodded, his eyes hooded, a resigned smile hovering on his lips. "That is the name she told me.

"You don't believe her?"

"How can I tell what to believe? The woman gained entry to my home using a letter from my deceased brother. Until she told me otherwise, I believed her to be my sister-in-law."

"She did eventually tell you the truth, then."

"Is it the truth?" His features guarded, Mendoza shook his head. "Tell me, Mr. Fergusson, what do you know about this woman?"

A fair question, and not easily answered. He believed she was not Elizabeth Mendoza, believed it to the very tips of his toes. But of Eliza Kent he knew nothing whatsoever. Except perhaps that her husband died after being gored by a bull. Or . . .

Nathan and Eliza Kent. Those were the names she'd given the victims of the accident, the names that marked their graves. Could Eliza's husband have been the coachman who died, and she herself Elizabeth Mendoza's lady's maid?

Mendoza cleared his throat. "Whoever the woman is, sir, she is a thief. That much is certain."

"I can scarce believe that." Or could he? Hadn't Eliza stolen not only Elizabeth Mendoza's belongings, but her identity as well? "Did she not come here to return your sister-in-law's effects to you?"

"Did she?" An ironic expression tugged at the corners of Mendoza's mouth. "Certain things have gone missing. Things that belonged to my brother and should by rights now belong to me."

"What things? Perhaps I can help."

"They are nothing of consequence to anyone but a Mendoza." The man inclined his head with a pained expression.

"The value is almost entirely sentimental, but to a man living far from the country of his birth, such trifles are worth more than all the riches of the world. But this is not your concern, Mr. Fergusson. Not your problem."

"Your lost property may not be my concern, sir, but the fate of an innocent woman is."

"And what makes you so certain she is innocent?"

"I know her." Dylan pushed to his feet. No matter her outward deceptions, everything else about Eliza—her wide-eyed amazement at Longfield Park, her generosity toward the children, her ability to ride astride . . . and the passion he'd felt come alive within his arms . . . those were all real. He would wager his life on it.

He'd already wagered his heart and lost it . . . to the woman now calling herself Eliza.

He met Mendoza's gaze with one as steady as he could manage in light of his feverish need to find her. "I am as certain of her innocence as I am that she is not your sister-in-law. If you know where she has gone, you must tell me."

"Indeed, Mr. Fergusson, I believe I can tell you exactly where the woman has gone." Calmly, slowly, the Spaniard gripped the arms of his chair and came to his feet. "If I heard the constable correctly, he has taken her to Newgate Prison, where she will remain until my property is restored to me."

Eliza pulled her feet up beneath her and huddled closer to the jagged stone wall. It was cold, so cold here, even with so many others crammed into the choked confines of the cell.

Ragged, dirty bodies ranged along the flagstone floor, talking, whispering, coughing. At least two dozen women inhabited the cell—old, young, pregnant, sick, and some, she suspected, who were dying. There were children, too, filthy ragamuffins who scavenged the slimy floor for crumbs and worse. Eliza tried not to look at them, tried not to envision their fates if they didn't escape this place soon.

Nor did she wish to dwell on her own fate, for what escape could there be for her? In a final warning before the constables dragged her away, Dr. Mendoza had threatened to press full charges if she didn't return the parts of the crest to him immediately. Before she quitted his house, she had written a letter to the Holbrooks at Longfield Park asking for the half of the crest she'd given William, but how could she return a stone she knew nothing about?

She tried but could not quite shake the memory of the scaffolding she had passed on her way into the prison. Did they still hang thieves? Would they, even if Dr. Mendoza recovered his crest and that damned stone? Who would speak in her defense?

Dylan could have no idea she was here . . . and even if he did, would he care? Justice would find her, he'd said. Indeed it had, more complete and appalling than she ever imagined.

She had thought London a loud, dirty, frightening place but this—this place was hellish. This would drive a person mad before too long. She shivered and drew her knees up close, pressing them to her chest. Someone had taken her shawl when she first arrived. They said it would be returned, then later laughed when she asked for it.

After searching her reticule, Dr. Mendoza had thrust it back at her, money and all. But now her money was all gone, used up on food rations, a blanket and the right not to be shackled to the wall like the wretched souls in the first cell she had passed on way to this one.

Her blanket hadn't lasted much longer than her money. She'd given it only minutes ago to a shivering child who had crawled in beside her, a waif of a girl no more than six or seven, all huge, liquid eyes and hollow cheeks and pointed chin. Eliza had taken one look into the shadows flitting across those wan features and saw hunger, exhaustion and the limits of endurance. She knew the signs, for she had once worn them as she now wore Elizabeth's flowered muslin, the dress Raphael had tossed at her after he tore the amber bombazine.

With a resigned sigh she had tightened the ragged blanket around her shoulders for one last instant, braced herself for the ensuing chill, and then wrapped it around the little girl.

"You have it," she'd whispered, afraid to speak louder for frightening so frail a creature. "I'm not cold at all."

No sooner had she tucked the blanket beneath child's chin than a jubilant smile had broken out across those haggard features. Eliza experienced a moment of contentment, reminding herself there could still exist the odd moment of cheer in this dismal world. But the child was already on her feet, already yanking the blanket from her lean figure. She hopped over several pairs of legs as she made her way across the cell.

" 'Ere, Mum, got another one." She handed the blanket to a hulk of a woman with a face that looked carved from a dried apple. The woman proceeded to hawk the scrap of wool for a fraction of what Eliza had spent for it.

Indignation propelled her to her feet. "Give it back—"

"You'll shut your yap if you know what's good for you." So swiftly Eliza barely followed the movement of her hand, the woman whisked a slender dagger from her bodice and waved it with a menacing flourish. Those nearest her fell silent and eased away. The woman's lips pulled to a snarl. "Nobody forced you to give it away. You did that yourself."

Half tucked behind her mother's begrimed skirts, the child smiled at Eliza, her eyes filled with the calculation of someone decades older.

After that Eliza pressed tight to the corner, her cheek turned to the harsh stone. A person could go mad . . .

"You there. In the frippery."

She glanced up, more an instinctive reaction to the grating summons than an assumption the guard meant her. And yet, from between bars of the cell door, one crooked finger poked in her direction. She pressed a hand to her chest and mouthed, *Me?*

"Aye, you." His sneer revealed missing front teeth. "Get your lazy arse up and follow me."

He led her along a dank corridor, barely wide enough for her to evade the hands groping from inside the cells. She pretended not to hear the shouted oaths, the licentious calls as they passed through the men's quarters. She ran to keep up, feeling the need to duck beneath the pinched shadows above her head.

An iron door opened onto the prison bailey, empty but for a handful of ravens, their black bodies dotting the ground like bits of discarded coal. They squawked and flapped away as Eliza and her guide traipsed among them toward another building, another iron door. He called into a grating set at eye level, and the door opened from within.

"In 'ere."

Up a flight of winding steps, down a stone corridor. There were no cells here, only solid oak doors lining the hall like sentries. One creaked open as she passed by, a single eye peering out at her through the narrow gap. Further along, a door stood wide and voices tumbled out. Eliza gazed into the room to see, to her astonishment, a small crush. Men and women, all finely dressed, stood around the room or lounged in easy chairs sipping tea. The aroma of freshly backed sweet rolls curled beneath Eliza's nose.

She hadn't expected madness to take hold quite this soon, but surely her eyes and nose deceived her.

The guard came to a halt before one of the doors. He waited, staring at Eliza as if she should understand what came next, what she should do, why he had brought her here.

When she didn't move he clutched her shoulder. "Inside, slattern. Can't stand about all day."

Swinging the door open with one hand, he propelled her inside. The door slammed at her back. She stumbled, caught her balance and stood dumfounded.

The room was not large, barely more than a quarter of the one she'd inhabited at Longfield Park. Like the cell she'd just left, the walls and floor were of the same inhospitable stone. But a mere two strides in, her feet met with the muffling cushion of a rug, faded, treadworn, but undeniably there to ward off the stony chill. And a bed, a real one hung with draperies, occupied a corner of the room. Beside it stood a wash stand with pitcher and bowl. And before a glowing brazier, an oak table offered—good heavens—platters of fruit, bread and cheese.

Yes, madness could be the only explanation.

"I would have been here sooner." The bed curtain stirred and, like an illusion conjured by the most forlorn hopes, a cloaked figure stepped out from behind one corner of the bed. His hand made a sweep of the room. "I had to make arrangements first. They won't let me take you from here—not yet— but I could make your stay a damn sight more bearable."

"Dylan." Eliza ran until she hit the wall of his chest and his arms closed around her. "I can't believe you're here. How is it possible?"

"Did you think I'd stay away forever? Ah, Eliza. Eliza Kent." Her name, formed so softly on his lips, was an explanation and an affirmation and a pledge. Her breath hitched in a burning throat. Dylan's hands framed her face and raised it from his shirtfront. "Mendoza told me where I'd find you."

"You believe me now."

"I suspect Elizabeth Mendoza's dresses fit her rather better than they fit you."

She laughed and shivered against him.

Without a word he released her and shrugged out of his cloak. It engulfed her like a swirl of ink only warm, soft . . . miraculous. His arms quickly followed, setting her quite firmly on heaven's most glorious cloud. He chuckled against her hair. "When will I ever learn to bring two?"

The jest traveled deep inside, tugging at that place where love and fear and joy and despair all dwelled, awakening all at once. She clung to him, pressing her face to the warm strength of his neck.

"Why did you pretend to be someone else?" he demanded, giving her a shake. "Why do such a foolhardy thing?"

"I was desperate. I wanted to live. I knew it was cheating but—"

"You didn't need to cheat, you little fool." His voice ran hoarse. "All you had to do was wait on that hillside for me. I came, didn't I? I rescued you."

"But I didn't deserve you. I—" Her words were stopped by the press of his mouth, by his incoherent murmurs against her lips.

His arms groped for better purchase and once found, he lifted her and swung her onto the bed. His lips became hot embers on her face, her neck, across her shoulders. "Do you think it matters to me if you are a lady or her maid?" He pulled back and his gaze, gray-green like the misty Yorkshire moors, held the quivering intensity of a lightning charge. "Did you think I wouldn't understand? Is my heart as unreadable as all that?"

There was something wrong in what he said; she felt it like a treacherous bog swirling round her ankles. Before she could fathom the cause, he swore and dropped his mouth to her bosom, sending hot desire melting through her. Another instant and nothing else mattered, not Elizabeth or the Mendozas or the charges against her. Only this—the sensation of Dylan's touch on her body, crushing her to the velvet lining of his cloak, still redolent with the heat and scent of him.

Her fingers wrapped in his hair. Roughly she steered his mouth to hers. His lips tasted of coffee, his tongue of passion. Eliza set about consuming the flavor, wanting all of it, wishing to drown in it.

She was only half aware of his hands tearing away at her clothing, of her own grappling with his as a frenzied need to feel him inside her took control. There came a rush of brazier-warmed air on her legs and the caress of a heated sigh against her breasts as Dylan shoved the last of her clothing aside. Her legs opened.

She heard his voice, wordless, resonant, like a rumble from the earth. Then he was inside her and there was nothing else, no past, no future, no prison walls holding her. There was only the force of his thrusts, the blending of their gasps, the rising fever of their joined bodies.

And riding the undercurrent of her ecstasy, a single thought soared. *He believes me.*

For that alone, Eliza loved him.

CHAPTER 18

Through a veil of Eliza's hair, Dylan watched frail sunlight reach timidly through the window grating set high on the wall. He inhaled the fragrance of their lovemaking and struggled against the sense of dread gathering in the pit of his stomach.

He hadn't yet told Eliza the thing he'd learned upon arriving at the prison, the hideous surprise awaiting him in the warden's office.

But tell her he must and now, before any more time passed. Before the guards came to convey her to trial, where she'd be forced to face this latest development alone and unprepared.

"Eliza, are you awake?"

The fingers of her right hand flexed against his chest, pulling at the hairs till his skin pricked. "Don't leave yet," she whispered.

She had guessed partly right. He would have to leave shortly to begin searching for a way to exonerate her. "You'll stay here in this room while I'm gone," he assured her, well aware that he continued to put off telling her the truth.

"This *cell,* you mean." She raised up and swept back her hair, uncovering both their faces. Myriad emotions tossed in her great golden eyes. "Thanks to you, I will be safer here, and fed and warm and dry. But this is still a prison, and here I must remain until your sister sends the crest I gave William, and until I can find a way to prove I never had the stone Dr. Mendoza spoke of."

His heart gave a twist. He pushed upright against the headboard. "Lass, has no one explained the charges against you?"

"Not in so many words, but before Dr. Mendoza sent for the authorities, he accused me of stealing from him. Then he made me write a letter to Longfield Park, asking that the crest be returned to him." She shook her head, and her hair streamed over one shoulder to shower across her breast. "I thought it worthless, merely a jeweler's mold, or I'd never have given it to William. Will he be terribly disappointed to give it back, do you think?"

"Eliza, William's disappointment or the lack of it is the least of your worries." He reached for her hand, drawing it to his lips while he battled his aversion to what he must tell her next. "Even if Mendoza recovers the items he claims are missing, you will not gain your freedom."

"What are you saying?"

"My darling . . . you are accused of the murder of Anselmo Mendoza."

The color leached from her face. "But . . . did you not tell me it was Elizabeth who is suspected of poisoning her husband?"

"Aye. And the authorities believe you are she."

The jolt that rippled through her shook his arm and traveled to his heart. "But Mendoza knows I am not. And you know I am not. You must tell the magistrate—"

He shook his head. "I did. It is not Raphael Mendoza who has brought these murder charges against you. He merely accuses you of theft. The authorities here had already been alerted to the possibility that Elizabeth poisoned her husband and fled from York to London. And they feel there is enough evidence to prove you are she."

"Who alerted them?"

"I don't yet know. But I promise you I'll find out."

"But . . . oh, dear Lord." She let loose a groan of dismay

and pressed her hands to the sides of her head. "The letter I sent to Longfield. I signed it in Elizabeth's name knowing to do otherwise would only cause confusion." Her brow puckered. "It's one more testimony to condemn me."

He drew her closer. "We will not let it. You must tell me everything you know about Elizabeth Mendoza."

"I know so little . . . Oh, there is something." Her eyes narrowed. "According to Anselmo's letter, his wife and his brother had never met. But Raphael Mendoza knew her, Dylan. I'm certain of it."

"You believe they were acquainted without Anselmo's knowledge?"

She nodded.

"Then Raphael has lied, and Elizabeth lied to Anselmo. Which certainly suggests she and Raphael conspired against him. I don't know how easy it will be to prove, but if they knew each other here in London, there should be some evidence of it somewhere." He smiled, hoping to offer encouragement.

"Here in London," she repeated somewhat absently. Then her eyebrows surged. "At the theater, perhaps?"

The suggestion triggered an unsavory memory—he'd met Isabel at the theater—but he pushed it aside. "Why do you ask?"

"Were you in Dr. Mendoza's drawing room?"

"I was, but—"

"Didn't you see all the handbills, the theater signs hanging on the walls? He told me the theater is one of his vices."

"And no doubt not his only vice. Perhaps this Elizabeth was an actress."

Eliza nodded emphatically. "That would certainly aid her in deceiving Anselmo. But how to prove it? There must be hundreds of actresses in London."

"And nearly as many theaters." The waxing optimism of a moment ago faded. Eliza, too, looked crestfallen. He cupped her cheek. "We're not giving up, lass. Tell me about Elizabeth. When did you first enter into her employ?"

"I never worked for Elizabeth."

"Of course you did. Your husband was driving the carriage."

She shook her head. "No. The driver was a man named John Howitt. I never knew either of them. I just . . . happened to be there at the time of the accident."

"What were you doing there?"

"I was . . . nothing." She looked away and shrugged. "I was just there."

"Just hanging about the moors?" Sudden perplexity sent his hand scraping through his hair. "Eliza, there isn't a farm or village for miles. If you're trying to distance yourself from the crime of murder, this is not the way to do it."

"I'm telling you the truth." Her expression turned indignant. She began tugging away from him, putting several inches of mattress between them. "I know it sounds mad. Perhaps I *was* mad at the time. But yes, I was out on the moors by myself when the accident occurred. I ran to help them, but it was already too late."

"And then you took her things and pretended to be her?" It wasn't a question, just a recounting of the bewildering details. "Eliza, do you know how *that* will look to the authorities? Why, they'll think . . . "

The rest hung in the air between them, laden with implications.

"Go ahead and say it." Her golden eyes crystallized to a cold, metallic sheen. "They'll think I had something to do with *her* death too. Hers *and* Anselmo's."

"The broken whiffletree and linchpin. Luke said they appeared tampered with."

"Yes." She sounded almost pleased but for the brittle edge to her voice. Her jaw squared. "It would seem I am already tried and convicted, by you *and* your brother-in-law."

"Lass, you needn't turn your anger on me. Based on the tale you spun, of course I assumed you were Elizabeth's lady's maid. If you say there is no link between you and the Mendozas I'll believe you. But it isn't me you need convince. The courts can convict you on precious little evidence. If the barristers are satisfied with that evidence, they will probe no further. They will not search for witnesses who can prove you are not Elizabeth."

"Will they let you produce one?"

Would they? Could a Scottish farmer hold sway in an English courtroom? Perhaps not, but he was not without resources. "If such a witness exists, I'll produce him and make them listen. Perhaps someone in your home village in Yorkshire?"

"No. I left Flaxborough nearly a year ago. There is no one there who can attest to my whereabouts in the weeks leading up to Anselmo's death."

"You didn't drop off the face of the earth during those months. Surely there is someone somewhere who can vouch for you."

"That time was . . . difficult," she said. "In truth I do not believe there is anyone who would be of much help. Oh, but there is a physician from York who knows of a certainty I am not Elizabeth, and I'm sure he could also attest to the fact that I never worked at Folkstone Manor. He told me he was Anselmo's friend and . . . "

"When did he tell you this?"

She hesitated, bottom lip inching between her teeth. Then, in the quietest of murmurs, "At the inn in Heverton Gorse. The morning we left. He'd come searching for Elizabeth."

"By St. George, woman, no wonder you were in such a hurry to be off." He remembered how vehemently she had insisted, even when he told her there wasn't so much as a wagon to be hired for the journey. He released a sigh. "Tell me his name."

"I don't know it. He never told me."

"How can I find a man if I don't know his name?"

She made a groping gesture at the air. "He's from York . . . ."

"There must be scores of physicians in York."

Her head went down, and her next words came from within the curtain of her hair. "Then there is someone else who can confirm that I am not Elizabeth, that I am neither a lady nor a lady's maid."

"All right then. Tell me *his* name and I will ride through the night to bring him here."

"You know of him." She lifted her face, now etched with defiance. "And he, my dear Mr. Fergusson, knows well enough of me. You will find him in Heverton Gorse, at the Raven's Perch Inn."

Her next words sucked the air from his lungs.

"He is the innkeeper, and he can tell you exactly who—and what—I am."

Dylan pressed his fists into the coach seat, ignored the bright foliage passing the windows on either side of the road and wondered if he would ever breathe freely again. The journey back to Longfield Park had done nothing so far to ease the grip on his chest, the one encompassing both heart and lungs. In fact, the nearer he approached his sister's home—in her husband's coach, he might remind himself—the tighter that stranglehold became.

Only now did he understand the magnitude of his transgressions against the Holbrooks, including how completely he had misread the woman he now knew as Eliza. Only now did he understand the extent to which she had deceived them all. And only now did he comprehend the depth and breadth of his feelings for her, feelings that persisted despite the reality that he must give her up.

Who and what I am. The innkeeper at the Raven's Perch Tavern knew, and now Dylan knew, too.

I could not have been traveling as Elizabeth's maid, you see, because the night before the accident, I went to the

Raven's Perch for the sole purpose of selling myself to the highest bidder.

He'd felt ill when she spoke those words, *wanted* to be ill, to purge his mind and body of a sickening truth about the woman he had been determined to marry. But how—good God, *how*?—could he bring such a woman back to Longfield Park as his wife, into the bosom of his family, all those faithful, genuine Holbrooks whom he always complained of, groaned over, and loved more dearly than his own life?

Now you know the truth of it. A farmwife turned laundry maid turned whore turned thief and murderess. Take my advice, Mr. Fergusson, get out now, while you still can.

He *had* got out—he'd run, out of the privileged quarters, across the bailey, past the Press Yard and the Keeper's Lodge with its perverse marketplace offering luxuries to the condemned. He'd kept on running, out through the Debtor's Gate and onto Old Bailey Lane, shutting his eyes as he hurried past the scaffolds, empty now but for the ghosts of the poor souls who had swung there through the years.

He'd run from the truth, from the ugliness of it. He hadn't been able to run from the pain in Eliza's voice, from the hopelessness tarnishing her golden eyes. He carried that pain with him now, mixed with his own, a tangled confusion of betrayal and hurt that seemed to have taken up permanent residence inside him.

He had been traveling with the windows open because the slap of cool air on his cheeks helped him hang onto what was real, what was now, rather than wallow in his past illusions of Elizabeth. But it was growing late and the sun had dipped below the trees. The air snapped with cold, and with no small twinge of irony he realized he'd left his cloak with Eliza.

The coach listed suddenly and he slid to one side. The view out the windows revealed Longfield's carefully manicured drive. He was here. In minutes he'd have to face his family.

He knew what he should say. The lines had rehearsed themselves in his head the whole way there.

*Forgive me. I was wrong. You were right. I won't make the
same mistakes again.*

Upon being admitted to the Grand Hall he asked the footman not to announce him. The man showed no surprise.
Dylan was, after all, part of the family.

Family. The very word sank like lead to the pit of his stomach. He had very nearly betrayed this family's trust.

I'm sorry. I was wrong. The words created a cadence in his
head that matched the rhythm of his footsteps through the
house. He made his way to the conservatory, where he'd been
told he would find everyone.

. . . A laundry maid turned whore . . . The words raked his
soul like the swipe of a doxy's fingernails.

As his shoes clicked against the conservatory's mosaic
floor, his nephew spotted him. "Uncle Dylan!"

A burst of blossoms went flying into the air and showered
the floor as William launched himself across the room. He
came at a dead run and propelled himself off his feet. Dylan
had no choice but to open his arm and feign an enthusiasm
that matched the boy's.

Lena and Lara came next, thudding into his legs and plucking at his trousers for their turn to be hoisted into the air. The
Westies, meanwhile, attacked his shoes. An instant later
David Holbrook came barreling around a row of potted
palms, and Dylan was obliged to set the twins down beside
their brother, catch their cousin up and swing him once
around in a wide arc.

From within the clamoring jumble of children and dogs, he
was aware of the adults at the wrought iron garden table pushing to their feet and making their way toward him, of excla-
mations of welcome he didn't deserve. Not this time.

His gaze found Charity's first. It was an instant of com-
munication perhaps only achievable by siblings, a wordless
acknowledgment of his transgressions, of her displeasure and

hurt. But as Sir Joshua shook his hand, Dolly kissed his cheek and Lady Mary surveyed him through her quizzing glass, the tight line of Charity's mouth softened. She offered a nod of acceptance, a shrug of forgiveness, and he drew his first complete breath in hours.

His gaze then fell upon Luke, who had been right about so many things for so many years. Dylan had believed Luke wanted to change him, make him a fitting brother-in-law for a duke. And he had parried every good suggestion with the headstrong indifference of a stubborn Scottish farm boy.

Only now did he realize Luke's purpose. Power. Not to rule over people—that was never Luke's way—but to protect them. To ensure the safety of those he loved, those in his care. Luke saw this as his greatest responsibility and his greatest privilege as both duke and head of the Holbrook family. He had merely wished the same for Dylan, and for the family that would one day be his.

The last of his youthful bluster now billowed away beneath the Duke of Wakefield's regard. Dylan swallowed a lingering taste of foolish pride and stepped forward from the gaggle of family surrounding him. The words of apology he'd rehearsed on the way there, however, fled his mind. He simply said, "I need your help."

Luke clapped a hand to his shoulder. "You shall have it."

Dylan reclined against the camelback sofa and pressed the heels of his hands to his eyes. His mind reeled with the revelations of the past twenty-four hours and from far too little sleep. Now, a day after quitting London, he was back in the city, this time in the home of Helena Holbrook's cousin, Tess Emerson.

That lady sat opposite him in a Louis Quinze armchair on the far side of the sofa table. Her husband, Charles Emerson, stood beside the hearth, elbow propped on the carved mantel. Luke and Wesley threatened to pace holes into the drawing room carpet while Helena was just then kneeling on the floor to tempt a fleecy cloud of a cat out from beneath the chaise longue.

Charity occupied the seat beside Dylan on the sofa. He felt uneasy about her having made the journey here. In fact he'd urged her to remain at Longfield, but she insisted being four months gone with child hardly precluded her from traveling. Stubborn of her . . . and he damn well appreciated it.

Mrs. Emerson leaned forward to place her teacup on the sofa table. Beside it, the ebony metal of the crest they brought with them from Longfield absorbed the firelight without a trace of warmth. Mrs. Emerson's brow crinkled in concentration. "You say Raphael Mendoza knew his sister-in-law?"

Dylan nodded. "Eliza seems certain of it. Something he said, a slip of the tongue. It's also apparent from his letter that Anselmo had no idea the two had ever met."

Mrs. Emerson sat back uttering a thoughtful *hmm*.

"Eliza also remembered seeing a good deal of theater literature in the man's drawing room," Dylan added. "Considering the role Elizabeth was playing as Anselmo's wife, there's a good chance she might have been an actress."

"Let us hope so. That would certainly narrow down our search," Charity commented.

"We'll need to know which theaters are popular among the university set." Charles Emerson paused to study the bronze mantel clock. He slipped his watch from his waistcoat pocket, flipped it open, and used his forefinger to push the big hand on the mantel clock ahead several minutes. Then he faced the others. "You say he's a professor of history. Then chances are he favors the classics—Shakespeare and Marlowe of course, but probably the Greek dramatists as well. That will narrow the possibilities considerably."

"The search could still take weeks." Dylan didn't mean to sound cynical, but Eliza's trial could begin at any time unless Luke managed to procure a delay.

"I know we're pressed for time." Emerson gave him a sympathetic look. "If anybody can do this, it's my wife and her battalion of spies."

Aye, Dylan knew the truth about Mrs. Emerson, about how she had once prowled London's most squalid streets in the guise of the mysterious Midnight Marauder. While society believed the Marauder to be murdering young prostitutes, she had in fact been rescuing such women from a hellish existence and reeducating them, preparing them for respectable and successful lives.

Women . . . such as Eliza. The thought made him queasy. Gripping the padded arm of the sofa, he pushed out a breath and with it a lingering, irrational wish to make Eliza Kent his wife. There was much he was willing to overlook, but this . . .

"Darling, you give me much too much credit." Mrs. Emerson smiled fondly up at her husband. "If anyone can obtain the answers we seek, it is Fabrice and Gwennie. They are the Midnight Marauder now."

Aye, Helena, too, claimed her cousin had retired from such dangerous endeavors prior to the birth of her child, leaving the Marauder's quest in the capable hands of her man-of-all-work and his wife. Luke, however, had more than once voiced his suspicion that Tess Emerson kept her finger close on the pulse of the Marauder's activities.

"It is through their contacts," Mrs. Emerson continued with the air of a seasoned professional, "that we'll find the link between Raphael and Elizabeth Mendoza, if in fact one exists. I should think by spreading the word of this trial, we may be able to flush out knowledgeable individuals. In my experience, there is always someone willing to divulge all they know on a subject, especially if that subject involves scandal and foul play."

"We'll need to see Mrs. Kent first," her husband put in, "for a description of the woman."

"Aye, we should have stopped at the prison earlier." Not for the first time, Dylan regretted the decision to come straight here upon arriving in London. True, it meant enlisting the Emersons' help that much sooner, but despite everything, he loathed the thought of Eliza waiting alone these past hours without a trace of hope. When he last left her, he had given her no indication that he still intended to help her. Now he sorely wished he had.

Frustration propelled him from the sofa. Charity started at his abrupt motion, then relaxed back against the cushions.

"We reached London too late today," she calmly reminded him. "We'll go tomorrow, when Luke can also petition the court for a continuance on the proceedings."

Luke ceased his pacing. "And with any luck, my men should have your innkeeper here by then."

Dylan didn't miss the ironic look that passed between Charity and Helena, perched now on the edge of the divan with the Emerson's cat snug in her lap and filling the room with purrs. Dylan understood that look. It had to do with Luke's use of the word luck when referring to the man who would, by necessity, reveal Eliza as a prostitute to the court.

The irony didn't end there, of course. There was also the matter of Dylan being publicly humiliated once it was revealed that he had been taken in and used, that he had championed a common whore. Rather like Don Quixote, wasn't he, tilting at windmills and defending his exquisite Dulcinea, in actuality a mere tavern wench.

He groaned, ignoring the sideways glances of the others and wishing he'd taken the quickest route home to Scotland a fortnight ago.

An hour or so later, Mrs. Emerson found him outside in the gazebo. He was half sprawled on one of the wrought iron benches, head tilted back against the latticed wall, an arm thrown across his throbbing temples.

"I'm glad I found you alone, Mr. Fergusson," she said, and climbed the steps to the bower's entrance.

He wasn't particularly glad at all, seeing as how he'd taken pains to slip away unnoticed. He lowered his arm and peered up at her, realizing how rude he was being in not sitting up, much less standing, but chalking it up to his being a barbarian Scot.

She smiled, seeming unperturbed by his slouch or at having found him in shirtsleeves. She joined him on the bench. "There's something I wish to say to you, and I thought it a matter best raised in privacy."

He swallowed a sigh and sat up straighter. "Please speak your mind, Mrs. Emerson."

"It's about this poor Eliza Kent."

He felt his back stiffen, his shoulders bunch.

"It's perfectly all right if you still care for her."

His stomach curled in on itself. He breathed in and out, willing the nausea away. "What makes you think . . . "

She waved a hand at him. "Please, Mr. Fergusson. You needn't deny or affirm it, and you needn't defend yourself. It's your business and certainly none of mine, except that . . . " She slid a few inches closer, bending toward him with an intimacy that rather exceeded the established boundaries of their acquaintance. "You seem so infinitely desolate."

His throat tightened and went dry—desolately so.

"Think about this, Mr. Fergusson. What separates me or even your sister—a duchess—from a woman who sells herself on the streets? Oh, don't be offended and don't look so shocked."

He eased the tension from his features. "I don't know the answer to that."

"Desperation, Mr. Fergusson. Of a sort people in our circle cannot conceive of. Add fear and hunger to the mix and you have an individual willing to do just about anything to survive." Her hand came down on his shoulder. "I don't want you to make the mistake of judging her too harshly. Nor do I wish you to beat yourself up for continuing to have feelings for her."

He opened his mouth to protest this last, but the knowing slant of her eyebrow coupled with his own conscience rendered the denial mute. Instead he offered a weak smile and nodded.

CHAPTER 19

A sudden thwack and the unceremonious intrusion of footsteps sent Eliza tumbling from the fragile comfort of a dream. She bolted upright in her prison bed and blinked at the surrounding curtains as if by doing so she should be able to see through to the commotion on the other side.

Raised voices sent her heart hammering against her ribs. That certainly wasn't the boy who emptied the chamber pots every morning. Footsteps thumped across the carpet, advancing toward the bed. With nowhere to hide, she tightened Dylan's cloak around her as she had countless times these past two days and pressed tight against the headboard.

A hand swathed in a fingerless glove thrust the curtains aside. The head prison matron, a stout, leathery woman with a grizzled thatch of hair knotted at the top of her head, flashed a spiteful grin. One eye peered at Eliza while the other rolled to stare at some point across the bed. "Let's go, duck."

She scrambled to evade the woman's grip. "Go where?"

"Courthouse." A second guard, a man with flaming orange hair shorn nearly to the scalp, leaned over the room's only table, reaching for a slice of the coarse brown soda bread brought in earlier for Eliza's breakfast.

Since Dylan's visit the nature of her confinement had changed considerably. No one had ever come to bring her back to the common cell in the women's wing and here she had stayed, in a room no one even bothered locking except at night.

She was free to move about the building during the day or wander outside to the bailey. She'd even had visitors, at least at first, other inmates with the means to buy a private cell and a measure of freedom. One woman had sauntered into her room the first night, gazing about with a predatory air. When she'd demanded to know what brought Eliza to Newgate, Eliza had replied in her sharpest, most curt voice, "Murder."

No one visited her after that except to bring her meals twice a day. And there was a boy, all sharp bones and matted hair, who came in the morning to empty the chamber pot beneath her bed.

All but temporary comforts. The appearance of these guards now served as a harsh reminder that though she might enjoy privileged prisoner status, she was in fact no more favored than any other accused wretch.

The one with the roving eye wrapped her greasy fingers around her forearm. Eliza yanked it from her grasp.

"You needn't touch me. I'll come along willingly."

The woman's grin displayed the blacked stumps of two front teeth. "Got to tie your hands, lovey."

Eliza whisked them behind her back. "Oh, please don't. I promise I won't resist."

"Rules is rules. Now hold 'em out like a good girl."

"At least let me pin my hair up first."

"No time," the flame-haired man said. "Besides, you're a right comely little dollop just as you are."

His cajolery sent a slithery sensation oozing down her spine. She offered up her wrists, and the woman wrapped a length of hemp around them so tight it bit into her flesh.

They brought her outside onto Bailey Lane, where the sun hit her full on the face. She marveled at how much warmer it was beyond the prison walls than within, as if the old stones held fast to the memories of a thousand winters past. Eagerly she filled her lungs with air no longer laden with dampness and decay, but her respite proved all too brief. No sooner did the guards point her in the direction of the courthouse than she found herself face to face with the taunting prospect of Newgate's public gallows.

The male guard tittered. "Not to worry, sweeting, there's no rope swinging from the crossbar. Leastwise not today." He and the woman shared a laugh while Eliza's stomach dropped to her feet.

Inside, a nearly empty courthouse gaped before her. She hadn't expected that, had envisioned a colorful throng swarming the benches and spilling into the aisles, dozens of heads craning for a view of the trial. A perverse sense of disappointment ebbed through her that no one cared about poor Eliza Kent, even now, with the lure of infamy attached to her name.

She stumbled as she crossed the threshold onto the wide-board floor, raising a clunk that echoed off the plaster walls. She managed to hoist Dylan's cloak along with the front of her skirts with her bound hands. A man in a powdered wig and a flowing black robe sat at a table in the open area just beyond the gallery benches. He glanced up abruptly at the report of her misstep, as if the noise had roused him from a particularly deep moment of concentration.

The back of another man's head caught Eliza's attention and she nearly stumbled again. Two rows back from the barrister's table, dark brown hair streaked with silver caught the dusty light of the gas lamps along the wall. Eliza's breath caught as Raphael Mendoza turned his head, spotted her and tossed shrewd speculation over his shoulder.

Then he hadn't gone to Yorkshire as planned, at least not yet. Eliza thought she detected a line or two of worry around his eyes, making him appear a good deal less confident than when she'd seen him last.

The prison matron nudged her from behind. As she started down the aisle the most contrary thought danced through her mind: *this is rather like a wedding and I'm the bride, only the hangman is the groom and the gallows my marriage bed.*

From the corner of her eye she noticed a man and woman

sitting side by side in the very back row, he all but concealed beneath a tweed great coat, she beneath a gray bonnet. Eliza rather wanted to stop and thank them for coming. The notion almost made her giggle. She pressed her lips together, held her head high despite Raphael Mendoza's persistent sneers and let the guards conduct her to the accused bench.

No sooner had she sat than she was prodded to her feet. Her two wardens stood directly behind her as if ready to seize her should she try to bolt. Another man in a powdered wig and rippling black robe entered the room with a resolute stride. Without looking at her or anyone else he stepped up to the hulking, oak-paneled bench, raised high on a platform at the front of the courtroom. Even standing, Eliza had to raise her chin to look at the man.

She couldn't tear her gaze away from him or shake the image of a general peering down from his fortress. With much of his person concealed by wig and robes, he seemed . . . inaccessible, impenetrable. Eliza had always heard that judges were supposed to be impartial. With his cool blue eyes and thin, colorless lips, this man appeared merely indifferent.

Eliza started to sit but felt a sharp thwack at the back of her head.

"Wait for the jury, stupid," the matron hissed.

A moment later six more men filed in. One or two studied Eliza as they crossed to a line of wooden chairs set against the opposite wall. Most seemed to be doing their utmost to avoid her gaze. Misgiving breathed a chilling breath across her shoulders. Had the jury already decided her fate?

With the clearing of a throat her trial began. The charges were read, not in the gentle way Dylan had explained them but a brisk, clipped recounting of her many sins, real or mistaken. There was no emotion, no sign of any tolerance for the follies of a desperate woman. She stole a glance at the jurors and saw burgeoning disapproval in the set of their mouths, the squint of their eyes.

Quite suddenly what had begun as a bad dream turned nightmarishly real, with a stark and crushing truth.

She would be found guilty.

Her lungs seized. Breathing became a frightening struggle while her heart thrashed so wildly her shoulders heaved with each beat. Raphael Mendoza was called to testify. As he sat at the witness stand and answered the barrister's questions, his elegant Spanish voice churned like a flooding river in Eliza's ears. She didn't know what he said. She only saw the judge's brow wrinkle while the jurors' gazes converged like a noose around her.

A letter was produced and read aloud. She heard Elizabeth's name, allusions to poison, a reference to her hasty departure from York. A physician's name was read at the end, a Dr. Henry Bowler. The same man she encountered at the Raven's Perch?

"Oh, but Dr. Bowler should be able to—"

"Silence!" The judge rapped his gavel several times, drowning out Eliza's voice. "You have no leave to speak."

"But—"

"One more word, Mrs. Mendoza, and I'll have you gagged."

She groped at the bonds holding her wrists while panic put dizzying spots before her eyes.

"The witness may step down."

Angling a gaze in her direction, Raphael returned to his seat. Eliza prayed her turn to speak had come. The thought both reassured and terrified her. She despaired of her ability to command her tongue around the words that might convince all these men of her innocence. In the silence broken only by the scratching of a quill while the barrister jotted down some notes, she shook back her hair, smoothed her skirts and prepared to make her stand.

But it was not her name the barrister called next. "Mr. Philipe Mendoza de Leone."

Another Mendoza? Craning her neck, Eliza saw the man at the rear of the gallery getting to his feet.

Realization thundered through her. *Bugger it!* The man who had accosted her in Wakefield. But the woman . . . ? Another memory flickered. When they'd first encountered this Spaniard, he'd been at the side of the road beside his coach, speaking to a woman inside.

He approached the front of the courtroom, sparing her only the briefest gaze as he passed.

"Señor Mendoza," the barrister, said, "do you speak English?"

"A leet-tle," came a heavily accented reply. As Eliza looked on in confusion, the man held up his hand, pinching a small space between his thumb and forefinger.

"Good. I will speak slowly. If you do not understand, please stop me." The barrister smiled, then proceeded to ask this Philipe Mendoza a single question. "Can you point out for this court the woman known as Elizabeth Mendoza de Leone, your deceased cousin's wife?"

Philipe's hand came up once more. His gaze centered on Eliza. His forefinger, like the barrel of a pistol, aimed directly for her heart.

"What do you mean you've never heard of her? She was brought in only two days ago." Flanked on either side by Luke and Wesley Holbrook, Dylan stood before the prison official and struggled to rein in his temper. They had just been to Eliza's room to discover it abandoned. There had been no sign of her in the bailey or anywhere else.

The warden scratched his head. "What's the name again?"

"Eliza Kent, you—"

Luke delivered a jab to his ribs, cutting short the rather unsavory epithet he'd been about to call the gray-haired man behind the desk.

"No one listed by that name, sir."

Just before another surge of frustration got the better of

him, Dylan realized his mistake. "Elizabeth Mendoza de Leone."

"Ah, right. Been brought over to the Old Bailey."

"The courthouse?" Dylan felt the blood seep from his face. "They can't have done, not yet. As I said, it's only been two days since her arrest."

"Been moved up."

"Now see here—"

Wesley's hand came down on his shoulder, yanking him a full stride backward. Luke stepped up to the desk.

"Can you tell us why?" he asked the warden while Dylan seethed and tried unsuccessfully to shake off Wesley's grip.

The official rustled through some papers in a box on his desk and scanned one of the pages. "Foreign Secretary got involved, asked to have the trial date moved up." He glanced up at Dylan with a grin of such genuine enjoyment Dylan wanted to knock him a facer. Something of that desire must have communicated itself through the muscles of his arm, for Wesley's grip tightened as the warden continued, "Seems the lady's quite the international celebrity."

"What the devil do you mean?" Dylan demanded.

The man shrugged. "Don't know much beyond that, sir. But for the Foreign Office to request an immediate trial . . . "

Dylan didn't linger to hear the rest. Breaking free of Wesley's restraining hold, he rushed through the dank corridors and toward the front gates, the Holbrook brothers trailing behind.

They caught up with him at the courthouse. Luke barred Dylan's way by thrusting an arm between him and the courtroom door.

"Keep your head in there. Acting the barbarian won't free Eliza."

He scowled at his brother-in-law but nodded. "I'll bear that in mind." Then he pushed his way past.

And stepped into pandemonium.

"But you don't understand," Eliza was shouting to be heard

above the pounding of the judge's gavel. "I am not Elizabeth. I'm Eliza, Eliza Kent," she insisted while the judge bellowed, "Silence! You will be silent this instant!" Meanwhile, the six members of the jury raised a buzz of astonished conjecture amongst themselves.

"Oh, but this is all a mistake," Eliza persisted as two guards moved forward and grabbed her elbows—elbows encased within Dylan's greatcoat. "A terrible misunderstanding."

It was then he realized her wrists were bound. Fury roared through him to mix with his fear. He started down the center aisle. Was he too late? Had Eliza already been convicted? "Your honor," he called out, "I have new evidence that supports this woman's claim—"

"Objection!" shouted a man, obviously the barrister in his wig and black robe. "Your honor, I must object!"

The judge's gavel reverberated like gunfire against the walls and beamed ceiling. He rained enmity down at Dylan from his towering perch. His voice boomed above the clamor, "Who the blazes are you and how dare you barge into my courtroom?"

The sight of Raphael Mendoza arrested speech for the briefest of instants. Then Dylan forced his gaze from the Spaniard. "Sir, I am Dylan Fergusson—"

"Who?" The judge shook his head as if at some insect.

At the sound of his voice, Eliza fell silent and ceased struggling with her gaolers. She stared across the room at him and he hesitated, lost for a moment in her great golden eyes. His mind fisted around the truth: she had lied over and over, deceiving him and his family, making fools of them all.

That much he might have forgiven. What he had failed to reconcile, much less find the strength to forget, was the notion of Eliza selling herself. He had believed she'd given herself to him out of a growing and very mutual love. But . . . the notion brought bile to his throat . . . could their lovemaking merely have been a means to an end, a way to reap yet more profits in her role as Elizabeth?

Those thoughts traveled through his brain in a matter of seconds. He knew why he'd come. No matter the sins committed by Eliza Kent, the murder of Anselmo Mendoza was not one of them. He opened his mouth to address the judge. He found himself confronted by Luke's solemn features instead. His brother-in-law had stepped in front of him and was now pressing his hands to Dylan's chest, urging him back.

"I'll handle this."

"No, Luke, I—"

"Dylan." An emphatic energy snapped in Luke's eyes. "You asked for my help. Let me give it as best I know how."

Wesley caught hold of Dylan's arm from behind and dragged him into the nearest row of benches. "Sit," the former army major ordered, "and shut up."

In the next moment Dylan witnessed a transformation he'd seen countless times before but which never failed to impress him. As Luke stepped forward, he seemed to grow in height, bearing and sheer presence. Upon reaching the front of the courtroom he was Luke no more but His Grace the Duke of Wakefield, a peer of England and a man of influence and authority. Something deep inside Dylan went very still, considering . . .

The judge pinned Luke with a simmering glower. "And who might you be?"

"Your honor," he said in as commanding a tone as he might have used to address the House of Lords, "I am the Duke of Wakefield." He paused as those simple words produced their immediate effect. The judge pulled up straighter while the anger faded from his eyes, to be replaced with respectful, if surprised, attention.

"There is indeed evidence that this woman is not, in fact, Elizabeth Mendoza de Leone," Luke went on smoothly, "and that she neither knew Mrs. Mendoza nor her husband, Anselmo."

Eliza gaped at him.

"Your honor," the barrister cried out, "this is highly irregular."

The judge held up a hand for silence and cleared his throat. "Your grace," he said a great deal more calmly than they'd thus far heard him speak, "these proceedings have reached their conclusion. The evidence against this woman is overwhelming. The court is in recess until tomorrow morning, when the jury shall announce its verdict."

"Nonetheless, your honor, I ask the court's indulgence in a single day's delay. Tomorrow I shall produce a witness who can vouch for this woman's whereabouts at the very time Elizabeth Mendoza would have been traveling south from York."

The judge drew a deep breath and let it out slowly. "One day, your grace?"

"Yes, your honor. That is all I ask."

Dylan started to stand, a protest hot on his tongue. Wesley gripped his shoulder and thrust him back down.

"One day isn't enough," Dylan hissed at him. "We need time to find out who the real Elizabeth was and how Raphael knew her. He's guilty as sin and can't be allowed to get away with it."

"Are you more concerned with freeing Eliza . . . " Wesley pinned him with a dead on glare. "Or getting even with Mendoza?"

Dylan scowled. Then his gaze drifted to Eliza. How young and fragile she looked with her chin and pinched features poking out from the heavy collar of his cloak. "You know the answer to that. But our so-called witness might not be enough to ensure a verdict of innocent. I've seen the man. He doesn't exactly inspire confidence."

"Trust my brother," Wesley whispered back. "We will proceed a day at a time. Once we prove Eliza isn't Elizabeth, we'll have all the time we need to find evidence against Raphael Mendoza."

Dylan gave a reluctant nod. Wesley continued staring at him, one eyebrow raised in speculation.

"What?" Dylan demanded.

"I suppose this means you still care for her."

Dylan pushed off the bench and headed up the aisle toward the door. He never made it out.

CHAPTER 20

"You." The sight of the mysterious Spaniard from Wakefield stopped Dylan cold. His hand swung up, forefinger outthrust. "Who the devil are you and—"

Wesley grasped his shoulder from behind. "Will you stop making scenes? It is not helping."

"That's the man who assailed Eliza in Wakefield."

"Then obviously his presence here is no coincidence." Wesley pulled him down onto a bench—again—then turned to regard the couple sitting at the rear of the gallery. "Did it ever occur to you that man might not be in the wrong? That he may be another of Elizabeth Mendoza's victims?"

The question penetrated layers of anger and frustration. As the ongoing conversation between Luke and the judge became a distant droning in his ears, Dylan's head drooped between his shoulders. The fatigue of the past forty-eight hours dragged at every muscle in his body. "No," he said to Wesley, "it didn't occur to me. I saw him grab Eliza and . . ."

"And you lost that Scottish temper of yours." Wesley peered over his shoulder at the couple in question.

Dylan stole another glance as well. From deep within her bonnet, the woman's somber eyes met his for an instant then darted away. The man was staring straight ahead, intent on Luke and the judge. He seemed to be straining to hear, a crimp in his brow suggesting he couldn't quite make out the words. Dylan couldn't help but acknowledge the pair appeared neither dangerous nor irrational.

"I believe it's time we all calmed down and had a talk with these people," Wesley said. "Perhaps they might enlighten us as to what the blazes is going on and why this broken crest is of so much importance to so many people."

"Aye, important enough to involve the Foreign Secretary." This most recent development posed the greatest mystery of all. What could be so compelling about the Mendoza family as to draw the interest of government officials?

Dylan's ponderings were cut short by an abrupt change at the front of the courtroom. Eliza's guards yanked her to her feet and prodded her into the aisle.

"Thank you," she whispered as she was bustled past Luke.

Before logic might dictate otherwise, Dylan was on his feet and blocking the way. She met his gaze with a puzzled frown as if to ask what he intended. Indeed, he himself didn't know. Surely no action of his could prevent her being locked away again. And neither had he anything useful to say. He'd fallen in love with a woman who practiced the oldest profession. Because of that, he must let her go. He knew it. She knew it. There was no other way.

Yet as the female guard nearly sent Eliza sprawling with a shove from behind, he opened his arms and caught her, then mustered a venomous a scowl.

"You'd do well to remember that no one treats an acquaintance of the Duke of Wakefield in a manner less than courteous," he growled to both guards. It was then he remembered to release Eliza, to unclench his hands from her slender shoulders. "Not if they wish to have employment come morning."

The woman's left eye reeled dizzily away, but her other eye squinted at him with sheepish comprehension. "Come along," she said quietly to Eliza, with a considerably more gentle prod.

Eliza's gaze clung to his until she passed. He stared after her, suspended in a haze of dismay. A burning sensation rose from his chest to sting his throat. A sense of hope-

lessness descended, as if he might never see her again once
she walked out the courtroom door, as though his very future hinged precisely on seeing her again.

The door closed softly on Eliza and her guards. The irony
of how easy it had become to invoke Luke's name for a good
purpose nudged Dylan's conscience, but that was something
he'd contemplate later. Instead he turned to regard Luke, to
thank him. Raphael Mendoza chose that moment to rise from
his seat and start up the aisle. This time Dylan stepped forward with a particular purpose in mind.

"Hold right there, sir,"

Mendoza regarded the hand Dylan wrapped around his
upper arm. "How dare you, señor. Release me at once."

"Not until I have some answers."

"Dylan." The cautioning voice came from Luke.

"You are a fool, Mr. Fergusson." Mendoza shook his head,
a mirthless smile curling his lip. "A fool for jumping to the
defense of a thief and a murderess."

Dylan's grip tightened. "You don't believe that any more
than I do."

Luke's hand closed over Dylan's with a pressure that threatened injury if Dylan didn't release the other man. When he
opened his fingers reluctantly, Luke addressed the Spaniard.
"You must forgive my brother-in-law, señor. He is . . . young."

"And rash, your grace, to risk bringing dishonor to his family's good name."

"We don't see it as a dishonor to defend an individual we
believe to be innocent, señor."

Mendoza studied Luke a long moment. "Do you have my
crest, your grace?"

"I have what appears to be half of a crest. I assume you
have the other."

Mendoza nodded. "Together they form the Mendoza coat
of arms." He held out his hand. "May I have it?"

Luke smiled. "I'm afraid I don't have it with me at the moment. But don't worry, it's quite safe."

"If you tell me where it is, I shall come by at the earliest convenience and pick it up."

"Not just yet, I'm afraid."

"Is this a jest?" Mendoza's dark eyes snapped with an anxious light. For the first time since Dylan met him, his steady calm appeared ruffled.

"No, señor, most assuredly not." Luke spoke as if the subject had begun to bore him. "That bit of crest shall stay exactly where it is until this matter has been sorted out."

"You cannot—"

"But of course I can. I have the authority, at least until this trial is concluded. Will you excuse me now, señor? I believe my brother is signaling that he wishes to have a word with me."

Wesley had, just then, raised a hand to hail Luke over to the bench where he sat with the two other Spaniards. Luke's departure left Dylan face to face again with Raphael Mendoza. The man was seething—face flaming, eyes blazing, breath slipping in short bursts between his teeth.

"I'm guessing that broken crest is worth more than it appears to," Dylan said with a smile.

"You will pay for this. You and your thieving whore."

That last word shredded any pretense of civility. Dylan grabbed handfuls of Mendoza's coat front and hauled him to his toes. "You'll find, señor, that I am not nearly the gentleman my brother-in-law is. Mention Eliza to me again and my fist will introduce your chin to the back of your throat."

He flung a dumbfounded Raphael Mendoza away from him. The man stumbled backward, his knees making sharp contact with a bench and sending it screeching several inches across the floor. Then Mendoza recovered his balance. Head down like a charging bull's, he hurried past Dylan and out of the courtroom.

Dylan's instinct was to follow. Before he could move in that direction, however, Luke gestured him over to the huddle he'd formed with Wesley and the couple from Wakefield.

"One of us should be keeping an eye on Mendoza," Dylan countered.

"Never mind. We know where to find him and I doubt he's going anywhere else too soon. Especially in light of what we've just learned. Brace yourself. You're not going to believe it."

Later that afternoon, Luke exited the Foreign Secretary's office no less perplexed than when he arrived. But the visit had confirmed what he'd learned earlier, a bizarre tale told in Philipe Mendoza's faltering English and Wesley's careful translations.

"It's all rather like one of those sordid novels Helena loves so much," he griped as he handed Charity, who had insisted on accompanying him, into their coach. "Feuding families and wills and hidden fortunes. . . ."

"Not to mention treason and betrayal. I daresay this would be one novel even Helena would long to put down." Holding her skirts, Charity slid along the carriage seat, making room for Luke beside her. "Imagine a family torn apart over money."

"There is nothing new in that, I'm afraid." As he settled next to her, the footman shut the door. The carriage jerked forward and started down the street, the clip clopping echoing along the building fronts. "What is surprising is how many years this particular feud has been festering. One would think after more than a decade the Mendozas would be willing to compromise rather than lose their inheritance."

"Yes, but apparently Anselmo Mendoza had decided to do just that. Return the stolen portion of the crest to his cousins, find the fortune together and share the rewards." Charity shook her head as if at an unsolvable puzzle. "No doubt Raphael balked at the idea, so he sent Elizabeth to steal the parts of the crest in Anselmo's possession and murder him."

"A brilliant deduction, Madam Bow Street Runner." He gave her a lopsided grin.

"And if Elizabeth fled York both to evade justice and to prevent Philipe and his sister claiming the crest, that would explain her carriage being hastily and poorly harnessed."

"I've no doubt you're dead on again, my dear. Her haste to quit York may indeed have caused her death. Unfortunately we haven't yet found a shred of proof."

"What more proof do we need than Anselmo being dead and Raphael demanding to know where the pieces of the crest are? Especially when those very pieces rightfully belong to his cousins."

"Or so they claim."

She leaned her head back against the seat, one hand smoothing absently across her rounded belly. "Sweet mercy, it's enough to make one's head ache. I'm beginning to wonder if this fortune even exists or if it's merely one of those wild rumors that spring up in the aftermath of a war."

"Apparently quite a number of people have wondered that very thing." Luke squinted as shafts of sunlight speared through the coach window. "Which is why the Foreign Secretary was willing to become involved. Even now, so many years after the war, this is a matter of great consequence to the Spanish crown."

"Because the Mendozas were accused of being Bonaparte sympathizers." Charity fell silent a moment. "Do you believe Philipe's claim that the charges were trumped up in order for the monarchy to seize their holdings?"

"It wouldn't be the first time a powerful family was taken down in such a way. Not to mention the confiscated property being a great boon to the Spanish crown, allowing the government far greater control over the border with Portugal."

"Good heavens. Poor Eliza, caught in the middle of such a tangle. It's one thing to be accused of theft by Raphael. It's quite another to face these murder charges levied by Philipe Mendoza."

"To be sure Eliza had no idea what she was stepping into when she assumed Elizabeth Mendoza's identity." Luke let out a weary sigh. "And neither did Dylan, I'm afraid."

"Yes, I worry for him, too. He's formed quite an attachment to Eliza despite all his protestations to the contrary. I don't for an instant believe he's simply going to forget her once the trial is over."

"Nor do I. I've seen the look on his face when he's near her—like he would move mountains or commit murder to safeguard her." Luke reached an arm around Charity and drew her to his side, breathing in the scent of her hair when she tipped her head against his shoulder. His free hand went to her belly, fingers spreading protectively over the fourth little Holbrook miracle growing inside. "When I see that look on his face I see myself, frantic to rescue you from Jacob Dolan all those years ago."

The memory of his erstwhile and corrupt solicitor hovered like a grim specter between them. When the man's illegal and nefarious activities at Longfield Park were discovered years ago, he had tried to kill Luke, not once, but several times. Failing in that, the solicitor had turned his malice on Charity in a desperate bid to escape capture. Only by sheer luck and the help of their two Westies had they and the rest of the Holbrook family emerged from the incident unscathed.

Charity drew him back to the present by lifting her face to his. "That being the case, darling, it won't be enough for Dylan to see Eliza exonerated."

"What are you suggesting?"

"I understand that Eliza's past is less than exemplary, but according to Tess even the most virtuous woman can fall to, shall we say, imprudent measures when other solutions fail to materialize. Call me insane, but wouldn't it be wonderful if there could be a happy end for both Dylan and Eliza? Together?"

"Perhaps, my love, but it's no business of ours."

"It most certainly is." She turned in his arms until she faced him head-on, appealing to him with one of her adoring looks meant to sway him to her cause. "As you once told me, my dearest, we're an odd scrap of family—"

"But a family all the same. Yes, I remember. But that doesn't give us leave to interfere in your brother's life. Especially his love life. And most especially when it comes to a woman who not only deceived him, but deceived us all."

Charity pulled back, eyebrows raised. "Surely you and I aren't about to condemn her for that?"

He blew out a breath. "I suppose given our history it would be hypocritical."

"Indeed. Now then, if we, as Dylan's family, don't interfere, who on earth will?"

Luke swallowed a groan and tightened his arms around her.

"It is a key."

At the sound of those words, Eliza jumped up from her seat beside the brazier. When her door opened she hadn't bothered looking around, for she'd assumed her visitor to be the ragged little boy come to take away the supper plates.

Now she swung about to find Dylan poised in the doorway. Shadows of fatigue plucked at his rugged features, and instantly her heart ached with the desire to pull him into her arms, smooth her hands across his face and draw his head against her bosom.

It was a notion no sooner formed than relinquished. Dylan Fergusson would find no peace at her hands. He had made that abundantly clear.

"What is a key?" she quietly asked, absently drawing his cloak closed around her. Whatever this key was, how could it possibly hold any consequence in her life unless it unlocked the prison doors holding her?

"The crest." He stepped into the room, his gaze flickering in acknowledgment of the cloak draped around her figure.

She started to slip it from her shoulders, but he held up a hand and shook his head. "I have no need of it."

Their gazes locked, seared, pulsated with emotions held in check. Eliza drew herself up inside his cloak and forced away the wish that it was his arms and not wool and velvet warding off the chill.

He scrubbed a hand across his fatigue-smudged eyes. "The two halves of the crest form a key held together by the stone Raphael claims you stole."

"But a key to what?"

"The answer to that is also hidden in the crest. Apparently, the carvings are symbols that give hints as to where Raphael Mendoza's grandfather hid what was left of the family fortune after the war."

"Good heavens. And to think I assumed it was worthless."

"Far from it. Sit." He strode further into the room. "This may take a while to explain."

The room held only one chair. She left it vacant for him and hopped up onto the bed. This brought a look of perplexity to Dylan's face as the memory of their lovemaking on that very bed simmered between them. With a ghost of a shrug, he dragged the chair closer to her, positioned it backward and straddled the seat.

"The close of the war ushered in many years of chaos in Spain," he began. "During those years the Mendoza family was accused of having been Bonaparte sympathizers, of conspiring to overthrow the monarchy. The Spanish crown seized their holdings and stripped them of all rights to their estates. Two Mendoza brothers were executed."

Eliza gasped, but he continued, "That left their children, three very young men and a girl still in her teens. At the end of the war, their grandfather stashed away a sizable fortune in the hopes of eluding the inevitable postwar pillaging. Or perhaps he *had* been a Bonapartist and feared the truth coming out.

"At any rate, he supposedly hid these assets in a vault

somewhere in a remote region of the Mendoza holdings. Then he had the crest forged and severed into parts. The children of his deceased younger son were given one of the two main sections. The children of his heir were given the other, plus the keystone that holds them together."

Eliza hazarded a guess. "Anselmo and Raphael are not the direct heirs."

"They are not, though apparently their grandfather meant for them to share in the Mendoza legacy."

"And this keystone. It's the stone Raphael claims I stole."

"Aye."

"But how did Raphael and Anselmo come to possess all the parts?"

"They stole them of course, shortly after their grandfather died. The Mendozas had escaped into Portugal, and Anselmo and Raphael used the upheaval in the family to their advantage before fleeing to England."

"Intending to someday return and find the fortune for themselves," she concluded. With both hands she swept her loose hair back from her shoulders. "But then Anselmo changed his mind. And that caused the rift between him and Raphael."

"Not only had Anselmo changed his mind," Dylan said, "he'd finally agreed to return the stone and the half of the crest in his possession to the rightful owners. He'd contacted his cousins for that very purpose."

"Then Raphael must still have the other half."

Dylan nodded. "He admits as much."

She considered these revelations with no small measure of astonishment. "How in the world did you learn all this?"

"From the children of the heir."

Her mouth dropped open. "You've spoken to them?"

"This afternoon."

"You can't mean . . . ?"

"The man who accosted you in Wakefield. And his sister. Philipe and Giacinta Mendoza."

Elizabeth's last words sprang to Eliza's lips. " 'Don't let them have it.' "

He frowned. "But it's rightfully theirs."

"No. Those were Elizabeth's only words to me. I thought she was trying to protect something from thieves. I never once thought she might be the thief . . . or a murderer."

"Aye. Philipe and his sister had arrived in England a few weeks before the accident. They traveled to York expecting to meet their cousin, but by the time they arrived they found Anselmo dead, Folkstone Manor shuttered, Elizabeth gone and no trace of the stone or the crest. They were tracking her to London when we encountered them in Wakefield." He drew a breath, his expression darkening. "It was they who alerted the authorities and brought the murder charges against you."

When she opened her mouth on an angry retort, he shook his head. "We can hardly blame them. They believed you to be Elizabeth. And they have every reason to believe Elizabeth murdered their cousin."

Eliza stared down at her hands, sturdy and callused but nonetheless honest hands, until that fateful day on the moors. "What a botched mess I've made. I thought because she was wealthy and beautiful her life would be charmed, as charmed as mine was cursed. And so I put on her clothes thinking to escape my own wretched, rotten . . . " She trailed off, attention adhering to a single thought.

"Lass?"

Beneath a sudden, staggering realization, it registered that he had called her lass again, the familiar term that had become so dear to her ears. But a much more pressing concern prevented her taking the time to acknowledge it.

She clutched her bodice. "Dylan, her *clothes*. It hurt when I first put it on, but it was the only one that fit. The others were too big and I couldn't lace them tight enough. So even though it poked my side I've been wearing this one ever since.

I thought it was a loose stay and some bunched cotton, but I became used to it so that I scarcely notice unless I twist . . . "

"What are you talking about?"

She slid to the floor and flung his cloak from her shoulders. "Quickly, help me take my clothes off."

"What?"

"Oh, don't look so scandalized. Help me off with this dress!"

CHAPTER 21

Scandalized? Hardly, but Dylan was glad she thought so. Because the expression that had dashed so blithely to his face had been one of eagerness, not scandal. He loathed his inability to conceal that particle of truth. Loathed, too, that his fingers shook as they closed on the first button of her gown.

He managed to work the topmost free, then took twice as long on the next. Hardly his fault, not with the nape of her neck mere inches from his lips.

Her impatience obvious in the hiss of her breath, she reached her arms over her shoulders to speed a process made nearly impossibly by his fumbling. His mystification grew as she clawed her arms free of the sleeves. When her bodice hung limp from her waist, she struggled to reach her corset laces.

Gently he pushed her hands away and began pulling the ties free of the eyelets. From over her shoulder he could see the tops of her small breasts pushing against her shift, her nipples dark and tempting beneath the wispy linen. Sudden desire sucked the moisture from his mouth. His hands stilled against the small of her back.

She turned, glaring at him and holding the loosened corset against her breasts. "This is not for your benefit."

"I know that."

"Do not forget it."

He nodded, feigning an innocent expression. She pulled the corset from around her waist, then further baffled him by tossing it onto the bed and running her palms over the padding.

"Eliza, would you mind telling me—"

"Here it is." Breathless, she turned to him flushed and wide-eyed. "I can feel it."

"Feel what?"

"Do you have a knife? Anything sharp?"

"Of course I don't have a knife. They make you leave all weapons at the gates."

She swung back toward the bed, snatched up the corset and began tearing at the lining with her teeth. A renting sound leaped through the air. Eliza slapped the corset back onto the bed, slipped a finger into the tiny hole she'd made and tugged. Threads ripped, but it took a great effort on her part.

"Let me." Dylan picked up the garment by its lining and yanked. Cotton batting floated to the floor. As he scooped out the strips from between the boned stays, something solid clunked beside his feet, bouncing once on the rug.

"That must be it." Eliza fell to her knees, hands rummaging through wisps of cotton. Then her fist closed and she grinned up at him. "Here it is."

She raised her fist and opened it. Her brow furrowed. "A rock. Just a worthless rock."

"Not worthless if it leads to a fortune."

She didn't comment. Staring down into her palm, she stood and moved closer to the taper burning on the table. "It seems to be some sort of crystal. See how it glitters in the light."

When he moved to her side, she caught his wrist and raised his hand, rolling an oblong object about the size of a raven's egg into his palm. Opaque and gritty to the touch, it appeared no more valuable than a large but badly cut marble.

He picked up the candle and held it so that its glow filled his palm and shined directly onto the stone. The greater portion of that light was absorbed into the lusterless surface. But here and there, rays of light speared outward to reveal a secret to the careful observer.

"Good God." He could scarce contain the excited tremble in his voice. He placed his free hand on the silky-warm expanse between Eliza's shoulder blades and felt a sudden tug deep inside. He steadied himself with a breath. "Eliza, if this is what I think it is . . . It's unpolished, practically still in its original condition to be sure, but . . . "

"An unpolished what?" As she bent for a closer look, her breath feathered against his fingers, grazed his wrist. His pulse jumped, but from her nearness or the revelation sitting in his palm, he couldn't say.

"I think it's a diamond, Eliza. An incredibly large, probably priceless diamond."

"Good heavens. Then . . . the other stones in the crest. I assumed they were glass but . . . could they be . . . "

"Precious?"

When she nodded, he was struck by a notion so astounding he wobbled for balance. "Supposing the crest doesn't lead to the Mendoza fortune at all. The whole story might have been a ruse to safeguard the truth. Perhaps the crest *is* the Mendoza fortune, or what's left of it."

"Do you think Raphael knows this stone is a diamond?"

"Oh, I'd wager the farm he does. And Philipe and Giacinta, too. Even if the supposed hidden fortune is never found, this diamond could very possibly bring hundreds of thousands of pounds. Who knows, perhaps millions." He ran his thumb over the diamond's rough surface. "That would certainly give Raphael a motive for murder, wouldn't it?"

"And me as well." Her tone was grave. "It was hidden in *my* corset. It would certainly appear as if I stole it."

He lifted her chin and held her gaze. "I don't believe that, and I fail to see any reason to divulge this information to anyone. I'll simply say I discovered the stone hidden within Elizabeth's belongings. Something perhaps left behind at Longfield Park." The suggestion, whether wise or no, came from the part of him that believed Eliza innocent of the charges against her, that was still determined to protect her at all costs.

She shook her head. "I won't have you lie for me. I won't allow you to compromise your honor for the sorry likes of me."

"Nor will I see you suffer for crimes you didn't commit."

"And yet my crimes are many, and I won't have your perjury added to the list."

"Stubborn woman, stop arguing with me." To silence her the swiftest way he knew how, he captured her face between his hands and crushed his mouth to hers. Her stifled cry warned that perhaps he was hurting her, but he pressed the kiss deeper because hearing her give up her cause so readily triggered an anger and an unbearable desperation inside him.

And then her lips opened beneath his and the sweet taste of her filled his mouth. Soon there was only the heat of her tongue to be savored, the exquisite melting of her breasts against him, and sweet whisper of her fingertips against his back as her arms went around him. Fear and anger and the urge to protect transformed into something else entirely, igniting desire, fueling his erection.

But like rats to a trash heap the truth scampered back. How many men had she done this with? How many others shared the knowledge of her charms? He loathed himself for wondering, abhorred himself even more for breaking the kiss, swinging away and addressing his next words to the uncompromising stones of the far wall.

"Forgive me. I shouldn't have done that."

He heard a rustle of fabric behind him. He stole a glance over his shoulder to see her arms snaking into the sleeves of her gown. Flames lapped at her cheeks.

"What will you do with it?" she asked in a voice gone flat.

For a moment he didn't know what she meant. He merely stood regarding her over his shoulder, his back remaining a wall between them. Wretchedness coiled inside him. Then he felt the cold weight in his palm and realized she'd asked about the diamond. "I'll bring it to Luke. He'll more than likely hand it over to the Foreign Office and let them handle the matter."

"The Foreign Office?"

"Aye. It was Philipe who first appealed to the Office for help in retrieving the stolen property when he discovered Anselmo had died. That is how you came to trial so quickly."

"Good Lord." She sank into the chair and gripped its wooden armrests. "Though I suppose involving the authorities speaks well for him, for his honesty."

"Perhaps. Or perhaps we've all been had by these Mendozas and their talk of hidden treasure. Perhaps it's been nothing more than a bid to possess this diamond."

"But if that's true, why wouldn't Philipe simply have sold the diamond while it was still in his possession?"

Dylan shrugged. "That was years ago, while Europe was still reeling from the war. He simply might not have found the opportunity." He moved back to the table, holding the diamond up to the candle and watching sparkles appear like glints of sunlight through a cloud. "Too bad their grandfather's legacy only made for confusion and deception."

"Yes. We were all confused. All deceived. How I wish . . . "

He couldn't help turning to face her, couldn't stop from asking what he surely didn't need to know. "What do you wish?"

"That we'd taken the time to listen to Philipe in Wakefield." She raised her chin, her eyes shimmering drops of amber in the candlelight. "It might have changed so very much."

He nodded and wished there was more to say. The moment stretched, marked only by the luster in her eyes and the growing ache in his chest. "I must go. Charles and Tess Emerson have been combing the city for information to link Raphael to Elizabeth. Perhaps by now they've found something."

It was her turn to nod. He strode to the door, determined to be gone before he changed his mind. Her voice stopped him on the threshold.

"I don't forgive you."

When he turned she raised a defiant glance. "You asked me to forgive you for kissing me. I do not. I cannot and never will."

Her gaze, her lips, her husky voice held nothing of blame and everything of temptation. He swore softly, threw the door wide and strode from the room.

A mist, as rank as only the Thames could produce, breathed a foul glaze across the coach windows. Waiting here on the side of the road just beyond the street lamp's heartening sphere, Charity felt hedged in and cut off, as she so often did on foggy London nights. Drawing the edges of her cape closed, she fought the urge to shiver, an urge she refused to indulge for it would only prove Luke right about her venturing out tonight.

He had asked her to stay home despite Tess Emerson's note. Tess had new information and expected to have yet more before the night's end. Charity's response had been to swing her cape around her shoulders and order the carriage readied. Luke's reaction had been to whisk her cape away and replace it with his arms. Following a lengthy kiss, he had attempted to persuade her not to go out on such a damp, chilly night.

But then he had left on an errand of his own, something to do with the Yorkshire innkeeper who would testify on Eliza's behalf. Moments after Luke departed Berkeley Square, another coach rolled to a stop outside the Holbrooks' door, and Tess had swept inside with her encouraging news. With Luke away and Dylan finally obtaining some much needed sleep, albeit on the drawing room sofa, Charity had been free to join her friend. Of course, she hadn't intended to journey quite this far across London . . .

Beside her now on the plush velvet carriage seat, Tess leaned to peer out the window in the direction her man-of-all-work had gone. A furrow in her brow conveyed both impatience and frustration, for there was little to be perceived through the dense fog. Fabrice had left them shortly after midnight to venture into the decidedly shabby theater across the street. The half-hour had struck several minutes ago, a single, forlorn note echoing across the rooftops from a few streets away.

The last of the patrons had long ago dispersed, a few straggling actors and theater hands following soon after. Since then, only the footsteps of the occasional pedestrian broke the unnatural stillness, a stillness accentuated by the foghorns along the river.

Goosebumps traveled Charity's back, though her apprehension was not for their safety. An armed footman stood guard directly behind them at the back of the coach. Despite the hour and the neighborhood and the concealing fog, she knew they were safe, or safe enough.

No, her concern, here on this side street off Drury Lane, was that Fabrice's errand into the seedy Pavilion Theater would yield too few results to be of use, and the morrow would bring Dylan naught but more disappointment and pain.

"Perhaps he's found nothing," she said, each word couched in puffs of steam. As the last dissipated, she regretted voicing her cynicism.

Tess closed gloved fingers around her own. "He's learned something or he would not be gone so long."

"Luke was right, I should have stayed home." Charity sighed. "My only accomplishment tonight is to plague you with my qualms. I should know better than to believe I can keep a level head when it comes to my brother's future."

"Your qualms are perfectly understandable, and I'm very glad you came along. We'll have some answers tonight. I feel it. My people have been snooping nonstop since yesterday, and more than one source has pointed in this very direction."

This much Charity knew. Armed with detailed descriptions of both Dr. Mendoza and the elusive Elizabeth, Tess's "people" had been asking questions both at the University College where Raphael Mendoza taught and, due to a lucky snippet of gossip, at the smaller theaters located on and around Drury Lane. Dr. Mendoza was well-known in this area. It seemed the man preferred his dramatic arts to be intimate and inexpensive, and his actresses accommodating in roles that exceeded the evening's performance.

Approaching footsteps cut Charity's thoughts short. She and Tess turned in unison and squinted in an attempt to see beyond the fog-kissed window.

The coach door swung open. Fabrice's dusky features were illuminated from beneath by the lantern he carried, his grin etched by the harsh union of light and shadow. Tess's head tilted. "So then, my dark angel, what have you found?"

He stepped aside and raised the lantern. "The answer."

CHAPTER 22

Today would not be a repeat of yesterday, Eliza resolved as she shook out her gown, carefully hung on a bedpost the night before. When the matron with the roving eye came to convey her to court this morning, she would be dressed, groomed and ready to enter the courtroom with her head held high.

Of course, that said nothing of how she would leave once the proceedings were over. But she would worry about that later.

With difficulty, then, she cast aside visions of shackles, bars and worse. She ate meagerly, picking at the fresh goat's cheese, hardboiled eggs and bread brought in this morning. Her stomach was not to be trusted and that was a shame, for who knew when she'd encounter another meal as generous as this. Never—if she was convicted.

Briskly she washed her face in the basin of warm water left for that purpose and dried herself on a towel of clean, if somewhat frayed, linen. Yes, thanks to Dylan her needs were tended as meticulously as a lady's. She combed out her hair until the last snarl smoothed, braided the length and pinned it in a coil at her nape. She stepped into her dress—Elizabeth Mendoza's flowered muslin—and lastly drew Dylan's greatcoat around her shoulders. After setting her door open, she sat near the brazier to wait.

Although she recognized the footsteps thudding down the corridor some minutes later, she nonetheless recoiled at the sight of the unfocused mirth dancing in the prison matron's roving eye. Then the matron angled her head, confronting Eliza with the callous regard of her good eye.

"Mornin', duck. Time to see if you'll swing."

Without a word Eliza stood, allowed her hands to be tied and suffered the woman's grip on Dylan's sleeve as they started down the corridor.

She might have made it all the way to the accused bench without stumbling were it not for the voices. Barely had Eliza taken a step inside the Old Bailey Courthouse when the tumult hit her full in the face. Had half of London turned out to see if she'd swing? When the matron opened the courtroom door and prodded Eliza inside, the answer seemed a resounding yes.

Good heavens. A colorful crowd filled the gallery, or so it appeared on first impression. The matron even had to swat a few stragglers away from the doorway for Eliza to pass through. Row by row the voices quieted as she proceeded past them to the front of the room. Yesterday she had lamented the poor turnout. Today dozens of faces swarmed before her and made her dizzy. She didn't recognize a one of them. Where was Dylan? When she reached the accused bench she remained standing, turning to view the assemblage.

A couple of rows back from her, Raphael Mendoza eyed her with ill-concealed loathing. Further back still were the other Mendozas, Philipe and his sister Giacinta. They, too, stared, but less with malice than mere speculation. And perhaps, just for an instant, a touch of regret? Or was that foolish sentimentality on Eliza's part?

Her gaze darted through the throng again, then a third and fourth time. Who in heaven's name were all these people?

It didn't matter. None of them were Dylan. Ah, what had she thought? That he would champion her right to the end despite how ill she'd used him?

Yes, a small voice inside her confessed. She had thought—or hoped—exactly that. Because she had grown so accustomed to leaning on him, to seeking shelter behind his unfailing sense of honor. But even Dylan Fergusson, she supposed, had his limits.

The side door opened and the jury streamed in, their surprise at the commotion registering on their faces. They took some moments settling into their seats, whispering amongst themselves, gazing out on the crowd with no small show of astonishment. For Eliza, however, they spared no more than cursory glances.

A good sign or bad? Had they made up their minds about her?

The side door again opened and the bailiff announced the judge, who strode in an instant later. He climbed to his perch, rapped his gavel twice and announced the proceedings underway. A rustle spread through the courtroom as the occupants settled down.

The barrister stepped before the judge's bench. "Your honor, the new witness promised yesterday has failed to materialize this morning. I hereby beg the court to delay no further and allow the jury to render its verdict."

A protest started Eliza to her feet, but the matron's fat hand landed painfully on her shoulder and shoved her back down.

The judge squinted out over the courtroom. "If the Duke of Wakefield has not returned—"

Behind Eliza, a door opened. She twisted round and was struck by a heady surge of relief. The Holbrooks—a good lot of them—filled the doorway. From across the sea of heads Eliza met Charity's gaze, strong and steady with encouragement, so much so Eliza's eyes brimmed. Through the tears she made out Wesley and Helena looking calm and confident, and beside them an unfamiliar dark-haired woman whose firm chin and decisive stance placed her undeniably among the Holbrook ranks.

Behind the others stood the duke. He, too, returned Eliza's gaze with a heartening smile that made her want to tuck her face inside Dylan's cloak and weep with shame. What could she possibly have done to deserve such support, such loyalty? Her thoughts drifted for an instant back to her days at Longfield Park. How she wished she had done everything—*everything*—differently.

There was movement among them. Her heart lurched as Dylan shouldered his way forward to stand beside his brother-in-law, bringing with him the grizzled innkeeper from the Raven's Perch Tavern. The skin at Eliza's nape prickled at the sight of the man while a stone fell to the very bottom of her stomach at the thought of his coming testimony.

Her gaze darted back to Dylan. He stared back with a hooded gaze, his expression unreadable. She searched for some hint of the feelings they'd shared, at least up until two nights ago. Had she entirely killed whatever regard he had felt for her? Was it merely that impeccable, larger-than-life honor that brought him here, and nothing more at all?

The Holbrook clan started forward like the small regiment they were. However, once into the courtroom, the greater portion of them moved off to find seats on the benches, leaving his grace to continue alone down the aisle. Only he wasn't alone, Eliza now noticed. Someone followed close behind, but all she could see of this individual were powder blue hems and the top of a matching velvet bonnet. Its dyed-lavender feathers bobbed above the duke's right shoulder.

"Your honor," he said in a voice that commanded immediate silence from the onlookers, "I should like to introduce a witness who can, without a trace of doubt, prove the accused is not Elizabeth Mendoza de Leone."

As he fell silent the crowd began to hum, their many voices gradually surging through the room. People began leaning, craning their necks not only to view the woman in the velvet bonnet but toss whispers to her. Eliza saw the bonnet tip this way and that in response.

The judge rapped his gavel. The barrister scowled and threw up his hands.

The judge motioned the duke forward. "Your grace may proceed."

The duke stepped aside, gesturing the woman behind him to come forward. As she did, Eliza's eyes went wide, filled with an image of the impossible. The air rushed from her lungs, the room went black and she felt herself tumbling down a void of confusion.

Dylan bounded over benches, hopped between spectators and created a fresh stir of excitement as he dashed across the courtroom to Eliza. The judge pounded his gavel and shouted for order, a demand for the most part ignored as people vied for a view of Eliza, prone on the courtroom floor.

The prison matron stood over her, fanning a broad hand back and forth near her face in an ineffectual effort to revive her. Dylan had been afraid of this, but there hadn't been time to warn her. Charity and Mrs. Emerson had brought the woman back to Berkeley Square late last night. They had awakened him from a particularly vivid nightmare only to confront him with what must surely be a phantom.

He had glimpsed Elizabeth Mendoza's face only once and only in death, but he had been astounded to behold this latest development. Not to mention utterly flabbergasted by Mrs. Emerson and her servant's ability to ferret out any secret and any individual concealed within the sooty labyrinths of London.

Now he dropped to the floor beside Eliza and drew her head onto his lap. Gently he untied her bonnet and set it aside. He ran his fingertips across her brow. Leaned low to murmur her name. Leaned lower still to press a kiss to her temple. Sat up quickly, mortified by what he'd just done, and in front of a courtroom full of onlookers besides. Some of them were tittering.

"Eliza, wake up." He tapped her cheek. Perhaps not hard enough to be of much use, but she was so pale, so wan against the black wool of his cloak he couldn't bring himself to jostle her to consciousness in any more earnest manner. Still, she stirred and made a little noise, a soft coo audible only to him.

"You fainted," he said when she blinked up at him.

"Dylan." His name tumbled from her lips on a whisper, triggering an instinct to lift her in his arms and carry her out of that place.

She tried to rise but faltered, sinking back against his thighs. Although the resultant warmth spreading through him was far from unpleasant, he was all too aware of the inquisitive stares at his back, the curious murmurs. Slipping an arm around her, he raised her to a sitting position.

She blinked again, her expression fuzzy, disoriented. As he worked the ropes binding her wrists loose, she glanced up at the matron, over at the judge. Her eyebrows converged as if at a sudden and quite troubling notion. Once her hands were freed, she struggled against Dylan's supporting arm.

He wrapped the other around her and held her fast. "It's all right. You've had a bit of a shock but—"

"That woman." She peered at him wild-eyed, then at the woman standing in the aisle near Luke. "That's Elizabeth. That's—"

"No." He placed a finger to her lips and shook his head. "It is not Elizabeth, but I believe you have just confirmed that she is indeed who she claims she is."

She shook her head in bafflement. "And who would that be?"

"Mrs. Kent and Mr. Fergusson," the judge bellowed to the accompaniment of his gavel, "may this court continue or must I have you both removed?"

"Begging the court's pardon, your honor." Dylan pressed to his feet and helped Eliza up beside him. "May I make a request, my lord?"

The judge rolled his eyes. "What is it?"

"May I remain here with the accused?"

He felt Eliza's gaze upon him, wide and golden and filled with questions. Having not the slightest inkling how to respond to those questions, nor indeed what devilish impulse motivated his present actions, he remained focused on the judge.

"If it would please your honor to allow it."

"Will you prevent her falling off the bench again?"

"I will, your honor."

"Request granted. Now then . . . "

Eliza sank onto the bench. Dylan settled beside her—close beside, as dictated by the short length of the wooden seat. The witness was called forward.

Dylan could not but admit this woman was a rare beauty, with eyes so large and blue even the shadows could not diminish them, skin as pure as porcelain and, blanketing her shoulders from beneath her bonnet, meticulous ringlets as deeply black as the midnight sky. She was a work of art, as classically enchanting as those Gainesboroughs Sir Joshua Livingston was so fond of. But like a work of art, she radiated without warmth, without those endearing imperfections that could make a woman so intriguing. So engaging a man could scarce think of anything else.

As the woman took her place at the witness stand beside the judge, a tremor coursed from Eliza's limbs to echo through Dylan's body.

"Please state your name," Luke gently commanded.

"Antonia Marvelle." She spoke in a composed, clear voice that effortlessly filled the room.

Luke nodded, sauntered toward the jury as if lost in thought, then spun about to face the witness. "Miss Marvelle, are you currently employed?"

"I am an actress, your grace."

A smattering of conversation rippled through the audience. The judge tapped his gavel.

Luke placed a hand beneath his chin. "Miss Marvelle, were you acquainted with the woman who came to be known as Elizabeth Mendoza de Leone?"

"My sister, your grace."

A single gasp rang out through the courtroom. Eliza

pressed a hand to her mouth. Dylan caught her gaze and nodded in confirmation.

"Were you and she close, may I ask?"

"We were close almost all our lives. But that changed in the last year or so before she left London." Her eyes fell closed, the sudden tucking of her chin and tightening of her posture telling of a freshly reaped sorrow.

"Your sister married Anselmo Mendoza de Leone of York?" Luke asked her.

"Yes."

"Please tell the court how you learned of your sister's marriage."

Miss Marvelle tilted her lovely face upward to regard Luke. "My sister Elizabeth disappeared from London quite suddenly a year ago last spring. At the time I had no idea where she went or why. Some weeks into the summer, I received a letter from her informing me she had married. And asking for my blessing."

"And did you give it, Miss Marvelle?"

"Reluctantly, yes." She paused, then continued in her impeccable diction, "But she was my sister. How could I have done otherwise?"

Luke crossed the floor slowly as if strolling without purpose. "Explain your reluctance, if you would. Was it the suddenness of the marriage?"

"That, yes. But also because before Elizabeth quit London, she'd spoken of her intention of marrying another man."

"Can you identify that gentleman for the court, Miss Marvelle?"

"Most certainly, your grace." She extended a fashionably gloved hand, her forefinger pointing over the first row of heads directly at Raphael Mendoza sitting just beyond. "That is the man my sister swore she would marry, but never did."

Mendoza glared back at her, giving no reaction beyond the twitch of a muscle in his cheek.

"Had your sister known Dr. Mendoza long?"

"More than a year. They met at the Pavilion Theater after one of our performances. *A Midsummer Night's Dream.* I was Hermia, she Helena. He told her she'd so charmed him some of Puck's magic must have lingered in the air."

An eyebrow raised, Luke stole a glance at Mendoza. "Would you say they developed . . . a relationship?"

"I certainly believed they had, your grace. They saw each other quite regularly."

"Is there anyone else who might corroborate this claim?"

"Indeed, your grace." Dylan thought he heard the faintest trace of laughter in Miss Marvelle's voice. Her gaze swept the courtroom. "The vast majority of the individuals filling this room have at some point over the past few years been either actors or stage hands connected with the Pavilion Theater Company."

A hum of agreement rose behind Dylan until the judge rapped his gavel.

"Interesting." Luke paused to consider. "What reason, may I ask, did your sister give for her sudden change of heart?"

"No reason. Her correspondence was all rather cryptic in nature despite my own letters being full of questions." Miss Marvelle shook her head and sighed. "It wasn't at all like Elizabeth to keep secrets from me, or at least it hadn't been when we were younger."

"Then you would conclude her behavior had changed in latter years."

"In that last year in particular, yes. Drastically."

"How so?"

"In the last months we were together, I felt I knew my sister not at all. She had begun to think only of herself, of her own needs. Hers . . . " Miss Marvelle turned a cool look on Mendoza. "And his. Raphael Mendoza's."

"Miss Marvelle, I must ask you a question that demands an honest answer. It may upset you, but please remember an innocent woman's life may be at stake."

Miss Marvelle nodded. Eliza drew in a breath that quivered. Dylan realized with a start he had slid closer to her, his shoulder and thigh meeting hers with a soft press of warmth. His better sense counseled him to pull away. He remained exactly where he was.

Luke cleared his throat. "You must have known your sister better than anyone else alive. Would you say, based on everything you know about her, that she might be capable, under dire circumstances, of taking another individual's life?"

"The Lizzy I knew most of my life was most assuredly not capable of murder. However . . . " She paused and once more regarded Raphael Mendoza. A black crescent of an eyebrow lifted.

A moment stretched to unbearable lengths. Dylan found himself pressing forward, straining to hear her answer. Somehow—he couldn't have said when or how—Eliza's hand had found its way into his. Their fingers locked, hers trembling, his stiff and aching. Behind them, the crowd waited in taut silence.

Miss Marvelle raised her chin. "At first I believed Elizabeth ran off to York to marry Raphael's brother out of spite, because Raphael hadn't wed her himself. But I came to believe she and Raphael may have had a specific purpose in seeing her married to Anselmo."

"Then, Miss Marvelle," Luke said quietly, "how shall you answer my question?"

"In this way, your grace. Raphael Mendoza wooed and won my sister's affections at a time when she was still young and untainted for all she was an actress. He came to possess her entirely, to consume her life and her heart until she had nothing left for anyone or anything else. Even the theater, her greatest passion all her life, no longer mattered unless his face peered up at her from the audience. Do I believe she would have done anything for him, anything at all? The answer is an adamant yes. I believe Raphael Mendoza possessed the power to persuade my sister to do murder."

A collective release of breath breezed through the room.

Luke approached Miss Marvelle until he stood quite close, one hand resting on the rail before her, his head bent to see beneath her bonnet brim.

"I have but one final question, Miss Marvelle." He pointed to Eliza. "Is the woman sitting on that bench your sister?"

Miss Marvelle's brow furrowed. "Good gracious, no."

Astounded, Eliza watched the trial proceed. Had she just been absolved of the charges? Should she allow a hovering sense of relief to sweep through her, or was it too soon? Beside her, Dylan sat perfectly immobile as if afraid to move. Yes, she felt the same. That attracting the slightest attention to herself might bring the fist of justice down on her all over again. After all, no one as yet had proclaimed her innocent. Not in so many words.

After the barrister asked Antonia Marvelle a few questions, several of the spectators were brought forward to verify her testimony, which each did without a trace of hesitation. Philipe Mendoza, too, was called a second time to speak of the lost Mendoza holdings, the hidden fortune, the severed crest. He recounted for the court the agreement he and his cousin Anselmo had reached, and how upon arriving in York he had discovered Anselmo dead and his wife gone.

Throughout the testimonies, Eliza stole repeated glimpses at Raphael Mendoza. The man she had once considered handsome and refined diminished in stature at every turn.

Finally, Luke Holbrook addressed the court. "I am pleased to report that the items reported missing by Dr. Mendoza have been recovered. They were, in fact, never stolen by Eliza Kent but merely well hidden by Elizabeth Mendoza and under our noses the entire time."

With no small measure of satisfaction Eliza witnessed the jolt that shook Raphael Mendoza's frame. He had ransacked Elizabeth's belongings and assaulted Eliza herself in search of the diamond. A pity he hadn't thought to search her corset.

"They are now safely in the hands of the Foreign Secretary who has agreed to act as mediator between the Mendoza family and the Spanish crown," the duke explained. "Work has commenced to decipher the coded instructions on the crest. Of course, having the item intact would make the task infinitely easier."

He stared pointedly at Mendoza as he said this last. The Spaniard's face turned an ominous shade of crimson.

"I might also add that the recovered pieces were never stolen from Dr. Mendoza as he has claimed. They in fact never belonged to him at all, but rather to his cousins. They are the victims here, and they have been wronged most grievously."

The duke crossed the floor until he stood directly in front of Raphael, separated only by a row of faces. "We owe you a great debt, Dr. Mendoza. Had you not prompted this trial by having Mrs. Kent arrested, a good many facts may never have come to light. Your cousins, quite deserving of good fortune in my opinion, would still be as far as ever from recovering their portion of your grandfather's legacy." He cocked his head and sniffed. "Your portion, however, may of necessity go unclaimed. You see, when you—"

The sudden opening of the rear doors interrupted whatever he was about to say. Four men in dark suits marched in, their footsteps loud and conspicuous on the plank flooring. They reached the front of the courtroom and came to an abrupt halt, standing at silent attention.

"What on earth?" Eliza whispered to Dylan. Indeed, whispers swarmed the air behind them. Dylan only shook his head.

"As I had been about to say," the duke said, his voice calm, his smile amiable, his eyes fierce, "when you chose to harass Mrs. Kent, you failed to take into account her many loyal acquaintances. You must now reckon with the Duke of Wakefield, sir, and I promise I will use every resource at my disposal to see you brought to justice."

Eliza raised her free hand to her mouth to press back a rising sob. It racked through her silently, painfully. Dylan's arms went around her, holding her tight.

"Besides being ordinary," he whispered, "they can, on occasion, be quite extraordinary."

She nodded agreement against his shoulder. Then she lifted her face from that bulwark of safety. The duke was speaking to the judge.

"Your honor, these gentlemen are from Bow Street. With your permission, I believe at this time they wish to convey Dr. Mendoza to their offices in order to proceed with a thorough investigation into these matters."

Raphael Mendoza leaped to his feet. "Yes, I knew Elizabeth. What of it?" Using shoulders and heads for leverage, he sidestepped toward the aisle, raising a chorus of ouches as he trod on several feet. "I never asked her to kill my brother. I foolishly confided in her about the crest, and she . . . she set out to steal it. We were all her victims . . . ."

As he reached the end of the row several spectators stood and surrounded him.

"Going somewhere, bloke?"

"Best if you calmed down, old boy."

"Wouldn't want to miss your chance to see Bow Street, now would you?"

The four officers moved to take possession of Dr. Mendoza. Then they raised inquisitive looks at the judge. He shrugged and gave two taps of his gavel.

"Permission granted to remove the witness. Charges dismissed. This court is adjourned."

CHAPTER 23

Dylan bounded to his feet, tugging Eliza up with him.

Was that it? Around them, the courtroom exploded into a confusion of shaking hands, hugging, laughing and enthusiastic congratulations on a job well done. There was even the occasional burst of song, snippets from arias. Miss Marvelle's fellow actors sought her out with cheers of *brava*, *viva* and *huzzah*, as if she and indeed all of them had delivered the performances of a lifetime.

And then he realized his arms were around Eliza, that upon gaining his feet he'd grabbed her and crushed her to his chest. She was still there, her cheek spreading hot moisture into his shirtfront, her hair tickling beneath his chin. Soft sobs—or was it laughter?—traveled deep into his bones. He held onto her and a single thought.

They had won.

They?

His hold loosened a fraction, though she went on weeping against him.

Aye. They. Eliza and the Holbrooks and the Emersons and . . .

And him, damn it. His arms flexed, pressing her petite form as close as possible, feeling the warmth of her through their clothing. He had won the very thing he wished for, prayed for, lost sleep over these past three days. Eliza was safe. She was free. Free to put the past and all its ugliness behind her.

Of course he should be happy for her sake. He *was* happy. Delighted. For himself. Because . . .

Damn. He brushed his lips through her hair.

Because her safety and her happiness mattered. To him. By God, by St. George's ear . . . his own happiness seemed to hinge upon hers. No matter what she'd done in the past. No matter how she'd deceived him.

He loved her. Undeniably. Inescapably.

He might as well tell her, then. After all, she was already in his arms.

But they were far from alone. In fact, within moments they were surrounded. Charity and Helena reached them first, followed close behind by Mrs. Emerson.

Eliza lifted a swollen face from his chest. "Thank you all so much . . . I can't ever repay . . . "

"We won't hear of it, dearest."

"All that matters is you're free."

"Yes, and now you must put it all behind you."

They all but pried Eliza away from him, pressing hankies into her hand and dismissing both her thanks and her apologies with a wrinkled nose, a wave, a shake of the head. They enveloped Eliza in their tight circle and swept her away, beyond Dylan's reach, leaving him standing alone with empty arms and a mouthful of unspoken promises.

It didn't surprise him. The Holbrook women were like that, especially when they closed ranks.

But damn it, why close ranks against him?

They bustled her through the crowded courtroom, acknowledging good wishes but shielding Eliza with their own persons from congratulatory sentiments that might perhaps become overly familiar. Dylan strode to follow, but found his path blocked by the innkeeper from Yorkshire. The sight of the weathered face with its grizzled, bristling whiskers startled him; he'd all but forgotten the man's presence here.

"Don't anyone want to hear what I got to say?"

Dylan recoiled at a blast of foul breath and bit back a retort.

The man had, after all, been conveyed all the way to London with barely a word of explanation. "It seems your testimony was not needed. But be assured you will be well compensated for your trouble."

He started to walk past when the innkeeper said, "Can't fathom such a fuss over a useless chit the likes of her. Indeed I can't."

Dylan knew he should walk away; knew better than to prompt the fellow for an explanation. But some odd twinge of curiosity held him motionless. "What do you mean by that?"

"Stood in my tavern half the night without buying or selling naught." His sloping shoulders rose and fell within the coarse weave of his homespun coat. "Takin' up space, she was. Finally ordered her out. Then she stood for hours under the old tree across the way, just standin' and starin' like she was growin' roots."

"You mean . . . " Dylan felt his heart rising in his throat. He swallowed hard. "She never . . . "

"Her?" The innkeeper screwed up his features. "Don't have the stomach for it."

Dylan already was off, shouldering his way through the courtroom and outside into the gray drizzle.

"Eliza!" he called. He spotted her standing with Charity beside one of nearly a dozen carriages lining the road. They were speaking to Antonia Marvelle, or rather Eliza was, her face raised to the taller woman's, lips working fast. Her voice carried on a gust though her exact words were lost in a sudden patter of raindrops hitting the ground.

Dylan went still, head bowed to the rain, understanding that this was a discourse he had no right to interrupt. Instead he watched as Miss Marvelle squeezed Eliza's hand and bent her head to convey some quiet message beneath their bonnet brims. Then the actress turned and with the help of one of Luke's liveried footman, climbed alone into the carriage. Lifting their hems above the swiftly spreading puddles, Charity and Eliza hurried toward a carriage bearing the ducal crest.

Dylan turned his coat collar against the rain and set off after them. He was determined not to let another moment pass in which Eliza believed he hadn't forgiven her, no longer loved her, didn't want her in his life.

Despite the rain churning the dirt road into mud, his feet felt weightless, his heart light, his mind freed of a loathsome image. Because Eliza hadn't . . .

Before he took many steps a hand stayed him, a slight but insistent grasp on his forearm.

"Mr. Fergusson, let her go for now."

He frowned into Mrs. Emerson's adamant features. A footman stood directly behind her, holding an umbrella over her head as the wind swept rain onto her skirts. Dylan sighed. "I wish to speak with her, Mrs. Emerson. I think I deserve that after all—"

"After all you've done for her, Mr. Fergusson, you deserve her undying gratitude to be sure but—"

"I don't want her gratitude, damn it." She winced at his curt tone, and he felt contrite. "Forgive me, Mrs. Emerson. I merely wish to have a word alone with Eliza."

"And you shall." She steered him toward another of the waiting coaches, drawing him under the protection of her umbrella and compelling him to accompany her or act the cad. "I wish to have a word with you first, Mr. Fergusson. And please, for Eliza's sake and yours, listen to what I have to say."

But just then a voice hailed him, and he peered around the umbrella to see Luke and Wesley exiting the courthouse, accompanied by Philipe Mendoza and his sister. They hurried toward him, shoulders hunched to the rain.

"Gracias, señor, for all you have done." Philipe Mendoza extended a hand.

Dylan shook it, regarding the man. "Will you tell me something, sir?"

"Si, señor."

"Is the story of the hidden fortune real, or simply a smoke-screen to deflect attention away from the diamond?"

Philipe looked confused until Wesley leaned in and quietly translated. The Spaniard's eyes flashed in surprise, then admission. "The stone . . . it is very valuable. But my abuelo . . . my . . . " He looked to Wesley for confirmation as he labored with the words, ". . . my grandfather . . . told of great fortune." He gestured with his hands as if digging. "Hidden. I believe him. I search for the sake of . . . mis niños. My . . . "

"Children," Wesley finished for him, and Philipe closed his eyes and nodded.

"I . . . restore the Mendoza honor," the Spaniard concluded.

"Fair enough." Dylan offered his hand again. "I wish you all the best."

Next, Giacinta Mendoza held out her hand to him. Dylan raised it to his lips and met her somber gaze deep within her dripping bonnet.

"My children and my brother's children thank you, señor," she said in her cumbersome English. "Que Dios te bendiga."

"She said 'God bless you,' " Wesley murmured as the pair hastened through the rain to their carriage. Watching them go, he wondered if Philipe and Giacinta were truly any more deserving than their cousin Raphael, or if this family would continue to feud over a fortune tainted by sins, both past and present.

He helped Mrs. Emerson into her coach and climbed in after, settling into the seat opposite hers. Her husband, it seemed, had got a ride with Wesley and Helena. Mrs. Emerson removed her bonnet and gloves, smoothed her dark curls and brushed droplets from the skirt of her gown.

"Now then, Mr. Fergusson, about Eliza . . . "

It had been an endless several days. Now, as evening settled over Berkeley Square, Eliza felt her last stores of energy drain away. Nothing seemed as enticing as burying her face in a pillow and sleeping. But, dressed in a simple blue frock borrowed from one of the duchess's maids, who matched her in height if not quite in slenderness, she steeled herself for one final confrontation.

That same maid now poked her head in the rear parlor doorway, where Eliza had retreated in order to snatch a few moments alone. "The gentleman is here, ma'am."

Eliza drew a long breath, held it, released it slowly. Then she clasped her hands at her waist and proceeded past the maid and down the corridor to the main portion of the house. At the closed double doors to the drawing room, she stopped to gather her final reserves of strength. This might very possibly be the hardest thing she ever had to do.

But it must be done.

She opened the door and came to a halt, arrested by the sight inside. Dylan stood in the middle of the room. He was smiling, the light in his eyes transforming them from misty green to glowing emerald. There were roses everywhere, red ones, more than she could count, in his arms, piled on the sofa table and end tables, stuffed into various vases around the room.

Hadn't Mrs. Emerson explained the situation to him?

He held out his arms, extending a bouquet in each hand. "You do like roses, don't you? I seem to remember you enjoying them on a previous occasion."

Apparently Mrs. Emerson had not done a thorough-enough job.

"I love roses," she admitted. *I love you.* The words resounded through her heart. But she didn't say them aloud, too afraid speaking them would shatter the resolve she'd reached but hours ago.

His gaze burned into hers a long, shimmering moment. "I'm sorry for everything."

Astonishment swept through her. "You're sorry? For what possible reason?"

He started toward her and she pulled back a step lest she

run into his arms and bury herself in roses and masculine strength.

He saw the movement and stopped short several feet away, looking puzzled, uncertain, a little hurt. But he stayed where he was, arms and bouquets falling to his sides.

"I'm sorry for not seeing who you were from the first," he said. "I'm sorry for not being the kind of man you felt you could trust with the truth. And when you finally did trust me, I'm sorry I didn't believe you. And I'm infinitely, painfully sorry I turned away from you that night at the prison."

"You had every reason to," she whispered, the shame of it a stone in the pit of her stomach.

He shook his head. "Why did you let me believe you'd sold yourself in that tavern in Yorkshire?"

She closed her eyes and breathed, then walked past him and sat down on the settee. "It is what I went there intending to do."

"But you didn't."

"Does that make so much difference?"

"Of course it does."

"Then perhaps we are speaking more of your pride than of my virtue." She raised her face to him, forcing her gaze to meet his without flinching. "That I didn't sell myself had precious little to do with morals and everything to do with cowardice. Make no mistake. Given a second chance, another night after another day of hunger, and I more than likely would have."

"I don't believe that."

"I suppose we'll never know for certain."

"No, we shall not." He moved closer and lay the two bouquets he held atop the others on the table. "Because I intend to see that you never face hunger or fear or danger again, Eliza." He circled the table and sank to one knee beside her. Her stomach tensed. He reached for her hand, and a sense of dread filled her.

"Please don't." She snatched her hand away, clutching it with the other.

"Ah, but I will, Eliza." His hand closed over both of hers, blanketing them in warmth, her soul in regret. "It is what I wish, and I believe it is what you wish as well. For there is no escaping that we are perfect for one another." He pulled closer, leaning until the heat of his lips caressed the pulse in her throat. "Marry me, Eliza Kent."

She sat very still. She would not cry—she would *not*. For to cry would be to unleash her weaker side and she must be strong. Thoroughly and unconditionally strong.

"I cannot marry you, Dylan." The words came as little more than a murmur but they were nonetheless clear and uncompromising. And quite the opposite of everything her heart clamored to say. Oh, but she must use logic now. Logic and common sense and everything she'd lost sight of since that day on the moors.

He pulled away. "Why can you not? Because Tess Emerson believes it would be a mistake? I listened to her arguments and have come to the conclusion she's wrong. Bloody damn wrong."

"This is not because of Mrs. Emerson." She drew a breath, ready to voice all the reasons she had weighed and agonized over these past hours. But he pressed his fingers to her lips.

"If you tell me you don't love me I'll know it for the sorry lie it is. If not Mrs. Emerson, who else has convinced you we must not wed?"

"No one at all," she was quick to say, remembering the duchess's counsel earlier that day. She had helped Eliza reach a decision, true, but not once had Charity Holbrook advised Eliza to forget her brother. "It is my decision and mine alone."

"And I have nothing to say about the matter?"

If he said much more she'd lose her resolve and do the entirely wrong thing. Wrong for her, wrong for Dylan. She slid her hands out from under his and gained her feet. Putting the length of the hearth rug between them, she turned back to face him.

"Will you listen to me for a moment and not interrupt?"

He nodded, but she saw the reluctance in his eyes and gave a sigh. "I have come to depend on you these past three weeks—"

"I love that you depend on me."

She frowned. "You agreed not to interrupt."

He pushed off his knees and slid up onto the sofa. Leaning back, he crossed his arms over his chest in a show of patience she didn't for a moment trust. "Go on."

"Thank you." She fingered the buttons on the front of her dress, then dropped her hands to her sides. "I depended on you, as I've depended on others my entire life. First my parents, then my husband. In a short time I found myself both orphaned and widowed with no idea how to survive in this world. Have you any notion of how perilous the way is for a single woman with no connections? How vulnerable such a woman is to the whim and will of those who hold her fate?"

"Aye, lass, and that is why—"

She gathered her brows and pinched her lips together. Dylan fell silent.

"I fell into such desperate straits that when I took a hard look at myself, I failed to see anything to depend on, anything to believe in. So much did I find myself lacking, I believed the only solution lay in death . . . or in becoming someone else entirely."

"Thank God you chose the latter."

"I didn't, not at first. But Nathan's old rifle was rusted and wet and the barrel was too long to aim at my head."

"My God." His mouth fell open and his eyes took on a bewildered glaze. "That is what you were doing on the moors . . . ."

"Yes. And then the accident happened right before my eyes, and an opportunity literally fell into my lap. Thus, once again, I depended upon another individual for my very survival. I depended on Elizabeth Mendoza's identity to keep me safe and well fed. I didn't think much beyond that."

"May I say something?"

That he asked permission reached inside her and found a note of laughter lurking in her heart. It was merely a weak smile, however, that made its way to her lips. She nodded.

"I don't believe you're that same Eliza Kent who failed to believe in herself. Since that day I found you on the moors, you've changed. Become stronger. Wiser. I saw the changes occur. I felt them. And as they happened I fell in love with you."

"And I fell in love with you." It was a truth that burned its way from her soul outward, to singe her throat and her eyes and set her chest to aching so sharply she despaired of it ever subsiding.

"Then you admit it?"

A laugh burst forth in spite of everything. "Oh, Dylan, how can I not? Of course I love you. I'll always love you."

"Then . . ." He stood, came toward her, stopped and looked utterly lost. "Isn't that reason enough to be with me?"

"No. It is reason enough to leave." She held up her hand to forestall the firestorm of arguments gathering in his features. "It is not enough to love you. I must learn to depend on myself and no one else. To know I can survive all alone if I must. To be a complete person and never wish to be another."

His hand fisted and released and groped at the air. "How blasted long will that take?"

Forever. Never. Long enough to break both their hearts. She simply didn't know. "I won't ask you to wait for me."

Flashing dangerously, his eyes narrowed. "The hell I won't."

And like a soldier, he pivoted and marched away, leaving her alone to fight a crushing deluge that very well threatened to drown her.

CHAPTER 24

Dylan stayed in England until September waned, waiting to hear from her, hoping her transformation into a better person would be swift. And why shouldn't it be? All Eliza needed was to realize how fine and strong and beautiful she already was; and that he needed her as much or more than she had ever needed him.

At least he entertained few worries for her welfare. She was no longer alone in the world but at the Emersons' country estate, where scores of women before her had acquired the very wisdom she now sought. As London's Midnight Marauder, Mrs. Emerson had used her manor in Surrey as a school of sorts, where even the most downcast women found hope and a future.

But as October arrived and no word came from her, Dylan admitted the time had come to return home, a journey begun and delayed so many weeks ago. Perhaps at home he'd find peace of mind and a sense of relief for this endless waiting.

He found neither. He gleaned little satisfaction in bringing the herds down from the summer pastures for the autumn breeding, felt only an offhand confidence that the spring lambing and sheering would be among their most successful ever.

Charity brought little news when she and Luke arrived with the children. Only that Eliza seemed to be thriving under Tess Emerson's tutelage. Bloody blasted well and good. What else, he wondered, would Eliza find in Surrey? Perhaps that she didn't need the likes of him, that she could make her way perfectly well on her own. It was a thought that left him feeling empty and obsolete. Christmas was bleak.

In January Charity gave birth to a baby boy. They named him Duncan, and holding the infant in his arms allowed Dylan to feel something of joy again, a stirring of optimism.

February brought news of Raphael Mendoza. With too little evidence to convict him of conspiracy to commit murder, he'd been deported to Spain. There he would soon face charges of fraud and theft. His cousins continued to search for their grandfather's hidden legacy, while the Spanish crown made small gestures toward exonerating the Mendoza name. Dylan wished them well but found he hadn't the enthusiasm to see their exploits through to the end.

Those months saw changes in his own life as well. Taking Luke's advice, he took careful stock of the family holdings, investments and prospects. It became abundantly clear the Fergussons were modest sheep farmers no longer. His family had amassed a fortune of their own that had nothing to do with crests or diamonds or decades old feuds, and everything to do with hard work, education and sound decisions.

If that alienated him from the neighboring farmers, he'd no longer apologize for it, neither to them nor himself. What he would do is step forward and voice their concerns where they would be heard. With wealth and privilege came responsibility. He understood that now. He was ready for it. Spring would see him back in London, at the opening sessions of Parliament.

It was there, in the Mayfair town house he purchased not far from Luke and Charity's, that a note sat waiting one morning on the silver post tray beside his breakfast plate. It had come, not from Eliza, but Charity. It contained two lines only.

She is in London, staying with the Emersons. She needs you.

He didn't bother ordering the carriage but took the streets on foot, causing a stir as he leaped over the street sweeper's broom, skirted footmen exercising dogs and dodged nannies pushing perambulators. He couldn't have said if the sun shone or rain hovered or if he had remembered to tie his cravat. He knew only that Eliza needed him, that she might be hurt or ill or in some kind of trouble again.

When he pounded on the Emersons' door, their man, Fabrice, admitted him into the foyer with a well-deserved frown of censure, he had to admit. The man stood in waistcoat and shirtsleeves as if his morning ablutions had been suddenly interrupted, though Dylan knew well enough this man-of-all-work started his days long before the average person arose.

"I'm sorry to barge in so early," he found himself apologizing, then remembered how Charles Emerson often joked about feeling the need to explain himself to his rather enigmatic, Creole-born manservant.

"Monsieur has raced the dawn to arrive here first."

"Indeed. But you see it's . . . " He had been about to say urgent, but surely nothing in Fabrice's composed manner as he closed the door indicated anything amiss in the peaceful shadows of the Emersons' home. "That is to say, I'd had a message this morning that . . . "

The man watched him expectantly, mouth raised in a half smirk no ordinary servant would have dared display.

"Damn it, Fabrice, is Mrs. Kent here?"

The smirk burgeoned to a grin tinged with the slightest hint of pity. "Would Monsieur like to see her?"

"I would. Is she . . . well?"

"As well as Fabrice has ever seen her. But perhaps it is for Monsieur to judge."

"What does that mean? She hasn't been ill has she?"

The man only gestured to the downstairs parlor. "If Monsieur would make himself comfortable, I will see if she is receiving visitors."

The wait was interminable, for all it lasted no more than a quarter hour or so. When Fabrice entered the parlor alone, a surge of disappointment brought Dylan to his feet.

"Will she not see me, then?"

"Mrs. Kent is waiting for you in the library."

All at once, he realized he hadn't the first notion of what he would say to her. Hadn't rehearsed a single rational argument because it had all been said before, to no avail.

Fabrice misinterpreted his hesitation. "Top of the stairs, monsieur."

"Right." He took them two and three at a time, stumbled once and kept going. He burst in through the library door with all the brute finesse of a barbarian and ground to a breathless halt.

"Eliza."

Seated behind the carved bulk of a mahogany desk, she smiled gently. "It's good to see you, Dylan."

She sounded different, her inflections smoother, less guided by the Yorkshire rhythms he'd failed to identify or understand when he first met her. He strode further into the room, peering through the dim light to see her, to make out minute details—the color in her cheeks, the shadows or lack beneath her eyes, the set of her mouth. Aye, she seemed fit enough. But the brocade curtains behind her were drawn, shutting out the morning and leaving him to curse the inadequacy of the single lamp burning on a side bureau.

"How have you been?" he asked.

"Quite well, thank you. And you?"

By St. George's ear, not at all well. He nodded rather than lie. "I'd heard you were in London . . . " He stopped just short of admitting he'd come rushing over like a madman.

The tilt of her chin told him she had already guessed that much. "Your neck cloth is hanging."

He raised a hand and indeed discovered the ends of his cravat trailing on either side of his neck. He shrugged. "Never cared for them much."

"Neither does your brother-in-law, from what I've gathered."

The mantel clock ushered by several otherwise silent seconds while they regarded each other. His eyes began to adjust to the dimness, but even so the desk hid most of her, along with the abundant folds of a paisley shawl that seemed rather more cumbersome than called for by the temperate morning.

Still, he became aware of a change that went beyond coloring or clothing or any other outward manifestation of the Eliza Kent he knew. This change radiated from the angle of her chin, the set of her shoulders, the evenness of her gaze. The alteration in her very bearing spoke of newfound confidence, of poise quite foreign to the frightened Eliza Kent she had been.

He wasn't completely sure he liked it.

"You wished to see me?" she said, and broke the spell of indecision that held him.

"Yes, damn it." She flinched at his sudden sharpness. He took a stride closer to the desk. "I wished to see you. All blasted fall and winter I wished to see you, Eliza. Why have you stayed away so long? Why have I had no word from you? What was so important you couldn't take a bloody moment to let me know you were well and not sick or dying or . . . "

He bit back the rest, the clamping of his teeth raising an ache in his jaw. His hands were shaking, his pulse bucking. He made a conscious effort to bring his breathing under control. Perhaps, after all, he should have rehearsed something rather more romantic and a tad less barbaric.

"I'm sorry. It's been a busy few months." She looked up at him calmly. "I've been studying the law."

"The law?" What kind of answer was that to his tirade? "Why? Do you have it in your head to become a barrister?"

She made a wry face. "I'm afraid society is not quite ready for women barristers. No, I've become what I unofficially call a legal advocate. I have infinitely more to learn, of course, but I've already helped my first clients."

"Your first what?"

"In Surrey, Dylan, there was a woman, a widow like me, who was about to lose her family's flour mill because her creditors claimed she could not make her payments. But there are ways to protect widows, you see, by establishing new credit terms and rates of payment."

"Really."

"Really. And do you know what else? That small triumph led to another, and then several. I've even been paid for my services."

Then it was true. She no longer needed him. Then . . . why had Charity suggested otherwise?

"What should I say, Eliza? Congratulations?"

She inclined her head. "That would be nice."

"All right, then. Congratulations for going off and achieving exactly what you wanted. You wouldn't marry me because you said you needed me too much. Well, obviously you no longer do, but did you ever once think that perhaps you'd got it wrong?"

"I know I was wrong about many things—"

"That perhaps you weren't the only person with needs?" He ploughed on, desperate not to allow her the chance to turn him away again. "That for instance I might have had a need or two, and that while you were away these many months becoming a complete, independent person, I've also made changes—changes that will prevent me ever feeling helpless again should a loved one of mine fall into desperate straits?"

"I did hear a thing or two from your sister. . . ."

"Has it even crossed your mind that I didn't return to London because I'd developed a sudden fondness for soot and shallow society? I'm here as chairman of the Committee for Scottish Agricultural Concerns—"

"To advise Parliament. Yes, Charity mentioned it. I'm so proud of you."

He released a breath. "I'm glad you're proud. You should be. Because it was due to you that I finally realized what my brother-in-law has been telling me all along. That a man must use all the resources at his command to protect his family and everything he holds dear. That to not do so constitutes the greatest of failures in a man's life."

"You could never be a failure."

"Eliza, can you understand what I'm saying? While you were off becoming a self-reliant person who no longer needs anyone else, I've been trying to become the sort of man a woman and a family can depend on and who can perhaps make changes in this dratted kingdom of ours that will make life better for all families."

"You're quite wonderful."

"I'm miserable!" She flinched again and a little voice cautioned him to stop shouting. He plunged on instead, finding himself utterly unable to heed his own wise counsel. "I've been miserable for months. Because none of it means a tinker's damn to me. I'm going through the motions. I've been alone, Eliza, and unneeded by the one person who made it all worth doing. Have you never considered that? You feared needing me, but did you ever once think of how much I might need you?"

His voice had risen steadily whether he willed or no. In fact, his intentions of winning Eliza's heart seemed to have disconnected from whatever the hell his mouth was doing. And just as steadily, Eliza had pulled back in her chair, tightening that blasted shawl's folds around her. Her eyes went wide, misty, magnified. The sight halted any further ranting quicker than sand bags against floodwaters. His blood froze; his heart went still.

"Eliza, forgive me—"

She was shaking her head, looking halfway between crying in earnest and leaping up and knocking him a facer. "What the buggery blazes makes you think I've stopped needing you?"

He stared down at her, mouth agape. "Do you?"

"Of course I do. As much as ever." She dabbed her eyes with the back of her hand. "I *have* learned a bit about making my way in the world. I'm not nearly as helpless as I once thought I was. But Dylan, it's the dependency I've conquered, not my need to have you in my life."

He was half-sprawled across the desk in an instant—circling would have taken too long. Eliza leaned to meet him partway.

"I love you." The words came in a rush from both at once, and as their mouths joined, a letter opener, a paperweight and a box of quills went scattering from beneath their elbows and onto the carpet.

It was a kiss filled with all the urgency of seven lonely, excruciating months apart, a kiss of longing, of promises yet to be made and kept and safeguarded forever. He inhaled the scent of her, swallowed the taste of her. He felt a welling need so great and so consuming his knees threatened to give way beneath the weight of it, and yet the touch of Eliza's lips made him buoyant, too.

When he pulled back to allow them both a breath, he saw a wealth of love in her golden eyes, in her sweet smile, and knew he'd never need, never lack for anything again.

But then she moved away further than he would have liked, sitting back in her chair. For a moment her bottom lip curled between her teeth. "There is something you should know."

He held out his arms. "Come tell me, lass."

Slowly she rose, at the same time slipping the shawl from her shoulders. She didn't need to speak a word of explanation.

"Eliza?" His voice came as a breathless whoosh of wonder.

"Yes." She pressed a hand to her belly. "Quite."

"But . . . " His heart filled his throat as he stared disbelieving at the strain of her dress across her stomach. He swallowed once, again. "Why didn't you send for me? Why have you waited so long to—"

"I didn't know if I could . . . if the baby would . . . " Her eyes brimmed and spilled over. "I was so afraid I'd lose it."

A cold and horrible misgiving gripped him until he feared so much as breathing. "Is it . . . all right?"

She nodded. A smile emerged through her tears. "Everything is fine. The doctor can even hear the heartbeat."

In his haste to reach her, he all but shoved the desk out of his way. Then he had her in his arms and against his chest, his lips pressed once more to hers. "A family," he murmured. The notion echoed through his soul. "I have a family."

Her laughter tickled his lips. "Not until you marry me, you don't."

"I'll have Luke arrange a special license tomorrow. Hell, I'm a man of authority now. I'll arrange it. That is . . . "

He dropped to one knee, then looked up to see a tear falling from Eliza's beaming face. It splashed his chin. "Eliza Kent, will you do me the honor of becoming my wife?"

Her reply was a laughing, hiccuping sob of a sigh, but she nodded. Vigorously. He wrapped his arms around her broad middle and pressed his cheek to the warmth of her belly.

"As for you, little one," he said, "are you listening? I want you to know I already love you. For you see, extraordinary though it sounds, I've learned it's quite possible to love someone before you even know who they are. Before you know their name or their favorite color or what they like to eat for breakfast." He gazed up at Eliza and glimpsed a lifetime of contentment. "It's just something you know deep down in your bones, right from the beginning."